The
END
of
ECHOES

Dawn Hosmer

ISBN 978-1-7374695-2-0 (paperback)

1st Paperback edition August 2019
2nd Paperback edition July 2021

Cover Design by: Monika Petkele
Interior Design by: R.F. Hurteau

Dedication

To those taken from us, far too soon.

Part I

I wanted a perfect ending. Now I've learned, the hard way, that some poems don't rhyme, and some stories don't have a clear beginning, middle, and end.
Life is about not knowing, having to change, taking the moment and making the best of it, without knowing what's going to happen next. Delicious Ambiguity.

~ Gilda Radner

People do not die for us immediately, but remain bathed in a sort of aura of life which bears no relation to true immortality but through which they continue to occupy our thoughts in the same way as when they were alive. It is as though they were traveling abroad.

~Marcel Proust

Do you remember me? Do you remember the way my hand felt as it brushed against your cheek? Do you remember the way you would look into my eyes and see the future? Do you remember the sound of my laughter? Does it echo through your mind as loudly as the pain? Is my voice ever louder than those shouting in fear, rage, judgment, and condemnation? Can you still see my smile and know it will all be okay? Can you hear me say I love you? Do you know I still mean it—no matter what?

ROBBY

22 YEARS, 7 MONTHS, 23 DAYS AFTER
OCTOBER 1, 2011

I slam the door to my apartment, shutting out the sound of my raging wife and crying son. I peel out of the parking lot, squealing my tires on the way. Why can't Carla ever cut me some damn slack? Why doesn't she know when to leave things alone? With her incessant nagging, all I want to do is slam my fist into something. Why can't she learn? Today was not the day for her to question me. I got a stack of letters from my *father* today. I didn't even make it a quarter of the way through the first one before needing a shot of whiskey. The second letter warranted a second shot. The third letter brought my lunch and the whiskey back up. I burnt the remainder in the kitchen sink, along with the first three.

Carla walked in with Jason in her arms as the smoke was still clearing the room. Her complaints about the smell started spewing out before she even got all the way through the door. I've promised myself, and her, so many times, that I wouldn't hit her again. This time, I tried to walk away, but she followed me. I meant to gently push her out of the doorway so I could make my escape. If she hadn't grabbed my arm, I could've left without anyone getting hurt. Instead, my instincts kicked in, and I did what it took to get her hands off me so I could get the hell out of there. In my blind rage, I forgot she was holding Jason, my brain fuzzy from whiskey, and the words my father had written. The punch landed square on her jaw, making both of them slam into the wall. On a different day, I would've stuck around to make sure my boy was okay. But today, I just needed to get out of there.

Where can I go? Somewhere to escape my father's letters, forget my past. I lift the whiskey bottle to my lips, take a long, burning chug, and head through town. I have no desire to go to the bar and deal with the small talk of the small-town drunks. Perhaps I'll drive and see where I end up. The idea of not stopping until I run out of gas sounds appealing. Wherever that is, maybe I'll stay. A new town could mean a new life since no one would know who I am or my whole life story. No one would judge me based on my father's mistakes. I could create a new me, be a different person.

I'm sitting at the last light in town before the freeway when I see her, jogging in place while waiting for the light to change with her little dog panting beside her. The hair on my arms and the back of my neck stand at attention, and a tingle races up my spine. It's like the meteorologists always warn people about as one of the signs they're about to be struck by lightning. I look to the sky— no lightning. I look back to the woman—she's absolutely stunning. I'm captured by her beauty, with her blonde hair, her petite frame, and those long legs. I've never had this type of instant attraction before—one where my whole body promptly responds.

The light changes to green. The woman takes a few steps into the crosswalk before stopping at the realization my car hasn't yet moved or the fact I'm staring intently at her. I glance at the light, then at the exit ramp towards the highway, half a block in front of me. I look back at her. I should drive away, leave this town behind me. Blue eyes, so deep, so innocent, bore into my soul. *Those eyes belong to me.* The thought comes from nowhere, the voice it came in—one from my past. I shudder. *I'm not my father.* Even as I glance away, eyes darting toward the exit ramp half a block in front of me, her gaze holds me in place. My hands tremble on the wheel. I should drive away, leave this town behind me. Not sit here like some sick pervert. A bead of sweat rolls down my forehead. It's hot in the car, too damn hot.

A new life, away from here, beckons to me. My old life, my father's words, my father's choices taunt me. A shudder works its way through me as I understand his desire. A yearning to have her next to me pulls at me as though it's a magnetic force.

She turns and quickens her pace in the other direction, moving away from me. Her dog struggles to keep up. The light is still green. She's now part-way down the block. She glances back over her shoulder, checking to see if I'm gone, or perhaps willing me to follow her.

The words from my father's letter burn my soul, *I know you're a lot like me. I hope it's not too late to change your path.* The two paths are clear in front of me…I just must choose which one to take. It's now or never. The fire within consumes me, making my decision clear.

TOM

WHEN the knock on the door comes, it has been exactly six thousand, eighty-one days, eight hours, and six minutes since I made the phone call that turned my nightmare into a reality. It was that long ago I lost half of my heart. Now that someone is offering to help heal my wounds, ones that have been with me for five hundred eighty-five million, nine hundred seven thousand and five hundred sixty seconds, the exact moment the offer is made is also burned into memory. I've mastered the art of losing myself in numbers throughout the years to protect me from a reality with no guarantees. Only numbers offer me the comfort of certainty, an answer— they are the only black and white in my world full of gray.

I answer the door to find Detective Bradley standing there. The two of us have only met a couple of times when he was first hired at the Fairmont County Police Department. He'd come to talk about the case and how he'd be proceeding now that he was in charge after Detective Sanders' retirement. He had assured me, using the same tired clichés, that he would personally see to it that every stone would again be overturned, and every possible witness questioned once more. At the time of those assurances, I couldn't help but shrug them off as they were promises made before—ones never resulting in any answers. Promises that left my wounded half a heart freshly bleeding each time I dared to get my hopes up. Instead of expecting to ever see the assurances fulfilled, I put all my hopes in a neat little box and stored it away on a shelf in my mind, telling myself I could move on. I could forgive without ever knowing the truth or having a person with a face and a name to which I would offer this forgiveness.

Until now, for exactly nine million, seven hundred sixty-five and one hundred twenty-six minutes, I truly believed I would be the first person to continue to live with only half a heart. I had desperately tried to convince myself, and everyone around me, I could carry on with only the memory of her—never knowing who or how or why. I fully believe my own lies until the second Detective Scott Bradley speaks the words I thought I'd never hear.

"We made an arrest today—we've got him," he says, beaming with a smile and eyes glistening with tears. My heart races and sweat breaks out across my brow as I struggle to comprehend his words. He embraces me so tightly it takes my breath away.

KENDRA

THE DAY OF
FEBRUARY 8-9, 1989

I can't find Chelsea. She's supposed to be snuggled safely in her bed, already surrounded by dreams. But, she's not there. Instead, her backpack lays where she should be. Her car isn't in its usual spot in the garage. It's eleven at night—she's always home from work by this hour on a school night. I fell asleep on the couch while reading and awaiting Chelsea's return from work. I always wait up for her so we can have a half-hour of uninterrupted catch-up time at the end of each day. With her school and work schedule, and my hectic working mother routine, I savor this time with her each night because it can be just the two of us. Tom and Kent are always in bed by nine-thirty, and Chelsea's always home by ten. But, not tonight. Tonight, she's not where she's supposed to be. I don't know where she is, and the panic rises with each step I take towards the bedroom to rouse Tom.

I flip on the light. Tom's faint snores fill the room. "Tom, honey." I gently shake his arm.

"Yeah. What's wrong?" he says, immediately reaching for the alarm clock on his nightstand.

"Did Chels call to tell you she'd be home late from work?"

"No. Why? Isn't she home yet? It's after eleven." Tom bolts upright, suddenly alert.

"She's not here. I fell asleep on the couch and just woke up. I hope her car didn't break down or something…there's several inches of snow out there." My heart races and my hands tremble as the image of Chelsea's car in the ditch pops into my head.

"Let me call her work. Maybe they had to stick around late."

Tom grabs the phone beside the bed and dials the number for *Landoll's,* from memory of course. After what seems like forever, he hangs up without uttering a word.

"I'm going to drive to the restaurant the way she usually comes home to make sure she hasn't broken down somewhere or slid off the road. Call Nicole. Maybe Chelsea called or stopped over," Tom says, already half-way out the bedroom door.

A tremble works its way through my entire body. I never realized before now that fear could make even your eyelashes quiver. *Focus, Kendra, deep breath. Call Nicole—maybe she's heard from her, or maybe her car broke down. She's probably sitting some-*

where waiting for us to come because she knows we'll notice she's gone. There's no need to get so upset. I utter the assurances to myself aloud as I rush to the kitchen to find Nicole's number.

After four rings, Mr. Spriggs answers with sleep heavy in his voice.

"Hi, John. It's Kendra Wyatt. I'm sorry for calling so late, but can I speak to Nicole? Chels isn't home from work yet, and I was wondering if Nicole's heard from her."

"Sure, Kendra. Let me get her up."

It takes an eternity for Nicole to get to the phone. "Hey, Mrs. W. What's up?" she says and yawns.

"Hi, hon. Sorry for waking you, but Chels hasn't gotten home yet. Did she call you?"

"I talked to her at about eight tonight. She called from work saying it was slow, so she wanted to kill some time. She said she might get off early if people didn't start coming in—all this snow probably kept them away. I hope she's okay," Nicole says without pausing for a breath.

I wrap the telephone cord, round and round my wrist. "Tom went to look for her in case she broke down, so hopefully that's all it is. Sorry for waking you."

"Please have her call me when she gets home—no matter when it is. I'm worried about her."

"Me too." My voice catches. "Alright, sweetie. Thanks."

As I hang up, my hands shake so badly it takes me two tries to get the phone back on the hook. I need to calm down and not get so easily panicked. This same issue has come up many times in my life. My first instinct is always to worry. I need to take a deep breath and calm down. But this is my daughter. She's not where she's supposed to be. I don't know where she is.

I tiptoe into Kent's room where he is sleeping peacefully. I sit on the floor beside him and take his hand, laying my head on the mattress. Where has the time gone? How did the kids grow up so quickly? It seems like just yesterday we brought Kent home from the hospital to meet his new sister, who was thrilled, at the age of seven, to finally be getting a baby brother. She wasn't thrilled about the brother part, but the baby part was good with her. She adjusted quickly to the idea of having a boy in the house though; except for the time when she watched him get his diaper changed that first week and got a nice warm stream of pee in her face. She decided that even though she loved her brother, boys were just plain gross.

God, please let my baby girl be okay. Where is she? Please let Tom find her. Protect her wherever she is.

She must be okay because I would know if something happened to my daughter. After all, Chelsea is my firstborn, the one who made me who I am today. With her birth, I became a mother. Motherhood is the only job I've ever had that comes as naturally to me as taking my next breath. Chelsea is as much a part of me as my own beating heart, as my left arm, as my eyes. Just as my arm couldn't get cut off without me knowing, something couldn't happen to Chelsea without my awareness either. Once she fell on the playground at school and cut her head so badly she needed stitches; at almost the exact same moment, even though I was at work, twenty minutes away, I had a splitting headache. When the school called, I had just taken two aspirin. Tom always laughs at my sympathy pains for the children, but it assures me I'll know when one of them is hurting.

I lie down in bed next to Kent, feeling some comfort the minute his warm body snuggles up to me. I listen to his breathing, feel the twitches in his legs as he dreams, but I'm aware of each passing moment—each second that goes by with no word from Tom. I stare at the clock on Kent's bookshelf, watching each minute tick by, trying to assure myself that all is okay, and we'll all laugh about my "freak-out" for years to come. But Chelsea isn't home. She's not where she's supposed to be. I don't know where my daughter is.

Finally, I hear the garage door open and run to the kitchen to find Tom standing there, with tears in his eyes.

"Her car wasn't at work. I took four different routes to and from the restaurant. I didn't see her car anywhere. I drove as slowly as I could to make sure she hadn't gone off the road. God, where is she?" he shouts, looking to the sky as if God will send down an answer. "I think we better call the police."

Tom speaks into the receiver as calmly as he can, despite his rising panic. "Um…yes. I need to report my daughter missing." The time on the clock reads 2:01 a.m.

My daughter, my Chelsea, my heart is missing.

BILLY

TODAY is my fifth birthday and, so far, it's been a great day. Mommy woke me up to a breakfast feast of pancakes with five candles resting on top of the stack, sausages—the long, skinny kind that look like baby snakes, not the big round kind that reminds me of a pile of dog poop—orange juice, and hot chocolate with whipped cream on top. My two favorite people in the world are eating with me, Mommy, and my little brother, David.

After we finish breakfast, Mommy goes into the other room and comes back singing *Happy Birthday*, carrying a wrapped box with a big red bow. I can hardly wait to see what's inside. I'm super excited because we don't get presents often.

"Happy fifth birthday, honey! I wanted to get you

something really special since you're a big boy now." She hands the gift to me and then quietly says, "Let's not tell Daddy about this, okay?"

"Okay, Mommy. I won't tell him, and neither will David." I shoot David a mean look to make sure he knows I'm serious. I'm used to keeping secrets from Daddy, so he doesn't get mad.

I tear the paper as quickly as I can and find a box of wooden building logs inside. "Oh, Mommy. Thank you. Now we can build a big fort. It even has little men with it. David, look! You can be that one and I'll be this one," I say excitedly, already starting to open the box.

"I'm glad you like it. Now, remember to only play with this when Daddy's not home. Since he's at work, why don't you two go play in your room?"

"C'mon David, I'll race you." I zoom off, holding the big box tightly in my arms.

*   *   *

We play together all day, building forts and bridges and castles. It's the neatest toy I've ever gotten. Big boy toys are so much more fun to play with than the ones for little boys. The only time we stop playing is when Mommy makes us come out for lunch. She fixed my favorite—macaroni and cheese with hot dogs. There isn't a better birthday lunch in the whole wide world. Even though it's my favorite, we eat quickly so we can finish making our kingdom.

We're in the middle of building the coolest fort ever

when we hear his voice. "Oh no! Daddy's home," I whisper to David. "Quick, help me clean up before he gets back here."

We scurry around the room gathering up all the loose logs and putting them into the box as quietly as possible. Daddy opens the door as we finish shoving the box underneath the bed.

"What're you boys doing in here so quiet? You must be up to somethin' if you're not making any noise," his voice booms.

"Just hanging out, Daddy." I stand and give him a hug around the legs. "Do you know what today is?"

"Of course, I know what today is. Do you think I'm stupid? It's Thursday." He grumbles and gives me a slap on the back of the head. My hand flies to the spot, rubbing it. Even though Daddy is only playing, it still hurts.

"No, Daddy. It's my birthday. I'm five today!" I wiggle five fingers in the air.

He nods and crosses his arms. "That must be why your mom's making such a big supper. To celebrate." Daddy pauses, with no smile, and says, "Happy birthday, William."

Daddy is the only person who calls me William. Everyone else calls me by my nickname, Billy. David tries to call me Billy, but since he can't say the letter l, it comes out sounding more like "Biwwy."

Daddy turns and leaves the room, slamming the door behind him.

"Is Daddy mad at us?" David whispers.

"No. He can't get mad on my birthday," I say with confidence.

Only moments after Daddy leaves, we start playing with our toy cars but are interrupted by Daddy yelling from the kitchen. Every word echoes throughout our small house.

"So, Ruby. Tell me, how much of my damn money did you spend on that little brat's birthday meal?" He pauses. "Answer me, goddamn it. Why's it that usually our suppers are macaroni and cheese or peanut butter sandwiches, but, because it's *his* birthday you spend money we don't have—money I've worked *my* ass off to make? To cook him a special meal."

Mommy apologizes, saying she thought it'd be nice for all of us to have a good dinner.

"You're sorry? How much did this spread cost?" Pots and pans bang around. "Let's see. What do we have here? A roast, potatoes, carrots, bread, a birthday cake. And you even got ice cream? Aren't you a great damn mother? How about you start being a great wife and getting your husband's permission before you go off spending *his* money on someone other than him? Do you hear me?"

David begins to cry, as he always does when Daddy gets mad. "C'mere buddy! Sit with me." I pull him onto my lap and wrap my arms tightly around him. "It's okay. You know how Daddy is. He'll get over it. Mommy will say she's sorry, and then everything will be okay."

I haven't even finished my sentence when we hear a loud crash from the kitchen. We both freeze.

Then Daddy's voice thunders as another crash comes, "Maybe this'll help you remember who the boss is in this house. Maybe next time you'll ask before you go planning a big birthday surprise." Another crash.

I turn to David. "You stay here. I'm gonna sneak out there and see if everything's okay."

"Don't weave me, Biwwy!" David sobs.

"I'll be right back... stay there. Here's my teddy. Hold him for a second."

I creep down the hallway as quietly as I can and peek around the corner into the kitchen. One of the kitchen chairs has been thrown across the room and is broken into three pieces. Mommy is on the floor by the refrigerator with Daddy standing over her, kicking her in the ribs. There's blood on her face. I don't know what to do. Daddy gets mad at us all the time, but I've never seen him hit Mommy before. I can tell she's hurt. I want to help her, but I'm afraid of Daddy. Remembering Mommy's words from this morning—that I'm a big boy now—gives me the courage I need. A big boy needs to protect his mommy.

"Stop it, Daddy! She's hurt!" I run towards her.

"Billy, go back to your room!" she screams at me from the floor.

"Oh no, you don't. You're a big, tough guy, huh? Trying to tell me what to do and not do? Well, c'mere birthday boy. I've got news for you," Daddy says, as he pulls me by my hair. It hurts so bad I want to scream. "Look at your mother. Do you see her?"

When I try to turn away, Daddy yanks my chin back, so I have no choice but to see Mommy lying on the floor, bleeding from her head and crying. Beside her is my birthday cake, smashed into tiny crumbs, the chocolate icing littering our white floor. I don't know what to do. I want to run to Mommy to make sure she's okay. I'm sad about my cake smashed all over the place. I didn't even get a piece.

"This is your fault, you little mama's boy! She spent all this money on you and look where it got her." Daddy screams as tears race down my cheeks. He's right—it is my fault. If Mommy hadn't cooked this meal for me, this wouldn't have happened. "She wanted to make you feel special, but I got news for you. You're not special. You're nothing but a piece of trash mama's boy."

My tears make him madder. "Why the hell are you crying? I'll give you something to cry about. How about your birthday spankin'? What are you, five now?" He rips off his belt and thrashes it across my bottom. "That's one." Another smack. "That's two." Another. "That's three."

The belt snaps back for the fourth, but it never hits me. Instead, there's a loud noise, and I turn around to see Mommy standing with a pan in her hand over Dad's body, now lying still on the floor behind me. Tears stream down her cheeks.

"Go get your brother, quick. We're leaving," she says as she grabs the car keys from Daddy's pocket.

I run to my room as fast as I can. I grab the box of logs from under my bed, my brother, and my teddy. When we come out, Mommy stands at the front door holding it open, telling us to get in the car. David and I pile into the front seat next to her. We drive off, leaving Daddy out cold on the kitchen floor.

I'm the first to speak. "I'm sorry, Mommy. I'm sorry I made him hurt you."

21

She stops the car and pulls me against her. "Billy, look at me. It is not your fault. It's his fault."

"Mommy, why doesn't Daddy love me? I love him," I say, crying against her torn shirt.

"Your father doesn't know how to love anyone, honey." She squeezes me tighter, pulling David into the embrace too. "I love you enough for both of us." She kisses each of us on top of the head and pulls back onto the road.

David says, "Mommy, where are we going?"

"I don't know, honey. Away. That's all I know. Just away."

It is my fifth birthday. It started out to be a very good day and ended up being the worst day of my life so far.

KENT

ONE HOUR AFTER

THURSDAY, FEBRUARY 9, 1989

I wake up to voices coming from downstairs. I glance at the clock beside my bed—it's three in the morning. *Why in the world are my parents up?* I lay there, trying to fall back to sleep, when I hear a man's voice I don't recognize. Deciding to investigate, I tiptoe down the stairs until I can see around the corner into the living room. There are two police officers talking with my parents.

Mom is crying, wrapped in Dad's arms. I turn around to wake Chels up when one of the officers ask how tall Chelsea is.

"Five feet, four and a half inches," Dad speaks up, with an exact height, of course. "And she weighs one hundred and nineteen pounds."

"Does she have any distinguishing characteristics such as birthmarks, moles?" The second officer asks. *What in the world is going on? Why are they asking about Chels' moles? That's just weird.*

"She has a small brown birthmark inside of her..." Mom covers her face with her hands. "I'm sorry. I'm really trying to keep it together. I just want you to find my baby girl." *Find my baby girl?* She pauses and blows her nose. "She has a small brown birthmark, shaped like a heart, on the inside of her left thigh and a mole on her left shoulder blade."

"What was she wearing when she left the house?" the tall officer asks.

Mom and Dad look at each other for a moment, and then Dad answers. "We don't know. Chelsea always leaves for work before we get home. I'm sure we can ask someone she works with..."

I speak up from my hiding place, interrupting Dad. I saw Chels before she left and, for once, I'd paid attention to her outfit since we were arguing, and I was doing what irked her most—making fun of her clothes and hair. "She was wearing that skirt you always say is too short." I glance at mom. "And her new purple sweater." Mom and Dad both turn towards me, their eyes wide with surprise to find me standing there.

"Oh, Kent, honey. Come here. I didn't realize you were up." Mom squeezes me into her arms. "Chelsea didn't come home from work; we don't know where she is. These policemen are trying to help us."

So that's what's wrong! I sit on the couch next to Mom, leaning into her, and I clutch her shaking hand in mine.

The officers' questions drone on and on. "Does she have a boyfriend? Who are her closest friends? Would she run away? If she did, where would she go? Does she have any enemies? Does she ever talk about anybody that's mad at her or doesn't seem to like her? Do you have any family members that live close? What are their names and addresses?"

At several points during all the questions, my eyes grow heavy, and I start to drift off, but I keep hearing Mom and Dad give bits of information about their perfect child, Chelsea.

"She's a good student and has put in applications to several universities. She's awaiting news on scholarship offers," Mom says.

"She's almost got a four-point GPA. Pretty impressive, huh?" Dad adds.

"She's been active in the drama club for the past four years and has a great group of friends. Her boyfriend is the quarterback—Brent Davis—and they've been dating for about four months."

I try to tune them out because I hate when they get started on their bragging kick about Chelsea. My parents think she's the perfect child, but I know better. I know the *real* her. Sure, she's smart and pretty, but she isn't always the best sister in the world. She can hit *hard* if she's mad enough. Like the time I took her bras and underwear and hung them in the tree, on the lamppost, in the bushes—wherever I could find a spot in our front yard. She woke up in the morning to her undies growing in trees for the entire world to see—or at least everyone who had to drive right by our house to get to the high school. It was hilarious, but she was ticked off. She chased after me and, as usual, caught me. She pounded on me for about twenty minutes, until Mom caught her and made her stop. We both got grounded for a week—me for embarrassing my sister and her for "using her fists to make a point." It was worth it, though, because Chelsea got teased by people at school for at least a year about her lacy panties hanging so graciously from the lamp post.

The more my parents and the police talk, the more my worry builds. Even though she can be a royal pain in the butt most of the time, she's still my big sister. She does occasionally let me in her room to listen to music with her. Once in a while, she lets me ride in her car, so I look like I'm cruising with an older girl. She even sometimes tries really hard to be nice to my friends who all think she's pretty. She gets a kick out of watching them blush. She gives me advice about when I grow up and how to treat a girl or get a girlfriend. Not that I care, since girls are disgusting. I don't want a girlfriend, so why would I care about keeping one? I can tell from the questions that the one officer thinks Chels has run away or is hiding somewhere with her boyfriend.

They don't know Chels like I do. She'd never make Mom cry like she is now. Or make Dad so worried that he looks like he's going to barf all over the living room floor. Even though she can be mean, I know she loves us. She wouldn't go somewhere without saying goodbye and tousling my hair like always and saying, "See ya later, little man!", which she knows drives me absolutely nuts especially now that I'm within inches of being her height. Or, at least, I always act like it does.

NICOLE

THE DAY AFTER
THURSDAY, FEBRUARY 9, 1989

I awaken in a panic remembering last night's events before my eyes open. Mr. Wyatt called and talked to my mom around four to let her know Chelsea was still missing. He said they'd spoken with the police who would probably meet with me at school today. I'm angry at myself because I overslept and now, I'll be late for school. It feels like I'm in a dream—in the real world, there's no way my best friend is missing.

I jump out of bed and throw on the first thing I see—my favorite jeans and a sweatshirt. I must get to school in the hope Chelsea will show up. If not, I have to be there to talk to the police in case they need information from me that will help them find her.

Chelsea has been my best friend for six years, since the start of middle school. We had four classes together that first year and hit it off immediately. We're like sisters but without all the arguing. We laugh at the same things, finish each other's sentences, eat the same foods, and can read each other's minds with just one look. We've been inseparable since day one. Every free moment we have, we spend together—which seems to be less and less now that we both have boyfriends, jobs, activities, and school.

Chelsea, where are you? Are you okay?

I walk into the kitchen to grab a piece of toast and beg my mom to borrow the car. Both of my parents are sitting at the table.

Mom pauses with the coffee cup an inch from her mouth. "Where are you going, sweetheart?"

"To school. I need to get there in case Chels shows up, or the police want to talk to me."

"Why don't you stay home today? You had a rough night last night, and if the police need you, they can find you here," Dad adds.

They both look as bad as I feel. "I really need to go. I'll be fine. Besides, this is probably all just some huge misunderstanding. Chels is probably sitting in Science class right now like she's supposed to be."

"I don't think it's a good idea but if you must..." Mom stands up, wraps me in her arms, and kisses me on top of my head. "Please be careful."

I grab the car keys, dangling them in the air like a ques-

29

tion. My mom nods to tell me it's okay for me to take the car. "Thanks. I'll be okay. Love you guys!"

I drive as quickly as I can to school and run directly into Science class without stopping at my locker or signing in at the office as I'm supposed to. I stop dead in my tracks when I see Chelsea's usual seat, the one right next to my own, is empty. The entire class grows completely quiet, and everyone looks my way. My nose tingles as it always does right before I cry, so I run out of the room and head towards Chelsea's locker. Once I get there, I collapse into tears, dropping my books beside me.

When the bell rings to signal the end of the period, I rush into the bathroom and sit in a stall, hoping to avoid any unwanted stares or comments. Within moments, others come in, their voices filling the air.

"I heard she ran off with this guy she met at work that's in the Navy," one girl's voice rings out. "I overheard my mom talking hushed on the phone this morning. She said Chelsea is a secret drug addict."

"I heard that too," another voice chimes in. "And that she OD'd last summer and had to get her stomach pumped."

"Some guys on the football team with Brent said she was knocked up and freaked out," a third voice adds. "Brent tried to tell her it would all be okay, but she was a mess. Maybe she ran away or killed herself or something."

"I guess little Miss Perfect isn't so perfect after all," the first girl snarls.

I storm out. "You don't know what the hell you're talking about. Everything you just said is total bullshit. You don't know anything about her if you believe crap like that. She's not pregnant; she's not a drug addict; and, she doesn't know a single guy in the Navy. Just shut the hell up."

My voice quivers. Snot drips into my mouth and last night's mascara streams down my cheeks. The girls stand there silently with their mouths gaping, shocked by my outburst. I can't quite believe it myself. I rarely cuss and try not to make waves. They step towards the door, but I push past them. I bolt down the hall and into the office, to call my parents for permission to go home for the day. I can't deal with seeing Chelsea's empty seat in all her classes. I definitely can't handle hearing more rumors and lies about her.

There are two people standing at the counter in the office talking to Mrs. Jarvis, the school secretary. "Oh, there she is now. I just paged for you … Nicole, are you alright?"

I run my hand through my hair and wipe my cheeks. "I'm fine, Mrs. Jarvis. What did you need?"

"These officers would like to talk with you for a moment if you're up to it."

"I'm fine." I force a smile and follow them into the principal's conference room. The room is dark and musty, with only a small window.

The female officer extends her hand to me. "Hi, Nicole. I'm Officer Radnor, and this is Detective Sanders." She points to the chair, and I sit. "Thank you for meeting with us today. As you know, we need to ask you some questions about Chelsea that may help us find her. Do you need anything before we get started?"

31

"No. I'm fine," I say and wring my hands.

"How long have you known Chelsea?" the detective asks, pulling a notepad and pen out of his pocket.

I force my voice past the lump in my throat. "For six years—since the beginning of seventh grade."

The detective holds his pen poised above his notebook. "Who are her other close friends?"

"I'm her best friend, but she has lots of acquaintances." I rattle off a list of names for them.

The officer brushes a strand of hair out of her narrowed eyes. "Does she have a boyfriend?"

"Yes. She's been dating Brent Davis for about four months." My leg bounces up and down with nervousness.

"Are she and Mr. Davis sexually involved, to your knowledge?" The officer asks and lowers her gaze.

I'm not sure how to answer. Officer Radnor senses my hesitation. She leans forward, touches my arm, and speaks in a soothing tone. "This interview and all of the answers you give are purely to help our investigation. It will go no further than this room."

I clear my throat while whispering an apology to Chelsea in my head. Answering truthfully feels like a huge betrayal of her trust, but it's worth it if something I say can help the police find her.

"No. Not yet. Chelsea has been debating about whether she's ready for that next step. She really loves Brent or else she wouldn't even consider it. He agreed to wait until she's ready."

"Does she have any enemies?" the detective asks, too

loudly for such a small, quiet room.

"Some people are jealous of her, but I wouldn't say there's anyone who is an enemy. She's nice to pretty much everyone. She isn't stuck up just because she's smart and pretty. She always stands up for people that are getting picked on and never makes fun of anyone." I rub my hands on my pant legs to make them stop shaking.

Detective Sanders peeks up over the frame of his glasses. "Has Chelsea ever taken illegal drugs?"

I shake my head. "No way. She's not that stupid."

"Does she drink?" he inquires.

Remembering their earlier promise to keep the information shared in this room, I answer. "Sometimes. We've been to our share of parties, and we've both drank several times. I've only seen Chelsea truly drunk once. She threw up all over the place, and I had to practically carry her to the car and to my bed to sleep it off. When she woke up the next day, with a serious hangover, she said she wasn't gonna be that dumb again. I've never seen her drunk since."

The detective's pen scratches out a rhythm on his notepad, then finally it stops. "When was that?"

"The end of the school year party last May, to celebrate us becoming seniors." Despite my efforts, my leg bounces again. I raise my hand to my hair, twirling a strand around my finger.

"If Chelsea were to run away, where would she go?" The woman's voice is so much more soothing than the detective's, which puts me at ease.

"She wouldn't run away—she has no reason to. If she

ever had an idea like that, she'd tell me."

"What's Mr. Wyatt like?" the detective barks.

Tears fill my eyes. "He's like my second dad. He loves Chelsea like crazy. You can tell he's so proud of her. To be honest, I wish he was my dad."

The detective exchanges a look with the officer before continuing. "Have you ever spent the night in the Wyatt home?"

"Of course, I've practically lived there over the past six years."

"Has Mr. Wyatt ever said or done anything that's made you feel uncomfortable?"

The question is like a punch in the gut because I know the implications of it. "No, he hasn't, and he wouldn't," I say and slap the table, not caring that my anger at this line of questioning is showing. "I hope you don't think he has anything to do with Chelsea being missing. He loves her and wouldn't do anything to hurt her... ever."

The officer reaches out and, again, puts her hand on mine. "Do you know anyone that would want to harm Chelsea?"

I shake my head and look to the ceiling, trying to keep the tears from falling.

"If you had to make a guess about her whereabouts right now, where do you think she is?" the detective asks, quieter this time.

This question catches me totally off guard, and a sob catches in my throat. "She has to be somewhere she can't get away. She'd never make everyone worry this way if she could help it." Speaking this truth pierces my heart in a way I've never felt before.

"Thank you for your time today. We'll probably need to talk with you again. We appreciate all of your help," Detective Sanders says, standing to signal the end of the interview.

All my earlier hopeful thinking has vanished, making it impossible for me to catch my breath as the words I just uttered hammer in my head. I know, deep in my core, something is terribly, terribly wrong.

KENDRA

12 HOURS AND 4 MINUTES AFTER
THURSDAY, FEBRUARY 9, 1989, 2:05 PM

I have no idea how to go about acting normal when it feels as if my whole life has been turned upside down. It's only been twelve hours since we reported Chelsea missing, yet it seems like it's been months since I've seen my daughter. I can't believe my lungs continue to breathe; my heart continues to beat; my eyes continue to see when the world as I've known it is so uncertain, full of so many questions. The simplest of tasks seem insurmountable—washing the dishes, cleaning off the counter, taking a shower—because every cell in my body is screaming over and over again, *your daughter is missing*. Is there a handbook somewhere to explain the correct way for a parent to face such a nightmare?

Since last night, I've had a tape on an endless stream in my head replaying so many moments of the past seventeen years. The first time I held her in my arms. Chelsea's first steps. The first time she said, "Mommy." Her first day of kindergarten. There are so many firsts to remember. Remembering them all only increases the fear that there may be an equally unending supply of lasts. The last time I touched her soft skin. The last time I looked into Chelsea's big blue eyes. The last time I heard my daughter's laugh. The last time I heard her say *I love you*. The last time I told her I loved her. I try to shake the thoughts from my mind—I'll never be ready to think about *lasts* when it comes to my children. Each second that ticks by with no news of Chelsea's whereabouts, my reality becomes grimmer, my fears larger.

The police said they'll be searching the area by the restaurant where she worked today in hopes of finding some clues as to where she could be. They'll be talking with her co-workers to see if she gave any indication of what her plans were after work and to see if they noticed anyone or anything suspicious last night. Tom left hours ago to do his own searching, saying he couldn't just sit at home when our daughter might need his help. I couldn't force myself to go with him out of fear of what we might find. There's some comfort in the questions left unanswered for what will we do, what will we become, if we get the answer we most dread?

Kent's in the living room watching something on TV like it's any other day. Tom allowed him to stay home today since he didn't get much sleep last night, which is good because I'm not about to let my other child disappear for even a moment when my daughter is lost.

The doorbell rings and Kent yells, "Mom, it's the police again."

Part of me wants to run to them, hoping they've found my daughter. The other part of me wants to run and hide, fearing they found my daughter's *body*. I can't make myself move in either direction.

"Mom? Did you hear me?"

Kent opens the door, and I hear Detective Sanders ask to speak with Tom or me. I wait, hoping to hear Chelsea's voice ring through the house, letting everyone know she's home and safe. Chelsea's voice doesn't come.

Kent leads Detective Sanders into the kitchen where I'm standing frozen in front of the sink full of dirty dishes. The detective asks me to have a seat with him at the table. I don't want to sit. Sitting always means something bad is coming. I want to scream at him to not tell me anything I need to sit down to hear. All I want to hear is my daughter's voice.

"Mrs. Wyatt, please…"

I reluctantly sit next to him as he reaches out to touch my hand. "We found Chelsea's car today. Someone set fire to it and left it less than a mile away from the restaurant."

I'm suffocating on his words. My chest tightens, making it hard to take a breath. The edges of my vision go black as if the world outside of this moment has ceased to exist. The truth of the situation comes barreling down on me. If Chelsea ran away, she wouldn't have burned her car. If someone burned Chelsea's car, it means they are trying to hide something. Her burnt car has no logical, happy-ending explanation.

"Mrs. Wyatt, I know this is hard. I'm so sorry. I promise we're doing all we can to find her. The lab will run tests on the car to determine if there's any evidence in it we can use…"

"Evidence? Do you mean my daughter's blood? Is that what you mean? Just say it like it is Detective. I'm a big girl. I can take it. Tell me exactly what you're looking for." I shout.

I don't realize Tom is home until his arms wrap around me, trying to protect me from the terrible truths of our reality. I don't want him to touch me. I don't want anyone's meaningless words and gestures of comfort. I push away from Tom's embrace, from Detective Sanders' compassionate eyes, from Kent's television program. I rush out of the kitchen, into the garage, slamming the door behind me. I get into my car with the intention of leaving, going somewhere, anywhere to get away from all of this. But where? *Where can I go that my daughter is no longer missing?* There is nowhere to escape this terrible, ugly truth. There's no place I can go to make me unhear the words that my daughter's car is burned beyond recognition. I lay my head on the steering wheel and don't even recognize the sounds coming from me— those filled with the sorrow of a loss so profound there are no words that can replace them. I pray for God to let my baby be okay, to please bring my daughter home.

BILLY

17 YEARS, 6 MONTHS, 24 DAYS BEFORE
JULY 15, 1971

WE'VE been gone from home for over a month now. The night we left, we drove and drove and drove. We ended up at Aunt Linda's house. David and I were excited because it was the first time we had been to another state, and neither of us remembered Aunt Linda. David had never met her, and Mommy said I was a year old the last time I saw her.

When Aunt Linda found us standing on the doorstep, her eyes went wide with surprise. She let us in and whisked Mommy away to get cleaned up. Aunt Linda got her fresh clothes and bandaged the cut on her head. The whole night, she kept asking Mommy questions about Daddy and if he knew where we went. It was obvious that Aunt Linda didn't like daddy much because whenever she mentioned his name, her face scrunched up like she'd just tasted a lemon.

We stayed with Aunt Linda and Uncle Joe for a couple of days while they helped us find our own place to live. It's a one-room apartment, complete with furniture, above a bakery. Even though it's small, I love it here. I love to smell the bread baking from downstairs; I love it because I can play with my wooden logs whenever I want; I love that we all sleep in the same bed every night even though it's tiny and pulls out from the couch; I especially love that there's no one screaming or hitting or crying. Mommy smiles all the time now and acts really silly, making us sometimes laugh until our bellies hurt.

The only thing I don't like is that Mommy has to work now. She's a waitress in a diner down the street from our apartment. Sometimes, when she goes to work, we stay with Aunt Linda, but, if she's busy, we have to stay alone. I hate staying alone, especially at night, because I get scared. I don't tell Mommy though because she seems so happy with her new job. She always puts on her pink waitressing uniform with the white apron, matching pink lipstick and has the biggest smile when she looks at herself in the mirror before walking out the door. After work, she always lets us help count her tip money. We have envelopes marked for each of the bills and Mommy divides the money between them. This is Mommy's first job ever, and she says she loves making her own money. So, even if I do get scared, I don't want to make Mommy worry. I like seeing her so happy.

Mommy always goes over the rules with us before she leaves … *Don't answer the door for anyone, even if you know them.*

Don't answer the phone. Don't go outside. Don't open the curtains. Don't use the stove. I know all the rules by heart now. When David and I are alone, I make peanut butter and jelly sandwiches on bread from the bakery downstairs. The owner's wife, Mrs. Lawson, gives us a loaf every other day. She's a nice woman and always tells Mommy what sweet little boys we are. I sometimes pretend Mrs. Lawson is my grandma because I think that's what a grandma would be like, with her gray hair, big belly, warm hugs, huge smile, and kind words. I've never met my grandma, but my guess is she'd be exactly like Mrs. Lawson.

While Mommy works, we play with toys or build tents over the furniture with blankets. Sometimes we watch shows that aren't too scary on the little black and white TV that sits on the stand across from our couch-bed. We usually stay so busy we don't have time to notice Mommy isn't home. But sometimes when she works the closing shift, we have to go to bed before she gets home. Those are the times I hear lots of weird noises and picture all kinds of scary creatures hiding in the closet or outside our apartment door. I never let David know I'm scared because it's my job to take care of my brother—I wouldn't be doing a very good job if I let him know I get afraid too. To help myself feel better, I make myself think of the bedtime stories Mommy tells us about princesses and princes living in great big castles. Most of the time, this calms me down enough to fall asleep.

Tonight is one of Mommy's late shifts, which means she should get home a little after eleven. I made Mommy teach me how to tell time, so I know when she should be home. Tonight, she's late. The big hand on the clock is on the nine, and the little hand is on the eleven, almost to the twelve. No matter how hard I've tried, I've been scared tonight, and nothing is making me feel better. David fell asleep beside me a long time ago and is snoring softly.

I carefully slip out of bed, so I don't wake him and get one of our books. I hope that maybe if I look at the pictures, I'll be able to fall asleep or Mommy will come home faster. I grab the book about the three bears. I know most of the words to this story because it's one of my favorites.

I look at it over and over again, trying not to hear the noise that sounds like scratching at the window or the thumping that sounds like footsteps coming from the bathroom. I try with all my strength not to look at the clock because Mommy is very late, and I'm scared she's not home yet.

Now, I hear talking outside of the apartment. I lay still, listening for Mommy's voice. I hear her laugh and instantly feel relieved. I look at the clock and see the little hand on the twelve and the big hand on the five. This is the latest Mommy has ever gotten home. But, she's here now, and that's all that matters. I flip off the light and cover up, so she won't know I stayed awake so late. As the voices get closer, I wonder who in the world Mommy is talking to. The key turns in the lock, and the door opens. I close my eyes as tightly as I can, not wanting to give my secret away but wanting to see who is with her.

As soon as the door closes, a man's voice says, "Ruby, I've missed you so much. I never wanna lose you again. I'm so sorry."

Then all I can hear are kissing noises. Then, the familiar

voice says, "You and the boys come home, and I promise things will change. I promise, Ruby. I love you more than anything in the world."

A million butterflies flutter in my chest at the realization of whose voice it is. It's Daddy. I don't know whether to jump out of bed and run to hug him or whether to bury myself further under the covers. I love and miss Daddy, but he hurt me. Even worse, he hurt Mommy. What if Mommy takes us back home? Will he be nicer to us? Will she still smile? Will Daddy hurt us again?

All of the questions tumble around in my mind, crashing into each other, when I hear my mother whisper, "We'll come home. I'll tell the boys tomorrow." Then, more kissing noises. "We've missed you too."

I don't know whether to laugh or cry. We're going home. I can't decide if that's good or bad. I fall asleep, with a mixture of fear and happiness, to the sound of my parents kissing and talking quietly on the floor beside me.

KENT

THE DAY AFTER
THURSDAY, FEBRUARY 9, 1989

I'M desperately trying to hear what's going on in the kitchen without being too obvious about my eavesdropping. I stay out of sight as the policeman tells Mom they found Chelsea's burnt car; I hear Mom yell and run out the door. I glance out the front window to see where she's gone and notice *them* instead. There are news station vehicles everywhere—parked in front of our house, in front of the neighbor's houses, down the street. *How cool!* I could be on TV, and all my friends would see me. I'd be famous.

"Hey, Dad. Come check it out." I wave my hand towards the front yard.

Dad approaches the window, wiping tears from his

cheeks as he squints at the chaos in front of our house.

"Oh, God. I can't take this. They're everywhere," he says and buries his face in his hands.

Detective Sanders comes up behind us. "I should've warned you—I'm sorry. The media is going to want to talk to you. When something like this happens in a town this small, they come out in hoards. I suggest you and Kendra do a press conference, make a statement for all of them at once."

"Can I be on the news with you?" I ask, excited by the prospect.

"Kent, calm down. Your mom and I need to decide if we're going to talk to them before I can answer that question." Dad turns to Detective Sanders. "I don't know if we can do this. It makes it all too real. I can barely talk to you without breaking down and Kendra…well, you saw how she's doing. What do we do?"

Detective Sanders puts his hand on dad's shoulder. "I suggest we hold a press conference. For one, it will get them off your back. Secondly, it'll allow you to plea to anyone out there that has information about Chelsea to come forward. Pictures of her and her car are going to be all over the news in a couple of hours. You can keep your statement brief but just appeal to whoever has your daughter, or information about her, to come forward," he says and then pauses. "Don't worry about crying; anyone would in your situation, and sometimes tears help appeal to people, encourage them to come forward."

*   *   *

TOM

Hearing the words, *whoever has your daughter,* breaks a new strain of grief loose within me. It makes everything too real. My mind instantly floods with images of a faceless person, with large hands, groping my precious daughter. Before hearing it, I could still pretend that maybe this is all a misunderstanding. Even with the news of the car, somehow, I was able to rationalize a mistake had been made. Maybe it wasn't even really Chelsea's car. How could they know for sure? The car was obliterated, down to the license plates. But with the utterance of those words, *whoever has your daughter,* it becomes painstakingly obvious that regardless of how I delude myself, the detective knows Chelsea isn't just off with friends enjoying a teenage stunt of running away from home for a while. It's now crystal clear that someone—whose name is unknown, whose face is unseen, and whose motives are unclear—has played a part in Chelsea's disappearance.

*　　*　　*

KENT

Dad breaks down sobbing. I've never seen him cry before. I rush to his side and wrap my arms around him. Dad has always been my protector—it feels strange for me to be the one comforting him. I always believed women are the ones who cry, and men bottle everything up and go about their business. Dad always stays calm in every crisis. As I cling to him, he sobs, lifeless, and not hugging me back.

Detective Sanders speaks softly to Dad while patting him on the back. "It's okay to break down. Anyone would in your circumstances. Why don't you go sit down for a bit? We can bide our time with the media—I *guarantee* you, they'll wait."

Dad sits on the couch, resting his head in his hands. Still sobbing, he says, "I'm her father. I'm supposed to protect her. How the hell can I protect her if I don't even know where she is? Who would do this to her? How could they do this to us? Where is she?"

I sit next to him, and this time he reaches out and puts his arm around me, pulling me close. "I'm so sorry, Kent. I don't know what to do. I don't know how to make this better."

"It's okay, Dad. The police will find her. We just have to pray, and she'll be okay," I say, believing every word.

"Kent, honey. God doesn't always answer our prayers the way we think he should. If He did, Chelsea would be home by now," Dad says quietly while stroking my hair like he used to when I was younger.

Dad takes a deep breath and turns to Detective Sanders. "Would you mind seeing if Kendra's still in the garage? Can you talk to her about the reporters and what we need to do? She might take it better from you."

"Sure. You and Kent hang out here, and I'll go talk with her. We'll get through this. We'll find Chelsea and catch this guy."

*　　*　　*

TOM

I nod although doubts ravage my heart, mind, and soul. I pull Kent close, trying to fill the emptiness within. When I replay the detective's words in my mind—*we'll find Chelsea*—another word is instantly added to that sentence. *Body.* A shiver works its way through me, realizing where my thoughts automatically go. Perhaps my mind is already starting to accept the facts that my heart can't even begin to comprehend.

WHEN you remember me, try to smile. I want you to remember the good times, those filled with laughter. The only way to lessen the pain is for you to cling to the happy times we shared. Picture me laughing so hard that tears race down my cheeks. Picture me running through an open field with dandelions all around and the sun beaming down on me. Even though I can't be with you, I'll always be a part of you and you, a part of me. The past can't be erased. The memories can never be stolen.

NICOLE

THE DAY AFTER
THURSDAY, FEBRUARY 9, 1989

I don't know how, but I made it through the day. Every part of me wanted to leave school early to avoid all the stares, rumors, concerned looks, and empty seats Chelsea should've been sitting in, but I couldn't make myself go. I kept thinking I'd stumble across Chelsea in the hall or class and holding onto the hope that she'd come running up to me, laughing and saying it was all just a big mistake. As I walk out to my car, I realize my hopes haven't come to fruition. Chelsea never appeared.

Brent comes running up, falling in step beside me. He looks as terrible as I feel. "Hey, Nicole. You hanging in there?"

"No. You?"

Brent shakes his head. "I'm worried sick. I've wracked

my brain trying to think of where she could be, who she could be with, who would want to hurt her. I don't have a damn clue. To make it all worse, the cops act like I have something to do with her disappearance. Like I'd hurt her. I love Chels."

"I know you do, Brent. *She* knows you do. The police are just trying to figure it all out."

"I know, but it hurts they could even think that." After a pause, he asks me to give him a ride home. "I was supposed to catch a ride with Sam, but I'm sick of everyone right now. I know you understand how I feel."

"Sure, and I do know *exactly* how you feel."

We get into the car, and I crank the heat to fight off the chill. "I blew up at some girls in the bathroom who were spreading shit about Chels— that she's on drugs, that she's pregnant, that she ran off with some guy in the Navy."

"Yea, I've heard my share of bullshit today too. Not one asshole could say anything true about Chels; like her missing gives them the right to make shit up. Ya know? The guys from the team had the balls to ask if the Navy-guy rumor was true! I didn't say shit because I would've lost it, but the look I shot them told them to back the hell off. Lucky for them, they got the hint!" Brent runs his hand through his hair. "As much as I didn't want to listen to the BS, I couldn't help myself, though, because what if someone said something that might help?"

As I drive, I scan the fields beside the road, the back-yards of each house we pass. "It's so freaking messed up. She could be anywhere right now. She could be in that house or that ditch or that field," I say as we pass each landmark. "How will they ever find her? She could be *anywhere.*"

"I don't know, but they have to. She has to be okay," Brent says, choking back tears.

Despite his efforts at stifling them, the tears escape. He wipes them away as quickly as he can. I've never seen a man cry before and don't know how to respond. We ride in silence until we turn onto Brent's street.

"They'll find her. Right, Nicole? You believe she's okay, right?" Brent asks as I come to a stop in his driveway.

"Do you want the truth?" Tears burn my eyes.

"I want you to say yes and that she's okay."

"I can't. I wish I could, but I can't. I don't think she is."

"Damn it, Nicole. She's going to prove you wrong. She's gonna be back any minute. You'll see." Brent slams the car door and takes the steps to his house, two at a time, as though he can flee the truth.

"I'm sorry for my doubts Chels," I whisper as I back out of the driveway and head towards home.

*   *   *

My parents are standing on the front porch as I round the corner onto my street. I instantly wonder if they found something out. I've barely opened the car door when they both come running towards me, my mother with her arms open to embrace me, my father shouting, "Where the hell were you? You're late."

"I'm sorry. Brent needed a ride home, so I dropped him off. Chill! I'm only ten minutes late."

"We were worried about you," Mom says, holding me

so tightly I can't move.

I push away from her. "I'm fine, Mom."

"We need to talk. Get in the house," my father orders.

I barely have a chance to sit before Dad starts ranting.

"Okay, new rules. One, you are to come straight home after school unless you have our permission ahead of time to go somewhere. Two, you need to quit your job—you're not working while some kidnapper is on the loose. Three, you're not to hang out with any guys until the police have figured out what happened to Chelsea." Dad's eyes never leave mine; the crinkles of worry at the corners aren't enough to keep my anger at bay.

I ball my hands into fists and raise my chin in defiance. Why are my parents treating me like I've done something wrong? "You're being unfair. I'm almost eighteen years old—these are stricter rules than I had when I was twelve."

"When you were twelve, your best friend wasn't missing. When you were twelve, none of your friends were possible kidnappers or murderers. When you were twelve, we were always with you to keep you safe." My father's voice gets shakier with each word.

Mom gently touches my arm. "Honey, we want to protect you. You don't really know who you can trust right now. The police are still trying to figure this all out. What if Brent had something to do with Chelsea's disappearance and here you are alone with him? He could've done something to you too."

"Brent had nothing to do with it. How could you even think that?" I throw my hands into the air.

Dad slams his fist onto the end table beside him. "Dammit, Nicole! Don't be naïve. You don't know who has Chelsea. It could be the guy you sit next to in Math Class, your favorite teacher, Brent, a customer from the restaurant, or even her father. You don't know; we don't know; the police don't know. The only person that knows is Chelsea, and she's not here to tell us." I almost don't recognize him as the same man who usually has less than three words to say to me each day. "You have to face the facts. Some sicko has Chelsea, and he could come after you next. And bad guys don't come with a warning label stuck on their foreheads. They look and act normal. Until this is solved, you should trust no one."

"Well, following your logic, that includes you. You're a man—you could be a sicko, too!" Sobbing, I run to my room before my father can yell at me anymore and tell me I'm grounded or wrong, or both.

*   *   *

I wake to my mom staring at me; the light on my bedside table casts a warmth to the room. The blinds are drawn as if that will keep out the dangers of the dark night—kidnappers who take people, like my best friend.

"Hi. Did you have a nice nap?" Mom asks, rubbing my back in small circles like she used to do when I was younger and having trouble sleeping.

I stifle a yawn. "I guess. Any news?"

"Why don't you come down and get something to eat? You've got to be starving," Mom says, averting her eyes, seemingly trying to avoid answering the question.

"You heard something, didn't you? What is it? Did they find her?" I bolt up and kick off my blankets.

"No, they didn't find Chelsea," Mom studies my comforter, smoothing out its wrinkles. "They found her car, though, less than a mile from her work. It was burned almost beyond recognition."

I gasp and feel like I've been stabbed straight through the heart. I grip at my shirt as I forget how to exhale. Every inch of my skin erupts in goosebumps. *Burned?* I frown, still unable to breathe.

My parents are right. No one knows who has Chelsea. It could be anyone. Faces flash through my mind, bringing an onslaught of fear. The janitor at our school who always smiles at us when we walk by. Mr. Sloan, our biology teacher. The guy who works at the *Taco Shoppe* next door to *Landoll's* that always offers us free drinks when we pass by. Brent. The guy whose locker is next to Chelsea's. Who can I *really* trust? As the faces continue to bombard me, I know that until the police find Chelsea, and figure out who the bad guy is, I'll do exactly as my father said and trust no one.

BILLY

17 YEARS, 1 MONTH, 8 DAYS BEFORE
DECEMBER 31, 1971

BEING home has been a lot better than before we left like Mommy promised. I wasn't sure about coming back because life was so much nicer without Daddy. I'm scared he'll hurt us again. Mommy promises she'll protect us and keep us safe. I don't really know what to think, but I know Mommy loves me, so I trust her.

I still miss some things about our time away. I miss sleeping with Mommy, the smell from the bakery, Mrs. Lawson, and the fresh bread she gave us. I miss seeing Mommy in her pink waitressing uniform and our trips to the playground at the school.

But there are good things about being home. Mommy

doesn't have to work anymore, which means no more nights alone, being afraid of monsters in the closet or noises echoing down the halls. Daddy's also been much nicer to all of us. For the first time ever, he took me outside when it was still warmer and played baseball with me in the backyard. Daddy doesn't stay out all night like he used to and when he's home, he doesn't smell like whiskey. He's nicer to Mommy too. He thanks her for dinner, helps her with the dishes sometimes, and tells her she looks pretty. Mommy smiles as much at home now as she did when we were in the apartment.

Today is New Year's Eve, and Mommy has been planning a celebration to *Welcome in 1972*. Daddy went to work at the factory today, but our party is planned for this evening. Mommy said we can stay up until midnight when it will officially turn from 1971 to 1972. I don't understand all that, but I'm excited about getting to stay up late, since my usual bedtime is eight-thirty. We went shopping with Mommy to get the party supplies. She's going to make chicken the way Daddy likes it, *dripping with grease*, macaroni salad, deviled eggs, Jell-O with fruit in it. She even bought us little noisemakers. Mommy is excited about our little party.

Mommy always has dinner ready for Daddy when he gets home from work. Yummy smells creep into my room while David and me play, and it makes my mouth water. I love deviled eggs and would eat them all if I was allowed, but Mommy will only let me have two because she says my stomach will get upset if I eat more. I try my best to ignore the smell of the food by building a bridge with David.

58

After what seems like forever to my rumbling stomach, I go to the kitchen to see if it's almost party time. The table is set with two lit candles in the middle. Mommy stands at the window, peering outside, and has a dress on I've never seen before. Her long, brown hair is braided down her back. I can't see her face, but I can tell she looks pretty.

"Mommy, when will it be time to eat?" I ask from the doorway.

"As soon as Daddy gets home," she says. "We can't start the party without him, now can we?"

"When will that be? I'm starving!" I say, sneaking towards the counter where the deviled eggs sit.

"Now, you, little man, stay out of the eggs." She catches my hand in her own, just as I'm about to snatch one.

"Just one, Mommy…please," I beg and give her my puppy dog eyes, knowing she can't say no when I give her that look.

"Okay, one." I grab one and shove it in my mouth whole, the yellow gooey filling dripping out of the corners, onto my chin. "Wipe your mouth, then go back and play until Daddy gets home. It should be soon."

I go back to complete our bridge. David and me run our cars back and forth over it, pretending there's a rushing river underneath that will sweep us away if we fall off. We play until our game escalates from driving on the bridge to destroying it with huge boulders of blocks falling from the sky. Once it's in ruins, I go back to see if Daddy has come home yet.

This time when I go to the living room, I count the

numbers on the clock; it's already seven. Daddy is late—way late. I look for Mommy, but she's nowhere in the house. Finally, I open the front door, and she's sitting on the front porch, right in the snow, with her head in her hands. She sniffles. Oh no! She's crying. Tears sting at my own eyes because I don't like it when she's sad.

"Mommy, what's wrong?" I sit and wrap my arm around her.

She wipes the tears away as she lifts her head and smiles. It's not a real one though—I can tell the difference. "Well, I think Daddy must have to work late so it will be the three of us for now." She pauses. "Are you still hungry?"

"Yes, I am," I say, rubbing my stomach. "But why are you crying?"

"I'm not. I just wanted to come out and get some fresh air. Now, let's go get your brother and have ourselves a party!" She stands and wipes the snow off the back of her dress.

I can tell she was crying though because her nose is red, and she has black streaks from her make-up under her eyes. But, I'm hungry and ready for our party, so I don't say anything else about it. Instead, I get David, so our fun can begin.

*   *   *

As Mommy promised, she lets us stay up until midnight. I manage to make it to watch the ball drop on TV in some faraway city, but David curled up with his blanket and fell asleep on the floor at ten. I wanted to wake him up at midnight so he could say *Happy New Year* with us, but Mommy carried him to bed. Mommy got up to look out the front window at least ten times during the evening. I wonder where Daddy is but don't ask because I don't want to make her cry again. I'm mad at him. He knew Mommy was excited about our party. Mommy even got a new dress and put on make-up so Daddy would say how pretty she was. Since Daddy didn't come home, I told her instead.

After the ball drops, Mommy gives me a New Year's kiss and tucks me into bed next to David. I fall asleep before she even makes it out of the room.

*   *   *

I wake up to my father yelling, in a voice I haven't heard since my birthday. Instantly, my entire body trembles. I lay as still as I can and squeeze my eyes shut, hoping I'm just having a nightmare.

"How dare you tell me what I can and can't do? The last time I checked, I'm the man of the house, and you're my wife. I decide where I go, when I go, and who I go with," Daddy rages. "I didn't want to come to your stupid party anyway. I needed a drink to stand being around you and those damn kids."

I lay quietly trying to hear Mommy's voice, but there's a loud crash, and then Daddy's ranting continues.

"You need to get this through your tiny brain. I work my ass off and put food on the table—not you. And if I want to go out and have a real celebration on New Year's Eve, I god-dammed will! You don't get a say so. I'm done playing your stupid game, woman. You obey me, not the other way 'round." Another crash scares me so badly I might pee my pants. "Stop trying to make me into a sissy choir boy."

Mommy's voice grows louder, begging and crying. My whole body trembles, from head to toe. "Please, Lee. Just stop. I don't want to wake the boys. Let's go to bed and talk about it in the morning."

"We'll talk when I say we talk and right now I'm talking. Got it?"

Mommy screams. I jump out of bed and realize David is awake too, lying wide-eyed and silent next to me. "Biwwy, please don't go. I'm scared."

"He's hurting Mommy, David. I have to help her." I say, already to the door. "Stay here. I'll be right back."

As I tiptoe down the hallway, Daddy is still yelling. Things are scattered all over the living room—my kindergarten picture frame is laying by the front door with glass everywhere, books have been tossed from the bookshelf, the candles from the table are thrown all the way to the hallway. There's a hole punched in the wall right beside the TV set.

Mommy sees me first. Blood trickles from her lip, down her chin, and her nightgown is torn. The skin around one of her eyes is red and swollen. Mommy notices me, and her eyes widen. She runs towards Daddy, who is still yelling at her, wraps her arms around his neck, and starts kissing him. With a hand, she motions to me to go away. I stand there, not knowing what to do. When Daddy pulls away, he speaks quieter this time.

"Oh, baby. I knew you'd see it my way. This is what a husband needs," he says as he pulls open her nightgown and starts kissing her neck.

Mommy looks at me and mouths the words *Go to your room now*. Daddy starts kissing her shoulders while she stands there staring at me with tears running down her blood-streaked cheeks.

I go back to our room, lay down next to David, and snuggle my three-year-old brother close to help him stop crying. I whisper the words to him I wish were true, "It's okay. Everything's alright."

TOM

THE DAY AFTER
THURSDAY, FEBRUARY 9, 1989

DETECTIVE Sanders has been in the garage talking to Kendra for over an hour. I can't imagine what's taking so long. I pace from the dining room, through the kitchen, to the family room and back again. It is twenty-two steps in each direction. Turn around, twenty-two steps back. I've walked back and forth fifteen times so far. Six hundred and sixty steps. Focusing on the number of steps keeps my mind from wandering to the what-ifs and the already-knowns regarding Chelsea. The counting keeps my fear and anxiety from consuming me.

I'm on my sixteenth trip to the family room when Kendra and Detective Sanders come back inside, almost hitting me with the door as it swings open. Kendra's eyes are puffy; her nose is rubbed raw, and there are red splotches all over her face. I've never seen her look so weary before. Of course, I've never looked at her before feeling such weariness within myself. Maybe what I see in Kendra is a mirror-image of myself; pain and sadness etched into every line on my face.

"Oh, Tom…" Kendra collapses into my arms, burying her head against my chest.

I hold onto her more tightly than I have in years. I wish I could protect her from having to feel any more pain through all of this. If only I can keep her within my embrace, maybe she'll be spared the realities to come. I breathe in the scent of her. Her hair still smells of berries from her shampoo. It's ironic such a sweet smell can come from a woman who has parts of herself dying and decaying before my eyes.

Kendra pulls back, taking my hands within her own. "Detective Sanders and I talked. We've got to do this press conference. To beg for someone to come forward with information that'll help us find Chelsea. To plead with whoever has her to bring her home. The not knowing's killing me, Tom. I think I can face anything other than another day of not knowing where my baby is."

"I know sweetheart. I know…" I pull her close again; her hot breath rushes across my neck.

Detective Sanders clears his throat, interrupting our embrace. "Let's sit down and come up with a statement you're comfortable with. Maybe we'll get some tips to help us out."

After a short discussion, we decide to do a press conference at the police station and deliver our statement to as many media outlets as possible. Detective Sanders sticks his head out the front door and every reporter on the block jumps out of their vehicle, circling like vultures, hoping to get a morsel of information.

"We will conduct a press conference at the Langston Police Department in one hour. We will fit in as many reporters as possible. See you then." Ignoring the slew of questions, Detective Sanders shuts the front door.

*   *   *

KENDRA

As we walk into the police station, I take a deep breath, trying to keep myself composed. How do I beg someone to spare my daughter's life when I fear it's already too late? How do I possibly plead with some stranger for information about my child that could lead to discovering the most devastating news of my life? How are Tom and I supposed to do this without crumbling into a million tiny pieces in front of a room full of reporters and cameras? Detective Sanders explained how important it is to show just the right amount of emotion—not too little, not too much. I wanted to ask if there's a formula for what the *right amount of emotion* is for those who've lost their child.

We take our seats at the front of the conference room, behind a large table. A hush falls over the room as all eyes turn in our direction. I search the faces staring at us and wonder if any of them really care or if this is just another story for them...a way to earn a paycheck. Do any of them care that they are witnessing a family being torn apart at the seams?

At exactly seven, Detective Sanders stands to announce the "rules" of the press conference, stating that Tom and I will speak first, taking no questions. Questions can be directed towards him upon completion, once we've left the room. We agreed this would be the least painful way to do what needs to be done. We won't have to hear the details of the case re-hashed, thus inflicting more pain to the wounds that have not even yet begun to scab over.

Tom, Kent, and I stand when Detective Sanders nods in our direction. Tom is the first to speak, while Kent holds up his sister's senior picture, taken only four short months ago.

"I am Tom. This is my wife, Kendra, and, our son, Kent." His hands shake as he points towards each of us. "The person missing here is our daughter, Chelsea. This is her most recent picture, taken only a few months ago. As you know, she never came home from work on February eighth. My wife and I reported her disappearance to the police yesterday. The only lead we have so far is the discovery of her burnt car less than a mile from the restaurant where she worked," Tom pauses, clears his throat, and takes a sip of water. "We're here to beg anyone that has any information about our daughter, Chelsea Marie Wyatt, to please call the Langston Police Department as soon as possible. Our family is falling apart without her."

I squeeze Tom's arm as we switch places; his eyes glisten with tears, threatening to fall. I clasp my hands together, trying to calm their trembling. My knees shake so badly I'm afraid my legs will give out. I lean against the podium to steady myself. "We want to plead with whoever has our daughter, to please bring her home. We love her more than you can imagine. Please return her to us. If anyone has seen anything they think may be helpful to the police, please report it. You never know how useful your tip may be. It doesn't matter how small the piece of information is, please call them—it may be the one thing the police need to find our baby girl." The tears waterfall, leaving a trail down my cheeks. "Chelsea, if you're out there and hear this, remember how much we love you. You're our angel. We'll be waiting at home for you, praying every moment you're okay. Please, bring Chelsea home."

I step back and wrap my arm around Kent while Detective Sanders nods and whispers, "Well done." We move into the open halls of the police station and huddle together in a hug, thankful it's over. We cling to each other as a way to hold ourselves upright.

NICOLE

2 DAYS AFTER
FRIDAY, FEBRUARY 10, 1989

THE sun, reflecting off the snow-covered ground, shines in my window, waking me at ten-thirty. I try to cover my head with my comforter to block out the light. If I could, I would stay in bed forever, or at least until Chelsea comes home. I don't feel up to facing the world right now. My parents and I agreed I should skip school today. Since I didn't have to get up, Mom gave me one of her Valium last night, and it did its job. It took everything away and quieted my mind, allowing me to get some sleep without thinking of Chelsea or envisioning her lying dead somewhere. I can't face everyone *except* Chelsea all day again. I can't bear to hear more rumors, especially in light of the police's discovery of her car. There's no doubt that the shit is flying all over school today.

I want to go back to sleep, but my thoughts are already racing out of control. I tug on some sweats and make my way down to the kitchen. I'm hungry, but everything is too much of an effort this morning. I grab a plain bagel and plunk down at the table. In front of me lies Chelsea's destroyed car, gracing almost the entire front page of the Langston Messenger with her senior picture next to it. Although the picture is black and white, I can see my best friend's light brown hair and sparkling blue eyes. I lightly touch the picture, wishing it was my friend instead of the ink of the newspaper.

I blink, trying to clear away some of the tears so that I can see the picture of Chelsea's car. It was totally destroyed by the fire, and I wouldn't have recognized it in a million years, even though it's the car Chelsea and I spent hour upon hour riding in talking about boys, our hopes, our dreams, our futures. I'm flooded with the memories—memories made with Chelsea in the car that's now plastered on the front page of every newspaper, in every home, in Fairmont County.

The many hours we went "cruising" flash through my memory. In a town as small as Langston, the cruising is limited to the local fast-food parking lots where car after car drives slowly through, occasionally making a stop to say hi to a friend or get the phone number of a stranger. My parents won't buy me a car, so it's always been up to Chelsea to do the driving. Our Friday night routine consisted of cruising in her car, looking for fun. Sometimes we'd pick up a couple of other people to hang with, but, most of the time, it was just the two of us, jamming to the radio so loudly we had to shout to hear each other. The two of us laughing hysterically—sometimes so much so that Chelsea had to pull off the side of the road to compose herself before driving on. One of the things I love most about Chelsea is her infectious laugh.

There are so many firsts for both of us that happened in that car. It's the place we tried our first cigarette. Both of us choked and gagged, thinking we were going to be the first people ever to die from smoking only one cigarette. Once we got the first one down, we threw the pack out the window, vowing not to do that again. We had our first double-date in that car with the Watson twins, which was a total dud. We were both so happy the other was along so we could share laughs about it later.

It was in her car that Chelsea talked to me about possibly wanting to have sex with Brent and the pros and cons of that choice. It was there we vowed to each other that we wouldn't let college separate us, and we'd follow the other one wherever they went. So many of my memories of the past two years are wrapped up in Chelsea and her car, now displayed on the front page for all the world to see. All those memories burnt to a crisp.

I hold the paper up so Chelsea's face rests against my cheek and I sob until I can cry no more. My whole body is tense with loss, grief, and fear. Chelsea's face is no longer visible on the paper as my tears have completely soaked through, causing the ink to bleed onto my cheeks.

I finally find the strength to get up from the table. I rush to my parent's bathroom, open the medicine cabinet, and quickly find the bottle I need. Inside is the pill that will take it all away for a while. I unscrew the cap, and this time take two. A little extra sleep will only make me feel better. I put the bottle back and head to my bed, hoping to feel the effects of the pills before the nightmares come again.

*   *   *

The Valium works. I manage to sleep deeply until seven, when my mom comes in to wake me. "Nicole honey, you need to get up. Detective Sanders is here to see you... he has some questions."

I try to open my eyes, but they are too heavy. "Tell him I'm sleeping. I'll see him tomorrow," I mutter and pull the pillow over my head.

"You can't tell a police detective you'll talk to him to-morrow. You have to wake up and meet with him... now. I'll get him some coffee and make small talk. Meanwhile, splash water on your face, get dressed, do whatever you have to do to pull yourself together enough to get downstairs to talk to him," Mom says as she yanks my blankets off. "You've got five minutes."

As soon as she leaves, I sit up, and the room spins. I plop back onto the bed, stare at the ceiling, and take a couple of deep breaths until the room steadies. Feeling a bit drugged may be a good thing—perhaps then I won't get so upset by the questions he might ask. I go to the bathroom and do as my mother sug-gested—splash water on my face, run a brush through my hair, and slip into jeans and a sweatshirt. I look awful with dark bags under my eyes and cheeks sunken in so badly that my cheek-bones practically stick out as far as my nose. It looks like I've

72

been crying for hours and haven't eaten for weeks.

I go down the steps slower than usual to make sure I don't fall since I'm still a bit light-headed. That would suck. Plopping on my butt right into the living room in front of the detective.

Mom meets me at the base of the stairs and hands me a cup of coffee. "Alright, I'll leave you two alone. Holler if you need anything."

Detective Sanders rises and shakes my hand. "Nicole, I'm sorry to bother you again so soon, but I have some more questions." He sits and clears his throat before continuing. "I've been interviewing some fellow students at the school. I have some names that have come up a few times. I wanted to run them by you to see if they are involved in any way with Chelsea. Or if you have any information that might be helpful."

I take a sip of coffee before answering. "Okay."

He pulls out his notebook and pen. "First one is Randy Stevens. What can you tell me about him?"

"Oh, Randy...he's a really sweet guy. He's had a crush on Chelsea since about the sixth grade, I think. He used to leave her love notes in her locker, on her windshield, taped to her front door. He wouldn't sign them, but we knew who they were from. He'd write these cute little messages that always said sweet things like she was as beautiful as a sunset."

Detective Sanders scribbles in his notebook as I talk. The writing stops, and he asks, "Did Chelsea ever date him?"

I shake my head. "He wasn't her type."

He furrows his brow. "What do you mean?"

73

"Well, Chels always attracted attention from a lot of guys. She really could have her pick of just about anyone, to be honest. Randy is quiet, smart, and doesn't have many friends. Chels is the complete opposite—she walks in the room and instantly commands the attention of everyone there without even trying. It just happens. She's like a light someone turns on in a completely pitch-black room. You can't help but look at it." I smile, picturing her.

"How does Chelsea feel about the attention she gets from Randy?"

"She loves it. She's always saying how sweet he is, and she feels sorry for him because he doesn't have many friends. She makes sure to say hi to him whenever she sees him and sometimes goes out of her way to walk down the hall with him."

"How does Randy seem to take it that Chelsea isn't interested?"

"I don't think he realizes it. When Chels is with you, you feel like you're the only person in the world at that moment. I'm sure that's how Randy feels whenever she's around too. He never asked her to go out or anything—we just know how he feels because of all of the love notes."

"How did you know they were from him?" He taps his pen against his lips.

"Well, one day, Chelsea got off work early. She saw Randy slipping a note under the windshield wiper. She ducked behind another car until he was gone so he wouldn't be embarrassed."

Detective Sanders' eyes narrow. "Were there lots of

notes left while she was working?"

I nod. "Quite a few. He seemed to always be able to find her car…" My voice trails off into thin air. "Is he a suspect?"

"We're trying to get some more information at this point. We don't have any official suspects," he says as he circles something on the page of his notebook.

"He seems so sweet. I really don't think he could ever hurt anyone, let alone Chels who he obviously cares about," I pause, hating where my thoughts are going. "But it's a little strange he can always find her car no matter where she parks. Once, she drove her parents' car to work, and he left a note on it, too. Kind of like he kept tabs on her. That's a little creepy now that I think about it," I say and wring my hands.

"That's *quite* interesting. Anything else you can think of?"

I shake my head as chills race down my spine. *Could someone as sweet and as seemingly innocent as Randy Stevens be responsible for Chelsea's disappearance?* I know Chels—if Randy had come up to her after work, wanting to talk, she would've made the time for him without a second thought.

I share this revelation with the detective and his eyes narrow with concern. He writes something else down in his notebook and says, "Okay, next name. Josh Lowry."

"What a jerk!" Heat rises to my cheeks at the mention of his name.

"What makes you say that?"

"He's a hood that smokes cigarettes and pot, drinks, beats people up. You name it, and he does it."

"Did Chelsea ever have any run-ins with him?"

"Yeah… a few," I pause, remembering the details. "Once, Chels was bent over at her locker, and Josh stuck his hand right up the back of her skirt. He laughed, saying he always wondered if she felt as hot as she looked. Chelsea was fuming and, of course, by the end of the day, it was all over school."

"What did Chelsea do about it?"

"Nothing. I tried to talk her into going to the principal, but she wouldn't, saying it'd only make it worse. Besides, Chels has this unbelievable way of feeling sorry for everyone who does bad things. She always says there must be something horrible going on in their lives for them to act that way. She said that same thing about Josh." I shrug and take another drink of coffee.

"Anything else with him?"

"There was another time Chels and I had to stay after school to meet with Mr. Thompkins, our art teacher, to work on a project. After we were done, Chels went to the bathroom; I planned to meet up with her there after I got my stuff from my locker. I waited for a few minutes, but she didn't come out. She was in the bathroom, crying in front of the mirror. Apparently, Josh had been hiding in the stall next to hers, and when she came out, he grabbed her and started kissing her neck, saying he wished she'd give him a chance. He told her he wasn't as bad as everybody thought, and he just needed someone like her to straighten him out. Chelsea said she told him she'd think about it and let him know." I pause and pick up my coffee cup, my hands trembling so badly a bit of it spills onto my lap.

"I told her he was a sicko and that she needed to go to

the principal, but she refused. She actually had the nerve to say maybe she should go out with him and help him get his life on the right track. I told her she was insane and needed to stay away from him."

Detective Sanders shakes his head and sucks in a sharp breath through his teeth. "Any other incidents that come to mind?"

"None in particular but, after that day, I saw a little change in Chels towards him. I think she took what I said to heart and every time she'd pass him in the hallway, she'd completely ignore him. I don't think he ever got the point though because he'd still stare at her or make little comments every time she was around."

Detective Sanders leans forward and rests his elbows on his knees. "Are you sure she never went out with Josh or took it any further?"

I nod. "I'm sure. She wouldn't have."

"Would she tell you, knowing how you feel about him?"

"Yeah. That's what best friends do—at least that's how Chels and I are. Even if we don't agree, we still stand by each other and let the other one make the mistakes they have to. She knows I would've come around or at least heard her out." I wrap my arms around myself, trying to calm the butterflies in my stomach.

"Do you think Josh would be capable of hurting Chelsea?" Detective Sanders asks with raised eyebrows.

This question takes my breath away as I realize the answer. "I know he could. He's really tough. I don't think he would though—he seems to really like her but doesn't know how to show it in the right way. I hope he wouldn't anyway."

"Would Chelsea have run away with him because she knew being with him would upset everyone?"

"No, she wouldn't. As I said, she's totally into Brent. She loves him. Besides, Josh was at school the day after Chels disappeared. A couple of people said he seemed pretty out of it and upset that day."

"Okay, one more to go. Do you need a minute?"

"Yeah. Let me get some more coffee. Would you like some?" I ask, standing with my cup in hand. What I really need is more Valium to calm my nerves, but I can't slip away to take them with a police officer sitting in my living room.

"No, I'm fine."

After I return from the kitchen, I sit as Detective Sanders speaks the third name. "Kurt Miller—what can you tell me about him?"

Hearing his name brings an instant jab of pain straight through my heart. I'd convinced myself I was over him. I fight back the tears welling in my eyes. "Kurt and I dated for a while right when Chels and Brent started going out. We always double-dated cause he and Brent were best friends too. It was going well—I was really into him, and I thought he felt the same about me. It started getting weird though—Kurt never wanted to go out when it was just the two of us. I started noticing he'd always watch Chelsea, talk to her, brush up against her when Brent wasn't looking. He paid much more attention to her than to me. When I'd bring it up, he'd laugh, tell me I was crazy, and say he was head over heels in love with me. So, I chose to believe him despite what I was seeing." Tears burn my eyes, threatening to fall. I look up at the ceiling to keep them at bay.

"One night, when we all went to the movies, his flirting with Chelsea just got out of control, and I ran from the theater in tears. Chelsea, of course, followed me. I exploded and told her everything I'd been noticing. She finally admitted Kurt had been hitting on her the entire two months we'd been going out. He once cornered her at Brent's house, when they were alone in the room, and kissed her. Chelsea slapped him across the face and told him never to touch her again, or she would tell Brent and me."

My heart sinks with the memories, and I wrap my arms tighter around myself. "Chelsea was upset and crying when she told me everything. She said she kept it from us because she didn't want to hurt either one of us—Brent by feeling betrayed by his best friend and me because she knew how much I liked him. We made a pact, there in the bathroom, to never keep secrets from each other again and she vowed to tell Brent the truth when they were alone. After our talk, Chels went back to tell the guys we were leaving, and I waited for her in the car."

The scratching noise of his pen finally stops, and he asks, "Did Chelsea tell Brent about Kurt?"

"Yeah. He and Brent had a falling out and haven't really been that good of friends since. They're still civil, but it's not the same with them."

"Did Kurt ever hit on Chelsea again or say anything to her?"

I grab my coffee mug and wrap my hands around it, trying to warm the chill inside of me. "Just little things, passing by each other in the hall or when he'd catch her eye in class. But nothing too blatant. As usual, Chels was able to let it go and move on, treating him okay when she saw him but not being overly friendly."

Detective Sanders closes his notebook and puts it back in his pocket. "Well, Nicole. Thank you for your time. This has all been very helpful. You've given me some great information to go with. I know it wasn't easy for you."

"I just want to help find Chels," I pause, trying to figure out how to phrase the question I need to ask. "So, do you think Randy, Josh or Kurt had something to do with this?"

"I'm not sure, which is why I needed information. Based on what you've given me today, they're all worth looking at further and asking some questions."

I don't know how to feel about this. These are guys I see every day sitting in the classroom with me, walking down the same halls, showing up at the same parties on Saturday nights. These are guys I wouldn't fear if I ran into them when I was alone. I know Chelsea wouldn't either.

I escort Detective Sanders to the door where my mom joins us. A blast of cold air takes my breath away. He thanks us and jogs to his car, leaving a trail of footsteps in the snow-covered sidewalk.

BILLY

15 YEARS, 4 MONTHS, 11 DAYS BEFORE
SEPTEMBER 28, 1973

THE sounds coming from my parents' bedroom tell me something is different about this fight. It happens so often now that David and I barely pay attention anymore when Dad's voice booms through the house, yelling insults and profanities at Mom. We never mention the after-effects of the fights anymore either—the black eyes, the busted lips, the broken furniture. I just accept that this must be what normal is for my family. I didn't give up trying to protect Mom easily, but my repeated attempts to intervene or to comfort her were always met with her pleading for me to stay out of it. She'd beg me to ignore our father when he's in his drunken rages because she doesn't want David or me to get hurt. She doesn't seem to understand I love her, too, and don't want her to be hurt either.

Each time the yelling begins, David and I try to find new ways to distract ourselves. We make up silly songs, singing louder to mask the sounds of shouting, or have pillow fights. We sometimes sneak out the bedroom window and wander to the farthest point in the yard, trying to count the stars until we hear quiet from inside our house. We make tents in our room out of blankets and sit underneath, pretending we're hiding out from the evil beast lurking beyond its walls.

We're experts at becoming invisible as often as possible whether Dad seems to be in a bad mood or not. It's much more peaceful and less tense when he isn't around. Our mom still tries her best to be a good mother, but she hasn't ever been the same since that New Year's Eve two years ago. A part of her died that evening—our dad beat the hope right out of her. When our father isn't home, she still plays with us, takes us to the park, laughs with us; but her eyes never sparkle when she smiles, like they used to.

As guilty as it makes me feel, I pray every day my father won't come home, or we can all run away again without him. I know we can find happiness again—we've done it before. My father drinks more and more now. The smell of stale alcohol is always on his breath, which makes me nauseous. He's even started drinking at home in the past year, which I really hate because at least if he goes out, we can relax while he's gone and pretend we're a normal family.

David and I have learned not to speak during dinner when he's home because we never know exactly what will set him off. But, when Dad is away, it's an altogether different story. All three of us talk more than we chew, with never a moment of silence. I love those dinners when he's gone and enjoy every laugh that comes from one of us. In a house like ours, you never know when you'll hear someone laugh again, so you hold onto each one as though it's something so fragile it could break with even the slightest twitch of one's finger.

So far, David and I have tried everything we can think of to distract ourselves from the yelling that grows louder with each passing moment, but nothing is working. David is more upset than he's been in a long time, and I don't know how to comfort him. I've just suggested we sneak outside when Dad slams our bedroom door open. He pulls our mother behind him by her long, brown hair. Her eyes are so swollen I doubt she can even see. Both of us freeze, staring up at our dad, waiting to see why he's interrupted his tirade to pay us a visit.

"Come with me boys." Dad drags Mom to the bathroom.

"What do we do?" David asks, trembling.

"I guess we follow him." I'm not sure if this is the right answer or not. In fact, I'm unsure if there even is a right answer at all. As we slowly make our way towards the bathroom, we hear the water running in the tub.

"Sit down, boys, where you can watch." Our father throws our mother onto the floor and places one foot on top of her chest so she can't move, even though she's not even trying to. We sit in front of the bathroom vanity as instructed.

"Are you ready to watch your mom die?" The coldness

in my father's eyes sends a chill down my spine, and the hair on my arms stands straight up. "Say goodbye, boys." With that, our father yanks our mother's head up off the floor and pulls her chin to face us.

"Daddy, what are you…?" My question is interrupted by him taking her head and plunging it beneath the surface of the water. This makes the life come back into my mother's limbs, and she starts kicking and flailing.

"Daddy, stop!" I lunge towards my father so forcefully, it knocks him off balance for a moment, and my mother slips from his grasp. She manages to give my father a strong kick in the stomach. Once our father regains his steadiness, he draws back, punching me so hard I fly back several feet, hitting my head on the edge of the bathroom counter. Blood oozes from my scalp. Before I can get up, he kicks me in the stomach, sending me hurling further back.

As I'm still struggling to get up, Dad again dunks Mom's head back into the water, holding her there until her legs and arms stop moving. When she's motionless, he lifts her out and tosses her onto the floor like a soiled dish rag. As he walks towards the door, past David and me, he kicks me one last time and says, "Clean up the mess your bitch of a mother made and go to bed. I'm going out."

David is the one to speak for once. "But…what…what do we do…what do we do with Mommy?"

"For all I care, you can bury the bitch in the backyard."

He stomps down the hallway and slams the front door behind him.

* * *

I must've passed out because I awake lying in a pile of my own vomit and to the sound of David's sobs. As soon as David sees that my eyes are open, his crying calms enough for him to say, "Biwwy, I think she's dead. She hasn't moved."

I push myself forward and move to our mother's soaking wet, still body, lying in the same position as it was before I blacked out.

"Mommy! Wake up, Mommy!" I say, leaning down to yell into her ear. "Mommy." I shake her, but she doesn't respond. "Mommy, wake up. We need you to wake up. Please wake up." I sob. My tears are so thick I can't focus on my mother's chest clearly enough to see if it's rising and falling.

I don't know what to do. Usually, I'm the one who can figure it all out, but this time, I can't. My head and stomach hurt from Daddy's kicks and punches. I do the only thing I can—I lie down on the wet floor next to my mother and curl up to her as closely as possible. The last thing I remember before I pass out again is whispering a prayer to please let me die with her.

* * *

I struggle to open my eyes to see who is shaking me, telling me to wake up. My one eye is swollen shut, and I can't force it open no matter how hard I try. I hear my mother's voice and wonder if God has answered my prayer to let me die with her. Then, I realize I also hear David's voice and a woman's I don't recognize.

Finally, I force my right eye open to see our neighbor,

85

Mrs. Jones, leaning towards me with her face only inches away from mine. "There you are. Can you try to sit up for me?"

"Where's my mommy?" I reach behind myself to feel if her body is still there. It isn't.

"I'm right here, sweetie." My mother's voice comes from the hallway outside of the bathroom.

Her voice snaps me back to my senses immediately, and I move as quickly as I can towards her. "Mommy, you're alive!"

She leans against the wall of the hallway with David nestled up against her. She pulls me into her embrace. "We thought you were dead," I say, starting to cry again.

My mother's eyes are swollen almost completely shut, and she has bruises in the shape of Daddy's hands up and down her arms and around her neck.

"It's okay. I'm alive. Are you okay, sweetie?" She leans and tenderly kisses me on the cheek.

David's whole body trembles, but he speaks up proudly, "When you wouldn't wake up, I went and got Mrs. Jones to help us." Mom leans down and kisses him on the head, saying how proud she is of him for acting so grown up and making such a good choice.

Mrs. Jones interrupts saying she thinks we all need to go to the emergency room. After inspecting the cut on my forehead, my mother reluctantly agrees. Mrs. Jones tells us to pack a few things because she isn't going to bring us back here and we can stay at her house for a while until we figure out what to do. Her plan might work because in all the time we've lived here, I've never seen Daddy even glance towards the Jones' house. It isn't a place he'd ever expect to find us.

BILLY

WE'VE been with Mrs. Jones for five days, and I don't want to leave. Mary, as she told us to call her, is a sweet lady and has taken really good care of us. She reminds me a lot of Mrs. Lawson at the bakery. She took us to the hospital that night to get taken care of. I had to get eight stitches in my head, and they kept Mommy for three days. Three of her ribs are broken, and her arm is sprained. She needed stitches on her head too, close to the same spot mine are—only four though. Mary agreed to watch us while Mommy was in the hospital and she promised Mommy over and over she wouldn't let Daddy get to us. Mommy almost refused to stay because she was afraid of leaving David and me alone, but, in the end, Mary must've convinced her she'd do a good job watching over us because she stayed. The hospital called the police to tell them about our injuries. They asked Mommy if she wanted to press charges against Daddy, but she said she just couldn't do it.

Mrs. Jones baked chocolate chip cookies and brownies with us. We played all the games that she keeps at her house for her grandchildren. She taught us how to sew buttons onto pieces of fabric, saying a boy should know how to sew on his own button. We must've sewn fifty buttons on the fabric swatches she gave us. When our fingers tired, we would dig through the box, searching for treasure. She had quite a collection, and we'd take turns picking out our favorites. Mrs. Jones had a story to go with each one. She'd tell us about the outfit it came from which would lead her to where she wore the outfit and who she was with when she wore it. We loved listening to her stories. What we loved, even more, was how quiet the house would be when we'd lay down each night to go to sleep—there were no crashes and screaming, only the sound of crickets chirping outside of the window.

Mary took us to visit Mom at the hospital each day, being careful to leave only after she knew Daddy left for work. Our mother looked terrible—she had a sling on her arm and bruises covering her body. She smiled great big at us whenever we visited, even though it had to hurt her battered face. The third day we went, Mommy was sitting up, dressed, and ready to leave with us.

Mary offered her house to us for as long as we need it, but Mommy says she doesn't feel safe being so close to Dad out of fear he'll eventually find us. Mommy also says she can't keep us out of school and hiding in the house forever. Aunt Linda's house isn't an option because Dad would know to look there since our apartment was close to her house, the last time we left. Mommy told Mrs. Jones that her sister would want nothing more to do with her because she'd allowed this to happen again. Mommy said Aunt Linda was mad that she went back home and told her not to show up, beaten to a bloody pulp when it happened again.

David and I are surprised when Mommy tells us we are leaving after breakfast. We don't know what decision she's made or where we'll be heading. All I know is I like it here and don't want to leave. I want to stay with Mrs. Jones, where we can talk, laugh, sew, and eat cookies. She's an even better adopted grandmother than Mrs. Lawson was.

I tell Mommy I don't want to leave, and David echoes my opinions. Tears build up in Mommy's eyes as we beg to stay. Mrs. Jones explains that Mommy is trying to do what she thinks is best for all of us, and we can come back to visit any time we want to. She assures us she'll save our favorite buttons for our next visit.

Mommy waits until she sees Daddy's car drive by on his way to work. She sneaks next door to get some of our things and comes back with our car loaded and ready to go. Everyone is in tears as we hug goodbye. Mrs. Jones gives each of us a big hug and a kiss on the cheek. She tries to be sneaky, but I see her push a wad of money into our mother's hand. She tells us she'll be praying for us and her door is always open if we need anything.

Mrs. Jones waves goodbye from her front porch as we pull away. I watch her until I can no longer see her past the trees.

*   *   *

We drive a couple of hours before Mommy tells us where we're headed like it's a big secret. When I refuse to stop asking, she finally reveals her plan.

"Well, boys. I think it's time you meet your grandparents—my mother and father."

"We have grandparents?" David asks from the backseat.

"Of course we do! Everyone has a grandma and grandpa," I chime in. "We just haven't ever met ours. Why haven't we, Mommy?"

"Well…it's a long story but let's just say we had a fight about something, and it's kept us apart far too long. It's time we all make up," she pauses. "They'll love meeting you guys. I'm sure the second they see you, they'll forget all about our silly fight." She smiles.

"Well, where do they live? It seems like we've been driving a long time." There's nothing but hills, trees, and fields outside of the windows. "Do we get to see another state again?"

"No. We're almost there," she says, but I can't imagine that we could be almost anywhere. "They live in a small town that's kind of in the middle of nowhere."

I didn't need her to tell me that—it's quite obvious.

"In fact, there it is." Mommy pulls the car to the side of the road and points back a long gravel lane to an old, white farmhouse with a barn out back and horses grazing in a pasture beside it.

"They have horses!" David exclaims. "Will they let us ride them?"

"We'll see, sweetie. Let's get settled in first. I'm sure we'll get to ride them sometime."

Mom sits there frozen for a moment, staring at the house. She moves the mirror and checks her reflection, brushing some hair back in place and putting fresh cover-up on the marks on her face. Even so, she still looks as though she's been in a brawl with her arm in a sling and swollen eyes.

She takes a deep breath before she speaks with a shaky voice, "Okay, boys. Let's go meet your grandparents."

We pull into the driveway and two big dogs bound towards us. David is scared of them, but I get out and start petting them right away. They cover me with kisses all over my face and arms. Once David sees they must not like to eat little boys, he gets out and lets them shower him with their wet doggy kisses, too. Mommy pets them and lets us enjoy the dogs for a moment before she shoos us along towards the front door with her.

She knocks, and we wait. The house is old and scary. It's probably haunted. As I'm trying to peer into the upstairs windows to see if I can spot a ghost, the front door opens.

A lady who looks like an older version of Mommy stands in front of us. "Ruby?" she says, opening the door to let us in.

"Mama!" Mommy walks towards her mother's open arms.

Mom hasn't yet reached our grandmother when a man's voice calls out from behind us. "Ruby, what the hell are you doing here?" His voice booms.

The screen door slams shut between us and our grand-mother, who stands frozen on the other side.

"Daddy! I wanted to come see you and let you meet my boys, David and Billy. I thought maybe we could make things right between us." Mommy takes a few steps towards him.

He holds out his hand to stop her from coming closer. "Are these Lee's boys?" he says with a scowl.

"Yes, Daddy. Lee's and my boys." Mommy smooths down her hair.

"Are you still married to Lee?" Our grandfather's voice bellows.

"Yes, Daddy, but…"

"That's all I need to hear. I told you when you wound up pregnant with that no good, piece of shit's child, you were no longer welcome in my house, and I meant it. You dug your grave when you started sleeping around with him. Now, you have to lie in it."

Tears fill our mother's eyes, and my grandmother gasps behind us but doesn't say a word.

"Daddy, please give me another chance. Me and the boys need you right now. We've got no place to go. Please, Dad-dy," Mommy says, raising her hand to her heart like she's saying the Pledge of Allegiance.

"I can't believe you'd bring that bastard's children here, expecting help from me. I told you from day one he was no good. You should've listened when it coulda made a difference."

"But Daddy, these are your grandchildren."

"No, they aren't. You stopped being my daughter the day I found out you were pregnant. As I told you then, I didn't raise a tramp. You and your kids best be running along now. There's nothing here for you," he says and points to the road.

Mommy seems more hurt than after even the worst fights with Daddy. She looks like she's been punched in the stomach and all the wind has been knocked out of her. She stands there, unmoving, as our grandfather pushes past us without speaking another word. He nudges his wife out of the way and slams the door behind him, leaving the three of us stranded on the other side.

I grab my mother's hand and lead her to the car.

*   *   *

We pull up in front of a place called Lakeview Motel, which is confusing because there's no lake in sight unless they consider the muddy water filling the pothole in the front parking lot, a lake. Mommy cried the entire hour it took to get here. She didn't speak a word as David insisted on asking a million questions, even though I told him over and over again to just be quiet and let Mommy drive. I have questions, too, but I know she's too upset to give any answers at the moment.

Why is grandpa so angry at us? Why didn't he even talk to us? When can we go back? Will we ever get to ride those horses? Where will we go now? Will Mommy ever stop crying? Why didn't our grandma invite us in and make cookies with us like Mrs. Jones does?

Through all the chatter, our mother just cried, without

making a sound, her tears flowing like a faucet somebody forgot to turn off. My mother's hands shook despite her tight grip on the steering wheel. They seemed to have a tremor that started at her fingertips and worked all the way through the rest of her body. Despite the warm fall temperature, it seemed like she was freezing cold. I cranked the heat up at one point to see if her shakiness would get any better. When it didn't, I turned it back down so I could breathe.

Our mom opens her car door and heads to the entrance marked *Office*. She doesn't tell us to stay there, as she usually does. She just gets out and leaves us without a word. I'm not sure whether we're supposed to follow or not, so we stay in the car and wait. After a few moments, she returns with a key.

For the first time since leaving her parents' house, she speaks. "Boys, we're in room ten. Each of you grab your stuff and come with me."

We each grab armfuls of our belongings. We don't have much with us, so we make it in one trip. The room is dark and dirty and reeks of cigarette smoke. The single window in the room is covered with thick, ugly drapes that block out every ray of sunshine. It reminds me of a cave. There are two beds in the room, a small table, a tiny television, and a bathroom.

Our mom puts down everything she's carrying and lays down on one of the beds without even taking off her shoes or pulling back the blankets. David and I stand there, not sure what to do since it's nowhere near time to go to bed. I suggest that we lie down on the other bed and read some books, which David agrees to. We look through three books, improvising greatly on the storyline, adding evil witches and monsters where none were written in, when we hear our mother snoring.

"Mommy's asleep?" David whispers. "It's too early to be asleep."

"Mommy's had a bad day. Let's watch TV or play until she wakes up."

We play, watch TV, read our books again, tell each other stories, check to make sure Mommy is still breathing, and then do it all again. Still, our mom sleeps. I look at the clock and realize it's very late—past our bedtime for sure and we haven't even eaten supper. The big hand is on the three, and the little hand is on the twelve.

We're both starving, so I rifle through our bags to see if there's anything to eat. There's a bag with ten cookies that Mrs. Jones must've given Mommy. Since I don't know when Mommy will wake up, I decide we better not eat them all. We each eat one along with some water from the bathroom sink and go to bed.

David falls asleep almost instantly, but I'm too worried. I've never heard of anyone sleeping this long. Is Mommy really dead and my eyes are playing tricks on me making me think she's breathing? What if she's sick and we don't realize it because we just let her lie there? What will we do if something happens to her? Where will we go? The questions race around and around, while David breathes deeply with sleep next to me. Unable to calm my thoughts, I finally climb into bed next to Mommy and put my hand on her chest, feeling her heartbeat. Convinced I can't make up a heartbeat, I finally fall asleep vowing to wake her up first thing in the morning, no matter what.

*   *   *

I awaken to a stream of sunlight coming through the now open curtains and to an empty bed. Mommy is gone. Panic fills me, thinking maybe she's been kidnapped or left us. Our things are still scattered everywhere, and David is sound asleep in the other bed. I tiptoe to the bathroom only to find it empty. I'm about to wake up David when the door to the room opens.

It's Mommy, carrying a cup of coffee and a box of doughnuts. She looks terrible with her hair sticking up all over, purple bruises covering her neck and face, and her dress very wrinkled.

"Hey, buddy! I got you some breakfast."

"Thanks, Mom. I'm starving."

Our voices wake David, and he jumps out of bed, heading straight towards the box of doughnuts.

"Sorry for sleeping for so long. I was just so tired…what did you boys do?"

We recount our adventures, which makes Mommy laugh. We sit at the little table and talk while we eat our breakfast. When we finish, Mommy announces, her voice dripping with sadness, that after she showers, we need to leave.

"Where are we going?"

"I'm not sure, Billy. I'm not sure." Her tears again flow. "I spent the money Mrs. Jones gave us on gas and this hotel room. I don't have anything left."

"What about Aunt Linda's house again?" I ask. "Or that

97

little apartment we lived in before?"

Mommy pats me on the head and forces a smile. "That won't work, honey. I don't know what to do. Let me take a shower, and I'll figure something out."

While Mommy showers, we gather up all our things. We're finished by the time she comes out. We load everything in the car and leave the little motel, still unsure of where we're headed.

We drive and drive and drive. Mommy is back in her trance of staring at the road ahead through her tear-filled eyes. Once again, she's quiet and will only tell us she doesn't know where we're going. Night falls, and I figure we must be getting close to somewhere since we've been driving all day. David is asleep in the backseat, and I feel myself giving in to the heaviness in my eyes. The movement of the car and the hum of the motor lulls me to sleep.

I jolt awake when the car stops, but I convince myself I must really still be asleep and dreaming. This can't be where she brought us. She wouldn't do this. She *couldn't* do this. As I rub the sleep out of my eyes, I look at Mommy, sitting still in the seat next to me, staring straight ahead with a blank expression. I blink several times to make sure I am seeing correctly. I realize I'm indeed staring at our house. She has returned home.

Do you remember the day we played in the park until the sun set and then raced home through the pouring rain? Do you remember how our laughter was the only way we could find one another? Do you remember our quest to come up with new ways to say *I love you* without uttering a word—three knocks on the wall after bedtime, holding up our thumb, index finger, and pinky and waving them high in the air? Do you remember the last time you saw me? Can you block that final picture of me from your mind? What would have become of you if you had been able to do so? What will become of you now, given the final picture of me burns so brightly in your mind even to this day? If I could erase those last moments for you, I would. Only you can choose to do that.

TOM

TWO DAYS AFTER
FRIDAY, FEBRUARY 10, 1989

IT'S only eight-thirty in the morning, and I'm already going stir-crazy. I don't know how I'm going to make it through another day of waiting. I considered going into work but decided I can't deal with the looks of sympathy I would get, the condolences spoken, the mention of prayers being said for our family. Kendra is still asleep thanks to the help of sleeping pills, but I can't risk dozing off and missing Chelsea coming home or a phone call from the police. I can't allow myself to drift away for even a moment.

It has been two thousand, nine hundred and eighty-five minutes since I last saw my daughter. This past Wednesday morning now feels like a lifetime ago. I was in the kitchen pouring a cup of coffee when Chels walked in, sleep still heavy in her eyes. It was already six forty-five, and she had to be out the door for school by seven, but she was still in her pajamas, hair unbrushed and no make-up.

"Running late, kiddo?"

"Yeah. I didn't hear my alarm," Chelsea said with a yawn. "Anyway, have a good day. I'll see you after I get off work." She grabbed a Coke out of the fridge and headed back down the hall to her room. I left for work.

I wish this scene were like one of those books where you get to choose an alternate ending. If I could, I would've stopped Chelsea from leaving the room so quickly. I would've taken her in my arms, looked closely at her beautiful face, and told her how proud I was of her, how much I loved her. For that matter, if I could choose a different ending, I would've skipped work that day, planned an impromptu vacation for the family, and headed out of town. Then Chelsea would've been nowhere near work that evening. No matter how much I long for it, real life just doesn't come with do-overs though. What is done is done. What is said is said. What wasn't said or done will forevermore remain that way.

My thoughts and regrets are interrupted by the ringing phone. As I've been doing consistently over the past two days, I let the machine get it. So far, we've received sixty-two phone calls offering support, prayers, meals, and help around the house. Most of them, I delete without even listening to the whole message. I can't bear to hear the sadness, pity, and concern in their voices when my grief is already such a burden to carry that I may buckle under the load. While I do appreciate the offers of help, what do I really need from anyone that they're capable of providing? How do you say to someone who's trying to be kind, "The only thing I need is my daughter—if you can't give me her, then there's nothing I want from you?" Kendra isn't holding up well, so I try to shield her from the messages, knowing each one she hears will also rip a fresh wound in her broken heart.

The only calls I bother to answer are those from the police. So far, there's been no news from them today. I didn't even bother to wake Kent this morning because I can't imagine letting my son leave the safety of our home until we have some news on Chelsea. The police have stated concerns about whether Chelsea's disappearance could be a kidnapping related to my job as Chief Financial Officer for the Ansley Corporation. The police said if it's a kidnapping for money, we could be expecting a ransom demand either by phone or mail within twenty-four hours of Chelsea's disappearance. So far, there's been no demand for ransom. I wish whoever has her just wanted money. I would get whatever sum is required to get my daughter back, even if it means breaking the law. Maybe today a call will come demanding money so I can buy back our daughter. I can buy back my life.

"Hey, Dad!" Kent's voice interrupts my thoughts.

"Hi, kiddo. How are you this morning?" I tousle his hair.

"Good. Why didn't you get me up for school?"

"I thought you could use an extra day off with all the stress and everything. You can go back on Monday."

102

"Thanks, Dad. I'm getting bored here, though. Can I hang out with Bill or Sam sometime this weekend?"

"We'll see," I say, when what I mean is there isn't a chance in hell that I'm letting him out of the house right now.

"Did they find Chels yet?" Kent asks innocently. Adults always assume the worst; kids in their naivety don't know how to do that yet.

"Nope. We still don't know anything," I say and rub the back of my neck. My muscles are so tight it feels as though they may snap.

"I wish she'd come home. I get lonely here with no one to fight with. Plus, you and Mom are so worried you're not much fun to be around."

"Sorry, buddy. We're pretty stressed out," I say, squeezing his shoulder. "And I wish she'd come home too. I miss her. I even miss hearing you guys yell at each other."

Kent grabs a glass of orange juice and heads to his favorite television-viewing spot on the couch. It's a little soothing to have some normal sounds in the house, even if only from the TV; something to hear other than the breaking of our hearts. My anxiety is consuming me; I've got to get out of this house. I need to do something besides sit around and wait.

"Hey, Kent. Tell Mom I went out for a while. If the police call, please get your mom up. Otherwise, let the machine get it and let her sleep."

"Alright Dad," Kent replies, not even glancing away from the TV.

I have no idea where I'm headed, but I can't stay within

the confines of our house anymore. I can't stand just waiting. I take off for nowhere in particular—for nowhere is much better than the somewhere Kendra and I are right now.

*   *   *

I find myself at the office. I instinctively pull into the lot, into my usual reserved parking spot. I sit there, watching people come and go from the doors I'm so used to walking through at least twice every day, six days a week, until the past two days. I fill with envy at the ease with which people manage to go about their business when my whole world is shattering to pieces. Part of me wants to go in, shut myself in my office, and go about my normal daily routine. The realistic part of me knows I will crumble the first time someone mentions Chelsea's name. Trying to maintain any semblance of normalcy right now is impossible. How can I possibly look at balance sheets, re-working the numbers over and over to find a missing dollar and twenty cents when I can't even find my daughter?

Frustrated by my lack of ability to plaster on a smile and walk through those doors, I leave, still having no destination in mind. I mindlessly drive, ending up in the restaurant parking lot, near where Chelsea would park for work. I watch people come and go from the stores and restaurants in the strip mall, some with packages loading them down, others with children, and some empty-handed. As I sit and watch the world pass me by outside of the car window, I start counting. Five men enter the restaurant. Two men exit alone. Seven women enter alone; three come out. Four women walk in the restaurant with chil-

104

dren. One walks out with their child in tow. Any one of these people could've been here the night my daughter went missing. Any one of them could have information to help lead the police to Chelsea. For that matter, any one of them could have my daughter. My anger swells at each person who walks in and out. Angry at the fact they still have their normal lives. Angry at the fact I don't. Outraged at the fact that one of them could have my precious daughter. Filled with rage that I can't—even though it's the one desire of my heart.

The anger swells until I can no longer contain it. I start hitting everything within my reach—myself, the steering wheel, the seat, the window. The shattering glass and pain in my hand, snap me back to the present where I sit surrounded by broken glass. My hand is bleeding, and my lip is swollen. Tears stream down my face. Sounds are coming from me that I've never heard a human being make—noises straight from the depths of hell.

KENDRA

2 DAYS AFTER
FRIDAY, FEBRUARY 10, 1989

I awaken with a jolt to tears running down my cheeks, soaking
my pillowcase. My brain instantly kicks into overdrive, screaming *Chelsea is missing! My baby is missing! Where is my daughter?* I
want to go back to sleep where I can dream my daughter is still
here, that my family is still whole. Getting my mind to quiet
enough for sleep to come again is impossible, though. Finally
mustering the energy to get up, I slip on jeans and a sweatshirt
and head towards the kitchen for some coffee. As I'm about to
pass Chelsea's room, I stop, unable to move any further. Slowly,
I open the door, hoping all of this has been a nightmare, and I'll
find Chelsea lying in her bed enjoying being able to sleep in. Her
bed is empty. I thought my heart was beyond hurting anymore,

but I'm wrong. A new wave of devastation crashes over me. This is no nightmare—this is our reality.

I flip on the light, shut the door behind me, and sit on Chelsea's bed. I breathe deeply, taking in the scent of my precious daughter clinging heavily to everything in the room. Why is it you never really notice someone's scent until they are gone? Like the lingering smell of Tom's cologne that remains on my dress after an embrace that I don't notice until I'm driving to work. The boyish smell Kent's sweaty head leaves when he leans up against me after a game of baseball that I don't notice until I'm changing my clothes for the night. The smell of something sweet—a mixture of flowers and vanilla—that emanates from every surface in this room that I never noticed Chelsea carrying on her when she was around. This smell is my daughter—a scent that floods me with thoughts of spring, of hope, of a future.

Her room shows the different stages of her life on every surface. On the top shelf of her bookshelf sits Fluffy, her favorite stuffed bear that she slept with every night from the age of two until she was twelve. On the floor next to her bed is the blankey she carried around with her everywhere she went from the time she was old enough to walk until she was about five. Even after she decided she was a "big girl," she still slept with it each night of her life up until the past two. I pull the blanket to my face and hold it there, breathing in the scents of Chelsea and her childhood. Breathing in scents that hold so many hopes and dreams.

As I cradle the blanket, I look at Chelsea's bulletin board covered with pictures of her and her friends. In all of them, Chelsea smiles radiantly, like she's having the time of her life.

Chels can light up a room just by walking into it. She can lighten the mood regardless of the situation with a simple laugh—how I would give anything to hear that laugh right now. Chelsea's bookshelf sits next to the bulletin board. She's a book lover and is never happy just getting them from the library. If it's a good book, she has to own it. Tom and I buy Chelsea a book for each birthday and another for Christmas, a tradition we started when she turned five. Some of my favorite memories with Chelsea can be found on her bookshelf. So many evenings Chelsea and I would curl up, each on one end of the couch with a shared blanket, and read. Me with coffee; Chelsea with hot tea, until recent years when she developed the taste for heavily creamed and sugared coffee. So many times, I would glance up from my page to watch her read and catch her crying or laughing as she perused the words before her.

On the top shelf are her framed prom photographs from her sophomore and junior year. My chest feels like its being crushed as I wonder if we'll be able to add her senior one to the collection. These pictures bring back every moment of the preparations for the big days with Chels. She had to look absolutely perfect, which meant a whole day spent at the salon getting her hair, makeup, and nails done. Months of planning went into prom—picking out the perfect dress, making sure her date had a perfectly matching cummerbund and bow tie with his tuxedo, and making sure the corsage had just the right amount of baby's breath with a matching rose.

God, please bring my baby home. I can't do life without her. Please, God. I beg, kneeling next to Chelsea's bed, sobbing.

I've always had such a strong faith, but right now, I don't feel like God is listening. If He is, surely Chelsea would be home by now. How could a God who loves me, allow me to suffer so much, to hurt so badly? *God, where is she? Where's my daughter?*

I crawl into her bed, cradle her blankey next to my cheek, bury myself under the covers, and wait for God to answer.

BILLY

13 YEARS, 9 MONTHS, 26 DAYS BEFORE
APRIL 13, 1975

TODAY has been horrible, and I just want to go home and hide from the giggling girls, the jeering boys, and the "concerned" teachers. Everyone has noticed my black eye, and most everyone has had something to say about it. My fourth-grade teacher, Mrs. Boyer, pulled me aside first thing this morning to ask what happened. I told her David and I were playing cops and robbers, and it got a little too rough. She listened attentively and then asked if there was anything else going on that I needed to talk about. I put on my best smile and said no, everything was fine. She insisted she was "here" for me if I ever need someone to talk to or confide in.

I chuckled when I imagined her face if I did speak up

and spill the truth. I could envision lifting my shirt to show her the bruises and welts covering my back and ribs. "Oooh…" she'd say, her lips pursed like a fish mouth.

Like there's anything she can do to stop it. No one can. Why talk about something that's inevitable? It's like talking about the rain falling from the sky, thinking by doing so, you can make it stop. I used to talk to my mom about these things after they happened. The talking changed nothing.

Of course, every bully in the fourth grade saw this as the perfect excuse to torment me, asking what the other guy walked away with or if I wanted my other eye to match. I've never been a fighter, but I was as tempted as I've ever been today to take them up on their offer. I'm sure I could kick the crap out of half of these tough guys if I'm able to stand up to my six-foot one-inch father so well. I didn't want to come to school today, but Mom forced me to, saying she'd help cover up the bruise and no one would be able to see it. That plan failed miserably. Like all of Mom's plans have lately.

When she first brought us back after the failed visit to our grandparents' house, she was distraught. She apologized for weeks, sobbing through the words each time. She explained she didn't know what else to do or where else to go. She said as soon as she could come up with a plan and stash some money, we would leave for good. We've now been waiting for almost two years. I occasionally ask her how much money she has saved or if she has a plan yet, but she always just says, "Not yet," with a faraway look.

In the meantime, while waiting for our escape, my father's violence grows. No longer is it only towards our mother, but David and me as well. That's how I got the great big shiner for all the world to see today. As usual, the fight started out between Dad and Mom. Actually, Mom is never really part of the fight, just the recipient of the anger spewing constantly from my father. I can never quite figure out what sets Dad off. Sometimes my mother doesn't even look at him, or utter a word, and he starts hitting her like he's pissed because she's still breathing.

Last night was one of those nights. David, Mom, and I were sitting down to our dinner of macaroni and cheese—all that was left in the cupboards—when Dad stumbled in, smelling like a brewery. Without saying a word, Mom stood and got him a plate of food. She went to put it down in his usual spot at the table, and he knocked it out of her hand, sending noodles and glass flying everywhere. She didn't say a word, just sat down and waited to see what her fate would be. That wasn't the right choice, I guess, because Dad yanked her to the floor, shoving her face in the spilled noodles and broken glass chards, telling her to "get off her ass and clean up the mess."

After he let go, without making a sound or letting a tear escape down her cut and bloodied cheeks, she got a broom and dustpan to clean it up. That wasn't the right choice either. Dad snatched the broom and started hitting her with it upside the head, along her spine, the back of her legs—wherever he could reach. Mom did the best she could to block the blows with her arms, but Dad was faster. At some point during the scuffle, David left the room. I did my best to keep eating and not watch or hear what was going on around me, as I've mastered over the past couple of years. I did my times-tables in my head to the sound of my mother's cries and gasps of pain.

My father seemed to be satisfied once Mom was a bloody mess, crying in a heap on the floor. He sat down at the table. "Where's your brother?"

"I don't know. He was just right here. He must've been done."

Dad stormed out of the room on the search for David, yelling, "Nobody's finished until I say so. David, get your puny little ass back out here."

I sat silently, listening for David's voice or cries. When I heard nothing, other than Dad's ranting about David needing to stick around to learn how to be a man, I went to the kitchen door to see what was going on. Dad had yanked David out of our room and was pulling him down the hall by his arm. David fell to the ground, and Dad started kicking him while still wearing his steel-toed boots. David was screaming out in pain, which further fueled our father's anger, making him kick harder and faster.

I looked to our mother for help; she was still curled up in a ball on the kitchen floor, sobbing. When I realized that, once again, she was going to be no help to us, I ran to try to stop Dad. I knew if I could distract him, he'd leave David alone. I'd done it numerous times before. I would much rather take my father's wrath than see David hurt since I've been his only source of protection for years. He's only seven and doesn't have an instinct in his body to defend himself—he'd lay there and let our father beat him to death without ever trying to get away or fight back.

I ran up and kicked Dad as hard as I could in the back of the leg. I knew my diversion tactic worked when I felt myself being hoisted and flung across the room. As I landed, Dad was there to catch my fall with his boot swinging against my ribs. Against my back. Against my head. Against my ribs again. Against my back. I lost consciousness before my father was done.

I was out until later that night when I woke in my bed with my mother sitting next to me holding an ice pack on my head. I opened my eyes and looked into hers, seeing more sadness than ever before.

"I'm so sorry, honey." She wiped the hair back from my forehead. "Are you okay?"

I wanted to tell her no. That none of us were okay. I wanted to tell her to look in the mirror, at her face covered in cuts and bruises, and ask herself the same question. I wanted to tell her she needed to get us out of here now so we can be spared my father's wrath. I wanted to tell her I was angry at her for not protecting us, as a mother should. Instead, I leaned into her open arms, breathed in the smell of her fear, and felt her trembling. After a moment, I looked back into her eyes and said I was fine.

KENT

TWO DAYS AFTER
FRIDAY, FEBRUARY 10, 1989

FOR about the hundredth time in the last hour, the phone rings. I'm sick of hearing it. I've managed, so far, to tune out the voices of those callers who chose to leave a message even though I'm supposed to be listening for a call from the police. But, enough is enough, I can't just let the machine get it. I want to tell whoever it is to stop calling, to leave my family alone, and to let me watch TV in peace. After all, what good is a day off school, if I'm constantly being pestered by the ringing phone?

"Hello," I say as meanly as I can, hoping whoever is on the other end feels my annoyance.

"Hi, Kent! It's Grandma."

"Oh, hi, Grandma." Instant guilt about my tone washes

over me. "Mom and Dad let me stay home today."

"Are either one of them there?"

"Well, Dad's been gone for a while. I'm not sure where he went. And I think Mom's still sleeping. I haven't seen her yet today."

"Oh, okay." I hear the worry in Grandma's voice. "Grandpa and I are coming to help out for a while. We'll be there tomorrow afternoon. Can you let them know?"

"Sure! I can't wait to see you. Maybe we can go do something fun. I'm so bored here."

"Maybe…see you tomorrow," Grandma's voice trails off.

"Bye, Grandma! Love you!"

"Love you too, sweetie!" she says with sadness in her voice.

I'm glad they're coming. Maybe they'll act normal because Mom and Dad sure aren't. Like now, it's almost one o'clock in the afternoon. Dad's been gone since early this morning, and Mom's still asleep. She never sleeps this late. I wish all of this with Chelsea would be over so life can get back to the way it used to be. Even staying home is starting to lose its fun because I'm bored. I'm sick of having no one to talk to and sitting inside all day.

I decide to check on Mom and see if she's awake yet. I go upstairs and knock quietly on her bedroom door. When no answer comes, I open it and see she's not in bed. I search her bathroom but still, no Mom. I hurry down the hall to my room, but she's not there either. Only one other room to check—Chelsea's. Her door is shut as it has been since Wednesday night. I raise my hand to knock as Chels always reminds me to do, but then stop because what's the point if she isn't here anyway? I crack the door open and see brown hair spilling out over her comforter, the corner of Chelsea's blankey sticking out from underneath. I run to the bed.

"Chels, you're home!"

At the sound of my voice, Mom sits up groggily, trying to shake the sleep off. "Oh, Kent, honey. I'm so sorry. You thought I was her." Tears fill her eyes.

I run to the bathroom, lock the door and, for the first time since Chelsea disappeared, I cry.

*   *   *

KENDRA

I could kick myself for upsetting Kent. I get up quickly, trying to catch him. I reach the bathroom just in time for him to slam the door in my face.

"Kent, honey, I'm sorry," I pause. "I didn't even think of how it would look if you walked in and found me there. I'm so sorry."

I wait for him to respond. All I hear are his muted sniffles. "Kent, do you want to talk about it?"

Finally, an answer comes from beyond the door. "No, Mom. I don't want to talk about it. That's all we've been talking about. Just leave me alone."

Kent's words sting. Even more painful is his attitude. He's always been a mama's boy and hasn't yet hit the stage where he mouths off with regularity. With coaxing, he always confides in me. "Okay, but if you change your mind, I'll be in the kitchen."

No reply comes, only the sound of Kent blowing his nose. I walk downstairs with guilt heaped onto my shoulders, right next to worry. How could I not think of the possibility that Kent might come in the room and mistake me for Chelsea? I feel even worse about the fact that, in reality, I haven't thought about Kent at all in the past two days. Regardless of what other roles I have to fulfill in life, I'm always a mother *first* and have worked especially hard at encouraging the kids to talk about their feelings. To realize I haven't even considered how Kent is holding up with Chelsea missing or even bothered to talk to him about it, other than sharing the facts with him, makes me feel like a failure. Maybe all of the good mothering skills I thought I had were a joke; it's easy to be a good mother when there's no real stress, no drama, just ordinary everyday life. When presented with the first real challenge in my parenting, I've not only failed Chelsea but Kent as well.

I need coffee. I wonder where Tom is as I dump the grounds in the filter. I want to ask Kent, but it's probably better to give him the space he thinks he needs. While the coffee brews, I sit at the kitchen table to wait. To wait for Tom to come home. To wait for Kent to want to talk. To wait for the police to call. To wait for Chelsea to be found. Waiting is now a part of me. There's no *doing* in our current circumstances, only waiting. I am a puppet with a faceless, nameless puppeteer holding my strings pulling me this way and that, thrashing me about, ripping me apart at the seams. I crave the ability to regain some control over my life, over our lives. But the puppeteer is in absolute control, allowing us no room for choices.

Lost in thought, I don't even realize Tom has come in until he sits down next to me, without uttering a word. His eyes are puffy, his lip swollen, his hand bleeding.

"Oh my God, Tom! What happened?"

"I don't know. I just lost it." His entire body trembles.

"Did somebody do this to you? Did you hurt someone?" I stand and embrace him, pulling his battered face against my stomach.

"No, I did it to myself. I went out for a drive and ended up at *Landoll's*. As I sat there, I got so angry. Before I knew it, I ended up like this with a busted-out window in the car." Tom weeps; his tears dampen my shirt.

"Oh, honey. This is so hard on all of us. I don't know how we're gonna do it, but we'll get through this. I know we will." Tom is usually the one who utters these types of responses when I break down about something. To have our roles reversed so drastically makes me feel even more unstable. I realize, even as I'm saying the right things to Tom, there are no assurances or guarantees. The stability we've always known, the strength we've always felt, the usual way we get through struggles, no longer applies. The rules have completely changed.

Kent walks in during our embrace. "C'mere hon," I say, pulling him close.

We cling to each other, hoping nothing further penetrates our circle of despair.

NICOLE

THREE DAYS AFTER
SATURDAY, FEBRUARY 11, 1989

I manage to sleep until eleven-thirty, thanks to two more Valium I coaxed out of Mom before heading to bed. I actually asked for one but took two instead and stashed three more under my mattress for when I need them. Mom won't notice—she only took a few right after my grandmother's funeral a year and a half ago. Two work much better than one in helping me to forget long enough to fall asleep, and well enough not to have images of Chels take over my dreams as they do over every waking moment. Since meeting with the detective yesterday, I can't shake the overwhelming feeling that whoever has Chels is in my circle of friends. What if it is Randy, Josh, or Kurt? How can I possibly pass by them in the hallway at school, not knowing if they are responsible for Chelsea's disappearance? How can I contain my fear?

Within minutes of waking, I have the strongest urge to get out of the house and search for Chelsea. I haven't seen the area yet where they found her car. I can't sit in this house anymore— I need to look for her. My parents will never agree to let me go by myself—as frustrating as it is, I do understand why. Chels' kidnapper could be there just waiting for another victim. Mom peeks in the door as I'm debating about asking her to go with me.

"Oh, you're up. Good! How did you sleep?"

"Pretty good—thanks for the pill. It really helps me to stop thinking about this mess."

"I'm glad they are helping, and you're getting some rest. I know how hard this must be for you. I'm so worried about Chelsea." Mom sits down and pulls me close.

"Me too, Mom." I sit in my mother's embrace for a few moments. "Hey, Mom? Can we go for a drive? I need to see where they found Chelsea's car."

"Are you sure that's a good idea?" Her face scrunches in worry.

"No, but I know I'm not up to sitting here worrying all day again. Worrying and waiting are the only two things I've done for the past three days." I wrap my arms around myself, trying to squash the feeling of doom that seems to be a constant now.

"I'll leave it up to you...if you need to do it, then we'll go."

"I do. Maybe we'll see something the police missed."

"Get dressed and come down when you're ready. I'll leave your dad a note, so he won't worry if he comes back before we do," Mom says, picking up an armful of my dirty clothes as she heads out the door.

I shower and get dressed in record time—thirty minutes. I don't bother to put on make-up or dry my hair. I ask Mom if I can drive so I have something to focus on besides my emptiness and fear.

I drive through town to Shannon Road, which is behind the strip mall next to *Landoll's* restaurant with a cornfield on each side. I look to the field on the right, knowing from the description in the newspaper, Chels' car was found about a half-mile down, right next to the river. I'm scouring the landscape for any signs of the fire, or anything else unusual, when Mom gasps.

"Oh, Nicole! Look!" She points to the field on our left. I come to a stop in the middle of the road, unable to move.

All the air escapes me, like I've been punched, with the realization that the sight before me can only mean one thing. Along the bank of the river are six police cruisers and an ambulance. They are loading a gurney with a sheet covering a body into the back. They shut the doors and pull away, without their sirens on. If the person were alive, they would be rushing to get to the hospital. There are no flashing lights, no sirens, no sign of a hurry whatsoever as the ambulance drives through the bumpy, rutted field and pulls onto the road.

As soon as the ambulance pulls away, Detective Sanders' car leaves the scene, with lights and sirens blaring. I follow behind, trying my best to tail him, but not able to go as quickly and have people pull out of our way to make it through intersections. We arrive at the Wyatt's as Detective Sanders is ringing the bell. We rush to the porch and get there as Tom opens the door.

Detective Sanders asks us to please give the family some time alone with him, but Tom interjects, saying I *am* family and to let me hear whatever needs to be discussed.

*　　*　　*

TOM

I can tell the news we're about to receive isn't good. Detective Sanders' face is strained and showing raw, fresh pain within its creases. Part of me wants to call for my family; the other part wants to run out the front door, never to return, if that means the news needing to be shared will never become reality. If escape were that simple, I would choose the latter without hesitation. This devastation will follow me wherever I run; the truth seeking me out like a shark hunts its prey. I tell everyone to make themselves comfortable while I go to get Kendra and Kent from upstairs. We're all seated in the living room within a matter of minutes.

Detective Sanders loosens his tie, seemingly trying to gain composure before speaking. Despite his attempts, his voice still quivers. "We got a call this morning at around nine. A man from the neighborhood behind the restaurant was walking his dog along the river this morning when he spotted a body in the water."

Kendra gasps and crumbles from her seat onto the floor.

I see her fall but can't make myself go to her. Instead, Nicole runs to Kendra's side and cradles her against her chest, as a mother does for her crying child. Detective Sanders' chin trembles as he quietly says how sorry he is.

"Please go on..." I say, suddenly feeling an overwhelming need to hear the rest of the story. To know my daughter's fate. To know my family's destiny. To know the extent of the grief I'm sure to face.

Kendra continues to wail and sob in a way that doesn't sound human.

Detective Sanders looks towards Kendra and quietly continues. "We immediately went to the scene and found what we believe to be Chelsea's body, underneath some branches, lying face down in about a foot of water. We previously searched this same area, but we may have missed her because of the snow cover and because her body was partially concealed."

Every muscle in my body tenses with a stress I've never known before. It feels as though I'm going to shatter into a million tiny pieces in front of everyone. I can't fall apart. I must be the strong one, especially since it is obvious Kendra isn't hearing a word being said. I must hold onto all the information the detective is offering. Kent scoots over to me and curls against my side. I want to be able to soothe my child, calm my wife, but I can't. The slightest movement will surely cause me to break. Just as I couldn't protect Chelsea from her fate, I can't protect them either. I let Kent snuggle next to me—the statue that's supposed to be his father.

"I'm so sorry, Tom." Detective Sanders places his hand

on my shoulder as if it could help the utter desolation that just destroyed my soul. Crushed my future. "I'm going to need one of you to come to the hospital to identify the body. We are fairly certain it is Chelsea because of the descriptions you've given us."

Detective Sanders pauses at the sound of a knock on the door. Nicole's mother gets up to answer the door, and Kendra's parents rush in.

Kendra's father halts; his brows knit together as he spies Detective Sanders wiping tears from his eyes. "What's going on, Tom?" Kendra's father asks.

I can't get the words out of my mouth. There is no way to put into words the cruel facts that were just delivered. How do I tell him I was just asked to go identify a body that may be my Chelsea?

"Oh, Daddy!" Kendra clings to her father's legs as though she's drowning, and he is her only hope of rescue. Both of her parents stoop down and pull her into their embrace.

I interrupt to tell Detective Sanders I'll accompany him to identify the body. At the words, Kendra's mother gasps and cradles her daughter against her as their sobs fill the room.

"I'll give you a few moments and wait outside. Just come out when you're ready." Detective Sanders leaves us to deal with our shock.

Feeling completely numb and void of emotion, I share the news with Kendra's parents and rise to get my coat. I'm amazed I can function so well even though I cannot feel any part of my body. My head feels like it's floating, suspended in a world of disbelief. Nicole's mother stands and announces she and Nicole are leaving, that they'll do whatever they can to help. Nicole reluctantly, and tearfully, allows her mother to lead her to the car. I want to be able to offer comfort to Nicole, but there are no words to give.

Detective Sanders says he thinks it's best if I ride to the hospital with him. I resist, arguing I'll be fine driving myself, but he insists. I don't have the energy or will to put up a fight, so I follow him to the squad car.

I cannot wrap my mind around the image Detective Sanders started to paint for us. I can't get the full view without more details.

"Was she clothed when you found her?" I force the question out.

"Mostly," Detective Sanders pauses. "Are you sure you want to talk about this right now?"

"Yes. I want to know," I say, but I don't know that *want* is the right word. I *need* to know.

"She had everything on except for her shoes. We didn't find those."

An instant wave of nausea hits me, and vomit rises into my throat. I choke it back down, crack the window, and continue. "How did she die?"

"An autopsy must be done to determine the cause and time of death."

An autopsy? Someone will be cutting apart my daughter's body. The body I held for hours on end when she was an infant; the body that endured countless cuts and bruises when I taught her to ride a bike; the body that turned from a child into

126

a woman before my eyes over the past several years; the body that will never again be my daughter. I feel myself starting to break but won't allow it. *Someone has to be strong here. You're the only one that can do it. Be strong, be strong, be strong*, I silently chant. I begin to count the houses we pass. When I get to twelve, I'm again calm enough to speak.

"Do you have any idea who did this?" I ask as a hundred faces flash through my mind.

"We have some people of interest we're talking to, but no, we have nothing conclusive right now. We're hoping we can get some additional clues from the autopsy report. We're working on it, Tom. I promise we'll catch this guy."

We pull into a spot in the staff parking lot at the hospital. He waits to speak until I make eye contact. "I need to warn you that this is going to be difficult. Not only because this is your child but because she's extremely bloated from being in water for so long. She will look nothing like the Chelsea you last saw."

I take a moment to try to absorb the information being shared, but I'm not able to, no matter how hard I try. The words don't register. "Are you ready?"

"Let's get this over with," I say, opening my door.

The two of us walk silently into the Staff Entrance on the bottom level of the hospital. An entrance I have never before seen. An entrance I've never before needed to see, as it is the one leading to the last place on earth I ever expected to find myself—the morgue.

*   *   *

KENT

I'm trying to focus on the game of rummy Grandpa and I are playing in my room, but all I can picture are the things described by the detective. My sister's dead body. My sister floating, eyes wide open staring up at nothing, in partially frozen, murky river water. Her hair tangled in knots of leaves and branches, floating behind her on top of the water. I keep trying to focus on the cards by repeating what I see in my head. *Ace of spades, ten of hearts, three of diamonds, four of diamonds...* but then instead of the Queen of hearts, I see my sister's haunting, hollow eyes staring up at me. I can't even picture her alive, but only as the images my mind is concocting.

I keep smiling and trying to chatter away like I always do when I'm with Grandpa, but he must realize I'm not okay because, during the middle of his turn, he lays the cards down and hugs me close. I don't remember the last time my grandpa embraced me like this—the older I get, the less my family members actually touch me. I wonder if it's an unspoken rule of the adult world that men don't need affection; or in my case, boys that are almost men don't need to be touched.

At first, I stiffen under the weight of my grandfather's arms and then, within seconds, my entire body goes limp against him. I can't hide my feelings any longer. We sit in silence, man and boy, each with a world of hurt within our hearts, but neither of us speaking it. For the first time since Chelsea disappeared, I feel like someone notices I'm still here. My parents wouldn't even notice if I disappeared too, because they have been so consumed with Chelsea. My grandfather's hug makes me feel like I still matter.

Finally, Grandpa speaks. "You know, buddy, I needed that."

"Yeah, me too."

"Now back to our game where I'm gonna kick your butt."

"Awful sure of yourself for an old guy, Pops!"

Our playful banter continues as we get back to the game. Thanks to my grandfather's warm embrace and all the love I felt in that moment, I'm able to focus on the cards in front of me for the rest of our game, momentarily released from the images of my dead sister filling my mind.

*   *   *

TOM

From the moment we step inside the threshold on the lower level of the hospital that will lead us to the morgue, I begin counting each step. Twenty-two steps down a hallway and then a left turn. Thirty-three steps to the large gray metal doors where Detective Sanders knocks. Four seconds until a man, who looks about sixty-five years old, opens the door. Ten seconds while the detective makes introductions. Eleven steps into the room where the silver, aluminum table is situated in the middle with a sheet pulled over the top of it. Five seconds of standing while the gentleman asks me if I am ready. One nod of my head. Three seconds for the sheet to be pulled back far enough for me to see her face. A milli-second for me to realize it is my daughter even though it looks nothing like her. A lifetime of moments flash before my eyes as I fall to the ground.

BILLY

THE second I enter the door, my mother thrusts a suitcase in my arms, telling me to gather up clothes for David and myself.

"Where are we going?"

"I don't know, but we need to leave as quick as we can. He just left for the store and will be back any minute." I know *he* means Dad.

"What about David?"

"We'll leave now and then go pick him up from school."

As I take the suitcase from her, I notice the new bruises on her left jaw, the purple handprints on her right arm, the swelling around her nose which makes it appear twice its normal size.

"What happened, Mom?" I gently touch her cheek.

"We just have to go. It's time."

I hurry to our room, shoving clothes for both of us in the bag, a couple of books, several of David's favorite toys. As I'm zipping it, I hear a noise that stops me in my tracks—a car's tires on our gravel driveway.

I peer out the window, and sure enough, Dad is already back. I rush to the door of my parent's bedroom where Mom stands with a suitcase.

"C'mon, Mom. He's home. We've gotta go." I pull on her free hand, which instantly starts to tremble. "When he comes in through the garage, we'll slip out the front door to the car in the driveway. Do you have the keys?"

She pulls them out of her pocket. We crack the front door open, waiting to hear the garage door shut, knowing that's the sign to make our escape. It's so quiet we can hear our hearts beating. *Thump, thump, thump...* We hear the garage door start to shut and bolt out the front door to the car waiting in the driveway. Thankfully, the doors aren't locked, and we're able to get in quickly, throwing our suitcases in the back seat. Mom sticks the key in the ignition and turns it. Nothing happens. She tries again—still nothing.

We don't have time for this. Dad is certainly almost finished searching the house for us. Soon, he'll look out the front window to see if the car is here. We have to be gone or almost out of the driveway by then. A third turn of the key. Nothing.

"C'mon, Mom. We've gotta hurry." My heart feels like

it's going to explode.

"I know. It won't start. Oh, God, it won't start. Please, God…" My mother's voice trails off as a sob catches in her throat. "Billy, what do we do?"

"Try again, Mom. Try again." My heart's in my throat and pumping like it does when I run really fast.

Another turn of the key. This time the engine roars to life. I breathe a sigh of relief and look towards the house as Mom slips the car into drive, slowly edging forward. The front door stands open, and Dad is barreling towards us.

"Go, Mom, go. He's coming." I yell, urging her to move forward faster.

She presses harder on the gas pedal. But she isn't fast enough. As she starts to move forward, Dad reaches the car, punching the driver's side window, shattering it. The shock makes Mom stop.

"Go, Mom! We can get away. Just go!" I shout.

Mom sits there frozen, contemplating her next move, which gives my father time to get in front of the car, kicking its bumper. He's yelling obscenities telling us to get out of the car.

"Just go, Mom. It doesn't matter if you hit him, go!"

"I can't hit him, Billy. I can't."

We sit there for what feels like a lifetime with Dad cursing and screaming, and Mom burying her face in her hands, crying. I feel more trapped than ever before. We're so close to escaping my father's wrath. I realize Mom can't bring herself to do what needs to be done. I will do it for her. As she sits there sobbing, I stretch my leg over to the gas pedal and push with all my strength.

The car lurches forward, knocking Dad to the ground. Still, I don't let up. It is either him or us. For me, there isn't really a choice to be made. Just as I accept that I have it in me to actually kill my father, my mother's foot slams on the brake while she simultaneously throws the car into park.

My head can't even wrap around it. "Mom, what're you doing?"

She opens the door, with tears streaming down her cheeks. "He's hurt. Oh, God, he's hurt." She rushes to the front of the car.

I cannot believe the scene playing out in front of me. My mother, who has endured broken bones, busted lips, blackened eyes, and a broken spirit at the hands of my father, is actually rushing to his defense. She's concerned about *his* well-being. My mother, who has for years, sacrificed herself and our safety to my father's rage, is giving up our chance for escape to make sure he's okay. I don't care if he's hurt. As my mother rounds the front of the car and stoops down to check on him, I say a prayer he's dead already. That her help is too late. I don't want my father spared of pain. I want him to feel every bit of hurt we've felt over the years. I want my father to feel the fear he's inflicted upon us more times than I can remember.

Within moments, my mother's head rises above the hood of the car, still bent over, looking towards the ground where my father would be lying. *Please, God, don't let him get up. Let him be dead.* I pray, holding my breath, hoping to see my mother's tears and know it's over. To know we're finally free.

Instead, I see my mother's hand linked to my father's, trying to pull him up. My heart sinks, and anger swells within me. I envision myself pushing the gas pedal down again, the car lurching forward to run over him. I imagine the relief I'd feel if he couldn't hurt us anymore. The only problem is how to do it without hurting Mom too. I can't bear to hurt her. If she'd just move out of the way. *Mom, move away... don't help him up. I'll take care of us. Please let me take care of us.* I pray for my mother to be able to read my thoughts and respond accordingly.

Instead, my father stands at the front of the car, holding onto my mother for support.

"Billy, come help me get your father into the house," she calls out to me.

For the first time I remember, I directly disobey my mother and, instead of getting out to help, I lock the doors and glare into my father's eyes.

"You heard your mother, get your sorry ass outta that car right now and come help," my father's voice echoes in my head.

I turn away from his piercing gaze and look out the window, watching the birds fly from tree to tree, the clouds move across the sky. My defiance enrages my father who begins screaming so loudly I'm sure the entire neighborhood can hear, and he pounds with both fists on the hood of the car. My mother tries to calm him, telling him she can get him into the house without my help. Through all of it, even though I'm fiercely trembling, I refuse to look back in his direction.

Finally, the yelling and pounding stop. Out of the corner of my eye, I watch my parents slowly make their way to the door. The car must've hit my father's right foot because he's limping, unable to put any pressure on it. But, as far as I can tell, that's the only real damage. *So much for God answering my prayers.* I can imagine how angry Dad is at our attempted escape, causing him pain for a change. I definitely don't want to be around to catch the brunt of his rage over this one. If screwing the toothpaste lid on the wrong way makes Dad mad enough to hit me with a belt until welts cover my back, the punishment for this will be far worse. Probably worse than anything we've endured so far.

I'm not going in that house. I'll wait on David to get off the bus, and we'll come up with a plan. I try to formulate a getaway in my mind. We'll grab our bag from the backseat and head south to Florida. We'll use Mom's stash of money to get into Disney World. We could hide somewhere really good when the park closes at night and sleep under the stars with Cinderella's castle looming over us. We could stay there as long as we want, riding rides, shaking hands with Mickey Mouse, getting food out of trash cans if we need it.

I'm so lost in my daydreams of escape; I don't notice the bus has dropped David off until he's standing next to the car. I nearly jump out of the seat when he raps on the window, expecting to see my father peering in.

"What're you doing out here?" David asks.

I tell him everything, and David just keeps saying over and over how mad Dad is going to be. I share some of my getaway ideas with him, but he keeps squashing each plan saying it'll never work. I'm angry he won't just play along and be willing to risk it. So what if we fail. At least we would get away from this house for a while. David puts an end to my fantasies by saying if we do run away, our parents will call the police who would find us and bring us back home. I know this is true and our punishment would be far worse for running away than it's already going to be.

"So maybe my plans won't work, but will you sit here with me for a bit and talk about them. Let's just imagine it together." I look at David, pleading with my eyes. I desperately need to escape this reality for a while, even if it's only through fantasizing about a new life—one where my father no longer exists.

David climbs in the car next to me, and for the next hour, we talk about what it would be like to escape. My stress lifts as we share our visions of meeting the seven dwarves and Snow White, riding Space Mountain until we puke, and sleeping under the stars in the happiest place on earth.

*   *   *

I finally come up with a realistic plan for tonight. I send David to Mrs. Jones' house to hang out until I can figure out how angry our father is. I'll get him or go over to stay, too, depending on the mood in the house. David will tell Mrs. Jones what has happened because she'll understand. Over the years, she's the only person either of us has trusted with the secrets lurking within the four walls of our house. She'll do anything she can to help us. Often, during Dad's rages, I send David to her house to keep him safe.

David reluctantly agrees, and I watch from the car as he makes his way across our yard, through the pine trees separating our property from Mrs. Jones'. When I can no longer see him past the tree line, I open the door and slowly make my way to the front porch. The closer I get, the more intently I listen, trying to see if I can hear Dad's voice. Complete and utter silence.

Once I get to the front door, I peer into the window beside it. My father sits on the couch watching television; his foot is wrapped with a bag of ice on it, resting on the footstool in front of him. Beer cans litter the floor around him. I figure Dad can't do too much harm, tonight at least, with his foot hurt and decide to go in.

I try to open the door as quietly as possible, hoping to sneak past Dad. The second I'm in the door, he speaks. He doesn't yell; he speaks. Hearing my father talk calmly is a shock. I can't remember the last time I heard his voice in anything other than shouts of rage.

"Son, come here where I can see you." I creep to the opposite end of the couch, trying to stay as far from him as possible. "You will be sorry for this. This is the biggest mistake you've ever made. I want you to know that you'll regret it."

The intensity in my father's glare, and the calmness in his voice, send chills down my spine and make the hair on my arms stand on end. There's no doubt my father has been sitting here planning his revenge just as I was earlier planning my escape. The difference is my father has the power to make his come true.

Later, as I'm lying in bed, I cannot sleep. No matter how I try, I cannot shake off the evening's events or the fear building inside at my father's threat. The whole night was strange. Mom carried out her evening routine like nothing out of the ordinary had happened, like we weren't just trying to escape our hell hours earlier. Dad ignored us for most of the evening, sitting on the couch, drinking beer, and watching television. He didn't yell at us, didn't scream his usual obscenities. Each time he spoke, it was with the same flat tone he used when issuing his threat of a payback to me earlier in the afternoon. I would've felt more at ease if my punishment were already out of the way, rather than lying in wait to see what plans my father has.

After Mom helped my stumbling drunk father to bed, I snuck over to Mrs. Jones' house to tell David to spend the night and took him a change of clothes for the morning. Mrs. Jones offered to let me stay, too, but I know if I disappeared, the eventual punishment would be worse. My father didn't even ask about David's whereabouts, so absorbed in his plot for revenge that he could think of nothing else. I did tell Mom where David was, whispering to her while we were getting dinner ready, which she thought was a good idea. I asked Mom why Dad was acting so strange; she simply shrugged and said she had stopped trying to figure him out years ago.

Is Mom as scared as I am? Did Dad also let her know our "crime" would not go unpunished? Does Dad know I was the one that pushed down the gas pedal, causing the injury to his foot? I have no idea what story my mother told him about where we were headed and why.

The silence of the night is killing me. I don't even know how I should be preparing to defend myself. Usually, Dad leaves nothing to the imagination where his anger is concerned. It is all yelled out, bouncing off the walls, the ceilings, the floors. There's never a doubt, thanks to the verbal and physical outbursts, how Dad feels he's been slighted or wronged. This time, however, everything is left to my imagination. The only thing I know for certain is this evening, and my father's coolness, is definitely the calm before the storm.

I'm afraid to shut my eyes—terrified of what I'll find when I open them. I try to focus on other things—our Disney World dreams, math problems at school. Concentration is impossible because every cell in my body is screaming a warning that danger is lurking around the corner, down the hall, in my parent's bed. In science class this year, we learned about the body's natural fight or flight response. Normally my body races into fight mode to protect David or myself. Now every part of me is screaming, telling me to flee. To run away from the impending doom. Even though I don't know his plans, my instincts tell me that, this time, I won't be able to fight back against my dad's wrath. I know his rage has grown each minute this evening when he didn't scream at us; his fury expanded with each sip of the beer he took instead of hitting us; his wrath swelled each time he watched Mom or me walk by. Most people would cool off about a situation if given time to think it through; however, my father isn't most people. Time, when it comes to his anger, is no one's friend. In this evening full of uncertainties, I know this for certain.

BILLY

I'M still awake when the sky shows the first hint of morning light. I couldn't sleep at all because fear consumes me. Now that morning is almost here, I finally feel like I can breathe deeply for the first time since I laid down last night. I watch the seconds tick by on the clock, waiting for six to come. Then I can get up, get dressed, and wait in my room until six forty-five when I have to leave for the bus. The house is quiet; my parents must still be asleep. I don't know how Mom manages to sleep in the same bed with that monster each night. How does she ever feel safe enough to doze off next to the person who has hurt her over and over again? I don't know why she doesn't put a pillow over his face one night and not let go of it until he stops breathing. I'm furious she even cared about him being hurt yesterday. How can she care about someone who has no regard for her as a human being? How can she worry more about his well-being than she does about her own or her children's?

I come up with no answers to the questions burning my soul. I do know my mother loves David and me. I've always believed she'd do anything she could to protect us, and I know many times, her beatings came as a result of offering herself as a sacrifice to spare us. Or because she spoke up in our defense. My father dying seems to be the only way to shelter us from more pain. I know in my heart, after our failed attempt yesterday, we'll never get away. Our future lies within these walls, suffering my father's wrath. I cannot fathom spending the next seven years, until I'm old enough to be on my own, watching my mother get hurt and lose what little light is left in her eyes. What will I do if she can no longer smile even in the moments my father isn't around? Won't there come a point where he's completely stolen her soul?

There's no way Dad will allow me to be the punching bag in David's place forever. David will never survive if he has to experience a quarter of what I've endured on his behalf. Even when I am eighteen, I'll never be able to leave David behind, so I'll have to go somewhere he can tag along. Maybe by then, my mother will finally be able to leave, to come with us. The question that keeps swimming through my mind is *How?* How will I make it through the next seven years when every day is such a battle, and each moment with my father around feels like an eternity?

*   *   *

School doesn't offer the distraction from my fears as I'd hoped. It's already eighth period and the end of the day rapidly approaches. Despite my attempts to focus on the English teacher's ramblings about subject-verb agreement, it's all starting to sound like a foreign language.

The only thing resonating in my mind is my father's threat and worrying that today will be the day he exacts his revenge. I want to figure out a way to disappear from this life, from this world. Or, at the very least, be able to figure out a way to not have to go home.

As the bell rings signaling the end of the day, my skin is clammy and my heart races. It feels like an elephant is sitting on my chest, making it hard for me to take a deep enough breath. I chant prayers inside of my head as I make my way to my locker… *Please God, let the bus break down on the way home…*down the hallway…*Or, let Mom be waiting outside school to take us away …* out the door of the school…. *Okay, she's not here. Let her be waiting in the driveway when I get home.* Let us get away this time. The closer we get to my bus stop, the harder and faster my heart pounds. The houses and trees whizz by outside of the bus window. As my driveway appears, there's no sign of Mom waiting there for me. My prayers continue as I stroll up the driveway. *God, let him be dead. Let him have died in his sleep from a heart attack or drinking too much. Anything, God. Just let him be gone.* I open the front door and peek inside, instantly realizing none of my prayers have been answered. My father isn't gone; my mother isn't going to whisk us away to safety. He is ready to make good on his threats.

I see Mom first. Her face is swollen and bloodied, almost beyond recognition. She sits in a kitchen chair in the middle of the living room. Sitting isn't really the correct word—she's slumped forward, barely able to hold her head up, with her hands duct-taped together behind the chair. Her feet are taped at the ankles to the chair's legs. I don't know why my father has gone to such trouble tying her up; she's been beaten so badly there's no way she can move, even if she tried. There are newspapers and books thrown everywhere, littering the living room floor.

I quickly move closer, hoping to free her when I see my father sitting against the wall in the far corner of the living room. He has an almost empty bottle of whiskey in his hand. I can't see him clearly because a shadow from the now-empty bookshelf conceals him.

Using the same calm tone as last night, he speaks. "Welcome home, son. We've been waiting," he chuckles. "Haven't we, Ruby? Haven't we been waiting on our boy here to get home?" He stands.

I instinctively flinch, keeping my gaze glued to my mother. I don't want to look in my father's eyes and see his rage and anger. I'm afraid to catch a glimpse of what's to come. My mother manages to raise her head slightly to look at me through slits in her swollen eyes. I can hear her thoughts... *Run. Get out of here. Now. Please, just go.* Regardless of what she wants me to do, I can't leave her.

My father plods towards me; my heart quickens with each step. Instead of retreating, as every bone in my body screams at me to do, I stand firm. "Well, thanks to your little act of bravery, trying to run over me yesterday, I haven't been able to do much besides think. Think about what punishment you and your mom deserve for trying to run away. For trying to kill me." Again, my dad lets out a sadistic laugh. "I couldn't wait for you to get home so I could show you what I came up with."

Mom whimpers. She's trying to talk but can't force any words out. Tears waterfall down her bloody cheeks, making it look like she's crying tears of blood.

"Come sit next to your mom. Your savior. The one who was trying to rescue you from the big bad wolf."

I hesitate. I want to be closer to Mom to make sure she's okay, but I'm scared to move any nearer to my father. My mother's screams throb inside my head... *Don't do it. Go now, Billy. If you love me, please go.* I force myself to take one step. Two steps. Three steps. Four steps. I quicken my pace for the last two, dropping to my knees in front of her. I lay my head on her lap and feel her quivering. She tries to lean down to me but can't because her hands are tied too tightly.

"I love you, Mom," I whisper as tears spill past my eyelids. As I raise my head to look at her, my father's kick lands squarely on my ribcage. The air is knocked out of me, and I fall to the ground next to my mom's bound feet. As I lie there trying to catch enough of a breath to get back up, my mother's whimpers turn into sobs that seem to come straight from her soul.

"Get up, you little punk." Dad stands over me, nudging me with his foot. "The best is yet to come."

I manage to pull myself up on one elbow as my father

grabs me, yanking me to my feet. There's another kitchen chair directly behind the one my mother is tied to. My father pushes me down and begins taping my legs. I frantically pull at my father's hair and try to scratch him, aiming for his eyes. My father responds with a punch in the face. The blood immediately gushes from my nose, and I know it's probably broken. The pain radiates up my nose, across my forehead, down the back of my neck. A blinding white light steals my vision, and the only thing I can focus on is the throbbing.

I don't realize I've lost consciousness until I awaken to find my hands also taped behind my back, my fingers interlacing with Mom's. Somehow, she's managing to stroke my hand. Each movement of her fingers seems to say, *I'm sorry. Please forgive me. I love you.* I jerk around, trying to see where my father is, what he's doing. I can't see him, but I can hear him. He seems to be standing on the other side of Mom. I hear newspapers rustling beneath his feet and something splashing, like maybe he's spilling his whiskey. Mom's grip tightens; it's no longer a smooth caress but a grasp full of fear and desperation.

The newspaper rustling, along with the splashing and sloshing of liquid, continues until my father is standing in front of me. A fresh bottle of whiskey in one hand and a can of lighter fluid in the other. He's drenching the papers and books with the fluid.

My heart sinks as my father's plan, and the depths of his evil, become clear. Mom frantically tries to loosen the duct tape wrapped around my wrists, her fingernails furiously working back and forth, back and forth, like she would use a steak knife to cut a piece of meat. Sobs wrack her body. I wish I could think of something to do or say to make my father stop. To help free my mother.

My father tosses the now empty lighter fluid can on the floor and stoops down to look directly in my eyes. I want to spit in his face. I wish I could free my legs to kick him, but they're tied too tightly.

"If you had just tried to get away, this wouldn't be happening. But you decided to be a big, tough guy and try to kill me. You're too weak, though. You're nothing but a momma's boy." My father's finger is inches from my face. I want to lunge forward and bite with all my strength, but I'm unable to move because of fear's grip on me. "This is your fault. You get your wish—you and your mom get to go away together."

With those words, my father steps back, pulls his lighter from his pocket, and opens it. My mother, hearing the sounds, screams. No words come, just the guttural wails of a woman who knows she's about to lose her child. My father backs away, towards the door, his eyes never breaking contact with mine. He gives a slight merciless smile, flicks the lighter, tosses it onto the pile of rubbish surrounding us, and shuts the front door behind him.

Instantly, fire is everywhere, following the path of lighter fluid my father surrounded us in. A thin line races into the larger pools of liquid which then spew their flames into the air. The heat surrounds us. I pull on the tape encircling my wrists with all my strength. Mom's sawing has paid off—the tape starts to give way.

Mom speaks the first words since the incident began. "Billy, pull. Quick. We have to get out of here! There's not much time."

Hearing the desperation in her voice, along with seeing that the flames have now spread to the surrounding carpet and furniture, gives me a strength I didn't know I possessed. I pull again on my arms—this time freeing them from their binding. Quickly, I lean forward to unwrap my ankles. The heat from the fire smothers me. It climbs the walls and licks its flames towards the ceiling. The smoke grows thicker by the second, making it difficult to take a breath.

Once freed, I stand, kick my chair out of the way, and begin working to free my mother's hands. Again, she speaks. "I love you, Billy. Don't ever forget how much I love you." As I work to free her, she keeps repeating those words, with a calmness I can't grasp given the desperation of our situation.

The flames singe the skin on my back, a pain like I've never felt before. I smell my burning flesh. The tape on my mother's hands won't loosen. I move to her feet in the hopes that if I can get them free, she'll be able to make it out.

As I move around to the front of her, there's an explosion of light and sound and fire. Its force pushes me backward. As I scramble to get up, the flames engulf my mother. Her screams of agony mix with the last words I will ever hear her say. "I love you, Billy. Run."

I bolt towards the front door, through the haze of smoke and wall of flames—skin burning, eyes searing, flesh cooking. When I reach the door, I turn as I stumble out onto the porch to get one last look at my mother. I can no longer make out her face, her body. The fire has devoured her. There is no longer a distinction between where she ends, and the fire begins. They have become one.

I lunge forward, away from the house and onto the grass. My body is wracked with coughs, trying to expel the smoke lining my lungs. I collapse onto the ground, watching the flames incinerate my house, my mom, my life. The tears fall from my eyes and burn my skin. They're boiling from the heat stored inside me. I no longer feel the pain from the burns covering my body. All I feel is my heart breaking into a million pieces, shattering inside of me. All I hear are the sobs of a boy who's lost the only person in the world who loved him enough to make him believe there was always hope. No matter how desperate the situation, she always made me believe that one day, it may be different. Before I pass out, the last thing I see is my hope going up in flames before my eyes, along with the rest of my life.

Part II

Grief can't be shared. Everyone carries it alone,

his own burden, his own way.

~Anne Morrow Lindbergh

Rest assured that in her dying, in her flight through darkness

toward a new light, she held you in her arms

and carried your closeness with her. And when she

arrived at God, your image was imprinted

on her joy-filled soul.

~Molly Fumia

REMEMBER me as the first raindrops of spring fall from the sky. Remember me when you hear the birds singing their melodies high in the treetops. Remember me when you feel the cool breeze of autumn on your face. Remember all the good times, the laughter, the joy. To do this, you'll have to let the painful moments slip from the recesses of your mind. Don't let the joy of our past be stolen from you as I was. I am still here even though you may not see me. Remember me when you look in the mirror, into your own eyes, and see me looking back at you.

KENDRA

4 DAYS AFTER
FEBRUARY 12, 1989

I stand frozen in front of Chelsea's closet, unable to decide which outfit to choose. Each article of clothing holds so many memories. Won't the good memories be erased if the final one created is so painful I cannot bear to think of it again?

The purple dress with the small pink and white flowers—the outfit Chelsea wore to her sophomore singing ensemble concert. Seeing it hanging there lifeless, I hear Chelsea's voice singing just a bit louder than the rest of the choir. I picture her dreamy expression as she sang the Latin words to the piece I assumed was a love ballad, simply by watching her expressions.

The navy-blue dress with the gold buttons—the one Chelsea wore out to dinner with us on her seventeenth birthday.

Chelsea got to choose the restaurant, and her pick was an up-scale steak house in the city. The meal cost a small fortune, but it was worth it to see her excitement over being treated like royalty throughout the meal. Chelsea joked saying she finally felt like the princess we always made her out to be. She looked radiant that night too. It seems like just yesterday I was feeling the bittersweet mixture of joy and regret as she came out of her room in this dress. The joy at seeing what a beautiful young lady she had become. Regret at how quickly the time had passed and how the moments already gone could never be recaptured.

I lean forward into the closet and breathe deeply, taking in the scent of my daughter. Taking in the scent of the memories. I have no idea how to go about choosing an outfit for my child to spend forever in. I can't envision Chelsea's lifeless body in any of the clothes hanging here. These are all items she wore while laughing, or dancing, or singing, or eating, or sleeping. She wore them while living her life, which is what she's supposed to still be doing.

I collapse under the weight of the memories, clutching whatever clothing I can reach as I fall. I hold my precious daughter's shirts and dresses in my arms and cry, soaking them with my tears. *I can't do this. I can't let her go. I can't see her with no life left in her eyes, with no smile on her lips. I can't possibly see her arms and not want to feel them around me. I can't know that she's been hurt and not want to hold her, kiss her cheek, and tell her it will be okay. I don't even know where she's been hurt so I can kiss it to make it better. I don't know how to live without being able to make her better.*

155

My thoughts are interrupted by my own mother's arms encircling my shaking body. How ironic that my mom is doing for me what I want so desperately to be able to do for my daughter. Her hands stroke my back. The heat from my mother's kisses warms the top of my head. She whispers, "Shhh… it's okay, honey. I'm here." My mom is doing things for me that I'll never again be able to do for my daughter.

"I can't do it, Mom." I manage to spit out between sobs.

"I know, honey." She continues to stroke my hair, my arms, my back. "We'll get through this. I don't know how, but we will."

"I don't want to get through it. I want to go back…" I gasp for a breath. "Back to when she was here. When she was safe. I want her back. God, please give me my baby back." I feel like I'm being ripped in two as I shout to a God that I no longer trust to listen or care.

"Honey, why don't you go lay down for a bit? Your dad and I will buy a new outfit for her to wear. We have a couple of hours before we have to be there."

I don't want to lie down if it means getting up to go see my daughter's lifeless body for the first time. I don't want to let my parents pick out clothing for Chelsea that she'll never get to wear as a living, breathing human being. I don't want to take another breath if I can't reverse time and go back to the place where our lives weren't filled with tragedy, when our family wasn't broken. When our daughter's future was somewhere other than inside a box that will forever be placed in the ground.

*   *   *

KENDRA

Without a memory of how I got to bed, I awaken to Tom's voice and his gentle shake on my arm.

"Honey, you've got to get up. We've got to leave in fifteen minutes."

I bolt up. "We can't. I don't have anything for her to wear. Oh God, I don't have anything to put on her." The tears well up.

Tom points to an outfit I've never seen before, hanging on the back of the bedroom door. "Your mom and dad picked it out. It'll be beautiful."

"You mean it would've been beautiful," I say as I take in the light green sweater and skirt ensemble. It actually looks like an outfit Chelsea would've picked for herself.

"Yes, it would have." Tom pulls me close. "Get ready. I'll wait downstairs."

I go to the bathroom and examine myself in the mirror, seeing the black circles under my eyes, the red splotches on my cheeks. If I cared, I could put on some make-up and look a little more presentable, but I don't. It doesn't matter if the entire world can see the pain written all over my face. There's no sense in putting on a mask when sorrow radiates from every pore in my body. Anyone within a mile of me can probably feel it in their own soul. There's no sense putting on make-up I'll be crying off within the next half hour. Instead, I run a brush through my hair, rinse my mouth with mouthwash, and go downstairs to join my family on our trip to hell.

*   *   *

TOM

I tried to talk Kendra out of going to the funeral home with us today, but she refused, reasoning that she's been involved with every major decision in Chelsea's life so far and that isn't about to change now. I'm worried about her reaction to seeing Chelsea's body. We were given a choice to see her today or wait until prior to the viewing when she'd be fully clothed and ready for "show." Kendra decided she wanted to get it over with today. I don't know if she'll be able to withstand making a decision about funeral arrangements or the casket that will hold our daughter's body for all eternity. Rebecca told me how devastated she was by just trying to select an outfit for Chelsea to wear—how can she possibly deal with everything to come over the next few hours?

I don't know how I'll react today to all the decisions that must be made, to once again seeing my daughter's still, bloated body. The one that looks nothing like her, yet the one that has stolen our entire future. I'm afraid I'll be able to see where the incisions were made to perform the autopsy. The images of them breaking Chelsea's body apart to explore its inner depths assault my mind. What if they didn't put her back together right or if she is even more disfigured than the last time I saw her?

My anxieties are compounded by the funeral director's explanation to me that we need to get moving quickly on the arrangements since it has been so long since Chelsea's demise. I found it funny he used the word demise instead of saying it like it was—her death, her murder, her end. Someone in the business of death should at least be able to speak the word. I know enough to read between the lines of what he said—we must hurry because Chelsea's body is starting to decompose. My stomach turns, wanting to vomit out the truth, each time the words decompose and Chelsea pair in my mind.

I cannot bear to take on the weight of Kendra's pain today, too; mine is already too much. There's no way I'll be able to handle the weight of her grief when my own is about to make me buckle. I'm glad her parents are going—if Kendra breaks down, they'll handle it. I'm usually the shoulder for Kendra to lean on, but now a simple lean from her will push me over the edge.

Everyone is silent during the drive, each lost in our thoughts, our memories, our fears. I finally speak when we pull into the spot in front of Simons Funeral Home asking Kendra if she's sure she's up to this. She answers by being the first one out of the car as if on a mission to prove her strength. As if there is a prize for being strong.

We sit in the lobby waiting for Shaun Simons, the Funeral Director, to come for us. I glance around the room taking in the floral wallpaper, the scent of flowers, the dim lighting, the decorative vases, the expensive furniture. It has the feel of an upscale restaurant, not a place of death. I vaguely recall the last time I was in a funeral home, attending my Great Aunt Wanda's funeral when I was seven. I remember playing hide and seek with my cousins while all the adults cried and talked about their memories. I wish I could be that carefree again, seeing death as an excuse to see people I'd lost touch with, to play, to laugh.

"Mr. and Mrs. Wyatt, I'm Shaun Simons." He walks towards us with his hand outstretched, a solemn expression on his face. "I'm so sorry for your loss."

I introduce Rebecca and Carl, and then we follow him into the inner sanctum of the funeral home—the last place on earth any of us want to go. It is full of caskets and headstones for us to choose from. The room is dim with a bright spotlight shining down to illuminate each one as if we're shopping for a new diamond and need to see how it reflects the light.

The room starts to spin, and I grab hold of Kendra's hand to steady myself. She squeezes it and leads me to a chair. She's talking, but I can't quite make out the words or respond. I think she's asking if I'm okay—I manage a nod. I sit there as her lips move, saying something, and then watch as she walks with her mother to the caskets on display. Her composure amazes me as she and Rebecca stroll with Carl and Mr. Simons behind them, examining each one. She strokes the silk linings as if she were picking out a new blouse, trying to find the softest one.

Mr. Simons spouts off details about each—words that don't register, no matter how hard I try to make them. Words like twenty-gauge, stainless steel, bronze, mahogany, cherry. Words used when purchasing household items like silverware or a new dining room table. Not words I associate with a box in which to bury my daughter. My head continues to swirl with the sights before me, the words being said, the new facts of my life without Chelsea.

To keep myself grounded, the counting begins. I read the names on the caskets. Batesville Primrose, eighteen letters. Batesville Alameda Rose, twenty-one letters. Jefferson Silver Copper, twenty-one letters again. After finishing with them, I move onto the grave markers. I read the inscriptions on each, counting how many letters they contain.

In Loving Memory of
Judith Sebold
Loving Wife and Daughter
Born April 17, 1932
Died January 2, 1983

Eighteen words, eighty letters, including the numbers. I wonder if Judith Sebold was a real person. If so, she lived fifty years, eight months, and sixteen days or eighteen thousand, five hundred, and twenty-two days.

Kendra interrupts my calculations to ask if I'd like to see her top three choices. I say yes when what I really mean is it's the last thing on earth I want to do. Kendra leads me to her selections, talking about the details she likes about each. The Batesville Primrose—one of her choices because of the roses, Chelsea's favorite flower, and because of its pink silk lining, Chelsea's favorite color. I tune her out, unable to listen as she leads me through her favorite aspects about the next two. Picking a casket for our daughter because the color was Chelsea's favorite, or because the flower on it was the one she loved the most, is absurd to me. Our daughter will never see the casket, even though it will be her home forevermore.

We finally follow Mr. Simons back to the desk to sit and discuss our final selections. He shares the prices of the three Kendra selected. The first is $1,295, not including the burial vault.

One plus two plus nine plus five equals seventeen—a good number. The second is $1,149. *One plus one plus four plus nine, equals fifteen.* I'm not fond of the number fifteen, so I quickly rule out casket number two. The third is the most expensive, $2,349— eighteen is the total, again a number I don't much care for. I state my preference for the first choice. Decision one out of the way.

Next, we discuss burial vaults. Applying my mathematical reasoning, I reach my decision in the same way. This time, I select the vault whose price adds up to twenty-one, a number which I also like. Decision number two done.

Then comes the headstone—the monument that will represent our daughter's life to the rest of the world. The stone that will summarize everything her life has been; everything it will ever be. I try to suppress my raging emotions by reducing the decision to a mathematical one, but my mind can't concoct a rationale that applies. There is no numerical way to signify my daughter's time on this earth other than the obvious... Born March 2, 1971. Died February 8, 1989. I wonder if we can add the phrase, *We think*, after the date of her death for will we ever really know when she took her last breath, when her final moment on this earth was? When trying to come up with wording, the numbers are all I can envision. *Chelsea Marie Wyatt— ONLY on earth for 17 Years, 11 Months and 6 Days. Or, Chelsea Marie Wyatt—STOLEN from her parents 152,272 hours after taking her first breath.*

Kendra looks to me for help in making the decision. It's as though I'm watching a movie. I see the tears stream down her cheeks; I hear the sobs rising within her; I feel her gaze boring into my soul. I can't help myself—I laugh and share my latest idea. *Chelsea Marie Wyatt – Time on Earth: 566,179,200 seconds Time in Heaven: Eternity.* I know instantly I shouldn't have spoken my thoughts aloud as Kendra slams her fist down on the desk and storms off in tears. I should follow her and apologize, see if she's alright. I can't, though. I have nothing to offer that she'd understand. I have nothing to give to help ease her pain. Instead, I get up and walk out the front door of the funeral home, down Eighth Avenue, headed toward home.

BILLY

11 YEARS, 8 MONTHS, 19 DAYS BEFORE
MAY 20, 1977

I wake up confused, unsure of where I am. I slowly look around the room and see the curtain hanging from the ceiling and the empty chair in the corner. Monitors beep in a steady rhythm next to the bed. An IV is inserted into the back of my wrist, pulling on my skin, and I feel a burn worse than any pain I've ever felt underneath the bandages on my arms. I can't figure out why I'm in a hospital bed, why I hurt so badly or why I'm all alone. Then it hits me—the memories barrel over me like a freight train. I scream so loudly nurses come running from each direction, hearing my broken heart echo down the hallways as I yell, "Mommy! Mommy! Mommy!"

*   *   *

When I wake several hours later, someone is holding my hand. Before I open my eyes, I say a prayer asking God to please let it be my mom—to allow all the memories swirling around in my brain to have been a terrible nightmare. I know immediately it was no nightmare when I see Mrs. Jones sitting there, watching me. My mom is nowhere in the room.

"Hi, sweetie! It's good to see those big brown eyes," Mary says with a slight smile. "How are you feeling?"

"Mommy. Where's Mommy?" I utter the only words on my mind.

"Oh, honey. I'm so sorry…" Mrs. Jones' voice trails off as she leans down to hug me. She's crying. "She didn't make it. She's gone."

The life leaves my body. I know, based on what I can remember, the likelihood of Mom surviving the fire was slim, but I still had hope that God worked a miracle and allowed her to live. As always, God hadn't cared enough to listen to my prayers.

Tears roll down my cheeks as Mrs. Jones explains what happened after I passed out in the front yard. She was the one who first noticed the smoke and called the fire department. After alerting them, she rushed over to see if any of us were inside and found me lying unconscious on the front lawn. She said the fire department and ambulance showed up quickly, but it was too late; the fire had spread too far. Our house was gone. My mom was gone. My dad was nowhere to be found.

I manage to ask where David is through the lump taking over my throat. Mary explains that David came home in the midst of the chaos of the firemen trying to put out the blaze, and he stayed by my side until the ambulance took me away. David's been staying with her ever since, while the police try to contact some of our family members to help out. Mary promises to bring him to visit soon.

"What's going to happen to us?" I cry. "Who will take care of us?"

"The police are talking to your aunt and your grandparents to see if you can stay with them for a while. If not, you can always stay with me. We can sew buttons and eat cookies."

For the first time since waking up, a bit of calmness washes over me. I like Mrs. Jones and know she'll take care of us. If I can't have my mom, my next choice would definitely be Mary.

"Our family won't want us," I explain. "We only met our grandparents once, and they didn't even talk to us. They made Mommy go back home even though she was really hurt." I pause, anger swelling in my chest at the memory of them turning us away. The realization hits me like a hurricane that Mom would still be alive if they'd allowed us to stay. "I hope we can stay with you—I don't like them."

"It'll all work out. I'll make sure you're in a good place."

"What about Dad? Do the police know he did it? He burned our house. He killed my mom," I sob.

"That's what they thought. They're still looking for him. Don't you worry; they'll find him. He'll never hurt you again."

I want to believe her, but it isn't true. Dad will cause me pain every day for the rest of my life because I'll no longer have

Mom. The anguish he's caused will never go away. Even if my burns and bruises disappear, my heart will never be able to put itself back together.

All of the talking and thinking has exhausted me. When I tell Mrs. Jones I need to go back to sleep for a while, she strokes my head like Mom used to do and hums me a song. Despite my fear and pain, sleep takes me away.

KENT

4 DAYS AFTER
FEBRUARY 12, 1989

I expected Mom to come back from the funeral home, crying, not enraged. She's the angriest I've ever seen her. In fact, until all the recent stuff with Chelsea, I don't ever remember my mom losing her temper. I'd overheard her and Dad sometimes arguing after Chels and I were in bed, about things like money or disciplining us, but she always tried to keep her cool when we were around.

I'm shocked by the raging woman who storms through the front door, hands on her hips, yelling straight at me. "Where's your father?"

I take a couple of steps backward and shrug. "I don't know. I thought he was with you."

She runs up the steps yelling Dad's name with a few cuss words after it. I've never heard my mom swear. Chelsea and I would get our mouths washed out with soap if we even muttered a word like stupid. I hear the doors opening and slamming shut, but I know Dad isn't up there. By the time Mom storms back down, my grandparents are standing in the doorway.

"Kendra, take a deep breath and calm down. You don't want to upset Kent," my grandmother says, moving cautiously towards Mom.

Mom throws her hands in the air. "Don't tell me to calm down. My husband just walked out on me during the worst moment of my life. He left me to deal with this by myself. I had to deal with seeing my dead daughter's body without him." Mom's crying, which makes her words even harder to understand. "I won't calm down until he looks me in the eye and gives me one hell of a good explanation for not only walking out on me but for bailing on Chelsea."

She storms into the kitchen. I hear the garage door open and slam shut, followed by the opening and closing of cabinets. I sure hope Mom hasn't lost it to the point she actually thinks Dad's hiding in a cupboard.

"What happened, Grandma?" I whisper.

"Kent, why don't you go to your room for a while until your mom cools off? We'll talk later," my grandfather answers.

I don't want to go to my room. I want to know what's wrong and why my mom is so angry. Instead of fighting it, I go, knowing no one will give me any answers anyway. I leave my door cracked though, trying to eavesdrop on the conversa-

169

tions from below. All I hear for the longest time is Grandma's calm voice met with silence from my mother. Not silence really, but no talking, just dishes being slammed around, chairs sliding across the kitchen floor.

I wish someone would tell me what happened. I've been nervous about it all day. Mom asked me if I wanted to go. Part of me did, but my fear took over, so I refused. I wanted to see my sister's body because my mind can't accept that she's gone. I keep thinking the dead girl they've been talking about must be someone else—it has to be a mistake. I've had daydreams over the last several days that it really is someone else's body, but everyone's too upset to notice. I imagine walking in, taking one look, and being able to say with certainty that it isn't my sister. Everyone would look closer, without tears in their eyes and hearts torn in two, and realize I was right. I would be their hero for noticing.

At other times though, all I can see when I close my eyes is Chelsea's face, covered in moss and leaves, staring at me with lifeless eyes, like zombies in a scary movie. In the nightmares I've had the past two nights, Chelsea rises out of the river water, covered in muck, calling out to me. "Kent, I need you. Please help me." In my dreams, her voice sounds different than in real life. She sounds scared, panicked. I can never force myself to move towards her. In one dream, I ran the other direction with her following after me, yelling for help. In the other, I started screaming so loudly that I woke up covered in sweat and shaking. I tried to fall back to sleep, but the awful images wouldn't leave, so I finally went into my parents' room and tried to wake Mom. Whenever I used to get scared, she was always the only one who could calm me down. She'd lay with me in my bed, rub my back, and sing me songs until I fell back to sleep. That night though, I could barely wake her, and when I finally managed to, she said I'm too old to be scared and to go back to bed. I don't know what was worse, my embarrassment at needing my mom's help, or her refusal to give it.

I lay on my bed and imagine what Chelsea looks like now. Will I be able to tell it's her? Has her body already started to rot? Will she stink like a piece of spoiled meat? I don't think I'll be able to make it through the calling hours tomorrow without crying. I'm scared of what my friends will think if I do break down. Will life ever get back to normal? I doubt it's even possible without Chelsea around.

Lost in my thoughts, it takes a moment for it to register that Mom's yelling again. I creep to the top of the staircase and lie down so I can see what's going on downstairs. Dad has just come in the front door, and Mom's going off on him, yelling, cussing, and screaming. My father stands there, expressionless, while Mom rants and raves. When Dad refuses to speak or offer any explanation for his behavior, Mom starts punching him in the chest. It continues until Grandpa finally pulls her away. The whole time, Dad just stands there, staring straight ahead, not reacting to her words or punches in any way.

Once Mom is out of his path, Dad retreats up the stairs without saying a word to any of them. He sees me get up from my belly at the top of the stairs, trying to sneak back to my room without anyone noticing. Usually, this would result in a lecture about respecting people's privacy or minding my own business.

Today, though, my father does nothing but simply looks at me with the same blank stare he gave Mom, opens the bedroom door, and lies down on the bed.

I don't know what to do. I definitely don't want to go downstairs because Mom's still really upset. Something is seriously wrong with Dad, but I know he won't talk to me about it. I don't feel like being alone with my thoughts again. I look at my father lying on the bed and staring up at the ceiling. Even though I may get in trouble, I lie next to him, curl up against his body, and rest my head on his chest like I haven't done for a long, long time. At first, Dad doesn't move. After a moment, without saying a word, my father's arm wraps around me and pulls me close.

BILLY

I sleep fitfully through the night. The nurses come in several times to give me medicine to help me calm down. Each time I do manage to drift off, the nightmares begin. The dream is always the same—Mom and I are alone in a room, surrounded by flames trying to consume us. We're too far apart to reach each other, and a wall of fire separates us. If I can just suffer the pain from the burning flames and get to Mom, everything will be okay. Each time, I summon the strength and courage to do so and force myself to push forward, to fight my fear. I'm in the midst of the fire, almost within reach of her, feeling my flesh burn off my bones. It's so real I can smell the searing of my skin. I can feel the heat of the fire, the smoke filling my lungs. I reach forward as she does the same. At the moment our hands meet, Mom vanishes. Each time she disappears, I wake up screaming and sweating. Every time I awaken screaming, I'm met with a nurse trying to make me go back to sleep, forcing me to return to my never-ending nightmare.

I wake up screaming again, only this time, I'm quieted by the voice of someone I don't recognize. A woman says it's okay and to take a deep breath, that it's only a dream. I force my eyes open and find a short lady with brown hair that I've never seen before, standing next to my bed. Her worried eyes study me carefully.

"Who are you?" I finally ask, still shaking from my nightmare.

"I'm Veronica Conley, a social worker with Children's Services." She touches my hand. "I need to talk to you for a bit. Would that be alright?"

I wonder if I really have a choice. She seems nice enough, but I'm scared of talking about everything, worried about reliving it all.

"I guess," I say, my voice quivering with uncertainty.

Veronica explains that her job is to ensure that David and I have a place to go now that our mom is "gone," which is the exact word she uses. Her word choice enrages me because it makes it sound like she left us on purpose, like she had a choice in the matter. "Gone" is where people go when they leave a room or go on a trip, not when they leave this world by dying. By being murdered. Hearing it upsets me so much I forget to listen to what she's saying. Finally, I tune back in at the mention of my grandparents.

I immediately interrupt, "I don't want to go with them. I don't like them."

"My job is to make sure you end up in a place where you'll be taken care of—where you'll get food, a place to live, someone to look after you. I have to try to find you a place to stay with relatives," Veronica pauses. "I talked to your aunt, and she isn't able to take you and David right now. She's worried about you, though."

"What about Mrs. Jones? Have you talked to her? She'd take good care of us—she said so."

"There's a process that must be followed before a non-family member can take you in. Mrs. Jones has started that process in case we can't find anywhere else for you to go." She leans forward and looks into my eyes. "Why don't you think your grandparents are a good choice?"

My chest tightens as I remember my grandfather's stern words to my mother and the way he walked right past David and I, without even a glance in our direction or a word uttered to us. I recall the devastation all over my mother's face as we drove away from there with nowhere to go, no one to turn to. I think of our time in the hotel room while my mother was so shattered by her father's refusal that she couldn't even move. I can't forget the despair I felt, and the hopelessness my mother radiated from every pore in her body, when we pulled back into our driveway at home, returning to my father.

Tears spill down my cheeks, as I finally say, "Because, if they'd taken us when Mommy asked, she'd still be here. She wouldn't be dead." A sob catches in my throat. "She needed them, but they wouldn't help. Please don't make me go there; they don't love me. They don't even know me. They didn't want her, and they don't want me."

"Billy, I'm sorry," she says as she leans close to wipe the tears from my cheek. "I'll do what I can to help you. Right now, you need to get better so you can get out of here."

Where will I go once I'm better and able to leave? I desperately want to be able to trust Veronica—she seems nice and has a look in her eye that tells me she cares about what happens. But I'll never again feel like I have a home if my mom isn't there with me.

* * *

Shortly after Veronica leaves, promising she'll be back soon to let me know what's going on, a police officer enters the room. As he approaches my bed, fear races through me. I don't like the police very much. I once overheard Mom tell Mrs. Jones she didn't call the police to help because they wouldn't do anything to stop my dad from hurting us since we were his family.

The officer's gruff voice breaks the silence. "Billy, I'm Officer Martin. I need to ask you a few questions."

I can't speak—not only does he sound mean but he's huge, the tallest man I've ever seen. He doesn't even smile when he introduces himself.

Officer Martin pulls up a chair and sits down next to the bed. I breathe a sigh of relief because he isn't as scary now that I don't have to crane my neck to look up at him. "How are you feeling?" he asks, and his eyes soften a bit.

"Not so good." My voice shakes as I answer.

"I'll try not to take up too much of your time because you need your rest, but I have to ask you some questions. Would that be okay?" I again wonder if I can say no but instead nod my head.

"Billy, can you tell me what happened the day of the fire?"

The day's events pour through my mind in an instant, like I'm watching a tape on super-fast forward. I don't even know where to start. Should I tell the officer about us trying to escape? Should I admit I tried to run over my father? Will I be able to make it clear to him how hard I tried to save Mom from the fire?

I start from the beginning and recount the events leading up to that day. When I get to the part about my dad throwing the lighter, I can't continue through my sobs. My mom's voice echoes through my head, along with the roar of the flames. The heat burns my skin all over again. My heart races with the same panic I felt that day.

The officer reaches out and gently touches my arm. "It's okay. You don't have to go on. I'm so sorry for all you've gone through."

"Did you find my dad yet?" I whisper, afraid of the answer.

"No, we're still looking. Maybe you can help with that... do you have any idea where he may have gone? Is there anyone you can think of that would take him in? Family? Friends? Someone he works with?"

After thinking for a moment, I tell him I have no idea. I don't know any of my dad's family, including my grandparents. I don't even know if they're still alive. The only thing I know for sure is my dad hates his parents. He'd always say things about his dad during or after the beatings, like how lucky I was it wasn't my grandpa doing the whipping or I'd be black and blue from head to toe. Or I wouldn't be able to sit for a month. He'd mention his mother when he'd yell at Mom, always telling her she was stupid and helpless just like his own mother. I share all of this with the officer, not knowing if it'll help.

Officer Martin thanks me, saying he appreciates my openness.

"What'll happen when you find him?"

"He'll be arrested and spend a long time in jail."

"Good." Hearing this brings me more relief than I've felt in what feels like forever. I hope they find him, and he goes to prison for the rest of his life—then I'll never have to see him or be afraid of him again.

"You'll be one of the first to know when we catch him." For the first time since the officer entered the room, he gives me a smile and a wink.

The only thing that keeps replaying in my mind, once I'm alone again, is the officer said *when* we catch him, not *if* we do. I decide to hold onto that *when* as my biggest hope.

NICOLE

5 DAYS AFTER
FEBRUARY 13, 1989

I wake up frantic, realizing I didn't hear my alarm which has been going off for over an hour. I'm supposed to be at the funeral home by noon, so my goal was to get up at ten to have time to get ready. I'm going early for the family viewing held before the doors open to the public at one. I now only have a half-hour to get ready to be there on time.

I took three Valium last night trying to find some peace. Since they found Chelsea's body, I've been a mess and have gone through the rest of my mom's bottle of pills as well as taken quite a few of the ones prescribed by my doctor. I don't have to hide the fact I'm taking them; Mom seems to feel helpless, so she offers the pills to me like parents offer candy as a bribe to make their kids behave.

When the drugs wear off, my mind races. I become obsessed with memories of Chelsea, wondering who killed her, picturing how she died, visualizing what happened to her before her death. Mrs. Wyatt told me Chelsea had been raped even though that was being kept from the public. The word *rape* makes me sick to my stomach, especially now that it's associated with my best friend. I remember all the conversations Chelsea and I had about whether or not she should have sex with Brent. It makes me cringe to realize Chelsea saved her virginity for someone so undeserving, rather than being able to offer it as a gift to someone she loved. No matter how hard I try, I can't shake the thought of her being violated in such a way.

I look forward to the numbness the pills offer. I know exactly how long it takes for the feelings to go away. It starts with a tingling in my fingers and toes. Then slowly it creeps throughout the rest of my body until every part of me can no longer feel—even though I never forget what happened, the pills give me a break from the emotional pain. The only part of me the pills can't deaden is my heart. Even though my brain no longer perceives the pain, my heart still bleeds, as it probably will forever.

I grab the outfit I wore for my formal senior picture. The outfit Chels helped me pick, saying how beautiful I looked. The one I promised to let her borrow whenever she wanted. The outfit Chels will never get the chance to wear.

My hands tremble as I think about the fact that I will soon see my best friend, dead. I'm shaking so badly I tear a hole in my pantyhose with my fingernail. Before I attempt another pair, I take two Valium hoping they'll help me get through the next several hours. I'll be able to function if I only take two since I've been downing three or four at a time for the past couple of days, every four hours. Three or four knock me out. Two will just take the edge off and make everything more bearable.

As quickly as possible, I get dressed and put on some make-up, which I haven't done for days. As I go through my normal routine, I wonder why it even matters how I look. No one will be looking at me; they'll be studying Chelsea's body to see if there's any resemblance to who she used to be, any clue that there used to be a funny, smart, kind person in the empty shell lying in the casket.

*   *   *

As soon as I step inside the funeral home, I'm assaulted with the thick smell of flowers, making me feel like I'm going to vomit. I never realized such a sweet smell could be so foul, so pungent. The only sound is the steady hum of instrumental music piping through the speakers. I quickly make my way to the room and see Mrs. Wyatt and Kent standing in front of the casket. I'm thankful they're blocking my view of Chelsea—I'm not ready to see her yet. I'm surprised when I hear Mr. Wyatt's voice call out from behind me.

He sits in a chair in the corner, as far away from the casket as possible. "Hi, Nicole. Thanks for coming. You're our first visitor."

The cordial nature of his greeting makes it seem as if

he's welcoming guests to a party at their home. "Oh, Mr. W." I quicken my pace towards him and fling my arms around him, the tears already starting to flow.

Tom pats me on the back, but there's no warmth in his embrace. It's as if I'm hugging a cold, stone statue. Tom's reaction, or lack of one, surprises me as it's definitely not the Mr. Wyatt I'm used to—the one who refers to me as his "other daughter" when introducing me to people. The one who I've secretly wished for years was my own father. The one whose little angel is lying dead at the front of the room.

Tom backs away. "Well, go take a look and see what you think. They did a pretty good job on her."

He's talking like Chelsea is a room he just painted or a meal he ordered. The strangeness surrounding Tom is overwhelming. I can't take it right now, so I leave him and force myself to move forward. Chelsea's grandparents stroll from one flower arrangement to the next, reading each of the little cards attached. I hope my mom remembered to send flowers; I asked her to send Chelsea's favorite, an arrangement of pink roses. I make a mental note to make sure to check later—now, I have to do what I came here to do. To see Chelsea. To start saying goodbye.

I walk up next to Kendra and Kent, intentionally avoiding looking at my friend. I want to say hello to them first for fear the words won't come out once I see Chels. Kendra pulls me into an embrace.

"Thanks so much for coming early. It means a lot to us you're here as part of our family," Kendra says.

My entire body trembles, and my words come out shaky. "It means the world that you included me."

We stand there a moment before she finally asks the dreaded question. "Have you seen her yet?"

I shake my head as tears pool in my eyes.

"Go ahead and see her, sweetie. You need to do this." Kendra releases her firm grip around me. "I'll be right here if you need me. Take a few minutes with her alone."

I don't want to leave the warmth and comfort of Kendra's embrace. I don't want to face the cold, hard facts laying before me in the pink and white casket with the huge spray of pink roses on top, embellished with a ribbon saying, *Our Beloved Daughter*. Mrs. Wyatt gently nudges me forward and leaves me no choice.

As I take a step towards the casket, I finally look. Lying before me is my best friend with her eyes closed. I don't care about the blank expression Chelsea wears, so unlike her in real life. The heavy make-up caking her face to cover the areas where her skin is starting to change color doesn't bother me. I look beyond Chelsea's face, swollen to about two times its normal size, and her hair that isn't fixed the way she likes it. The only thing I'm aware of is my best friend, the one I haven't been able to see or talk to for what seems like forever, is lying less than a foot in front of me.

I do what any best friend would do. I run forward and embrace my friend who's unable to hug me back. I kiss her on the cheek, feeling its coolness against my lips. I lay my head on her chest until my tears leave a wet spot that will always be a part of her, my anguish forever remaining with my friend. My sorrow isn't only for myself and my pain but for the future Chelsea will never have.

I stay with her until Kendra comes over to tell me it's almost time for the viewing hours. Kendra wraps her arm around my waist and leads me to the bathroom to help me put myself back together before everyone arrives. I have no idea how someone can put a puzzle together when such an important piece is missing. I'll never be whole again with the huge, empty space now inside of me that used to be filled with Chelsea.

BILLY

11 YEARS, 8 MONTHS, 16 DAYS BEFORE
MAY 23, 1977

I hear them coming and know immediately who it is even though I can't see them. I'd know David's voice anywhere. I can't make out what he's saying, but I know he's close. I've never gone so long before without seeing my brother, and I've missed him terribly.

There's a knock on the door. Before I can say *come in*, it opens a crack, and Mrs. Jones peeks in.

"Hi, sweetie! You're awake. I've got a surprise for you today." She pushes the door open the rest of the way to reveal David standing next to her.

As soon as David sees me, he lets go of Mary's hand and runs to my bed. Ignoring the pain, I manage to lift my bandaged arms to pull him into an embrace.

"Oh, Billy. I missed you so much. I was scared." David says, crying into my neck.

"I missed you too, buddy. I'm so glad you're here. I've been dying to see you."

David sits back and looks at me. "What's a matter with your arms and face?"

"I got burned from the fire." I hate mentioning it because he has to feel the same pain and loss as I do.

"Does it hurt?"

"Yeah—it hurts real bad, but the doctor says it'll get better. I'll be okay. I may look a little funny from scars, but it'll stop hurting at least."

"Can I sit up there with you?" David says, pointing at the bed.

"Sure, I'll scoot."

David hoists himself up and lies down next to me. He thinks the bed is fun and spends time playing with the buttons to raise and lower it. Even though it hurts to have him leaning up against me, I refuse to say a word about it. It's refreshing to have him here; I'm not about to let pain get in the way. We've slept in the same bed for almost nine years, which has made it doubly hard for me to sleep since I've been in the hospital. Maybe the nightmares wouldn't plague me as much if I had my brother's soft snores to focus on or his cold feet pressed up against my leg.

"When do you get outta here?"

"I don't know yet. The doctor says I'll probably have to stay another day or two to make sure my burns are healing okay and I don't get an infection."

"Oh." David pauses, and his eyes fill with sadness. "Billy, did Daddy do this? Did Daddy start the fire?"

"Yeah. He did." I pull him close again.

"Mommy's dead. Did you know that? He killed her. He killed Mommy." David sobs.

"I know. I tried to save her, but I couldn't get to her through the fire. I'm so sorry… I really tried." An image of my mother engulfed in flames assaults me.

"Mrs. Jones says we can live with her. Do you want to, Billy?" I nod. "Won't that be fun?"

I replay yesterday's conversation with Veronica but can't force myself to shatter David's hopes by sharing my fears that it won't be allowed to happen. Instead, I play along, letting myself imagine the possibilities.

"We could make cookies every day after school," I say.

"And sew buttons. Maybe we can even learn how to sew something else too. Can we, Mrs. Jones?"

Mrs. Jones wipes the tears from her eyes and pastes on a smile. "Of course, I'll teach you to sew all kinds of things."

"We could help Mary with her garden," I add.

David's eyes go wide, and he smiles. "Ooh… and we'll play lots of games."

We continue dreaming aloud about our futures with Mrs. Jones. She says maybe we can get a dog or cat. I've always wanted a dog, but I would settle for a cat. We talk for a long time about what kind of dog we want, what we'd name it, the tricks it would learn.

We're so deep into our fantasy world with our new dog that we don't hear the door open, not realizing anyone else has joined us until she speaks.

"I'm glad you're all here so I can talk to you all at once." Veronica stands at the foot of the bed. She has a look in her eyes that tells me whatever she has to say isn't good.

I want to tell her to go away. To leave us alone. To let us dream. To let us hope. Instead, I say nothing and lean my head against David's, trying to brace myself for whatever she has to say.

She pulls a chair up next to Mrs. Jones.

"Remember how I told you that part of my job is to make sure you have someplace to go where you'll be taken care of?"

Everyone nods.

She clasps her hands in her lap. "I've been able to figure some things out in the past couple of days, and I wanted to talk to all of you about the plan."

She won't meet my eyes. Instead, she looks from David to Mrs. Jones, never letting her gaze meet mine. She was different the other day. I yearn for her kind eyes to look at me and show me that everything's going to be okay.

"As you know, I've been trying to get into contact with your grandparents to see if they'd be willing and able to take you in. Like we've talked about, I had to talk to all of your family first, before making any other decisions or exploring any other options, like Mrs. Jones." Veronica pauses and pulls some papers out of her briefcase. "Well, yesterday, I was finally able to meet with your mom's parents, Marilyn and George, and I've got good news…"

"They don't want us! We get to live with Mrs. Jones?" My excitement is immediate as this must be it because Veronica knows how I feel about my grandparents after our last conversation. She'd never use the words *good news* if they wanted David or me.

"Well, not exactly. Let me finish, Billy." Even though she's talking to me, she still won't glance in my direction. She shuffles the papers on her lap.

My heart sinks at the words *not exactly*.

"Your grandparents have agreed to have one of you come live with them… specifically, you, Billy." For the first time, she meets my tear-filled eyes.

"We can't be apart. I have to be with Billy. Where will I go? I need my brother," David yells.

Veronica leans forward and pats him on the arm. "David, I've managed to work it out for you to stay with Mrs. Jones."

"I want to be with Billy…" David screams, clinging to me as though I'm a lifesaver, his only hope to keep from drowning.

I can't breathe. It's as if someone is holding their hand over my nose and mouth, smothering me. It's the way I used to feel when my father kicked me in the ribs over and over again. Only this time, the pain isn't in my side, it's in my heart. I don't know how a heart so shattered can still feel anything. My ears ring so loudly my head feels as if it's going to split apart, spilling out my brain and all its memories, on the hospital floor. Mrs.

189

Jones' mouth is moving as she rushes over to me, but all I can hear is the ringing. No words, just ringing.

David draws closer to me, his tears soaking through my hospital gown. The warmth of those tears tries to reach the coldest places within me. The places so frozen, they'll never have the chance to thaw.

I close my eyes and wish it all away. I imagine David and me in our bedroom underneath our tent of blankets, pretending we're pirates searching for treasure. I feel my mother's warm breath on my neck as she pulls me into her embrace, whispering goodnight into my ear. I smell the heavenly scent of chocolate chip cookies coming from Mrs. Jones' kitchen and the baking bread coming up through the vents in our apartment from the bakery. I hear my mother's laugh echoing in my mind as she listens to the story David and I made up about a boy named Cleo and his dog.

I'm jerked away from my memories, back to the reality of the present, when the ringing clears enough for me to hear Veronica say, *they'll be here tomorrow to pick him up.*

No! I want to scream. *You can't make me go there. You can't take me away from David. He's all I have left. I trusted you. How could you let this happen?* But I can't find my voice amidst all my despair.

I taste the saltiness of my tears and realize I'm crying. Veronica stands alongside my bed and finally looks me square in the face. How could I have been stupid enough to trust this woman? The woman handing me over to the devil.

She wrings her hands. "Look, Billy. I'm sorry. I know

you don't want to go there, but I don't have a choice. If there's family that wants you, I have to send you."

I sit in silence, wondering if she's waiting for me to lie and say it's okay. I refuse to give her that. It isn't okay. It never will be again.

Tears fill Veronica's eyes. *Good. She should feel bad. I hope she feels bad forever.*

"Billy, it's my job. I have to do my job. If I had a choice, I wouldn't make you go, but I don't."

I want to scream loud enough for every nurse, doctor, and patient in the hospital to hear. *Your job? It's my life you're tearing apart, and you're worried about your job? You don't have a choice? What about me? Where are my choices?* Even if I could muster the strength to shout the words, they'd make no difference. They never do. Talking never resolved anything. My mother tried to calm my father down for years with words. The result—a worse beating. I offered consolation to David over the years, telling him it was okay, and everything would be fine. The result—a dead mother, a murderous father, and being stolen away from my brother. Words are meaningless.

Veronica turns to Mrs. Jones. "I'm sorry. We'll talk. I've got to go…" she says and leaves the room. Leaves us to pick up the pieces of the mess she left behind.

David and I cling to each other, crying, unable to speak of our new truths. Mary leaves the room without saying a word, shortly after Veronica. We lay there, each lost in our own thoughts, our own memories, our own fears. Each of us unable to put words to them. Each hoping if we hold on tight enough, no one will be able to separate us.

After a while, Mrs. Jones returns announcing that she talked to the doctor and he's going to let me out early so I can spend the night with David at her house. She intentionally doesn't state the obvious—this will be our last night together before my grandparents come and take me away forever.

I should be happy to get out of the hospital. I should be excited about getting to spend time with David and Mrs. Jones, even if only for one night. Instead, all I feel is afraid and alone. Very, very alone.

KENDRA

5 DAYS AFTER
FEBRUARY 13, 1989

MY shoulders relax, and I breathe a deep sigh of relief as the last of the visitors leave from the afternoon viewing. There was an endless line of people from the time the doors opened until a moment ago when Mr. Simons informed the last few stragglers, co-workers of Tom's, that it was time to go, to allow the family time to relax in between calling hours. As if relaxing is possible given the circumstances.

The number of people who came through today to offer support and kindness was astounding. I wish that even a minuscule amount of the well-wishes was able to rub off of each person so I could collect it all and wave it around my family like a magic wand— to offer us healing, to fill our emptiness, to take our pain.

It seems like a lifetime ago since I'd last seen or spoken to my colleagues at the Davy Corporation, where I'm the Human Resources manager. The company must've allowed everyone some time off to stop by as there were well over thirty people here from work, from the girls in the office, to the guys who work on the factory line pumping out auto parts for eight to ten hours at a time. I almost didn't recognize some of the men without their typical covering of grease and smell of sweat.

Kent and Nicole stayed by my side the whole time, shaking hands, giving hugs, crying with those who wept, drying tears of the inconsolable. Nodding their heads when someone said how beautiful Chelsea looked even though they had to be thinking what I was—the body in the casket looks nothing like her. We made a good threesome since we each broke down at different times, leaving the remaining two to share strength with all those who passed by.

I saw Kent's embarrassment when one of his buddies walked up, as tears streamed down his face. Kent couldn't see the empathy in his friend's eyes, but it was there. He only saw his friend and fears he'll be made fun of for being a crybaby when he returns to school.

"I'm gonna run to the bathroom, and then we'll head out to grab a bite to eat before we have to be back," I say.

When I'm halfway to the back of the room, I realize I should've gone the other way because, on this route, I'll have to walk right past Tom. I can't even fathom looking at him right now since he, again, abandoned me to deal with everyone while he sat in the back corner, as far away from us as possible.

"Where the hell were you?" I hiss, even though I had no intention of looking at him, let alone speaking.

"I was right here the whole time. Do you know how many people came through here today?' he says with a smile.

"A lot. I was up there shaking all their hands, remember? Standing next to my dead daughter, welcoming guests, smiling, making small talk while you cower back here in the corner."

"To be exact, there were two hundred fifty-seven people in two hours. Imagine how many there'll be tonight." A shudder works its way through my body, realizing that Tom actually sounds excited.

"What the hell is wrong with you? Our daughter is dead, and you're counting how many people came, anxiously awaiting the next round? You're sick." My anger rises, and my head feels like it's going to explode. I walk away, knowing I'll go over the top if I have to continue conversing with the stranger that's supposed to be my husband.

"Where are we gonna eat? I'm starving," Tom says as I'm almost out the door.

That's it. I can no longer contain myself. I shout without caring who hears. "Nicole, Kent and I are going to eat. The three of us who were actually present today and talking to people, crying with them. You … I don't care what the hell you do, as long as it's nowhere near me."

I run the rest of the way to the bathroom, locking the door behind me. My anger swells as tears in my eyes and a lump too large to swallow in my throat.

What the hell is wrong with him? How could he do this to me…to us? He sits back there like it's not his daughter that's been taken. He lets me handle it all, thinking I'm strong enough to do it. I'm not… I can't take it. I can't do this alone. If he makes me go through this alone, I'll never forgive him. God, help me. I can't do this. I need him to take me in his arms and make me feel safe… like it's all going to be okay. I need him to be the strong one because I can't do it. Why isn't he helping me? Why is he leaving me alone to deal with this?

I finally let the tears of desperation fall that I worked so hard at holding back all afternoon. I successfully put on the mask I needed to wear to get through the day, but now it's crumbling off. My baby is gone. There's nothing I can do to bring her back. Everyone provided a distraction today, forcing me to look elsewhere, anywhere other than the one place I wanted to look, knowing it would be one of my last chances. For soon, I'll never be able to see my daughter again.

Without trying to hide my tears, my pain, I run from the bathroom back to my daughter. I stroke her cheek, touch her hair, hold her cold hand. I lean and kiss her on her hard, lifeless lips. I tell her how much I love and miss her. I beg her to please come back. To please just get up and come back to her mommy. I tell her how badly I need her. I whisper how sorry I am over and over again. Mostly I cry tears that burn my cheeks—ones straight from my raging soul.

Kent places his hand on my arm, and I pull him into an embrace. I bury my face into his hair, wetting it with my tears. "C'mon, Mom. We gotta go. We don't have much time."

196

"I don't want to leave her, Kent. I can't." I cling to him, staring at my daughter's face.

"I know, Mom. She'll be here when we get back. Promise."

After a few seconds, I loosen my hold on Kent, bend close to Chelsea as though I'm telling her a secret. "We'll be back, baby girl."

Kent guides me to the door. I look back to see my daughter one last time; instead, I see Tom, still sitting in the same seat staring off into the distance with a slight smile. A smile that can only belong to a crazy man and one that chills me to my core.

Do you remember me telling you I love you more than the moon, the stars, the sun, and the sky? Do you remember how you'd giggle and say, *But I love you more*? Do you remember sharing your dreams of the future with me? Do you remember believing in yourself enough to think that anything you dared imagine might be possible? Do you remember me saying you could be whoever you choose? Do you remember when you realized you might not know what you wanted to be, but you definitely knew what you *didn't* want to become? Have you become the person you wanted to be? Have you given up on your dreams? Do you still hope for a better future? Do you know it's never too late to choose a different path?

BILLY

11 YEARS, 8 MONTHS, 16 DAYS BEFORE
MAY 23, 1977

IT feels so good to be out of the hospital and back with David. I'm thankful Mary "pulled some strings" to get me out in time to spend the evening with David and her. Mrs. Jones told us she had to get Veronica's permission and the doctor's okay, but both were willing to give their consent with only a little begging on her part. The doctor sent me home with instructions on how to care for my burns, what I need to do for follow-up to make sure they heal okay, and two bottles of pills to keep the infections away. Mrs. Jones kept everything and told the doctor she'd make sure my new caregivers were aware. I can't associate the word "caregiver" with the people I met that were supposedly my grandparents. The word implies that the person actually cares.

From what I saw of my grandfather, I don't think he cares about anyone or anything if he was able to turn his back on his beaten, desperate daughter without a second thought.

I force myself to stop thinking about them and focus on David instead. I want to enjoy every minute of my time with him. Mrs. Jones made sure David and I ducked down in the backseat of the car, while she passed by what used to be our house. She didn't want us to see what remained, or rather, what was gone. She didn't want us to be flooded with the memories and our pain. I was happy we didn't have to see it—I don't want anything to take away from this time. I'm afraid it may be the last time I ever feel loved and safe.

We play every game Mrs. Jones has; we sew buttons on every piece of fabric we can find. We build tents with blankets over the living room furniture. We enjoy a huge dinner of lasagna, bread, and salad with brownies for dessert. After eating, David announces he has a present for me from him and Mrs. Jones. He zooms out of the room and returns a moment later, holding a wrapped package. Inside is a new set of wooden logs, with more pieces than the one Mom bought me years ago.

"We figured even a big boy like you would still enjoy playing with these from time to time. David told me how much you enjoyed your old set."

"Yeah. I told her they got burned in the fire, and you'd be sad," David says with a smile.

My eyes well with tears—only this time, not from sadness. Tears from feeling loved. Tears from feeling like someone in the world actually thinks about my feelings and knows how important such a small thing will be to someone who has lost so much.

"Thank you. I love them…" I wipe my eyes. "Do you want to go build something, David?"

"Yes, sir!" David runs into the living room, and I follow, after giving Mrs. Jones the biggest hug my sore arms can give.

We're able to build bridges and castles twice the size of those we could with the old set. We stay busy for hours until Mrs. Jones finally interrupts, telling us it's time to go to bed. It's midnight, but I don't want to go to sleep. Rather, I don't want to wake up to tomorrow and everything it will hold.

Mary must see my fear because she apologizes for having to end our evening and says she wishes she could let us stay up all night.

"Billy, you can sleep with me—the bed's a big one," David says.

He doesn't comprehend that going to sleep means waking up tomorrow, the day I'll be taken from him. He's just excited to have his brother back, and I don't want to steal that from him. Burying my anxiety, I follow him into the bedroom, and we nestle under the covers as we've done for most of our lives.

I can't sleep with all the thoughts racing through my mind. David, as usual, has no trouble; his soft snores fill the room within a few minutes of burrowing ourselves under the covers. I felt so alone in the hospital without the sounds, smell, and heat of David next to me. How will either of us survive when we no longer have the other to lean on? Even though I'm the older brother that always protects David, I need him as much, if not more, than he needs me. For years, I felt like I was doing something good by protecting him, even though I couldn't do the same for Mom. Taking care of David is the one thing I've done well in my life. I'm not a good student and hardly ever earn above a C on my grade card. I'm not a good son, because if I were, my mother would still be alive; my father wouldn't have had so many reasons to "teach me a lesson" over the years. I don't make friends easily and am often taunted by my classmates for being a weirdo. The only thing I've done right, and that I'm good at, is being a big brother. If I don't have David, I'll have nothing left.

I'm glad David gets to stay with Mrs. Jones because I know I can entrust him to her care. I wish, more than anything, that I could stay with them. I can't figure out why in the world my grandparents agreed to take me, why they want me. And why choose only me? Questioning their motives plagues me throughout the night, keeping me from sleep. I decide one thing while lying there next to David; I'll do whatever it takes to convince my grandparents to return me to my brother. I'll make them see I need to be with him.

*   *   *

The sun is starting to rise, and I can't stand watching my brother sleep any longer. I tickle him awake. He starts laughing before his eyes open. One of my favorite sounds in the world is when his giggles make his whole body shake. How long will it be before I get to hear that sound again?

Our tickling frenzy is interrupted by Mrs. Jones at the

door. "Boys, I made you a special breakfast. Are you ready to eat?"

The smells from the kitchen are wonderful. I know whatever she's made will be good because everything she cooks is.

"What'd ya make us?" David says as he hops to the floor.

"My special sausage gravy and biscuits. It's a recipe from my mom and the best I've ever tasted." She pats me on the head. "You'll both love it."

We race off towards the kitchen, leaving Mary trailing behind. By the time she reaches the kitchen, we're seated at the table, forks in hand, waiting for our food. She barely finishes filling my plate when I dig in. Mrs. Jones is right—this is one of the best things I've ever tasted. We rush through our first helping, and Mrs. Jones readily serves us each another biscuit smothered in gravy. Once our eating slows down, she makes herself a plate and joins us.

For a while, she just sits back, eating, watching, and listening. Finally, she speaks. "Boys, I hate to interrupt your fun this morning, but we have to talk about the plan for the day."

Her words send my mind racing. By "plan for the day," she really means, the plan for sending me off with my grandparents. I don't want to know the plan. I want to sit here with my brother and Mrs. Jones, enjoying our breakfast, and laughing. I don't even want to think of the people coming to take me away from the one person I have left on this earth.

Mrs. Jones seems to be able to see my thoughts written all over my face. "Billy, I'm sorry. I don't want to have to talk about this any more than you do, but we're running out of time." She envelops me in her arms. I'm struggling to keep the tears at bay while in the safety of her embrace.

She continues to hold me close while she speaks. "I worked it out with Veronica that your grandparents will come here to pick you up, so we can see you up until the second you have to leave. Plus, I want to meet them and let them know I plan on having you and David see each other a lot. Veronica will meet with us here to make sure everything's done by the rules."

"Wh…wh…what time are they coming?" David says, with a stutter that only comes when he's really stressed.

"They'll be here at one." Mrs. Jones glances at her watch. "You have five and a half hours."

Five and a half hours. Only five and a half hours left to spend with my brother. Then, who knows how long it will be until I see him again. I believe Mary means what she says about trying to make sure we see each other often—but often isn't every day. I've had my little brother by my side every day for as long as I can remember. Being around David for the past day is the only thing that's helped me so far forget, for even a moment, what happened to Mom. How will I keep the nightmares away and the memories from haunting me if I don't have David to play, laugh, sleep, and grow older with?

As hard as I try to hold them back, the tears won't stay in. They fall so quickly that nothing can stop them.

"Billy, don't cry. It's okay." David comes to my side to comfort me, his words breaking my heart further because I'm usually the one offering such words to ease his worries.

"I'll miss you so much. I don't want to go. Please let me stay here," I sob.

"I'd give anything in the world to keep you guys together. Believe me, if there were something that could be done, I'd do it." Mrs. Jones is crying too. "I'm sorry, boys. This is just terrible. I'm so, so sorry."

Mrs. Jones pulls both of us into her embrace, as though she's trying to absorb our tears and pain. Even though I'm overwhelmed and sad, the feeling I get from being in her arms is one I haven't felt often in my life. The feeling of being safe, protected. If only I could remain right here in the circle of Mary's arms, with my brother by my side, everything would be okay. This is the way I used to feel with Mom when I was young and believed she'd never let anything bad happen to us. That feeling faded through the years as she became less like herself, allowing us to be hurt repeatedly by my father. I realize now how much I've missed the feeling of absolute security. As quickly as I recognize it, Mrs. Jones' words pull it away.

"Okay, boys. I know we're all sad, but I'm not gonna let you spend your last five and a half hours together crying. Go play. Have fun." She pats us both on the back with a little push away from her embrace. "It's a nice day out. Why don't you go build a fort?"

I'm not sure whether to run after David, who is making a beeline towards the front door, or cling to Mary as tightly as I can, hoping she'll spare me from what's to come. I turn towards her, the words stuck in my throat. The words I want to shout and scream and yell—she has to protect me; she can't send me away;

she can't let my grandparents take me. I want to plead with her to keep me wrapped in her arms where I'm protected and safe. Instead, all I can do is look at her, unable to speak, unable to move.

"Billy, go play with your brother," Mrs. Jones says in the sternest voice she's ever used with me. "I know this is hard. He needs you to go play with him."

I head to the front yard where David waits for me with a baseball, glove, and bat. The words I didn't say, stuck inside forever.

TOM

6 DAYS AFTER
FEBRUARY 14, 1989

I wake up before the alarm goes off. It's only four-thirty in the morning, and I question whether I've slept at all. I tried, but my thoughts were racing, my mind unable to settle. I kept picturing the lines of people at the funeral home and re-counting those I could remember. I can't be absolutely sure the numbers I came up with last night were correct. It seems like I keep forgetting to add some of them. Last night, I counted three hundred ninety-five visitors, but when I replay it all in my mind, it seems like there were four hundred and two, but maybe it was only four hundred.

My counting starts again as soon as my feet hit the floor, trying to recall each person. As I start a pot of coffee, I realize we have only five and a half hours to go before the funeral. I wonder how many will show up today to pay their respects. I'm amazed by the number of my co-workers that came. The office has a total of fifty-six employees, and forty-seven of them visited yesterday. Perhaps the other nine will show today. Even if they don't, an eighty-three percent show rate isn't bad.

As the coffee brews, I try to talk myself into being more supportive of Kendra today. She's mad at me and hasn't uttered a word to me or glanced in my direction since she blew up yesterday at three twenty-two, thirteen hours and fifteen minutes ago. Several times yesterday, I tried to make myself go to her, to offer comfort. Each time I got distracted by a new person coming through the door or a new flower arrangement being brought in.

I know how hard this is on Kendra and I want to be there for her. She's really falling apart. I'm amazed at how well I'm holding up. Every once in a while, the reality of my daughter's death hits me with a stabbing pain in the chest, making it impossible to breathe for a moment. Mentally, however, I'm functioning fine. I haven't broken down other than the passing out episode in the morgue. My mind isn't being overtaken by sadness and memories—I'm still able to focus on my surroundings just fine. My ability to continue doing such complex mathematical equations, despite the fact I've lost one of the most important people in my life, amazes me.

The coffee finishes brewing after seven minutes, and I get up to pour a cup. I'm startled by Kendra's voice.

"What're you doing up? Do you know what time it is?" Kendra says too loudly for such an early hour, in a quiet house.

"I couldn't sleep. Of course, I know what time it is. It's four forty-two…unless, of course, you're in Tokyo and then it's six-forty in the evening." I didn't even realize I knew such things.

"Why the hell do I care what time it is in Tokyo? What's wrong with you?"

"Not a big Tokyo fan? What about Australia? In Melbourne, it's eight forty p.m." I clear my throat, impressed by my knowledge. "Nothing's wrong with me. Just trying to get ready for the day."

Kendra paces and gestures wildly with her hands. "You make it sound as though we're leaving on a family vacation, Tom. You act like none of this is a big deal, like our daughter isn't dead. You didn't shed a single tear yesterday. You never even looked at her." Kendra's crying. "How can you be so cold and heartless about all of this? Our daughter is dead! She's dead. Today is the last day we'll ever be able to see our baby's face. Do you get that?"

I want to be able to wrap my arms around her and ease her pain. I want to be able to tell her I'm sorry and promise to be more supportive today at the funeral. I want to be able to say or do anything to ease the tension between us.

What comes out of my mouth does none of these things and surprises me almost as much as the slap that lands across my cheek before I even finish my sentence.

"It's already eleven-forty in Bucharest. Imagine, if we lived there, we'd already be done with the funeral and able to put it behind us."

*   *   *

KENT

I just want today to be over. I'm not going to be able to make it through the funeral without breaking down. Lots of my friends and their parents will be there to see me lose it. They'll think I'm a big cry baby and I'll be the talk of the school for weeks—how Kent Wyatt bawled like a baby at his sister's funeral. How will I ever be able to show my face at school again?

Mom's making me wear a suit and tie. It's the first time I've ever worn a tie, and it feels like I'm being choked. The lump in my throat is bad enough—adding the noose around my neck isn't helping. The silence between my parents is making the situation worse. I sneaked into the doorway of the kitchen from my bed on the sofa this morning just in time to hear Dad rambling about the time in Bucharest… where in the world is Bucharest anyway… and to see my mother land a smack square across Dad's jaw. I crept back under the covers in the other room right before Mom bolted up the stairs, into Chelsea's room where she slept last night, slamming the door behind her. I'm glad it was me camping out in the living room rather than my grandparents, so they didn't have to witness the whole fiasco. I don't imagine they'd be too happy with my slap-happy mom and wacko dad.

Mom insists on the three of us riding to the funeral home together, although I have no idea why. Maybe so she can shoot daggers with her glares at dad the whole way there, hoping one of her mean looks will snap him back to reality. It's made for a tense ride, that's for sure. I can't wait to get out of the car, so I have something to focus on other than the tension.

The only words spoken on the ride were when Dad looked at me in the rearview mirror and said, "Happy Valentine's Day." I almost burst out laughing when I saw Mom's face in response to that. It was pretty bizarre. Here we are headed to my sister's funeral, and that's all he has to say. Why in the world would any parent choose to bury their daughter on Valentine's Day anyway? Why forever ruin the holiday devoted to love with memories of the day your child was buried?

I don't think I'll ever understand my parents again. Chelsea used to tell me that someday I'd feel this way when I'd ask her why she got so mad at them. She'd always tell me to wait until I was a teenager and then I'd understand. She'd sometimes make fun of me for how much I seemed to idolize our parents and assured me it wouldn't last forever.

Dad has just put the car in park when Mom bolts from it, towards the funeral home, without saying a word to either of us. I sit there a moment waiting for my father to give a signal it's time to head in. He doesn't say a word or make a move to get out of the car.

I put my hand on his shoulder to get his attention. "Dad, should we go in now?"

"You go ahead. I'm gonna sit here a while," he says.

"What time is it? Aren't we supposed to be in there early?"

"It's a little after nine. You go on in. I'm going to sit here where I can get a good count of how many people show up," Dad pauses, pointing towards the building. "You see, right there's the door. I can count people as they walk in, rather than

211

trying to see them all once they're seated."

I can't comprehend what in the world my father is saying; it's so bizarre. "Mom's gonna be really mad if you don't get in there."

"She'll be okay. She'll understand."

Hearing Dad say this confirms he's officially lost whatever was left of his mind. There's no way he can really think Mom won't blow her top over this one. How can he even begin to think Mom understands anything about him right now, seeing as how she's turned into a punching, slapping, screaming maniac around him?

I gently touch his shoulder again, but he doesn't seem to notice. "Alright. I'm going in. I'll save you a seat next to me."

"Yeah. Okay." Dad peruses the parking lot, eyes darting back and forth as if he's afraid to miss anything.

I walk to the front door of the funeral home, glancing over my shoulder at my father. He sits staring at the entrance to the parking lot, seemingly trying to will cars to drive in.

I honestly don't know what the hardest part of all of this is—losing my sister, Dad going nutso, or Mom becoming a violent lunatic. I'm the only one in my family who hasn't lost it. I wonder if my parents will ever be normal again.

BILLY

DAVID is the first to hear it—the sound of tires crunching on the gravel driveway. We're in the side yard gathering sticks to make the final wall of our fort when David freezes, nearly dropping his armful of twigs.

"Billy…" David's voice shakes. "Did ya hear that?"

I hadn't heard anything as I was lost in our world where all that mattered was making a fort to withstand the enemy attack. I quiet and hear the unmistakable sound of a car, knowing the enemy is fast approaching, despite our best efforts of concealment.

"Do you think it's them?" David asks.

I start shaking from the center of my stomach clear

out to my fingertips before my mind deciphers what the sound means. Once the thought registers, the quivering intensifies, and fear consumes me. David wraps his arms tightly around my waist.

"Let's go hide so they can't find us. C'mon." David pulls me by the hand to the tree line. We duck under the boughs of the biggest pine tree, hidden under its sagging branches full of needles and cones. From our hiding spot, we watch and listen. We hear a car door shut, but then nothing.

"Remember how you wanted to run away to Disney to get away from Daddy? Let's go now. We can do it. We'll wait here until it gets dark and then take off," David whispers and grabs my hand.

I want to get lost in this dream with David, but I can't. The fantasy didn't work before; it won't work now. Instead of Disney World, we ended up with a dead mom and me being shipped off to our grandparents. I wish I were older so I could get a job to take care of us. Then, we wouldn't need any adults to make decisions for us.

"Say we can go there together. Say you won't leave me." David's grasp tightens on my hand as he starts to sob.

Two sets of feet emerge from the back door. One pair I recognize as Mrs. Jones with her black, old lady shoes. I duck lower so I can peek below the branches to see who the other feet belong to. Their owner is Veronica from Family Services—I forgot she was coming today too.

"Billy...David...where are you?" Mrs. Jones shouts.

"Shhh...don't answer," David whispers.

214

"They're gonna find us, ya know?" I respond.

"Not yet… don't answer yet," David pleads.

"Billy…David… Ms. Walters is here to see you. C'mon guys. It's time to come inside," Mary shouts.

Mrs. Jones and Veronica step off the porch and move around to the back of the house, both of them calling our names.

I grab his arm and force him to look at me. "David, we have to go out there. They're gonna find us, and then we'll be in trouble."

"Let's sneak out the other way and take off. We won't have Mrs. Jones, but we'll have each other. That's all we need."

I like the sound of David's idea. As long as we're together, we'll be fine and able to handle whatever comes our way. We've done okay so far. I don't know how we'll survive, or where we can go, but we'll figure it out.

"Okay, we'll go out the other side of the trees when we're sure it's clear. When I say go, take off running. Okay?"

David agrees, and we fight our way to the other side of the tree. We have to scrunch low to the ground to fit underneath the branches that cut into our cheeks with their prickly needles. In the distance, Veronica and Mary call our names, their shouts now coming from the front yard. I pause a moment, listening again for the echoing voices.

"One… two…three…Go!" I yell. We scurry from underneath the tree and take off in a full-force run, still crouching towards the ground.

As we free ourselves from the branches, we stand to run faster. As soon as we're both upright, preparing to run full speed

215

ahead into a world where we can be together forever, we stop, unable to move any further towards what lays before us. The charred remains of our house.

Before this moment, neither of us have seen the evidence of our father's wrath. The place our mother died. The place where her remains still lay.

"Oh, God. Look at it," I say, grabbing David's arm to keep myself from falling over from shock.

Mrs. Jones told us the house had been destroyed, but those words hadn't prepared us for what we now actually see. Our once white siding is blackened and charred in the places it's still hanging. The roof is virtually non-existent. There are holes in the front of the house, allowing us to see clear through to the other side. I know, peering through one of those holes, that I'm seeing through the living room, right past the spot where Mom and I were sitting when my father started the fire. Right past the spot where I last saw my mother alive, where she took her last breath.

With my eyes fixated on that place, I walk forward.

"Billy, what are you doing? We can't go there," David sobs.

I say nothing and simply hold onto David's hand, pulling him alongside. After a moment, he gives up his fight to move forward and falls into step next to me, walking towards what was our home only a few short days ago. Towards what used to be our life.

The smell of burnt wood becomes more overwhelming with each step. It smells as strongly as if the fire is still raging before us. My eyes tear up, and my nose burns. This is the smell I will forever associate with death.

The house is completely destroyed, yet not even twenty feet away sits the car we tried to use for our escape, completely unharmed. Our home is scorched, yet the square cement front porch is hardly touched by the devastation. The remains of the potted pink geraniums Mom planted sit on the front step, their beauty a stark contrast to the ruined house beyond.

I let go of David's hand and quicken my pace for the last few feet. I climb onto the porch peering inside the hole that used to be our front door. The interior is unrecognizable. There's no evidence of the chairs my father tied us to. Other than from memory, I can't tell where our final moments together were spent. The only piece of furniture I can make out is what remains of our couch—I wouldn't have recognized it had I not spent my entire life in that room, on that couch. Mrs. Jones told me the fire had spread rapidly, and the fire department had a hard time getting it under control. I had no idea what that looked like. I now realize how quickly I would've had to act to spare Mom's life. I see what a miracle it is that I wasn't devoured by the flames, as well.

"Billy, can you see her? Is she in there still? I wanna see her." David stands beside me, trying to look past me into the house.

David's question sucks the air from my lungs—he can't comprehend that our mother's body is no longer lying on the living room floor. In his innocence, David presumed our mother's body remained intact somehow, even though the fire destroyed much more solid items like walls, roofs, and furniture. My brother is unable to imagine that our mother's body—the one that held us, laughed with us, cried with us—no longer exists. It has simply vanished from this earth in a puff of smoke and pile of ash. I'm envious of his lack of understanding.

I sit on the porch, coaching David down next to me and pulling him close. "No, kiddo. Her body's gone. It's not in there anymore."

"Where did it go? I wanna see her."

"She's in heaven now. Remember how she told us about heaven and how beautiful it would be. That's where she is."

I feel some of the tension leave David's body at this revelation.

"What do you think she's doing there?" David asks.

"Hmmm…probably looking down through the clouds at us and waving. She's probably smiling, too, and telling us she loves us," I say.

"I bet they've got lots of chocolate chip cookies in heaven," David adds.

"Probably any kind of ice cream you'd want too," I say. "Mommy loved dessert so she's probably eating all the sweets she can."

"Billy… I miss her," David says and leans his head against my shoulder.

"I do too. I miss her a lot."

"Do you think she looks the same?" David asks.

"She's probably prettier than ever, and I bet she smiles all the time now." Picturing her smile makes one spread across my face, despite my sorrow.

"Because she doesn't have to be scared of Daddy anymore, huh?" David says.

"Nope. She doesn't have to be scared of anything anymore."

David sniffles. "Do you think she's scared about us not being together?"

I don't know how to answer this. Our mother would never approve of us being split apart. I'm sure she'd be happy her parents agreed to take me at least; but I know she would've rather I stayed with David and Mrs. Jones. Mom trusted Mary, and there's no way she could trust her parents anymore after the way they treated us.

"I don't know. My guess is she'll make sure we're okay no matter where we are," I finally add, wishing I believed it.

"Can she be with both of us at once?"

"She's an angel now, so yeah. Angels can be everywhere all at once," I say in a voice displaying much more confidence than I feel.

"Cool! I bet she has wings—big shiny ones that let her fly through the sky. She probably uses the clouds as a bed." David chatters. "Look at that huge one. Maybe she's up there right now."

"Or maybe she's on that one," I add, pointing to one on the other side of the sky.

We look from cloud to cloud, trying to find evidence of our mother's existence. We're unaware of the passing of time, lost in our world of heavenly possibilities. Our daydreams are interrupted by voices calling our names. Mrs. Jones, Veronica, and two others stride across the yard towards us. It takes me only an instant to realize the two "others" are our grandparents.

We make no efforts to meet our search party. We sit quietly, arms around each other, watching the adults' approach. David starts crying when he realizes we've been discovered; my shaking resumes.

Mrs. Jones stops the group and comes towards us by herself.

"Boys, it's time to go back to the house and get everything together. Your grandparents are here," Mary says.

"Yeah, I see," I say, but refuse to make eye contact.

"He's not going. He's staying with me. We're running away," David adds, sitting up straighter as he says it.

"None of us have a choice in this. Billy, you've got to go with your grandparents. David, you're staying with me. I wish you could be together, but the decision's been made, and there's nothing I can do about it. Believe me, if there was, I'd do it," Mary pauses waiting for a response. When none comes, she continues. "Boys, it's time to go. Everyone's waiting."

Mary re-joins the group of betrayers.

"David, we've gotta go." I stand, but David refuses to budge.

He still hasn't moved as I walk towards the people who hold my future in their hands. I glance over my shoulder at him, but he turns his head away.

"David, come on!" I yell across the yard.

"I'm not coming," David answers without a glance in

my direction.

"Fine. You won't get to tell me goodbye then," I shout, hoping to motivate him to get moving. Still nothing.

I don't understand my brother's newfound stubbornness. I don't want to leave either, but I wouldn't throw a fit and miss the chance to tell him goodbye. David acts as if his life is over; at least he gets to stay with Mrs. Jones instead of being shipped off with strangers. By the time I reach everyone, I'm fuming at his selfishness.

"Just leave him there, Billy. He'll make his way over before you leave." Mrs. Jones wraps her arm around my shoulder.

Veronica looks completely out of place, dressed in her nice suit and high heels, standing in the middle of a yard with a burnt-up house. "Let's all get back inside so we can talk through some things."

We make our way back towards Mary's house. My grandfather hasn't glanced in my direction once, and he wears the same stern expression as the day he refused us. Our grandmother looks at me once and offers a slight smile. I try to force one in return but can't make myself. I have no kindness to offer to the people ruining my life.

Once we're seated, Veronica starts with all the formalities and introductions. It's pretty stupid she's introducing me to people on the same day I'll be sent to live with them. Obviously, I'm being sent to live with strangers. How can Veronica think "Marilyn" and "George" will love and care for me just because we're related? She'd find better luck picking two strangers walking down the sidewalk and shipping me off to be with them.

Veronica also goes over all the details about my need for medical treatment and follow-up for the burns. Mrs. Jones shares her ideas on visitation and contact between David and me, stressing how important it is that we're able to spend as much time together as possible, especially on important days like Christmas and birthdays. Mary says she's willing to drive down to their house to get me often and allow me to call collect so I can talk to David whenever I'd like. She says she'll do whatever it takes to ensure that we stay in touch. I watch my grandparents closely as Mary talks, hoping to see something in their expressions to give me faith they'll follow her plan. My grandmother nods often, but my grandfather just sits there stone-faced, like he's not even listening.

Mary ends by asking if Marilyn and George are planning on holding a memorial service for my mom.

Finally, my grandfather speaks. "No point. Not like there's a body to bury or anything."

I'm shocked by his blatant display of coldness. It was his daughter that died in the fire. He doesn't even seem to care.

"I think it's important for the boys to have some closure. I'll plan a service of some sort and keep you informed of the plans. Could you please make sure Billy can attend?"

Again, nothing from my grandfather and a nod from my grandmother. I wish my grandfather would say something or show some emotion so I could get a feel for what my life is about to be like. The stone-faced man before me is completely unreadable.

Veronica has forms for all the adults to sign. While

they're occupied, I go to the bedroom to collect my belongings, fitting everything I own into one small bag. At the last moment, I decide to leave my wooden log set for David. He'll enjoy it, and maybe it'll give him some good memories of our time together. As I'm about to leave the room, I pick up David's pillow, breathing as deeply as possible so as not to forget the scent of him. The smell of sweat, dirt, and a warm spring day.

By the time I get back to the living room, bag in hand, my grandparents are waiting by the front door with Mrs. Jones. Veronica is gone now that all of the "official" paperwork is done to lay out the rest of my life. I'm disappointed in myself for ever trusting that woman—the traitor who didn't even stick around long enough to say a formal goodbye.

I manage to get through the hug goodbye with Mrs. Jones without shedding a tear. I'm numb from the disbelief that I'm really being ripped out of my brother's life by these strangers. I'm finally convinced I'm out of tears, that there's no capacity left for sadness or grief. As I'm encircled in Mary's arms, I look around the room behind her to see if David has come back yet. There's still no sign of him. Maybe leaving will be easier on all of us if I don't have to say goodbye to him face to face.

My grandfather picks up my bag and opens the front door—his sign it's time to go. My grandmother gives Mrs. Jones a hug, thanking her for everything, and promising to be in touch soon. I follow them to the beat-up car sitting in the driveway and get in the back seat. My grandfather starts the car, which rumbles loudly; it sounds even worse than it looks. The car lurches forward as if it's debating about whether to go. I hope it stalls right in the driveway. Then we'd be stuck here until the car could get fixed, which would give us more time. These hopes vanish quickly though as the engine quiets a bit and the car moves forward a little more smoothly.

When we're almost to the end of the driveway, I turn around to get one last look at the life I'm leaving. David runs full speed towards the car, yelling as loudly as he can and waving his arms.

I can hear him, now that I'm aware of his presence. "Please stop. I wanna say goodbye. Please stop!" David repeats the words over and over again.

"Can you please stop so I can say goodbye?" I ask quietly. "David wants to say goodbye."

For the second time today, my grandfather speaks in his cold, heartless manner. "He had his chance and missed it. Too late. We gotta get home."

Without slowing, he pulls onto the road. The tears, I thought were gone, fall freely now as I watch my brother grow smaller and smaller until I can no longer see him at all.

NICOLE

6 DAYS AFTER
FEBRUARY 14, 1989

THE funeral home is already packed. I arrived later than originally planned because I couldn't decide what to wear. Each outfit I tried on didn't seem right to wear to my best friend's funeral. Since we shared all our clothes over the years, everything I own has been worn by Chelsea, too. Each outfit brought a fresh wave of pain as I remembered her wearing it, realizing that, from now on, my clothes will be worn only by me. Chels is wearing the outfit she'll wear for all eternity.

Mrs. Wyatt asked me to show up at nine to give me time to say a private good-bye before the funeral. I check my watch—I'm thirty minutes late. Every seat is already filled, with a line starting to form at the door. Mom grabs my hand and pulls me through the crowd to find the Wyatts. To get through the morning, I took four Valium. They aren't doing their job though. My body and movements feel sluggish, but my emotions are still raw, as though they're on overdrive. I fear I may crumble to pieces at any moment.

As we work our way towards the front of the room where our seats have been saved, I can't help but scan the faces in the church. Is Chelsea's murderer sitting here in this room? I saw Randy Stevens waiting outside amongst the other mourners. He didn't look guilty, only sad. Sitting towards the back of the room, next to Brent, is Kurt Miller. There's no way to judge Kurt's mental state, seeing as how he's already conned me once before; he could do it again. Is it possible Brent could've taken her life? Does he have a dark side no one knows about, but Chelsea came to see? There are so many people I don't recognize. How can I possibly be able to spot the one—the one who took Chelsea from me?

By the time we reach Mrs. Wyatt, her parents, and Kent, I'm shaking. I want so badly for Chelsea to speak to me from the other side and point out who the bad guy is. I just need a sign so he can be caught and punished. If he is, maybe the nightmares will stop. The ones from which I awaken screaming and dripping with sweat. A different face appears in each one as the person hurting my friend. Some I recognize; others I've never seen before. I'm afraid of whoever could do such a thing. Since there's no name to place with the act, I am afraid of everyone.

I offer quick hugs of condolences to each family member then excuse myself, rushing off to the bathroom. Once inside, behind the safety of the latched door, I take two more pills, hoping they take the edge off my fear. I return and find my place next to my mother and the Wyatts. In front of me sits the casket. It has already been closed. I missed my chance to see my friend one last time, to say my final goodbye.

*   *   *

KENDRA

I search frantically for Tom amongst the sea of people behind me. The room is filled to capacity with people in chairs, along the walls, sitting on the floor, and still more lined up at the doorways trying to get in.

I'm touched that so many people seem affected by my daughter's life. I wonder though if it's only her death they're moved by—the fears it creates in their own hearts, minds, and souls. Did Chelsea's death rock their boats? Ones they were convinced could never be overtaken by waves of destruction. Living in such a small town has its benefits, but I've wondered over the years if the people living here are too protected from real-world issues. Real-world issues that have now claimed my daughter's life. The town's safety net and protection were yanked away just as Chelsea was.

I can't find Tom anywhere. Even if he were in the room, there's no way to see through the wall to wall people. The service is going to begin in two minutes. Rage trembles through me. How dare Tom not come in early as planned, before they closed the casket for the last time, to say good-bye to our daughter? Thank God my parents are here to hold onto me, offering their

227

comfort through my sobs and grief. Grief so deep I never imagined it would be possible to feel it and continue living.

Kent broke down, too, but I had nothing to give him. My heart's broken into too many pieces to be able to stop the bleeding and pain in my son's. Instead, my father is Kent's comforter, wrapping his solid arms around his shaking body. Tom should be the one to be here with our son, telling him it'll be okay, offering his arms for comfort, his shoulder for tears. My father is such a solid, reliable, and strong man. The kind of man I thought I was married to. I'm astounded at how radically Tom has changed in such a short time. He's become someone I could never, in my wildest imagination, have envisioned him to be.

"Where's Tom?" My mom whispers. "The pastor just walked in… it's about to start."

I shrug, having nothing to offer in his defense. Kent leans his head on my shoulder. I refuse to let my anger at Tom deflect my focus on the last event I'll ever participate in for my daughter.

The organist's music begins playing Chelsea's favorite church hymn, *Amazing Grace*. I brace myself, wrapping my arm tightly around Kent's shoulder, knowing how hard the next hour will be for both of us. As the tears flow freely down my cheeks, I glance at the empty chair beside me, wishing Tom were here to help me through. Wishing doesn't do any good—if it did, none of us would be in this godforsaken room staring at the pink and white casket holding my daughter's body.

*   *   *

TOM

I stayed in the car longer than I originally intended. There were so many people that my entire focus was on counting, not losing track of my place as each new person walked up the steps, into the doors. There wasn't even a moment's break in the crowd during which I could check the time. If I looked down for even an instant, surely I would've missed someone.

As the arrival of guests comes to a halt, I finally sneak a glance at my watch and see it's nine fifty-seven—only three minutes before the service is scheduled to begin. I scramble to get out of the car and into the church so I can find my place next to my wife and son. As I push my way through the crowd, I repeat the final count to myself, to make sure I don't forget. Five hundred and eighty-three people. Five hundred and eighty-three.

Now that I'm inside, I'm sure my numbers are off. There are far more than that in the room. How could I have miscalculated by so much? There are at least a hundred more than my last count. I quickly scan the room, realizing some people must've entered from the side door, rather than the main one. How could I have forgotten there was another entrance? Now, I wish I would've come in and sat in the back of the room, so I could've ensured that I didn't miss anyone.

The organist begins playing *Amazing Grace*—my cue to get to my seat because the service is officially starting. There are so many people, though. I manage to push forward only to be stopped by a face I don't recognize, one I haven't yet counted. I add each new one to my list.

Our pastor's voice rings out, opening the service with

229

the reading of the twenty-third Psalm as Kendra requested.

"The Lord is my shepherd, I shall not be in want…"

I want Chelsea back. I take another step. Another strange face greets me. *Add one to the list. New total five hundred and eighty-five or was it eighty-six?*

"He makes me lie down in green pastures, he leads me beside still waters, he restores my soul."

Still waters. My baby girl's body was floating in water. Another step, another person, another addition.

The pastor continues with the scripture. "…Even though I walk through the valley of the shadow of death, I will fear no evil, for you are with me; your rod and your staff they comfort me."

I push forward as my thoughts whirl back and forth between numbers and the words I'm hearing. *Five hundred and eighty-seven, eighty-eight, eighty-nine…Fear no evil? What about the evil that steals your child? What about the evil that alters your entire life, your entire being, in only an instant? Can I fear that evil?* I frantically start pushing through the masses in front of me.

My own voice resounds in my ears before I'm even aware I'm speaking. "That's my daughter. I've got to get to my daughter. Please, let me get to her. Get out of my way."

The crowd accommodates, parting like the Red Sea.

* * *

KENT

I hear the murmur of voices behind us, making it hard to focus on what the pastor's saying. Even without the buzz of the crowd, it's hard enough to hear the words in relation to my sister and figure out what they all mean. I can't believe people have the nerve to whisper during a funeral. Even I know better. Then, I hear the voice, knowing it's him before I have the chance to turn around. Mom's grip tightens around my shoulder, and I know she hears, too.

My dad's voice grows louder and louder. "Let me through. That's my daughter. I've got to get to my daughter."

I want to disappear. It's bad enough my friends have seen me cry, but now my dad is yelling out, acting like a maniac in front of everyone. For the first time ever, I think I actually hate him. How could he embarrass himself, and us, like this?

"Please, let me through. I need to get to my baby." Dad yells, his voice becoming more urgent by the moment. "Six hundred, you're number six hundred."

People scatter, trying to move out of the way of the madman. The pastor keeps reading the scripture as if the room isn't falling into absolute chaos. The pastor's voice rises, trying to cover the shouts of my father and the whispers of the crowd.

Dad is now within feet of us. He's completely disheveled, nothing like the man who always has his shirts neatly pressed, his shoes perfectly shined, every hair in place. The one who always preaches to Chelsea and me about how important appearance is because first impressions can never be undone. His shirt is untucked, tie hanging loosely around his neck. His hair looks like it hasn't been washed or combed in days. His eyes are crazed, and there's actually drool coming out the side of his mouth. I want to disappear. Please, God, don't let him come sit next to me. I don't want to even be associated with this man who is supposedly my dad.

Finally, the preacher realizes the senselessness of continuing to talk over the racket and stops. The organist starts playing again, this time a song I don't recognize. The preacher steps from behind the podium, towards my father.

They are close enough that I can hear Pastor Ramey speak.

"Tom, why don't you go sit with your family?" He reaches forward to try to take Dad by the hand. "We can talk after the ceremony is over."

Dad jerks away. "I don't want to sit. I need to see my daughter. I need my daughter."

His voice echoes throughout the now silent room. Even the organist stops playing, intrigued by the scene. Dad lurches forward towards the casket, causing it to sway a little as the force of his body meets it. The only image circling around in my mind is my father knocking it over, spilling my sister's body onto the ground. I don't know if I'd laugh or cry if that happened. *Why me? Why is this happening to me? Isn't it bad enough that my sister's dead? Why can't my father act normal? Why is he embarrassing me like this?*

I bury my face in my hands, hoping that if I can't see what's happening, it will cease to exist. I know this isn't the case when the crowd gasps behind me. I slowly raise my head to see my father trying to pry open the casket. He mumbles incoherently—something about getting his daughter out of the box. Finally, he succeeds and lifts Chelsea's lifeless body into an em-

232

brace. Mom rushes forward to meet her husband and daughter in front of the sea of visitors. I can't take any more and run from the room out into the cold, winter air, not caring what anyone thinks of my early departure. As I begin walking towards nowhere in particular, I wonder how long it will take for anyone to even notice I'm gone.

REMEMBER me as the first snowflakes fall from the winter sky. Think of the times we spent amongst the drifts building snowmen, throwing snowballs, and seeing who could make the best angel. When you hear the summer wind rustling through the willow trees and feel its warmth, imagine it as my breath on your cheek offering a kiss full of love. When you notice a butterfly floating through the air, think of me flying now as lightly as it does. I have been released with wings to carry me to a place without pain, fear, or sadness. Free yourself from the burden of sorrow you carry because I'm no longer with you. I am free, and I am soaring.

BILLY

11 YEARS, 7 MONTHS, 16 DAYS BEFORE

JUNE 23, 1977

I'M standing by the fence, feeding an apple to the horse I named Brownie when my grandmother calls out from the driveway.

"There's a letter here for you, Billy."

I let Brownie finish her treat and then sprint to meet my grandmother.

"It looks like it's from David," she says as she passes it to me.

"Thanks." I race towards the big tree in the front yard, the one that's so tall it must be at least two hundred years old. It's my favorite place to sit on hot days; its shade almost completely blocks out the sun's burning rays.

This is the first time I've heard from David in the month I've been here. It's hard to hear from anyone since my grandparents don't have a phone, and they never take me anywhere I can find a payphone to sneak off to. I've memorized Mrs. Jones' number in case they take me on an impromptu trip somewhere there's access to one. Mary told me to call collect anytime and taught me how to do it.

I rip open the envelope, wanting desperately to see what my brother has to say.

Dear Billy,

Hi! It's David here. Mrs. Jones is writing this for me since my writing isn't so good. I miss you lots. I think about you every day and night. Thanks for leaving me the log set. I play with it all the time. It's not the same without you here, though.

I hope you had a good birthday. Did you get to have a party? Did our grandmother make you a good cake like Mommy used to? I miss Mommy. My 9th birthday is soon. Guess what we're doing for it? We're going to visit Mrs. Jones' grandkids and daughter in Illinois. They live close to Chicago, a big city Mrs. Jones says, so we'll get to visit there and eat in a fancy restaurant to celebrate. I'm excited to see a really big city with super tall buildings. Her grandkids are Maria, who's 11 like you, and Jared, who just turned 9 too. Jared and I will get along and play a lot. Mrs. Jones says you can ask to see if you can come with us. Please ask. I don't want to have a birthday without you.

Why haven't you called? I tried to call the number our grandparents left, but they must have written it down wrong. So, you call and give me the right number.

They knocked our house down. It makes me sad to see it gone. Mommy's gone. You're gone, and now our house is gone, too. Did you know they caught Daddy? He's in jail now. I hope I never see him again.

My mouth hurts from all this talking, so I've gotta go. Call or write soon. I love you and miss you. I hope our grandparents are nice.

Love,

david

Mrs. Jones added a note at the end saying they miss me and want me to come visit soon, along with a reminder to call collect anytime with her number printed across the bottom of the page.

I'm so happy to finally hear from David. His life sounds like it's going well. Even though my biggest wish is for my brother to be taken care of, I also feel a stab of grief and pang of jealousy after finishing the letter. I want to be with Mrs. Jones and David, going to a faraway city like Chicago. I want to be with someone who loves me and bakes me a cake for my birthday. My grandparents hadn't even acknowledged mine. I doubt they even know or care when it is. I didn't tell them, knowing it wouldn't make a difference. I don't even have to ask about going to Chicago because my grandparents would never let me go, even though it'd mean getting rid of me for a while.

When I first got to their house, I asked nicely when I could go visit David or if I could call. My questions were always answered with a stern look from my grandfather, directed towards my grandmother, and her un-reassuring response of, "We'll see. Maybe soon." End of discussion; it never went further.

My grandmother tries to be nice when my grandfather isn't at home. Whenever he's around, she acts like a completely different person. My grandfather acts as if I don't exist unless he's barking orders at me of chores that need to be done. It's fine with me; I don't want to have anything to do with him. I do my chores, as told, and then retreat to the field with the horses or underneath the tree to daydream.

My room used to be my mother's; it still looks like a girl's room with flowery wallpaper and a light pink bedspread. It makes me feel a little better to sleep in the place that my mother did when she was younger. It's like having a piece of her here with me. Sometimes, when I wake up scared from the nightmares, I look around the room and imagine her lying there years earlier, seeing the same wallpaper and furniture, hearing the same crickets outside, feeling the same breeze blowing the curtains back from the window, smelling the same hot, stale air. If I imagine long enough, sometimes it's as though she's lying in bed next to me, telling me everything will be okay, even though I know it never will be again.

I read the letter a second time, trying to hear David's voice saying the words on the page. I'm already starting to forget its sound. How could I hear someone's voice every day for nine years and start to forget what it sounds like in only a month? I still hear my mother's as clear as though she were standing next to me. Why can't I do the same with David?

I go into the house to find a piece of paper to reply, deciding to make David think everything's fine here and that I'm getting along okay. I don't want him to worry. I think up interesting things I can write to make him believe I'm doing well—I'll tell him about the horses, especially Brownie. I'll tell him I've made some friends and that we play cowboys and Indians together in the woods. I'll write about the wonderful chocolate cake my grandmother made for my birthday and the new log set they got me, knowing I missed the old one. I'll write that our grandparents aren't so bad, and they may let me come to Chicago, but I'll have to call later to let him know for sure. I just won't mention our lack of phone or the "wrong" number they gave to Mrs. Jones.

Once I sit down to write, the lies flow easily since I already drafted them in my head. Even though lying is wrong, I figure it's okay, this time, since it's to help my brother feel better. The imaginary life I create on paper makes me feel better too.

KENDRA

13 Days After
February 21, 1989

A week has passed since the day of Chelsea's funeral—the hardest day of my life. I could never have imagined how difficult it is to bury your child. I've known people that have been through the death of their child and always felt empathetic, or so I thought. Now that I've lived through it, I realize my sympathy never came close to the true feelings a mother experiences through the loss. It's as though half of me is now gone—like the entire left side of my body is in the casket with Chelsea. I have no idea how to function with only one side of my body, and I need to relearn the simplest of tasks, like how to take a shower or fold laundry.

My parents decided to stay "as long as they are needed," in their words, which is a good thing with Tom out of his mind. He lost what was left of it at the funeral as he pulled our daughter's casket open, clinging to her as though he could bring her back to life. My father was able to drag Tom away, back to the safety of our home, away from all the shocked guests.

My mother and I made it through the rest of the service without Tom or Kent. I had to stand by my daughter's graveside without my husband to support me through the life-shattering realization that it would be my daughter's home forevermore. Going through so much of this alone, makes me realize I have more strength than I've ever given myself credit for. It became evident in the fact that I simply made it through the service. Not without tears, not without pain, not without my heart being ripped from my body—but I made it through without losing my mind, like Tom. If I'd been presented with this scenario in the past, I would've bet my life that it would've been me to go crazy with such a loss.

I'm completely void of all emotion except the anger at Tom that wells inside me, threatening to boil over at any moment. He's taking the easy way out, retreating into himself and his insanity, as a way to avoid facing the cold, hard facts and feeling the pain that goes along with them. My mother has tried incessantly over the past week to calm me down and soften me towards Tom's "breakdown," repeatedly saying it isn't something he's choosing, that it's beyond his control.

Each time, I tell her, in no uncertain terms, I simply don't buy her line of reasoning because if I could keep myself

241

sane through the ordeal then, by God, so could Tom. Each time I see him curled up on his side, lying on the couch or bed, biting his fingernails and murmuring to himself, I have the overwhelming desire to kick him as hard as I can, hoping to shock him back to his senses. I don't understand how my mother can be sucked into believing he could go from a professional, successful man to a blubbering idiot within such a short time. If the circumstances alone were enough to warrant such a transformation, then I should be curled up next to him, murmuring, and biting my nails. I don't buy the "out of his control" thing. He's choosing this—the path of least resistance, the easiest way.

One of my parents contacted Dr. Sloan about Tom's "condition" on the day of the funeral. He made a house call the next morning to check on him. My parents begged me to stay for the appointment, but I refused and went to visit my daughter's grave instead. My mother relayed the prognosis later that evening, even though I made it clear I really didn't care to hear it. Dr. Sloan concurred that Tom was suffering from a "nervous breakdown" and needed to seek hospitalization where they could try to help him work through it with medication and therapy. In the meantime, he prescribed Tom heavy-duty drugs to calm him down and help him sleep.

The drugs do help him sleep, but I see no evidence of him being calmer when he's awake. Even though he barely moves, he seems agitated, constantly rattling off numbers to himself, gnawing on his nails so much the skin around them has started to bleed, or so my mother told me. I can't bear to get close enough to him to see his fingers for fear of my reaction and what harm I may do to him. Everyone is better off with me just keeping my distance.

Meanwhile, while Tom sleeps, mumbles, and gnaws, I'm fighting a desperate battle to try to learn to live with half of my body missing. I have no choice but to carry on—washing dishes, cooking dinner, doing laundry, looking after Kent, preparing to go back to work. Of course, my parents offer to take care of all of the household tasks needing to be done. I can't imagine sitting around letting them take care of me while I wallow in my misery like Tom. That isn't the path for me. For me to learn how to live as half a person, I have to do it right away, or else I'll curl up and die. Not that I haven't seriously considered that option. It would be much easier to swallow a handful of pills and end it all than to live the rest of my days without my daughter. The idea crosses my mind several times a day, and it offers some comfort to know that death is always an option, a way out. The fantasy always ends abruptly, slamming me back to reality, when I picture Kent's face. I can't leave my son, no matter how much pain I'm in, no matter how badly I want to avoid feeling it. Kent is my sole reason for carrying on, for facing another moment, for forcing myself to learn to live feeling so empty and lost.

I've decided to return to work tomorrow. My parents think I'm going back too soon. They don't understand I can't handle another day within the confines of this house with Tom's body sitting only feet away, but his mind seemingly lost for good. I can't wait to have a sense of normalcy to my days again, something to focus on besides my anger and loss—first, the loss of my daughter and now the loss of my husband, both of which fill me with rage.

TOM

2 MONTHS, 24 DAYS AFTER
MAY 2, 1989

I reach out for Kendra. Instead of feeling the warmth of her skin, lying next to me, I find air, nothingness. I open my eyes and explode into panic when I don't recognize my surroundings. The familiar sight of my ceiling spackled with the starburst pattern and the overhead light with a brass ring has been replaced by darkened fluorescent light strips. To my left, where the flowered curtains should be hanging over our bedroom window, there's a drab, gray wall. What happened to the curtains Kendra so proudly made? More importantly, what happened to our window?

I sit up and take in the entirety of the room. A bed with railings on the side, dim gray walls, the stale smell in the air. The memories start filtering in. An image of Rebecca and Carl leaning over me lying on the couch at home, shouting and asking me if I'm okay, telling me to talk to them. Their voices distant, as if they're traveling through water trying to reach me a million miles away. I remember trying to answer them, but the only sounds that would come forth were a string of numbers. Numbers only I knew the meaning of. Numbers that outsiders wouldn't understand. Numbers that kept me locked in, safe, protected.

A picture of Dr. Sloan then rushes into my mind. He's standing next to me, as I'm strapped into some white contraption that kept me from moving my arms and legs. I remember feeling trapped, confined, unable to move or catch my breath. I recall the doctor explaining to a nurse about my "condition." I struggle to remember the words used that day, but only fragments come. Words like delusional, hallucinations, loss.

Kendra's face and voice fill my mind, nothing but anger conveyed from both. I recall her standing next to me, as I'm lying in a bed. Was it this same bed? I wanted to embrace her to take away her anger and allow her to consume my pain. But I was unable to respond the way I wanted to. Instead, I was stuck, unable to move, staring at the wall beyond her while she yelled. I only remember bits and pieces but do recall her saying I need to snap out of it and take care of my family. I don't know what I'd been doing if not taking care of my family. Hasn't my job always been to take care of them? Have I failed somehow?

I try to fit the puzzle in my mind together to make sense of where I am and why I'm alone. There's a chalkboard on the wall to my left that says

Nurse: Lucy

Today's date: May 2, 1989

My heart instantly races upon seeing the date. *May 2, 1989.* Someone must be playing a joke on me. There's no way it can be May 2nd. The last I remember it was February 3rd or maybe February 4th. There's no way three months could've passed that I have no memory of. I have no idea why I'd be somewhere that I need a nurse named Lucy. I do a once-over of my body, and it seems I'm physically okay, all in one piece. No bruises. No casts. So why do I need a nurse? If I have a nurse, I must have a button to push so that Lucy can come and explain a few things to me, like where I am and why I'm here.

I search and can't find the button to call her. I walk to the door, try to turn the knob, but it won't open. I'm locked in this room. My anxiety grows as I work the doorknob, trying to jiggle it free. Nothing. The door holding me captive has a window at the top with bars instead of glass. I'm stuck, trapped, like a caged animal.

"Lucy!" I yell through my barred escape. "Nurse Lucy… I need help. Please help me." My voice echoes down what seem to be empty hallways, void of people moving about.

My cries are met with those of others in the hallway, seemingly as trapped as I am. I understand some of the voices; others are just wails and moans. The whole hallway comes alive with noise and cries for help. Still, no one comes.

"Lucy!" I scream, trying to make my voice louder than the others. "Where am I? I need to know where I am. Please tell me where I am."

"You're in hell, pal," a voice screams out followed by laughter.

The shrieks of my unseen fellow prisoners become so loud that I can no longer hear my own voice. I quickly realize the futility of continuing to yell when no one can hear me and, if they can, no nurse named Lucy is coming to offer an explanation. The cries make my head throb. I have to stop the noise. I retreat to the corner, stoop, and cover my head with my pillow. It does nothing to dull the screeching and wailing.

The only thing that offers the silence I crave is the wall in front of me. Pounding my head against it until the pain overtakes my ability to hear.

NICOLE

4 MONTHS, 3 DAYS AFTER
JUNE 11, 1989

THE day I've anticipated for so long is finally here… Graduation Day. The day that symbolizes becoming an adult, of being able to make my own choices. I'm so relieved to be done with high school. The past four months without Chelsea have been unbearable. I've tried my best to become better friends with many of my acquaintances. People have been more than willing to take me under their wings. Everyone feels sorry for *the girl whose best friend was murdered.* But no matter which crowd I immerse myself in, or who I hang out with, no one can replace the friendship Chelsea and I shared. I often find myself in a crowd of people and hear myself laugh while my mind wonders what in the world I find so humorous. My laugh never reaches my soul anymore. I don't know if I even have a soul left or if I've killed it off with the Valium, along with the fear and sadness I've been trying to rid myself of.

I've been anxious about how I was going to hold up during the ceremony, but with the help of my little yellow friends, I make it through the moment of silence and speech in Chelsea's honor, without breaking down. After the ceremony, I head to the cemetery and leave my cap and tassel sitting atop Chelsea's grave. Remnants were left by other visitors today— pink roses scattered one by one around the headstone, a graduation program, a poem written by one of our fellow classmates in Chelsea's memory.

I sit amongst the mementos and talk to my best friend as I've done several times in the past few months.

"Chels, I wish you were here. We always talked about graduation and how we couldn't wait for it. It wasn't the same without you. Nothing is anymore. I feel lost all the time now. It's like I don't even know who I am without you. Now I'm done with school and don't have a clue what to do next." I wrap my arms tightly around my knees. "We always talked about going off to college together. I don't want to go without you. I can't. I have nobody to talk to anymore that really knows me. I'm just lost, Chels. Lost and afraid… afraid of everyone and everything. I wish you were here so I'd be okay; it'd all be okay."

When I have no words or tears left, I rise and walk towards my car, knowing I'm headed to places Chelsea definitely wouldn't approve of. There's a big Graduation party tonight at Joe's house. Joe is known for being a hard partier and is someone

Chelsea and I would've never socialized with before. But now, Joe is definitely into me and hasn't been shy about his intentions for commemorating this special day. I intend to do whatever it takes to make the pain go away for the rest of the night. *If only Chelsea were here, I wouldn't be acting so stupid* I tell myself as I play out the nights' events. I don't know if it's funny or sad how much I've changed in such a short time. I always thought I knew what I wanted out of life, who I am, what I stood for, right from wrong. Now, I'm a stranger to myself. I have no path anymore. I'm lost. Chelsea wouldn't even recognize me based upon what I've been doing and the people I've been hanging with.

As I pull into Joe's driveway, I take a deep breath and feel a moment of relief as I anticipate the night before me. I'm ready for the drugs, the sex, or both, to take me away from my fear, my thoughts, my memories, my pain, and the person I'm becoming without Chelsea.

KENT

1 YEAR, 7 MONTHS, 7 DAYS AFTER
SEPTEMBER 15, 1990

I STAND by my locker until the bell rings, signaling that all students should be sitting dutifully behind desks, waiting for the teachers to start their preaching. Instead, I'm waiting for the halls to clear so that no one will witness my escape out the side door. It's taking forever for the halls to empty, but then, finally, my chance comes. I burst out into the too-bright sunlight and warm, muggy air. Once outside, I finally feel like I can breathe. That building and those people are draining me of everything I have. Life, in general, feels that way most days. Nothing seems to be okay since Chelsea was killed.

I hate middle school. In fact, it totally sucks. It doesn't help that everyone still refers to me as *the boy whose sister was murdered.* Some people try to befriend me only to get the scoop. Others treat me like a freak—like my sister's murder might be contagious or something. I don't trust anyone's motives for wanting to be my friend, and quite frankly, I don't have the energy or desire to deal with anyone. Right now, all I want is to be left alone. Which is why I'm headed to the woods behind the school instead of to math class where I'm supposed to be. I've only been in middle school a couple of weeks and have hated every minute of it.

I know the school will call my house and leave a message letting my mother know I've skipped classes again and will be forced to serve an in-school suspension since it's my third offense. I also know that, as with the previous two times, I'll delete the message before Mom has the chance to hear it and I'll be able to adequately forge her signature on the note sent home notifying her of my terrible crime. I've signed her name so many times now it's almost an exact match.

As I draw nearer to my favorite spot, a large oak tree that towers over everything else, I finally feel some of the tension ease from my neck. I always have a headache nowadays unless I'm off by myself, forgetting the real world I've left behind. Sometimes I daydream everything is the way it used to be—that my life hasn't unraveled by the seams. I pretend that Chelsea is still alive, picking on me, teasing me about my terrible table manners, mothering me by correcting my grammar as I tell stories about my day. I envision our family sitting down to dinner as we did in the old days …before. Before Chelsea was murdered. Before my dad went nuts. Before my mom decided to work all the time. Before

I became non-existent.

Today I'm flooded with memories of my father's time away from home. Mom actually forced me to go visit Dad a couple of times in the four and a half months he was in the loony bin, until I refused to go any longer. I couldn't stand it there. One, it stunk. Two, my dad acted sane compared to some of the psychos in there with him. Three, I didn't see the point in spending time with a man who did nothing but talk about numbers. The number of miles between the hospital and our house. The number of cars traveling on the American freeway system on average per hour. The number of tiles in the ceiling of the visiting room.

Whenever I was around him and he'd start his ramblings, it made me want to scream. I'd envision grabbing my father by the shoulders, shaking with all my strength, and telling him I didn't give a shit. I wanted to yell that he needed to ask me about school or how I was feeling. I needed him to talk to me about anything besides his stupid numbers.

I vividly remember the shock on my mother's face when I refused to accompany her any longer. She came to my room, something she rarely did anymore, telling me to get ready to leave for our visit. I simply looked up from my magazine for an instant, refused to acknowledge her in any other way, and then resumed my reading. My mother demanded a response from me, asking if I'd heard her. As her demands grew sterner, I stood up, pushed past her in the doorway, headed down the stairs. I didn't speak until I'd opened the front door. "You're on your own. I'm not going."

I heard my mother screaming at me between the moment I stepped out and the one where the door closed behind me. "Wait a minute young man. Who do you think…?" Then, silence. She could've come after me and would've caught me. But she didn't. I knew she wouldn't, so I didn't even bother quickening my pace as I made my way down our street, away from our house of silence and pain. My old mom would have made me pay severely for my act of defiance, grounding me of all privileges, demanding work around the house; but, then again, the old me never would've been so outright rebellious. My new mom, the one who doesn't seem to care about me one bit or even notice I'm alive, never spoke another word about the incident. Nor did she ever again talk about her visits with my father or ask me to accompany her. Even though Dad has been home for a while, he still isn't right, and I do what I can to avoid him.

The tension returns to my shoulders. My escape from the confines of school isn't giving me its usual distraction from reality. I desperately need away from it all before it sucks me into the black hole of misery that's becoming my life. Instead of sitting under the old oak tree, rehashing things in my mind, I wander towards the neighborhood on the other side of the forest.

Once there, I find a new way to ease my mind of anxiety, this way working better than any I've found so far. Destruction. First a rock through the picture window of the house with the green shutters and perfectly manicured lawn. Next, a dumped trash can in the yard with the purple flowers, leaving refuse thrown about. Then, my house key scraped down the side of the cars parked along the street. As I meander through the neighborhood, towards home, I leave a trail of misery behind me.

BILLY

10 YEARS, 9 MONTHS, 25 DAYS BEFORE

APRIL 14, 1978

ON my way from the bus stop, I leaf through the stack of mail and spot David's handwriting. I run towards the front door, anxious to see what's new in his life. I hate that the only way we have to communicate is through the mail since our grandparents won't arrange visits with David or make sure I get to talk to him on the phone. It's been almost a year since I've heard my brother's voice. Has it changed? Would I recognize it if I overheard him in a crowd? Mine is starting to crack into a high-pitched squeal every once in a while, which is terribly embarrassing when it happens at school.

Once inside, I toss the mail on the end table and head upstairs to my room, taking the steps two at a time. I like to be alone to read David's letters so I can cry or laugh without having to answer to anyone. I usually read each letter four or five times trying to picture the brother I remember, doing the things he's written about, before drafting my reply. The more time that passes, the harder it is for me to envision him.

By the time I reach the top step, I've already opened the envelope and unfolded the letter. I step inside my doorway when my grandfather's voice booms up the stairs.

"Hey, boy! Get down here. Got some work for you to do."

My grandfather hasn't once used my name in the ten and a half months I've lived here. It's always "boy," or "stupid" or some other degrading name. I don't even know if he remembers my name and at times, I'm tempted to remind him. No doubt that would result in punishment. I haven't learned much about my grandfather, but I can tell he's someone who won't put up with backtalk. It's safest to just silently comply with his demands.

Even after living with my cruel father for so many years, I'm even more frightened of my grandfather. The fact that he never says much, communicating mostly with glares to his wife or a heavy-footed walk, keeps me on edge. If people use words, I can at least tell what's going on in their heads. I always feel like I'm trying to read his mind, which keeps me constantly on eggshells, watching every word, facial expression, and movement around him.

"Be down in a few minutes…"

I can't even finish my sentence before my grandfather's

"Now!" booms up the stairs.

I toss the letter on my bed and lay my backpack over it to conceal it, in case my grandmother comes into my room. I don't want to chance her reading it because I'm sure David will reference life here "on the farm" as we refer to it. Of course, any mention he makes would be based on my complete fabrications shared in my letters to him. I don't want to have to explain to anyone why I don't just tell him the truth. I don't even fully understand it myself.

I think the only reason our grandfather agreed to take me was so he'd have someone to do all the dirty jobs around here. I've become his chore boy, his free labor. I reach the front porch where he waits impatiently, holding the door open.

"Hurry it up… we ain't got all day," he says as he heads towards the side of the house with me trailing behind.

"See all this junk. Pile it up over there." My grandfather refers to sticks, wood, and other debris that's blown from neighbor's trash cans or from the street where people threw litter out their car windows. All of it now clings along the property's fence line. It's been there for a long time as the weeds have actually started growing through some of the paper bags clinging there.

"Gotta get all this out so I can fix the fence. Got holes all through it," my grandfather orders.

I don't understand his desire to fix the fence or clean up the trash. It all blends in quite well with the surroundings. The farmhouse is in desperate need of a new paint job. Most of the shutters are barely still attached. The roof has obviously been patched many different times over the years by someone who didn't make much of an effort to ensure it matched.

"What are you gawking at? Get busy." My grandfather thrusts a pair of work gloves into my hands and heads off towards the barn.

I work until dark, unweaving trash from the fence, moving the debris to the spot in the field where my grandfather had indicated. I'm so lost in thought I don't realize how late it is until I trip in a hole I couldn't see because there's no longer enough light. I head towards the house, my stomach growling, and hope my grandmother saved me some dinner since no one bothered to call me in for it. She probably wasn't allowed to interrupt my work. My grandfather wouldn't have seen the necessity of me getting dinner. I'm torn between my need for food and my desire to read David's letter. I had to fight the urge, as I worked, to sneak inside and read it. I knew better than to attempt it, though, because my grandfather must have superhero vision and hearing. Anytime I try to take a rest during my "assignments", my grandfather hones in on me immediately telling me to get back to work, reiterating his policy of, "No breaks till the job is done."

I walk in the front door, and my dilemma is solved for me by my grandfather. He's sitting in his recliner, reading the paper. "There's a plate of food in the kitchen. Hurry up and eat. There's more to do."

"It's pretty dark out there. I can't see a thing. Can I finish tomorrow? I got homework, too."

He lowers his paper, glaring at me. "Is that backtalk I hear? Mark my words, you best not be back-talking me."

"No, sir. I just…"

"You'll just go eat your supper and do as I say. You got five minutes."

As I hurry to the sink to wash my filthy hands, my grandmother sits the plate of food on the table. She gives me a slight smile and a nod as I sit and begin to shovel the food in. I'm half-way through the meal before I even stop to ponder what I'm eating. Everything my grandmother makes tends to taste like the meal before, if being tasteless is considered a taste. My growling stomach dictates the need to finish the meal anyway. I would kill for a plate of Mrs. Jones' sausage gravy and biscuits.

I've just finished the last bite and am emptying my glass of milk when my grandfather yells from the other room, "Time's up."

I don't know what the big rush is on this job and what's left to do tonight when we can't even see. I want to read my letter from David, do my homework, and go to bed. A reasonable man would respect me for wanting to follow through on my school obligations, but not my grandfather. Being reasonable isn't his specialty.

My grandfather says he has to get something out of the barn and to meet him by the pile. I kick dirt into the pile, fuming at his unfairness. Most kids complain about their parents making them do their homework and go to bed early. I just want to be able to get mine done. What's so important about this job that it must be done tonight and it all must be done now? I am tired.

The smell hits before I'm aware of my grandfather's

presence. Gasoline. The sloshing sound of it against the pile of rubble echoes in my ears. The smell and sound together turn my stomach as I realize what's coming next. I try to turn away before the match my grandfather throws bursts into flame, but, I'm too slow. The whooshing sound of the fire beats inside my chest and head. Regardless of the heat generated, a chill races up my spine. I faintly hear my grandfather yell something, but I'm unable to make out the words. Instead, all I hear as I run towards the woods—away from my grandparents, away from the fire, away from my painful memories of the past—is my mother's voice screaming out in agony from within the flames.

Part III

What is history? An echo of the past in the future; a reflex from the future on the past.

~ Victor Hugo

Grief is in two parts. The first is loss. The second is the remaking of life.

~ Anne Roiphe

KENDRA

18 YEARS, 6 MONTHS, 27 DAYS AFTER
TUESDAY, SEPTEMBER 4, 2007, 10:08 A.M.

TOM answers the door, and then I hear a man's voice but
can't make out what's being said. I finish washing off the
counters so everything will be tidy when we return from Tom's
doctor's appointment. I head to the front room to see who is
visiting us on a Tuesday morning when we would typically be
at work. Tom, with tears streaming down his face, is wrapped in
the arms of a man I don't recognize at first.

Dear God, please don't let anything be wrong with Kent.
"Tom...is everything okay?" My voice cracks as I touch him on
the shoulder.

The man hugging my husband turns, allowing me to see
who is attached to the large frame. It is Detective Bradley.

"Kendra..." Detective Bradley removes one of his arms from around Tom and rests it on my shoulder. "We found him. We made an arrest this morning. We've got Chelsea's killer."

My mind instantly speeds into overdrive, and I must remind myself to take a breath. I can't comprehend what I'm hearing. "What?"

"They caught him, Kendra. After all this time, they found him. Can you believe it? Our prayers have been answered." Tom pulls me close. A smile beams across his tear-covered face.

A million questions race through my mind—ones I've had eighteen and a half years to form. They pour out before I have the chance to filter them.

"Who? Why? How did you catch him? Why our baby?"

"Let's sit down. I know you must have a lot of questions. I'll tell you everything I'm able to at this point," Detective Bradley says as we each take a seat.

I shake my head, at a loss for words. In some ways, I want the detective to share everything as quickly as possible, so my questions will finally have some answers. Another part of me isn't sure I can handle knowing. I've learned to find safety and comfort over the years in not knowing; it has become a part of me. I've filled in my own blanks many times throughout the years. For a long time, I truly believed the worst part of losing Chelsea was never knowing the details. But now, when the answers are so close I can reach out and touch them, I realize that I've long ago accepted the facts—the fact that my daughter is dead; she's never coming home; someone killed her; her murder forever altered the course of my family's life. It's taken years to accept these facts and to believe that I've forgiven the nameless, faceless person who did this to our family, who stole our child.

The details scare me. They are the only unknowns left in the madness surrounding Chelsea's death. What if the details crush me? What if they, once again, steal Tom's sanity? Will the "forgiveness" I've granted Chelsea's killer continue once he has a name, a face, a history and a life he's lived freely in the years since I've lost my daughter? Or will the rage return? The rage that consumed me for so long after Chelsea's death. The rage that destroyed my relationship with Kent and almost stole my marriage. I'm much more afraid of my internal fury than going on forever without knowing the specifics.

Tom's arm wraps around my shoulder, and I lean into him as Detective Bradley begins to speak.

"The department received a call a couple of months back from the Bureau of Criminal Identification and Investigation saying they matched DNA evidence from a robbery last year to DNA evidence in Chelsea's murder. As a result of that call, we did further testing on the suspect who was in our custody on another charge." Detective Bradley leans forward, his arms resting on his knees. "We got the call yesterday which confirmed the man we have is indeed the same man responsible for Chelsea's death. God must've been smiling down on us with this one as he was scheduled to be released on his other charges this afternoon. Instead, we're able to hold him on the charges related to Chelsea."

"Who is it? Is it someone police investigated before?" Tom asks as I start mentally listing some of the two hundred potential suspects the police have interviewed over the years, wondering if one of them is the person responsible.

"No. It's actually someone who has completely avoided our attention in this matter until the DNA match. We're not even sure he knew Chelsea. His name is William Lee Dunkin. Does that sound familiar?"

I scan my memory for any trace of familiarity with the name. There is none. Tom and I both shake our heads, coming up empty-handed. Neither of us has ever heard it before.

"We can't give you a lot of details now as it's an ongoing investigation, but I can tell you he's forty-one, so he would've been about twenty-two when Chelsea was murdered." Detective Bradley scans the notebook in his hand. "He's currently serving time for breaking and entering, but he's got a rap sheet a mile long. He's divorced with six kids, but with as much time as he's spent locked up, I doubt he has a relationship with any of them.

"We're still trying to piece everything together and will need to talk with some of the people we originally interviewed to see if there's a connection we're missing. Right now, though, we really don't see an obvious one."

"Is William from around here? Why Chelsea? Why my baby girl?" The questions pour off my lips as my mind tries to wrap itself around this new information.

The detective shrugs and shakes his head. "I wish I could give you those answers. From his file, it seems like he showed up in this area about the time he was sixteen after living with his grandparents for a while. Not sure why he picked here, but this is where he stayed, unfortunately for us."

I'm consumed with disbelief. Why is this happening now, after so long? A part of me has always believed this moment would come, but now that it's here, I don't know what to do with it. I'm not ready to have my life unravel again by having to relive everything that happened almost nineteen years ago... the pain, the loss, the uncertainty. We did what we had to do to move on, to rebuild a life for ourselves, even though a vital piece was missing. We've all been through so much—Tom's nervous breakdown, my rage, Kent's rebellion. We stitched everything back together the best we knew how and created a tapestry of lives torn into a million little pieces that February night, eighteen and a half years ago. I can't have it all torn apart again.

"Do you have a picture of him?" Tom asks.

Detective Bradley pulls one from his file and hands it to Tom. I try to force myself to look at the man on the sheet of paper Tom is holding, but I can't. I cannot force myself to look at the last face my daughter saw. I run upstairs, needing to escape. As soon as I reach the bathroom, nausea overtakes me, and I vomit, trying to void my body of the fear consuming me.

*   *   *

NICOLE

The phone call brings the world around me to a screeching halt. I still hear my daughters in the background laughing with their father. I feel my feet on the kitchen floor and smell dinner cooking on the stove less than a foot away. None of it is the same though, as it was only ten short minutes ago. I don't know whether I should laugh, cry, or hit something. The feeling of helplessness overwhelms me —something I haven't felt for quite a while. The feeling that scares me most of all threatens to take over, rattling my already jumbled thoughts. Even though I haven't done so for years, the thing I want most at this moment is a drink or a pill—something to take the edge off the swarm of emotions invading my soul, taking over my entire being, and shaking the world I've worked so hard to create.

"Mommy, I said what'sa matter?" Isabella, my six-year-old daughter, tugs lightly on my arm, trying to pull me back to reality.

I plaster on my mommy smile. "Nothing honey. What do you need?"

"I asked you a million times if you would come in and play Go Fish with me."

"Give me a few minutes to talk to Daddy first, okay?" I say, trying to ignore the cravings overtaking me.

"Okie dokie. I'll get it set up for us."

I lean down and give her a kiss on the cheek, amazed I'm still able to perform such a normal function when everything around me now feels crazy, like I don't belong in my own skin anymore.

"Steve, can you come talk to me in the bedroom a minute?" I yell into the living room as I walk down the hallway to our room.

"Now that's an invite I'll never pass up... a bedroom meeting," he jokes and then turns his attention back to our nine-year-old daughter. "Chelsea, I'll be back in a minute."

I drop onto the bed and wrap my arms around my

stomach, trying to suppress the feelings consuming me. Steve smiles as he walks in the door, but it fades as soon as he sees me.

"Hey, babe. What's the matter?" Steve asks and sits next to me.

"Just hold me, please." I lean into his embrace, and the tears begin to fall.

After a minute he says, "You're starting to scare me. What's wrong? Who was on the phone?"

I pause before saying the words I thought I'd never have the chance to say. "That was Tom Wyatt. They caught Chelsea's murderer."

"Oh my god. When? Who is it?"

I repeat the information Tom shared, hoping with every word that the news will feel more real. Instead, the more details I share, the more my body shakes, the harder my tears fall, the more Steve's eyes fill with concern. I finish telling him everything and fall back onto the bed, covering my face with my hands.

"Hon, this is great news. The Wyatt's must be so relieved to finally know who's responsible. Now, they can get some answers." He pauses for a moment, and when no sound escapes me except for my continued sobs, he says, "What's wrong, Nicki? Aren't you thankful they caught him? You never thought this day would come."

"I don't know what I feel right now. I think I'm just in shock and need some time to let it sink in."

"Why don't you lay down for a while and I'll entertain the girls? Maybe some quiet will help you feel better." Steve caresses my leg.

"I can't. I promised Isabella I'd play *Go Fish* and I need to make dinner, go to the PTA meeting, and help the girls with homework. I don't have time to just lay here." I sit up and wipe my tears.

"I can help with homework, play *Go Fish*, and call Sharon to let her know you won't be at the meeting. We'll order pizza so we don't have to worry about dinner. I really think you need some time to process all of this."

"What's to process? Chelsea's still dead. They caught the guy. Now, we'll all have to live through this nightmare again. Lying here, crying my eyes out isn't going to do a thing to change the situation." Anger spews from me even though I know Steve is just trying to comfort me. "I don't have time for this right now."

I leave him sitting there and stomp off to the kitchen to follow through on the commitment I made to my daughter to play *Go Fish*.

I'm relieved when the evening finally comes to an end. I forced myself to do all my normal activities—I cooked dinner, played *Go Fish*, helped with homework, and went to the PTA meeting. And, I was able to fake a smile and good attitude through most of it. Steve tried to talk to me again after the girls went to bed, but I told him I wasn't ready, and we'd talk later.

Now it's eleven-thirty; everyone is asleep, and I can, at last, be alone with my thoughts. Now that I'm able to think, I'm not sure it's a good thing. My thoughts from earlier instantly come back to, *if only I had something to take the edge off, I could get through this, and figure out what I'm feeling.*

272

I haven't touched a drug or alcohol in over eight years, since my oldest daughter, Chelsea, was one. I don't really remember my last use, but I do remember the after-effects, ending up in treatment, and Steve taking me to my parents until I could get myself together. From what Steve told me later, he came home from work to find me passed out on the floor with Chelsea crying hysterically, covered in her own filth. He found an empty bottle of vodka and an open bottle of Valium lying on the floor beside me. Even though we fought about my drinking and use for years, this was the last straw for him because it affected our daughter. Chelsea could've eaten some of the pills, and they surely would've killed her.

At that time, I realized how sick and tired I was of feeling sick and tired, so I agreed to seek help. Plus, I didn't want to lose my family. I already had one failed marriage; I wasn't up for another loss. I went to a small residential treatment center about an hour from home and stayed for nine weeks. During that time, I worked through a lot of the feelings I'd been trying to avoid by staying high. All of them stemmed from the same thing—the loss of Chelsea. Because I started taking the pills right after Chelsea's murder, I never really grieved her loss, and I never faced all the fears Chelsea's murder had invoked. Fears that kept me stoned out of my mind for over a decade. Ones that kept me from being able to give or receive love. Fears that kept me locked in my own prison, unable to live.

I finished treatment successfully and left as a new person. I finally believed I deserved to live, even though Chelsea never got the chance. I understood why I was so afraid to love anyone, including my husband and child. I gained insight into some of my obsessive-compulsive behaviors such as always leaving a note or a voicemail if I went anywhere so that if I never returned, my loved ones would know where I had been, where to look for me. Those nine weeks offered me the time to grieve that I should've taken ten years earlier rather than numbing myself out.

The only people who visited me regularly during that terrible time were Tom and Kendra Wyatt. Every weekend during Sunday visitation they would show up and offer their hugs and words of support. They were the only people who seemed to truly understand my pain and why it was still so intense after so many years. Everyone else had given up on me, but not them. Prior to my treatment, they tried to stay in touch, but I was usually so ashamed of myself and my life that I only maintained limited contact. I felt like my failed attempts at college, a marriage, success of any kind, were a disappointment to them because instead, I should be living the life Chelsea didn't get the chance to live. I should be making them proud since they'd never have a daughter to experience these things with.

Tom and Kendra came to the hospital after I had my first daughter, Chelsea. They cried tears of joy as they held her, knowing she'd forever offer a remembrance of their daughter's life, if only in name. The demands of parenting and the depression the first year after Chelsea was born made me spiral downhill faster than I knew was possible. Treatment helped me see my fears were even more compounded by the fact that I had a child to protect and love when I was clueless on how to even do that for myself.

Now, reflecting back on the last eighteen and a half years, I'm so angry with myself for feeling so helpless, so afraid. I'm furious that my first instinct is to pick up a drink, take a pill. The harder I try to make sense of my feelings, the stronger the urges become. Just one beer won't hurt. It will help me sleep, and I can deal with all this emotion tomorrow.

Steve occasionally drinks beer and keeps some in the refrigerator in the garage. Having it in the house never bothered me once I got sober. God removed all my urges to drink or use, once I surrendered it all to Him.

As I make my way towards the garage, my thoughts spin out of control, with two distinct voices inside my head. They talked about this in treatment, the addictive voice and the recovery voice battling it out, but I'd never experienced it before. The voices talk over one another, making either hard to understand.

I'll just have one. **You know you can't stop at one...you're an alcoholic.** *No one will have to know.* **Steve will know with one look at you.** *It's just to help me get some sleep. I won't be able to stop these thoughts without something.* **Is one night's sleep worth destroying your family?** *Just one... one won't hurt anything.* **You can't have just one... one will become five which will turn into ten which will lead to the pills.** *Everyone's allowed to have one once in a while.* **Not you...** *I'll feel so much better.* **Will you feel better if you lose your husband and kids?**

There's a twelve-pack in the fridge. I grab one and hold it in my hands, enjoying the cool feel of it against my skin. I can almost taste it. I imagine the relief it will bring, even as the voices continue battling within my mind. I dig through the kitchen drawer to find the bottle opener; my hands tremble in anticipation of that first sip. I pop off the lid, the smell instantly filling me. As I lift the bottle to my lips, I glance at the refrigerator plastered with pictures of Steve and my girls, and finally, my eyes come to rest on the one I've had the longest—Chelsea's senior picture, staring back at me, peering into my soul.

No, I won't do this. I won't throw it all away. I'll go through the pain and the sorrow for Chelsea. At least I get a second chance even though she didn't. I'm not going to blow it. I pour the beer down the drain and wipe the tears from my cheeks.

As I crawl into bed, my husband's body automatically curls itself around me. The warmth from his skin and his breath on my shoulder calms me. As I listen to his breathing, the voices quiet until they are drowned out by my husband's embrace and memories of Chelsea.

*   *   *

KENT

The phone rings for the fourth time in the past half hour and, again, Mom's voice echoes through my apartment from the answering machine.

"Kent, honey…it's Mom again. I know you're there, so pick up. I need to talk to you. Pick up…Fine, I'll stay on here and keep talking until you can't stand it anymore. The weather's awful today…it's raining horribly. The weatherman said there's a possibility of…"

276

"What Mom?" I reluctantly give in, lifting the pillow from my head. I can't take the sound of her voice anymore with this pounding headache.

"There you are. I know I didn't wake you since it's almost two in the afternoon. You have to be at work soon, so I knew you'd be up."

"I'm takin' the night off. Whaddya want?"

"You're not sick, are you? If so, I can bring some dinner over." The forced sound of concern in her voice makes me cringe.

"Mom, I don't need dinner. Now, why'd you call me a million times? What's the big deal?"

"We've got some good news that I wanted to share with you before you saw it on TV."

I can just imagine the news she has to share that's so important it'll be on television— Dad's business made a charitable contribution to a hospital for homeless, orphaned children. My mother's church group sewed blankets for a bunch of invalid veterans returning from Iraq. My best friend from high school received the Nobel Prize.

"It's about Chelsea." Mom's words bring my racing thoughts to an abrupt stop. "Detective Bradley came by the house this morning. They caught him."

"Caught who?" My voice is barely audible over the beating of my heart.

"The guy who killed Chelsea. He committed an armed robbery not too long ago, and the DNA he left at the scene matched the DNA from Chelsea's case. He's sitting in jail already, so they were able to hold him based on the DNA match."

277

"Who is it?" My mind replays images of all the "persons of interest" we've heard about over the years. Their faces flash through my mind. Was one of them able to fool the cops all these years? Adrenaline surges through me, along with anger.

"It's someone we don't think Chelsea knew. His name is William Dunkin. Does that sound familiar to you?"

"Uhm...no...I don't think so. Did you see his picture?"

"Your dad did, and he didn't think he'd ever seen him before. I couldn't bear to look... at least not today. I'm sure it'll be plastered all over the news tonight though."

I'm at a loss for words. All my thoughts are on a train barreling straight towards my forehead, ready to crash through at any minute. The headache I felt before talking to Mom was nothing compared to the pain thundering there now.

"Aren't you going to say anything? I thought you'd be happy. I thought maybe this news would help you move on."

Help me move on? A wave of anger that I've tried to keep from surfacing through the years, ripples through me. *Help me move on? From what? From the fact that my sister was stolen from me? From the fact that my whole family was destroyed by some sicko? From the fact that my mom cared more about her job and her church than she did her only remaining child? From the fact that my father has never again been quite right? From the fact that I'm almost twenty-nine years old and a complete failure?*

"Kent, are you there? Kent..."

Instead of saying all the things I want to, I simply say what she needs to hear. "I'm in shock, Mom. Yea. It's great news. Look, I've gotta go. I'll call you later."

"Alright. Let me know if you change your mind about dinner. Hope you feel better."

I'm surprised my voice didn't betray me, allowing my anger to seep through the phone lines straight to my mother's heart. Of course, my mother hears only what she wants to. Obviously, she wanted to hear that now everything will be okay, and I'll stop being such a screw-up.

My parents have had their passive-aggressive ways of letting me know throughout the years exactly what they think of my life.

We'd be happy to pay for you to go to college, so you don't have to work such strange hours. When what my father really meant is, please go back to school so you can have a reputable job for me to tell my friends about.

Honey, is there anyone special in your life? My mother meant different things on different occasions with this, from are you gay? To why are you such a slut? To you're our only hope for grandchildren. I don't want to be their only hope for anything, but too bad for me—that was a role passed on to me eighteen and a half years ago by this man named William Dunkin.

I know I'm a disappointment to them. Hell, I'm a disappointment to myself. I'm not living the life I pictured for myself—then again, neither is my sister. My childhood dreams were of becoming a police officer, a firefighter, or a businessman like Dad. But those dreams were long ago buried with my sister. Most of the time, I can pretend I'm happy with my life. I have no attachments, no one's heart to break. No one to break mine. I've already let my parents down too many times to count, so there's no pedestal left from which to fall. I'm a great bartender, and the ladies love me. Nothing makes me feel better than a beautiful woman smiling at my jokes. Well, nothing other than the feel of a beautiful woman's body lying naked next to me. I've had many women interested in commitments over the years, but marriage and children aren't for me. I don't want the pain that comes from caring beyond a couple of nights. I've held a job. I pay most of my bills. I make my once a month appearance at my parent's house for Sunday dinner. I have my women; I have my booze; I have my buddies. What more do I need?

Although, at the moment, I wish for nothing more than to have someone I love wrap their arms around me and tell me everything will be okay. There's no such person to fill that role though. Instead, I do the one thing that always brings some momentary relief from my emotions, I punch the plaster wall above the bed until the pain stops every thought, every need, every feeling.

*   *   *

BILLY

I'm stuck in that place between consciousness and sleep—the one I'm in most days in here; the place between my nightmares of the past and those of the reality I'm currently living. I never know whether it's best to stay in my dreams where my fate has already been decided or to rouse myself and deal with all the uncertainties of the present.

The noise coming from my pod mates makes the decision for me. I can't block out their curses and yells any longer. I lift the pillow off my head—at least that's what they call it here even though it's as flat as a sheet of paper and about as comfortable as one. As always, my first thought is of wanting. Wanting a drink or hit. Wanting out of this cell. Wanting to be able to go back in time. Wanting a different life.

If I were free, I would've had my first drink before my feet hit the floor. My family thinks the drinking and drugs destroyed me, but I know the truth—they are the only things that kept me alive this long. The numbness they provided is the only thing that enabled me to face another day for all these years. Now that I don't have my aid to forgetting, I have no idea how to get through the next thirty seconds, let alone another twenty-four hours. Not that I have a choice. I've given up that right many times over the years. This time it's the biggie I'm facing— one of the two events in my life, I would give anything to undo. But, no bargains with the devil are being offered.

I've been in the Fairmont County jail for over six months, and it's been almost as long since I've had a drink or drug. I hate facing the real world with all its painful memories and hard truths. I hate that most of those truths, I played a huge part in creating. I realize day after day, when not one person shows up to visit, how alone I truly am. I have fathered six children, divorced two wives, and not one of them has bothered to take the time to come see me. I can't blame them after everything I've put them through. This is just another one of my many screw-ups to them. I wonder if they know yet just how badly I've messed up. If not, I'm certain it will hit the news soon, and then there will be one less secret that I carry within.

281

They are officially charging me with murder today in a case that's remained unsolved for almost nineteen years. My face and name will be plastered all over every news channel and paper around. People will scream for my head. Her murder rattled this quiet, calm town to its core. No one forgot. Certainly, no one will forgive. I can't; how can they? I'm dreading my pod mates finding out about the charge since some of them probably remember when it all happened and want to seek vengeance for the pain I caused them, their girlfriends, or their mothers.

"Dunkin...visitor," the guard's voice booms from outside the door. It takes a moment for the words to register, as my attorney is the only person who ever visits me.

The guard leads me down the hallway to the visiting area. Who in God's name would be coming to visit me? I don't want to see anyone because I don't want to have to lie any more.

"Have a seat...you got twenty minutes," the guard we've all nicknamed Horse, because of his extremely large front teeth, mutters at me.

I sit and look through the glass at the person sitting before me, without recognizing him. I pick up the phone as the stranger does the same.

"Billy?" the voice says.

"Yea?"

"Do you recognize me?" The voice pauses for a moment awaiting a hint of recognition. When none comes, he continues. "It's David...your brother."

A lump the size of a baseball forms in my throat keeping me from speaking or swallowing or breathing. My thoughts jumble together, not being able to put the person in front of me with the words coming out of his mouth.

David leans forward, his brow creased with worry. "Billy, are you okay? If you want me to go, I can... I just needed to see you."

I'm finally able to speak. "No, that's okay. I just didn't recognize you. You're all grown up, and I wasn't expecting you and no, you don't need to go. How ya doin' little bro?"

David's eyes fill with tears. He shakes his head to compose himself. "Well, I'm not sure how I'm doing. When I set out to find you, I certainly didn't expect it to be in here. You haven't been easy to track down."

"Well, now ya know where I am. I ain't going anywhere soon." I force a laugh. "Why ya lookin' for me? How'd ya find me?"

"It's been a long time. You dropped off the face of the earth, and I wanted to see you, see how you were, find out what's gone on in your life, and why you disappeared. I eventually was able to get in touch with your son, Robby, and he told me you were here. Why are you here?"

I can't believe this man is David, with his thinning blond hair, his weathered and tanned face, his sad eyes. I can't find the little boy in him anymore. I can't even remember the last time I saw my brother.

"Hey, when's the last time we saw each other? I can't seem to remember."

David half-laughs, half-sneers. "Not surprising. You were drunk or high out of your mind. You showed up at my college dorm room, causing a huge scene. I took you to my room to stay until you sobered up, but you snuck off in the night with all my money. Let's see, that was what? 1995? So, it's been twelve years. I started trying to get in touch with you about a year ago... but, as I said, you haven't been easy to find."

I remember bits and pieces of the scene David describes. Mostly, I remember waking up in my brother's room, unsure of where I was, but knowing I needed a hit. I had the shakes and knew before long I'd be hurting badly. I remember seeing my brother lying there, sleeping so peacefully on the floor next to the bed he had given up for me. I remember wishing I wasn't about to walk out again on the one person I still loved in the world, wishing I wasn't going to violate him, too, by stealing from him. I sought David out as an attempt to save my own life. I was so strung out and lost; I was ready to end it all. I'm not sure if I told David this, but showing up at his college was my attempt at sparing my own life, if only for another couple of hours. I also remember knowing, as I slipped the money out of his wallet and snuck out of the room, that I wouldn't be seeing him again. I couldn't stand to see his disappointment at who I'd become. I couldn't bear to be another person on the list of people that had let him down.

My shoulders tighten with the memories. "Hey, listen, I'm sorry about that...."

"About which, taking my money? Leaving me not knowing if you went off and killed yourself somewhere, like you were talking about? Not being in contact for the past twelve years? Which are you sorry about?" David raises his voice, which makes the guard announce over the loudspeaker for all visitors to keep their voices down.

"About all of it... I was kind of... I mean, I am kind of a mess." I clear my throat. "So, I'm sorry. Just didn't want you to be brought into it."

"That should've been my choice. You're my brother. We're supposed to stick together, right?"

"Yeah, I guess." I look away from David's piercing stare. "So, enough about me...tell me about you. What'cha been doing these past twelve years?"

"Well, let's see... the quick version so we can get back to you is... finished college, went to law school, became an attorney, got married, just had a baby. Now, why are you in here?"

"Wow...my bro's a lawyer? What kinda lawyer? Can you help get me outta here?" I laugh.

"Sorry, I'm not a criminal lawyer. I work as a corporate attorney—you know figuring out how the rich can keep their money in a legal way. So...about you?" He leans closer, resting his chin on his hand.

"Who'd you marry? Anyone I know? And your kid— how old's your kid?"

"I married a woman named Rachel—we met in law school. My son is seven months old. His name's Brandon... Brandon William Dunkin." David looks away. "So, anyway... no more about me. What happened? Why are you here?"

God, I don't want to have this conversation. I don't want to look in his eyes and tell him what a fuck-up I am. "A lot of things, really. Like I said, my life's been a mess. I got in with the wrong crowd, started doing the wrong things, ending up in the wrong places... like here. Not much more to it than that."

David raises his eyebrows and sits back in the chair. "I've done some checking since I found out you were here. Armed robbery isn't just ending up in the wrong place at the wrong time. That's pretty serious stuff."

"Yeah, I know. Hey, are you going to be in town long?"

"For a week or so. I want to see you some more, maybe meet some of your kids. Sounds like you have a baseball team of them scattered around. Why?"

I study my hands, not willing to meet his eye. "Some more stuff's going to be coming out about me soon, and I don't want you to get too upset. I was um...I was brought up on some new charges that'll probably be all over the news by lunchtime today. I just want you to know. I don't know." I try to swallow the lump in my throat. "I wish you'd leave town and never look back. Just pretend I died that night because nothing good is going to come outta you finding me again. It's only going to hurt you more to know all this ... to see me in here...to hear what they're going to be saying about me. I'm not the person I used to be."

"Neither am I. For instance, twelve years ago, I did pretend you died and closed the door on you and the rest of my past. I let go of everything with Mom, with Dad, with you leaving. I locked it up and put it on a shelf tucked neatly away in the back of my mind. I stayed in touch with Mary and her family, and they were all I needed. My life's been good, and everything's been going just the way I wanted it to." David's eyes glisten. He clears his throat several times and loosens his tie.

"But then, recently, since I've had Brandon, I don't know...the past is coming back to me and I've been trying to make sense of it. Part of making sense of it involves you because you were the only other person there. You lived it with me. So, I needed to find you. I need to be able to talk through some of this with you. Sometimes I hold Brandon, and I love him so much. Then I'm struck with this overwhelming fear of what happens if I end up like Dad? What if there's this violent, horrible person in me that could hurt this little boy I love so much? Is it possible that Dad loved us, like I love Brandon, yet still hurt us so badly?" David rubs his forehead. "So, anyway I just needed to talk to you and figure some of this out. It keeps me up at night."

"Visiting time is over in one minute..." a voice announces through the phone line.

I'm not sure how to respond. I want David to leave and never come back. I can't let him down again and don't want him to learn of my newest charge. I want to say something, anything, that will make him walk away without regret. Yet, at the same time, I want to reach through the glass and take my brother in my arms like I used to do when we were small. I want to tell him I know what it's like to be kept awake at night by things on your mind.

"David, you don't have to worry about becoming Dad, because that fell to me. I am him. You'll see what I mean if you stick around. Watch the noon news and then leave. Just put that box up on the shelf in your mind and go take care of your wife and kid. You aren't him—I am."

287

I put the phone down, signal for the guard, and stroll away without looking back, even though I desperately want to see my brother one last time before he certainly walks away for good.

D o you remember the stories we read about kings, queens, princes, and princesses in their giant castles? Do you know that you were always my little prince? Do you know how proud I always was of you for being so brave and for being such a good big brother? Do you know how special you were to me? Do you know how sorry I am about the way things turned out? I wish I could have protected you from all that you had to see, hear, and live through. I wish I could go back in time and be as brave as the queens always were in the stories we read. I wish I could return to our past and protect you from all the pain you had to experience. I'm sorry I left you. I'm sorry you blame yourself. Please know that no matter what your heart and mind scream out to you, it is not your fault. I'm sorry I wasn't strong enough to leave. I'm sorry I let my fear dictate my choices and keep me from doing the right thing. Please don't let your fear hold you prisoner, as it did me.

KENDRA

18 YEARS, 11 MONTHS, 23 DAYS AFTER
JANUARY 31, 2008

TOM has the car warmed up and waiting for me in the driveway. My breath freezes in my throat as I head out the front door and adjust to the shock of the icy air. This has been one of the coldest January's I can remember. Thankfully, Tom got an early start on shoveling, clearing the sidewalk and driveway of the eight inches of snow that fell over the last day. The clouds are still blackened with yet another round to come.

"You ready for this?" Tom asks as I shut the door to the frigid air.

I have no idea what the real answer to that question is. If the question is…am I ready to face the living, breathing human being responsible for taking my daughter's life, who witnessed her last breath? Then my answer is a definitive no. Am I ready for justice to finally be served on Chelsea's behalf? Absolutely.

Instead of asking for further clarification, I simply state, "I guess—we'll see."

As we drive out of our neighborhood, I realize school must be canceled for the day. Children are out everywhere—sledding, building snowmen, making snow angels, pelting each other with snowballs. As we pull to the last stop sign in our neighborhood, I notice a young girl and a younger boy building a fort made of snow in their front yard. A woman, probably their mother, stands by, snapping pictures of their fun.

I'm sucked into memories of Chelsea and Kent enjoying their snow days so many years ago. They'd be up before the sun, waiting for the news to announce the cancellation for the day. Once their school's name appeared on the TV screen, their whoops and hollers would begin. They'd start planning their day's adventures before I finished my first cup of coffee. Their plans always included trying to build the biggest family of snowmen on the block, a fort for each of them to hide in as they bombarded each other with snowballs, snow angels to decorate the yard, and steaming cups of hot chocolate, with lots of marshmallows, for the breaks in between.

It used to be so frustrating for school to be canceled because it meant either Tom or I had to take the day off work. Usually, the job fell to me, despite the countless arguments with Tom about it being his turn. Now I would give anything to be able to have a day with my children doing nothing but watching them play, listening to them laugh, and taking in their happi-

291

ness. I would give up everything in my life—my home, my job, my friends, my health—to be able to go back in time and savor one more snow day with both of my children.

Lost in thought, I don't hear Tom talking to me until he pats my hand that's balled into a fist on my leg. I snap back to the present, realizing we're over half-way to the courthouse.

"I asked if Kent was coming today. Did you talk to him this morning?" Tom asks, withdrawing his hand from mine when I refuse to respond to his touch.

"I talked to him yesterday but forgot to call this morning. He said he'd try to make it," I pause. "I'm sure he'll be there. He wouldn't miss this."

"Let's hope he has enough sense to show. We really need to all be there to see this through to the end. We need the judge to see our family, so he knows whose lives William's actions destroyed," Tom adds.

Tom's voice is heavy with disappointment, as it always is when Kent's name comes up. I feel it too, but I hide it better than Tom ever does. I try to keep my worries from Kent because every time I mention them, he becomes vacant and further shuts me out of his life. He leaves phone calls un-returned, Sunday dinners unattended, and disappears from our lives until I'm able to track him down and guilt him into further contact. Will the judge take one look at us and see that we're no longer really a family, even though we can sit next to each other, shedding tears over all we've lost?

I don't even know if Kent considers our lack of a relationship a "loss" since it's all he's known for most of his life.

William Dunkin stole what our family should've been, by taking Chelsea. I have many friends with children in their late twenties, like Kent. Many of them are married with children and on their way to successful careers. I overhear colleagues' stories of spending the weekend with their grandchildren and the funny things they said or did. The life they talk about is supposed to be mine. It would've been had I not been robbed of it.

Chelsea would probably be married by now with a couple of children, like Nicole. Tom and I would have the kids over all the time for sleepovers and take them on family trips to Disney World or the beach. I would help my daughter through the frustrations of being a mother and the demands of managing a family. I would have been able to watch my daughter mature alongside my grandchildren, as she learned about life through her children's experiences.

If Chelsea hadn't been murdered, Kent would be completely different now, too. Instead of working at a bar, he'd have a day job probably as an engineer or a doctor. He'd have a wife, or at least a girlfriend he wasn't ashamed to bring around—one he met somewhere other than the bar. He'd stop over "just because," without me begging and pleading. He and Chelsea would be close as they were before Chels hit her teenage years. They'd laugh at their childhood memories—trips we took as a family, stupid parenting decisions Tom and I made, secrets they'd kept hidden from us throughout the years. If Chelsea hadn't been stolen from us, Kent would've had a childhood with parents who weren't so scarred by their own pain that we forgot he needed us. William stole our entire family's future. I have nothing but hatred for the man whose face I'm about to see. I despise what he's done to our family.

As we pull into the parking lot, Tom says, "Well, no surprise...don't see Kent's car. Should we wait for him or go on in?"

I look at the clock and see it is already quarter-til ten.

"We need to go in since we've only got fifteen minutes. He'll find us," I say, sounding much surer of myself than I am. How can he find us when he is so lost, even to himself?

*　　*　　*

TOM

As we walk into the courthouse, I reach for Kendra's arm, not as a measure of affection, but one of desperation. My legs can't carry me without the support of Kendra's strength and rage to lead the way. In our silent march down the snowy sidewalks towards the courthouse, I retreat mentally, counting each step, knowing each takes me one step closer to the beginning of the end of this nightmare. The one that started eighteen years, eleven months, twenty-two days, seven hours, and forty-six minutes ago. How much more time will pass before it is truly over? Will it ever really be over for Kendra and me?

Today is just the first step in the long process to come. Mr. Lockhart, the prosecutor, explained that the whole ordeal could take years, and after today, a court date will be set for William if he pleads not guilty. The prosecutor also explained that defense attorneys are masters at getting one continuance after another, which can delay the process by a year or more. I can't wait that long to know the fate of my daughter's killer.

Now that everything has been brought back to the surface and my emotions are again raw, every additional minute of waiting for that next step feels like an eternity. We now know who took Chelsea's life, but we still don't know why. For every small question answered, it's replaced by a million new ones.

Mr. Lockhart has spent numerous hours with us in the past four and a half months, explaining each step and what to expect. Today, William will be presented to the court via satellite from the jail. The thought of seeing his face, hearing his voice, looking into the last eyes my daughter saw, shakes me to the core. Will I be able to see the reflection of my daughter's last moments if I peer closely enough into his eyes?

We enter the already full courtroom with at least fifty people already filling the seats. Thankfully, the first row is reserved for us, or else we wouldn't have a place to sit. Nicole is already sitting on the bench, awaiting our arrival. I peruse the sea of faces for Kent, but he's nowhere to be found. The section reserved for media personnel is filled to capacity, leaving standing-room-only for several of the reporters. They'll be watching our every move, searching us for a show of sadness or a posture of hatred that they can report to their followers.

I'm thankful to the media for the job they've done throughout the years to keep Chelsea's face in the news, her unsolved murder in the minds of the people watching or reading. Every year, the local paper ran a story on February 8th, re-hashing the details and asking for information to help find Chelsea's killer. I always dreaded seeing the front page of the paper or tuning in to the local news stations that day as my daughter's face would be there smiling at me from beyond the grave. Each year I would vow to avoid the media. I would swear to myself, as I'd wander down the often snow-covered driveway towards the newspaper, that this year, I would have the strength to throw it, unopened, into the trash.

During year thirteen, I went the longest without actually opening the paper—twelve hours and five minutes. I'd gotten the paper at five after six in the morning. Instead of putting it in the trash can as I'd intended, I left it in its wrapper and laid it on the kitchen table. Throughout the workday, my mind kept returning to it, wondering if my daughter's face looked any different, if the author of this year's article managed to write anything that would evoke a long-buried memory for someone reading it. Or, if this would be the year that Chelsea's killer felt overwhelming remorse for his actions and, after seeing her again, would come forward and confess. By the time I got home from work, my heart was pounding in anticipation of what the words in the article might hold. Tracking muddy footprints through the house and leaving my wool coat on, I headed to the table. Feeling the pull of the information held within, and the hope it could bring, I took the paper out of its wrapper and stared into the smiling face of my daughter, forever seventeen. It was the same picture we had framed and sitting on the end table in our living room but, for some reason, the one in black and white hurt so much more to see. The face smiling back at us from the living room, made me think of spring, sunshine, and flowers blooming—of memories. The one in the paper made me think of screaming, pain, loss, a future with no new memories to be created. My beautiful daughter's picture should not be studied by every person with the fifty cents to buy a paper. It should be reserved for the ones who loved her, who remembered her. The fact that thousands of people held her picture in their hands each year made me feel as if I had to share so much of my daughter with so many people, there was nothing left that belonged to me alone.

After reading the article, I realized that again, the same words were used by a different author. No new chapter had been added—the ending was still the same with no happily ever after offered. My despair was always the greatest each year from the time of the article through the first promise of spring, when I would be forced to accept that another year had passed without Chelsea and without answers.

I step towards Nicole and notice the reporters scribbling furiously on their notepads, yet I have no idea what they are observing that's noteworthy. Are they noting the way the grief of the last eighteen years is etched into each line on our faces? Are they remarking on how there's no light left in us even though everyone expects us to feel relief?

I hug Nicole tightly before sitting down—the scent of lilacs envelops me. I close my eyes and hold her closely, trying to let myself believe, just for a moment, that it's Chelsea standing in my embrace. That the scent filling me is her future.

*   *   *

NICOLE

The air in the room changes before I'm aware that Tom

and Kendra have arrived. It's like a jolt of electricity has been sent throughout the courtroom causing everyone to become restless, stir in their seats, and lower their already hushed voices. I stand so they can easily find me, rather than get lost in the crowd. There is raw pain on their faces—pain they have learned to cover up so well over the past eighteen and a half years, but now brought fresh to the surface again. Since William was caught, they both look like they've aged twenty years. I wonder if people see the same when they look at me, although my face could never show the depth of the pain raging in my battered soul. When Tom reaches me, he practically falls into my embrace and clings to me as though I'm his only hope of making it through today without drowning in a sea of emotion, anger, and uncertainty. I try to absorb some of his pain to ease his load, but I can't because there's no room left for any but my own.

"Thanks for saving us seats, honey. You look beautiful," Kendra says, taking my hand as we sit.

"Thanks, Kendra. I saved enough room for Kent too," I pause. "Is he coming?"

"He said he'd be here..." Kendra's voice trails off as she scans the courtroom, her eyes locking on the monitor at the front. "Is that where we'll see him?"

"I think so," I answer as the screen changes from black to a brilliant blue, indicating that someone has turned on the monitor.

Within seconds, the bailiff's voice booms, "All rise for the honorable Judge MacAfee."

Everyone in the packed room rises to their feet, sitting

298

again once the judge is seated at the bench.

"The only matter set before the court today is the arraignment of William Lee Dunkin," the judge pauses as the monitor flashes to life with the faces of William and his attorney. Kendra gasps at the sight of William. She grasps my hand firmly, seemingly trying to anchor herself to the bench. Tom stares, unblinking, at the screen.

"Appearing via satellite for today's proceedings are William Lee Dunkin and legal counsel, Ron Chesterfield. Mr. Chesterfield, is the feed coming through alright on your end?" Judge MacAfee inquires.

"Yes, your honor."

I study the man before me. William seems much older than his forty-one years. I suppose that spending as much time in jail as he has over the years, ages a man. I saw his face in the paper, but seeing him alive and breathing right in front of me is different. He keeps his eyes lowered, not once looking into the camera that's broadcasting his every move to a courtroom full of people. Each time he makes the smallest move, like blink or tilt his head, shivers race up my spine.

"Thank you, Mr. Chesterfield. We will proceed then in the matter of the State of Indiana versus William Lee Dunkin," the judge pauses, shuffling the papers in front of him. "Mr. Dunkin, you are hereby charged with one count of aggravated murder, one count of murder, and one count of forcible rape, all of which are first-degree felony convictions. How do you plead on the charges set forth by this court?"

"Not guilty on all counts, your honor," Mr. Chesterfield

speaks for his client, who does not acknowledge in any way that he even heard the judge's voice.

I try to will him to look into the camera from where I sit. I firmly believe the eyes are a window into the soul and if I could look into William's, only for an instant, I could gauge whether there's any sorrow there for his actions. I would be able to see if he wears the guilt of Chelsea's murder like a chain around his heart. I would be able to discern, with one simple gaze, whether there's any soul left in him. That, he refuses to give though.

"On the matter of bail, the court has determined that due to the nature of the crimes with which Mr. Dunkin has been charged, the fact that he's evaded law enforcement for almost nineteen years on these charges, and the fact that he has no verified home address at this time, making him a flight risk, bail will be set at one million dollars," Judge MacAfee states. "The grand jury hearing has been scheduled for February 8, 2008. Anything further, Mr. Chesterfield?"

"No, Your Honor," Mr. Chesterfield speaks from beyond with a glance towards his client.

Judge MacAfee pounds his gavel and announces the adjournment of court as the screen on the monitor returns to its previous blue. As soon as the judge exits the courtroom, the life returns to it, with voices buzzing throughout.

It's hard to breathe. My lungs feel constricted with the weight of the world. Kendra sniffles, and I turn to her. Tears stream down her cheeks, dripping onto the lapel of her crisp, blue suit. Sensing my gaze, Kendra leans into me, resting her wet cheek on my head.

"I didn't think this would be so hard," Kendra says through her tears. "I didn't realize that seeing him would hurt this badly, would make me so angry."

"I know. It all feels raw—like it just happened yesterday, doesn't it?" I add. "I just want to know why."

Kendra straightens, wiping the tears from her face. "I don't even care why anymore. For years, that's what I wanted to know, but it doesn't even matter to me now. All that matters is that he pays for what he stole from us. He needs to pay for the pain he caused my baby. I'll do whatever I can to make sure he feels the same loss we have." The sadness in Kendra has been replaced by pure rage, each line around her eyes and mouth hardened with it.

I don't know what to say to help lessen her anger. I turn to Tom, hoping to get a response from him that helps. He hasn't moved from the position he's been sitting in, throughout court. He sits dazed, staring at the blue screen in the front of the room.

"Tom, you okay?" Kendra asks. When he doesn't respond, she gently squeezes his hand and asks again.

Tom startles back to the courtroom. "Yeah. I'm okay, just surprised. He's just a man. A man like I could see anywhere I go in this town—the bank, the grocery, church." Tom pauses. "I'm shocked that he's not the monster I've pictured in my mind over the years. He's just a man."

"He is a monster, regardless of what he looks like. He's the monster that destroyed our family. He may appear normal on the outside, but inside he's that monster," Kendra speaks too loudly, causing those exiting the courtroom to stop, listening in

301

on our conversation.

"Kendra, I know what he did. I'm just saying, we don't know. He's a man that looks like he's been through his fair share of hardships over the years. I guess I expected something different."

Kendra stands with her clenched hands on her hips. "I'll meet you at the car. The difference between us is that I could care less about what made him kill our daughter. The fact that he did is enough—the why simply doesn't matter."

Kendra pushes through the crowd at the door; her heels echo down the hallway as she makes her escape. Again, I'm unsure of what to do or say. I haven't even had the chance to sort through my own mixed feelings, let alone know how to intervene in the confusion between Tom and Kendra. I understand Kendra's rage, but I also have been filled with Tom's questions throughout the years.

I stand, holding out my hand for Tom. "Let's go. I'll walk with you to the car."

Tom pauses before standing and says, "Nicole, he may have killed my daughter, but he's not a monster—he's just a man." The shock of this epiphany is displayed through Tom's every gesture and facial expression.

Hand in hand, we make our way through the courtroom, the crowded hallway, and out into the snow, heading towards Tom's car.

* * *

KENT

The ringing phone rouses me from sleep. I reach over to check the time. Eleven twenty-five in the morning. As I hear my mother's voice echo through the apartment from the answering machine, I put the pillow over my head, attempting to block it out. My elbow bumps into a person in my bed. A woman is lying next to me; her blond hair spills over the pillow. I try to remember her name or where I picked her up, but last night is a total fog. I remember leaving work early and having a few shots in the crowded bar. I remember getting into my car, thinking I was heading home, but I must have made a couple more stops along the way. The woman lying naked next to me must have come from one of those stops.

She opens her eyes, seeming to sense me watching her.

"Hey, you," she says and reaches out to touch my arm.

"Hey," I say, letting my eyes wander. She's quite sexy, and I'm sure I must have had a good time with her. I feel myself getting aroused and pull her to me, deciding names don't much matter.

Things are quickly heating up when the phone rings again. My mother's voice echoes throughout the apartment.

"Hang on a minute. If I don't answer her, she'll keep calling until I do or, worse yet, show up at the door."

I grab the phone and say an abrupt hello to let my mother know exactly what an interruption she's being. The nameless woman runs her hands up and down my body, stopping at all the right places. I'm thoroughly enjoying it until I hear my mother's voice.

303

"Where the hell were you today?" she screams.

"I, uh, had to work late last night and am just waking up." I try to stall to figure out why she sounds so enraged. The mystery woman is still caressing me, and I want nothing more than to hurry this call so my wonderful wake-up can continue.

"Just waking up. For God's sake, Kent! Did you totally forget what today was even though I've called you and reminded you every day for a week now?" Mom yells, her voice cracking with anger.

The realization finally hits me, and I stand, pushing the clinging woman behind me, away. "Oh, God, Mom. I'm sorry. I forgot," I stammer. "As I said, I had to work late last night and forgot to set my alarm."

"Yeah, right. You worked late—just like you always say. Tell the truth, you got drunk again, have a hangover, and wouldn't have heard the alarm even if you did set it," Kendra rages. "Enough with your excuses. You knew how important it was to have you there. Again, we don't even show up on your radar." The truth of her words sting. I didn't realize she knew me so well.

I interrupt. "Look, I'm sorry. You know I wanted to be there. What happened?" The nameless woman stands in front of me, kissing my neck, and pushing her body against mine, trying to distract me from my obvious tension.

"If you really gave a damn about what happened, you would've been there. Obviously, your sister and your parents don't mean anything to you as long as you have your alcohol and women." My mother slams down the phone.

I throw the phone at the wall across the room, causing

the woman to take a step back.

"C'mon...let's go back to bed. I'll take your mind off everything for a bit," she says as she pulls me back towards it.

I give her a slight push, and she falls back onto the bed.

"You need to go." I pick up her clothes from the floor, thrusting them towards her. She sits there stunned, just looking at me.

Suddenly I'm enraged. "Get the hell out...okay? I want you to leave." I jerk her by the arm to a standing position, stuffing her pile of clothes in her arms.

She slowly starts to get dressed as tears fill her eyes. I hate that I'm taking this out on some stranger who doesn't deserve my anger.

"Look, I'm sorry. I need you to leave, okay. I have some things I need to deal with," I say more calmly.

She doesn't say a word; rather gets dressed and calmly walks to the door. "Hope you had a good time last night..." she pauses. "And for the record, my name's Christy." She slams the door shut behind her.

I sit on the sofa and bury my face in my hands. I should go after her. I don't know if she has a car or a way home. I can't remember if I drove her here or not. I don't even know if she really knows where she is. I can't make myself go, though. The realization of screwing up, yet again, with my parents hits me like a two by four upside the head. The weeks' worth of phone calls from Mom flood my mind. Everything she said while begging me to go to court...*we need to present a unified front... to honor Chelsea...to show her killer who he hurt by taking her...* are

305

pounding against my already aching head.

I start laughing and crying at the same time. I grab the dirty dishes from the coffee table and throw them against the door Christy just closed.

"Unified front," I scream as two-day-old coffee and toast splatter to the floor.

As I recall the last eighteen and a half years, I conclude that any phrase including the word *unified* to describe my family, since Chelsea's death, is laughable. There's nothing unified about our family without the glue of Chelsea to hold us together. My father lost in his own mind. My mother lost in her work and church activities. Me lost in my booze and women. How could three people so absorbed by their own worlds even pretend to put up a unified front? We could sit together on a bench, hold hands, and cry together, but anyone watching closely would be able to see the cracks in our facade.

I'm relieved that Chelsea's killer has been caught, but it doesn't change a damn thing about our lives. Chelsea is still dead. My relationship with my parents is still beyond repair. The past years full of hurt, shame, loss, and embarrassment still exist. Catching Chelsea's killer doesn't suddenly undo the years of suffering. My mother seems to think everything will be reversed if the killer is punished.

I don't give a damn that I wasn't there to paint the pretty picture of my family that Mom wants to portray to the world. I honestly don't know what purpose it serves to have everyone look at us and say, "Oh, how sad for them," as though having someone say it legitimizes our pain. Our pain isn't only the loss of Chelsea; for someone to truly understand its depths, they would have had to walk alongside our family for the past eighteen and a half years. It's not only William Dunkin that stole our picture-perfect family. We each played a part in giving it away.

BILLY

19 YEARS, 8 MONTHS, 9 DAYS AFTER
OCTOBER 17, 2008

IT'S been a week since I've been able to sleep or eat, knowing the trial is scheduled to begin tomorrow. I've had numerous conversations with my attorney, Ron Chesterfield, in the past year, but still don't feel ready. Since the charges were filed, I've been on an emotional rollercoaster with no drugs or alcohol to numb my pain or fog my memories. I read the papers and watched the news reports about my arrest and know the public wants me to burn for killing Chelsea. I read the quotes in the paper from Chelsea's mother, saying she'll spend every bit of energy she has, to see me pay for my crimes. What I wish I could tell them all is that I've paid every day of my life and will continue to do so until I take my last breath.

Initially, the prosecutor looked at the legalities of seeking the death penalty. Oddly enough, when I contemplate the possibility, the only thing I feel is relief. I'm not afraid of death in the least; in fact, I've spent most of my life trying to find it. I've looked it square in the face and gazed into its sorrowful eyes. I've smelled death and breathed in its scent of rotting flesh, broken dreams, and bitter regrets. I've tasted death's burn down my throat, searing my lungs. I've heard death's screams—angry, scared, and lost. I've felt death stealing one's last breath. Death is an old friend. I've relived the experience day after day, night after sleepless night. I do not fear death's finality. I fear re-living death over and over as I've done now for so many years.

Mr. Chesterfield told me that after researching, the prosecutor could not seek the death penalty because he had to go by the laws in place when the crime was committed—meaning the maximum sentence I face on the charges is twenty-five years. He didn't understand the reason for my tears as I sat there listening to him. Ron didn't know what to do with the tears and the silence, so he simply kept telling me it was good news. I know better, though. The only thing that has gotten me through many of my days and nights in jail is the hope that there'd be an end in sight. I was hoping death would be that end because it's the one I truly deserve.

Thinking of sitting in a courtroom full of angry glares boring into my soul, hearing every detail of that day so many years ago, finding out every specific about the girl whose life I took, sickens me. I run to the toilet to throw up, wishing I could void myself of my past the same way my body rids itself of food.

I'm rinsing out my mouth when the guard calls, "Dunkin, visitor."

I wipe my mouth on my sleeve and turn in shock towards the officer at my cell door. "For me?"

"No, dumbass, for your roommate with the last name Dunkin," the guard says with a sneer as I move into position to be handcuffed before the door is opened.

The last visitor I had was David, and as I expected, the murder charges kept him away. I can't blame him for wanting nothing more to do with me. If the roles were reversed and I had David's life, I would've written off my bum of a brother a long time ago. David has to be reminded of our father every time he thinks of me, and neither one of us wants to think about him.

The guard leads me to the visiting area, and I sit behind the glass in the first seat. Within seconds, my visitor is buzzed in. I'm surprised to see my brother's solemn face as he takes his seat. David has aged tremendously in the year since I last saw him. The lines around his mouth and eyes seem to spell out pain or shame; I can't tell which.

I pick up the phone, but David hesitates a moment before lifting his handset, looking intently at me. Finally, he speaks.

"Billy. How are you?" His voice has no life left in it.

"I'm okay. The question is, how are you? You look like you've been through a war lately." I chuckle, trying to lessen the tension.

"Hmm...You could say that. I came here for a couple of reasons. First things first," he pauses. "Dad's dead."

Before I even process the information, I say, "Finally."

David continues without commenting on my snide remark. "He died about a month and a half ago. He had a massive heart attack and died in bed. The mailman called the police after noticing he hadn't gotten his mail for over a week."

A heart attack in his sleep was much too painless of a way for our father to die. He deserved pure agony as he faced death's door. He deserved the suffering he dished out to us over the years.

"Anyway, since you're in here and I'm his only other living relative, I got to do the honors of dealing with his estate, which trust me, has been hell. He didn't have much, but it was up to me to clean out his apartment, settle all of his affairs, plan his funeral."

"You're a bigger man than I am because I wouldn't have done it. I would've left it all there for someone else to deal with, let him be buried in a little wooden box in a pauper's graveyard somewhere," I say, anger at our father pumping through my veins, straight to my heart.

"Yeah, I know, and maybe it's what he deserved, but I couldn't do it. I guess I had questions I was hoping I'd find answers to that would give me some peace." David clears his throat. "Anyway, I ended up having him cremated. I haven't decided what to do with his ashes."

I catch myself laughing before I stop to consider how it will come across to my brother. "How ironic, both our parents ended up a pile of ash. Too bad Mom had to feel herself burning, and Dad didn't."

"I know you've got a lot of anger towards Dad and so

do I, but he's dead now. The suffering he caused everyone is over. Like you, I wished for years that he could've died a slow, painful death and experienced half of the misery we felt, but that's not how it happened. I guess we don't get to play God. Maybe that's a good thing."

"And seeing as how Dad got to live a long life and die peacefully in his sleep, maybe God isn't such a God of justice after all." I shake my head.

"Anyway, we don't have time to debate right now, but I wanted to let you know. I found some things when I was cleaning out his apartment—letters he'd written to us over the years while he was locked up. Prison seems to have changed him in some good ways. Having all of that time to think made him realize how badly he'd screwed everything up with us." David looks down and continues to speak, refusing eye contact with me. "He tried to call me several times over the years, but I never returned his calls. Every time I knew he found me, I'd change my number. Each time, he'd track me down again, and I'd go through the same routine of becoming untraceable for a while. I wonder now if I should've called him to see what he had to say."

I slam my fist on the table. "Hell no, you shouldn't have called him. He killed our mother. He beat us as though we were nothing more than piles of trash. He tried to kill me too." The guard reminds me over the loudspeaker to keep my voice down. "Sorry, but a few years to think and realize you were an asshole that destroyed everyone in your life, doesn't mean he gets automatic forgiveness."

"You need to apply your logic to your own situation

and acknowledge what you've done to your family, to that girl. If we all followed your line of thinking, I definitely shouldn't be sitting here with you." David's words sting to the point that I'm speechless.

"I'll hold onto the letters for you in case you decide someday that you want them. He died a very lonely, old man."

"He deserved to die a lonely, *young* man," I add. "He had no one to blame for being alone other than himself."

David clears his throat. "We only have a couple of minutes left. The other reason I came is that I've been following your case and I want you to get a new attorney."

"Easier said than done, bro. When you got nothin', you get who they give you," I say.

"That's why I wanted to talk to you. Dad had some money tucked away, about twenty thousand dollars. He left it to us. I've used it to retain a real attorney for you, one who'll do a good job," David speaks without making eye contact.

"I don't want his money. I'll make do on my own with the attorney I got," I shout. "How can you even suggest I use his money? What the hell's wrong with you?"

David's face hardens, and he leans forward, stopping only inches from the glass. "No, what the hell's wrong with you? You're facing murder charges and a long time behind bars. Dad didn't do much for us but cause us pain. Hell, if it weren't for him, you probably wouldn't even be here right now. The least we can do is put his money to good use by getting you a good defense attorney. He never helped you before; let his money help you."

I sit there stunned beyond words. I want to stand up and walk away, pretending we never had this conversation.

"Just think about it, Billy. That's all I'm asking. I've already spoken with a friend of mine from law school that practices criminal law. He's willing to take your case at a drastically reduced rate. I know you're not up on these matters, but your defense is going to cost a lot more than what Dad left us—that's just a drop in the bucket. I'm willing to cover anything above and beyond what he left."

My entire body shakes with rage. "I don't want you doing that for me. I'm not your problem. You need to spend your hard-earned money on your wife and kid, save for college or a bigger house or something. Hell, add the twenty grand from Dad to it, and you'll have a nice little chunk right off the bat," I say.

"Just stop and listen..." David says.

"No, you listen. It doesn't matter how much money you spend on fancy attorneys to represent me; I'm going down. I'm going to be locked up for a long time. Put your money to better use than me. Spending it on me is like throwing it away. Give it to Brandon; tell him it's a gift from his waste of an uncle if it makes you feel better. Use it where it'll make a difference, cause here it won't." Tears burn and threaten to fall, but I refuse to release them.

"Think about it, okay? The attorney, Charles McCabe, is going to stop by this afternoon and say he's your new counsel. If you decide to take me up on my offer, then meet with him; otherwise, don't, and stick with Mr. Chesterfield. I've already paid him his retainer," David says.

"Get your money back, David. I'm not gonna change my mind," I speak firmly.

"Billy, your trial is slated to begin tomorrow; this is your only chance to change your mind," David pauses as his eyes fill with tears. "Regardless of what you've done, I love you. You're my brother, and nothing will change that. I haven't asked you for anything over the years, but I'm asking you for this. Please do this for me... and for Mom. It's what she would've wanted."

The buzzer sounds and the phones go dead before I have a chance to respond. I'm glad because I don't think I can speak past the lump in my throat. Any words spoken would be mixed with tears and grief.

My emotions are on overload. How can I possibly deny my brother the one request he's made of me in his adult life? How can I take money from the man who ruined our lives, who killed our mom? Wouldn't that be a form of forgiveness, which certainly does not reflect the condition of my heart? How could I possibly know what my mother would want—she wouldn't want me to be here in the first place? I wouldn't be in this position had things turned out differently. The questions pound inside my head, every thought crashing into the next conflicting one. The entire afternoon, my brain is assaulted with questions for which I have no answers.

For the second time today, I hear the guard call my name. "Dunkin, your new savior's here to see you."

My heart throbs as though it's going to beat its way right through my chest. I'm getting ready to tell the guard to send him away when suddenly everything within me grows still—the racing thoughts calm, my heart rate slows and, as clear as I can see the bars in front of me, I hear my mother's voice.

Go, Billy. For me, please go. It's not too late... The voice fades as quickly as it came.

Despite the sweat which has broken out across my brow, I feel an overwhelming sense of peace as I get into position to take the walk down the hallway, to meet my new attorney.

Tom

KENDRA yells from downstairs as I'm knotting my tie.

"I'll be down in a second; let me finish my tie," I shout in her direction.

She yells again, and I'm immediately frustrated by her impatience. I'm anxious to get this over with too, but I'm not taking it out on her. I give myself a once-over in the mirror, deciding I look presentable enough in my gray suit, maroon and gray paisley tie, and crisply pressed, white button-down.

I'm almost to the bottom of the stairs when I realize that Kendra isn't yelling at me, but at whoever has the misfortune of being on the other end of the phone line.

"What in the hell do you mean, it's been postponed?"

Kendra pauses. "That's not a choice. Do you understand me? We're ready now. We've waited long enough already."

I ask who she's talking to, but rather than answering, she thrusts the phone at me and runs out of the room.

"Um...hello?" I say not knowing who to expect on the other end.

"Hi, Tom. It's Justin Lockhart. I was trying to explain to Kendra that the trial's been postponed. Mr. Dunkin has obtained new counsel who needs time to review the case prior to moving forward."

I'm speechless, now understanding where my wife's wrath originated this time.

"Tom?" Justin says.

"Yeah, I'm here. Wow! Postponed?" I pause and start pacing. "Do you know when the new court date will be yet? It shouldn't take long, right?"

"We should know within the next month or so when the new trial is scheduled; but, I have to warn you, sometimes attorneys find reasons to delay for a long time. So, even if we get a new date, it doesn't mean it's set in stone," Justin explains. "I know Kendra's upset, but I tried to be open and up-front with you both from the beginning so we wouldn't be caught off guard by delays. Trust me; it's frustrating for me too."

"Yes, you've explained all of this; we still didn't expect it. We're ready to have this trial over and done with."

"I'm very sorry about this," Justin says. "Listen, I've gotta run, but I wanted to personally call you to let you know. I'll have my secretary contact you as soon as we've got a new date, and I'll be in touch."

The phone clicks in my ear as I'm saying goodbye. I hold it, listening to the dial tone, unsure of how to approach Kendra with this. I know the delay is beyond everyone's control. I also know that it will be completely unacceptable for Kendra. She's been counting down the days for this trial to start since we first learned of it after the Grand Jury Indictment on February eighth. She's spent eight long months preparing herself for what she'd hear in the courtroom, for being forced to re-live Chelsea's disappearance and murder. Her anger towards William Dunkin grows with each passing day. Kendra constantly talks about the trial—who she thinks will be called as witnesses and what information they'll provide. I tried, at first, to add my comments or suggestions to the conversations, until I realized that her rage doesn't leave room for my opinions. Mostly, I just listen to her rant.

Kendra's anger scares me. It grows with each passing moment; she is angrier now than she was at the time of Chelsea's murder. While having some of the questions answered surrounding Chelsea's death has given me more peace than I've had for years, each answered question seems to make Kendra come up with a thousand more whose answers will never satisfy her. The only question remaining in my mind is *why*, and I'm hoping that the answer can at least partially be revealed during the trial. According to all the information we have so far, there's still no known connection between Chelsea and William. The biggest question I have is whether fate caused their paths to cross that night or whether Chelsea's murder had been pre-meditated. The postponement of the trial means I'll have to wait a while longer to get these answers.

"Kendra," I yell as I head up the steps, loosening my tie along the way. When no answer comes, I call her name again.

As I walk into our room, I see her lying across the bed, her suit crumpled beneath her, her body wracked with sobs.

I sit on the edge of the bed, pulling her into my arms. I smooth her hair away from her tear-soaked cheek. "I'm sorry, honey. Justin said he'd let us know once a new date has been set." Kendra continues to cry in my arms. "I know you're upset, but Justin told us this could happen; these things usually don't go smoothly."

Kendra pushes away and stands in front of me. The rage works its way through her body from her clenched fists to her glaring eyes.

"I know what he said, Tom. I'm not an idiot. That doesn't make it any better," she spews each word at me with such venom that were they able to puncture my skin, I'd be a dead man. "Of course, you did nothing about it, did you? You prob-ably told him it's all okay, right? Just like always, everything's all okay with you? You can't be a man and put your foot down, can you?" Spittle flies from the corners of her mouth.

I throw my hands in the air. "What exactly did you want me to do? I can't force them to move forward with court, can I?" I speak as calmly as possible, hoping if I don't match her intensity, she'll see how ludicrous she's being.

"You could've tried something. Did you tell him the hell the last eight months has been on us, on me? No, of course

320

not. Did you tell him how I didn't sleep at all last night preparing for today? Did you tell him we've waited *almost twenty years* for this day, and he needs to do whatever he needs to do to make this happen? Of course, you didn't. I'm sure it's all okay with Tom. You'd be okay waiting until hell freezes over for this trial, wouldn't you?" Kendra screams, pacing back and forth in front of me.

"I want this to be over as badly as you do." I reach for her hand.

She jerks it away. "Like hell you do, Tom. You don't even talk about it; you push it aside and leave me to deal with it. Just like you did when she died—left me to deal with all of it. I'm not going to sit by and let you do this to me again."

She grabs her purse off the chair next to our bed and runs out the door. She's reached the front door by the time I get downstairs.

"Kendra, where are you going? Just stay here. You shouldn't go anywhere when you're this upset," I say calmly, but inside I'm furious. I want to grab her by the shoulders and shake some sense into her.

"Don't tell me what to do." She slams the door behind her.

The tires squeal as she pulls out of the driveway. I should go after her but know I'll never catch up. Even if I could, there isn't a thing I could say or do to calm the storm raging within her.

*　*　*

NICOLE

I've been at the courthouse waiting for the trial to start since eight, even though it isn't slated to begin until nine-thirty. I was hoping that having some time to myself would give me the strength I'll need to deal with the events that will unfold today. I would've loved to stay home, curled up with a blanket and a mug of hot coffee in my favorite chair, but getting quiet time in a house with two kids is as difficult as figuring out the exact shape of a snowflake before it melts. I can hardly finish a thought at home on a normal day, let alone on one where my thoughts are waging a war inside my head. I left Steven in charge of getting the girls ready and headed here after a quick run through my favorite coffee shop, trusting a hot latte will give me the energy I need.

I sit in the empty courtroom trying to process my thoughts about the trial starting, the last two decades, the impact Chelsea's death has had on my life, seeing William Dunkin for the first time in person. My addictive thoughts have spiraled out of control several times over the past few months, preparing for today. I even went so far as to go to a doctor who wasn't familiar with my history, to get a script for Valium. I dropped it off at the pharmacy and was told it would be ready in fifteen minutes. I went to the gas station next door while I was waiting. The anticipation of some relief from the pills made me shake, so much so, that I dropped change while attempting to pay for my gas. The woman behind me picked it up, and our eyes met when she handed it back to me. I recognized her from AA, although Sue looked much different than the last time I saw her at a meeting months ago. Her face was gaunt, with a yellowish cast; her eyes sunken with dark circles beneath.

Instead of rushing to the pharmacy as I previously anticipated doing, I waited out front for Sue. We had spent many nights after meetings drinking coffee and talking about our families, our addictions, our recovery. Sue was obviously drinking again, and I recalled from our talks what would happen if she didn't maintain sobriety. Instead of picking up the pills, Sue and I went for coffee, and she told me about her relapse which caused her to, at least temporarily, lose custody of her children, get arrested for drunk driving, lose her job, and now drink daily again—all within a matter of months.

I realized then that God put Sue in my path at that exact moment to keep me from heading back down my own crazy addictive path and losing everything I've worked so hard to build for myself. I called my sponsor from AA, who picked up the pills for me and disposed of them. I also confessed my struggles to Steven. Since then, he's been supportive by helping with the kids so I can go to meetings or out to coffee with my sponsor; although, I can tell my confession worries him. He's reminded me several times he won't stay with me if I start using or drinking again and gave many subtle reminders about what our life used to be like. Sue has been back to meetings several times, but she still hasn't quit drinking again.

Even though I would prefer to be numb to get through events like today, I'm grateful for my sobriety. I've learned through the years that no matter how much I numbed myself out after Chelsea's death, it all came back in full force the moment I got sober. It would have been much easier to deal with the emotions back then, as they came, instead of trying to deal with years of them all at once.

I think about Chelsea. Even though so much time has passed, I can still picture her smile and hear her laughter as though she were sitting right next to me. What would've become of our friendship had she not been murdered? Would we have gone to college together as we planned? Would we still be friends, getting together for coffee and ranting about our husbands? Would I keep everyone at a distance like I do now, out of fear that I'll care too much about someone and they, too, will be stolen from me? I've never found a replacement for Chelsea and doubt I ever will. Other than my family and my sponsor, it's impossible to truly let all my walls down with anyone, and it's much easier to be a loner. I've come to understand through years of therapy, and countless discussions with my sponsor, that my fear keeps me locked inside my own little prison. I must battle my fears daily over losing my children or husband to some random act of violence; I can't imagine wanting to take on the stress of worrying about anyone else.

My sponsor offered to come to the trial today, to be here for me in case it gets too hard. I declined, knowing I'll be surrounded by Chelsea's family and old friends from high school who will come because Chelsea's death rocked the foundation of this entire town, especially those of us who went to school with her. Many of them also had to deal with the same fears I've had for years about who killed Chelsea, the lack of trust in anyone, the realizations of their own mortality at such a young age, the understanding that the world could be a cruel place and everything you thought you understood about life could come crashing down around you in an instant. The news of William's arrest sparked many calls from people I haven't heard from in years. Sometimes it's a relief to talk to those that lived through this with me; other times, it's too painful, realizing everyone had the chance to grow up and raise families when Chelsea didn't.

I'm startled from my thoughts by the door to the courtroom opening, the bailiff stepping inside. I glance at my watch and realize it's already nine—only a half-hour to go.

"Ma'am? Are you here for the Dunkin trial?" The bailiff asks.

"Yes. It's scheduled for nine-thirty, correct?" I reply.

"I'm sorry you're just now getting the news; it looks like you've been here a while. The trial's been postponed," the bailiff informs me.

I collect my things, asking why and if it's been rescheduled. The bailiff apologizes saying she really can't answer questions as to why and a new court date hasn't yet been set. I thank her and head out the door, pressing a hand to my stomach to try to calm my nerves. I'm ready for this to be over and for all the anxiety to go away.

I make a stop in the restroom to compose myself, not sure what to do since I've requested the next week off work in anticipation of the trial lasting that long. I decide to stick with my plan of taking today off at least. I'll go home and take a nice long nap while the house is still quiet.

I descend the front stairs of the courthouse and hear

someone call my name from down the street. Kent walks quickly towards me.

"I think you're headed in the wrong direction," he laughs.

"Oh, I guess you didn't get the news. The trial's been delayed," I say, taking in the sight of Kent, clean-shaven and in a suit. I can't remember seeing him in one since Chelsea's funeral. "You look nice, by the way."

"Thanks, but why's it delayed? Are my parents here? Do they know?" Kent rattles off questions, obviously having poured as much emotional energy into preparing for today as I have.

After talking for a few minutes, I suggest we go eat breakfast and drink lots of coffee so that I can catch up with my "little bro," what I've called him for as long as I can remember. Kent takes my arm, and we head into the *Jury Room*, the diner next to the courthouse.

*   *   *

KENT

The waitress fills our mugs with coffee and takes our orders. My order of three eggs over easy, two slices of bacon, two sausage links, three slices of toast, hash browns, and three pancakes, surprises Nicole. It's a feast compared to her order of oatmeal and side of fruit.

"What?" I say to her raised eyebrows after the waitress walks away. "I'm famished."

Nicole chuckles, "I guess so. Are you eating for two?"

"Ha! Funny one," I reply. "The stress of waiting for to-

326

day has bolstered my appetite."

Nicole becomes serious. "How are you doing, Kent? I mean, really. You don't look like yourself."

"I'm fine," I say, after taking a drink of my coffee. "And, usually when someone says something like that, they really mean you look like shit. So, thanks!"

"I'm serious. How are you really doing with all of this with the trial and William and your parents? It's got to be hard on you." Nicole reaches across the table and takes one of my hands in her own, forcing me to make eye contact. "Remember, it's your big sis you're talking to here."

I take a long, slow drink from my coffee, nearly finishing it before answering. "I don't know, really. I try not to think about it too much or let it all get to me. It's been a long time. What good is it going to do to worry about any of it? It won't change a thing."

"I agree with you that it won't bring Chelsea back," Nicole adds, "but, I don't see how you can just not think or worry about it. Chelsea being murdered changed your entire life. William Dunkin killed a part of you, the rest of your family, me, right along with Chelsea. It's got to affect you."

I glance out the window as Nicole continues talking, trying to hold back whatever is rising in my chest—sadness, fear, loss, grief—I don't really know what it is.

"Look, I gotta run to the restroom, I'll be right back." I get up and rush away before my emotions have the chance to spill over.

I go into a stall and lock the door behind me. What

the hell's wrong with me? She just asked how I'm doing; why is that making me feel like a ball of mush? I'm fine. None of this really matters. The fact they caught William won't change a damn thing. Chelsea will still be gone. My relationship with my parents will still be non-existent. I'll still be left with no one. It doesn't matter.

I sit there for several minutes repeating this mantra to myself of it not mattering, until I start to believe it again, and head back to the table where Nicole and my feast are waiting. Nicole must sense a change of subject is in order because the rest of our meal we talk about her kids, my job, her husband—anything but Chelsea and the trial.

Despite my protests, Nicole insists on paying the bill. As we head back towards our cars, it hits me just how much I've enjoyed our time together and how nice it was to have someone to talk to that wasn't judging me. I can't remember the last time I had such an easy conversation when I wasn't plastered. I can't remember the last time I felt like someone actually cared about me.

I stop and draw her into an embrace.

"What was that for?" Nicole asks, still in my arms.

"To say thank you."

"You've already thanked me way too much for breakfast. It really wasn't that expensive, even though you ate like a pig," Nicole jokes.

"Not for breakfast. It was good to see you and have someone to talk to, ya know?" I say as my eyes well up.

"Oh, Kent! Anytime. I wish we saw each other more.

Anytime you need anything, call me. My home's always open to you, and I'm only a phone call away," Nicole adds.

"Thanks, Nicole. I know you mean it. I want to stop by and see your girls—it's been a long time. Too long. Give them big hugs for me, okay," I say.

I open the car door for her. As she's about to sit, she stops and gently touches me on the arm. "I need to say one thing, and I promise it's not meant in a negative, judgmental way at all, okay? Remember, I've been where you're at—with the drinking and the lifestyle. If you ever want to know how I got to where I am now, I'd love to talk to you about it, okay?" Nicole pauses, and I can tell broaching this topic makes her fear that she'll make me run away again. "I love you, and I want you to be okay. Remember, I'm always here."

I give her another hug and promise I'll remember her offer. I joke as she's getting seated about showing up at her house every night, right around six, in time for dinner, which she says is fine with her.

As I watch her pull out of the parking spot, the loneliness I'm so accustomed to feeling slices right through my soul. You don't really miss something that's never been there until you get a taste of it. Today, I spent time with someone who really loves and cares about me; someone who's truly concerned. Her concern isn't like my parents'. Half of the time I wonder if they are worried about me because of what I'm doing to my life and how lost I am in my own world, or if it's because of how my life appears to their friends. I have no doubt that Nicole's worry is because she loves me and has nothing to do with her own

329

self-interests.

As I drive towards my apartment, I replay Nicole's last comments in my mind. She can see straight through my *It doesn't matter to me* façade, into the pain that lies beneath. She can tell I fight a daily battle of burying my sadness through whatever bottle, drug, or woman is closest. I realize as I pull into the liquor store parking lot that looking at me must be like looking into a mirror, seeing her own past reflected in my eyes.

I pick up a fifth of vodka and head to the counter, promising myself to someday take Nicole up on her offer and talk to her about how she stopped the crazy lifestyle. But that won't be today. Today, what I need is to go home and drink until I no longer remember the emptiness inside.

* * *

KENDRA

The amount of rage still pumping through me, even though eight hours have passed since this morning's phone call, amazes me. Today was supposed to be the day that Chelsea's vindication began; instead, it was a day like we've seemingly had thousands of in the past nineteen years. One of waiting. Many times today, I asked God the same question I've shouted at him countless times throughout the years—why? Why are we forced to wait again, when all we have done since the day of Chelsea's disappearance is wait? Wait for them to find her body. Wait for them to determine the torture she went through in her final hours and her cause of death. Wait for her funeral. Wait for the police to get a new promising lead. Wait for them to catch her killer. And now, wait for that killer to be brought to justice. Why is it too much to ask for just this one phase of the whole enormous process to go smoothly?

I spent the morning driving to no place in particular, trying to calm myself down. When that didn't help, I tried shopping as a distraction, which only increased my anger. Each salesperson I encountered, each mother with a child, each happy couple shopping together, only increased my fury. How do these people go on with smiles plastered to their faces, enjoying life when, once again, mine has been slammed to a screeching halt by William Dunkin? As I perused the purse selection in the department store, I imagined killing William myself. I wouldn't do it quickly though; I'd plan a slow, painful death, making sure he suffers every bit as much as Chelsea did in her final moments. I was completely lost in my fantasy world until a salesclerk forced me back to reality by gently taking my arm and asking if everything was okay. I heard myself answer as if it were coming from a million miles away, telling her no, everything is not okay. I dropped the purse and bolted out of the store, deciding that shopping wasn't the answer either.

Now I'm in the car again and at a complete loss as to what to do, where to go. I briefly consider going home, but I can't deal with Tom. Once again, he's abandoned me to deal with everything on my own. Tom doesn't even care that it was delayed, using his usual mantra of, *It's out of our control.* For once, I wish he'd exercise some authority to make the people in charge see how important it is to us to have this trial over and done with. It's as if I've been holding my breath for weeks in

331

anticipation of today. Rather than finally being able to breathe, I'm left waiting for how long to inhale? A week? A month? A year? Again, I'm left with more questions—never answers, only a growing list of uncertainties. I want to make them stop; I need a few moments of peace without the pounding in my chest and head. I want to be able to breathe. For this to happen, I need to know the punishment William will face. I need to know how he'll pay for the pain and anguish he's caused. Then, and only then, will I be able to breathe.

As I drive off, again with no destination in mind, it hits me that I didn't call Kent this morning to tell him about the delay. Guilt stabs me at forgetting Kent, yet again. I wonder if he showed up and how long he had to wait before he heard the news. I wonder how he took it, knowing that the anticipation of the trial starting had to have worn him down too. I now know where I need to go, to check on Kent as I should've done this morning. I can't do anything right when it comes to mothering him.

I'm an hour away from his apartment but decide to pick up dinner for both of us. I actually feel myself calming down when I envision us sitting together at his table, sharing a meal, and having a real heart to heart talk. I don't even know my son and have wanted to change that for years. I'll force myself to just listen to what he has to say, not make any comments that he'd see as judgmental. Maybe we can begin to rebuild our relationship. I'll do everything in my power to keep the focus of the conversation off Chelsea or the trial, and, for once, it can be on Kent or the weather or politics—whatever he wants to discuss.

I'm ready to really hear what he has to say and listen for clues to tell me who my son has become.

I'm growing more optimistic as I pick up fried chicken, mashed potatoes, gravy, biscuits, and coleslaw to take to Kent's, remembering it was one of his favorite childhood meals. Even though this day started off with disappointment, it can end on a good note and be the first day of a new start with my son. I'll ensure that something positive comes out of this otherwise terrible day.

I arrive at the apartment and ring the bell, my arms full with our dinner. When no answer comes, I ring a second time and wait. Again, there's no answer, so I put the bags down and knock as loudly as I can. I know Kent didn't have to work today as he'd taken time off for the trial, but again, only silence greets my knock. I dig through my purse for the key I've never used before; the one to his apartment, that he gave for "emergencies only." He must be gone, but I let myself in to set up dinner and wait for him to come home. Maybe I can do some cleaning or laundry until he returns.

Once inside, I place the food on the one empty spot I find on the table. The room is littered with empty liquor bottles, pizza boxes, and about a month's worth of dirty laundry. I can definitely put myself to use while I wait. I pick up handfuls of empty bottles and see the figure on the couch, mouth open, slobber running from its corner.

A rush of adrenaline fills me until my mind has time to process the scene. Once I realize it's Kent, I move slowly towards him, so I don't startle him. I sit on the edge of the couch and see the empty vodka bottle lying next to him like a sleeping baby would, nestled against his side.

I bend close. "Kent, honey. It's Mom."

He stirs but doesn't awaken. I'm reminded of the boy I rocked each night, who I watched sleeping once he got too big to hold. In sleep, his face still has that look of innocence, the one I never see any more when he's awake. I smooth his sweaty hair back off his forehead, causing him to stir again.

"Kent, are you okay?" I speak softly.

His eyes open and take a moment to adjust. "Mommy," he says, using the name for me that he hasn't uttered since he was about seven years old. He grabs my hand. "Mommy, is that you?"

His voice sounds so weak and shaken—like a lost little boy. As soon as the thought registers in my brain, the truth stabs my heart—he is lost. He was lost to me years ago.

"I'm right here, baby. Right here." Tears well in the corners of my eyes.

"Stay with me, Mommy. Don't leave me," Kent says, lifting his torso off the couch and leaning into my embrace.

"I'm right here. I won't go anywhere. I'm right here," I keep uttering the words over and over as my son drifts back into his stupor, wrapped in my arms.

I had prayed all day for the rage to leave me, never knowing it would be replaced with such a terrible sense of grief. For once, the heavy sense of loss inside me isn't only for my daughter, but for my son as well—the one who is now passed out and able to, for this moment, forget just how forgotten and overlooked he's been.

REMEMBER me despite the clouds of despair that overshadow your memories of the past and your hopes for the future. Even though the storms of rage fill your soul, remember all is not lost. I am no longer with you, yet I am not gone. Make sure I live on by creating a family that can love, laugh, cry, and remember together. Love each other despite your pain. Wipe each other's tears on those days it all seems unbearable. Forgive, for it is the only way you will ever be free. Don't let my death be your end, for it wasn't mine. I'm still shining brightly—an eternal flame. Remember me on your journey, for I'm with you on the mountaintops and in the valleys. I have never left your side. When the storm passes and God places a rainbow in the sky as his promise to you, remember what that promise means. You won't be destroyed. He has been with you throughout your quest. While he carried you, I walked alongside, holding your hand, and whispering truths I hoped you could hear.

BILLY

19 Years, 10 Months, 9 Days After

December 17, 2008

M R. McCabe somehow arranged for David to sit in on today's meeting to discuss our strategy. I mostly sit, staring at my palms, while the two of them talk about my options in their legal jargon, as though I don't exist. Some of their words register, like plea bargain, insanity plea, but mostly they just float in the air of the conference room, never fully penetrating my mind.

"Billy, what do you think?" David asks, interrupting my intense memorization of the lines on my left palm.

"I'm actually wondering which of these is my lifeline. Do either of you know?" I ask, making eye contact with David. His face wrinkles with disgust at my question.

"Billy, Mr. McCabe and I both have other things we could be doing right now seeing as how Christmas is a week away. We're here to try to figure out the best course of action for you, and I feel like we're wasting our time. You don't even seem interested," David says in a raised voice. "You can either contribute or Charles and I will leave."

"Sorry. I'm kinda lost in my own world," I say. "Plus, I can't understand half of what you're saying. Can you put it in real language and stop talking over my head?"

David's face softens. "I guess we are talking in legal-ese—sorry, I don't even realize I'm doing it. Charles, can you explain the options?"

Mr. McCabe begins. "Well, William, as David and I were discussing, we've got several options in how to proceed with your case, and we need to do so quickly to satisfy the court by getting a trial date scheduled." Charles looks at his notes and continues, "Option one is for you to plead not guilty by reason of insanity. That would involve you undergoing psychiatric evaluations by someone chosen by our side and someone chosen by the prosecutor's team. Essentially, we must prove you weren't mentally capable of knowing right from wrong when Chelsea was murdered. The prosecutor will have to prove that you did. David's got some valid points about how your past could have contributed to a psychotic break, which led to Chelsea's death."

"And the other options?" I ask, again studying my hands but, this time, understanding and hearing every word spoken.

"We don't use the insanity defense and move forward with a trial. I've got to tell you though, the evidence against you is overwhelming, with your DNA being found *inside* the victim." Charles words make me wince like I've been punched in the stomach. "This option is the most expensive, timely, and potentially costly for you. If the jury finds you guilty, you could be facing upwards of twenty-five years behind bars."

"Plus, I'd have to sit through a trial? I'd have to listen to everyone's theories about what happened and why, right?"

"Exactly," David says.

Charles clears his throat. "The last option would involve some cooperation on the part of the prosecutor, but I think Mr. Lockhart would go for it. That's for you to plead guilty to lesser charges and possibly get a reduced sentence. But this would be completely up to Mr. Lockhart, and then the judge would decide your sentence. There are no guarantees how a judge will go on sentencing even if you've made a deal with the prosecutor."

"So, basically, I say I'm guilty and killed her but claim I was crazy at the time and still have to sit through a trial. Or, I say I didn't do it, but sit through a trial anyway, hearing every shred of evidence they've got against me. Or, I just admit guilt and see what the judge decides," I summarize.

David nods. "Exactly."

"What do you think I should do?" I direct my question to David.

"I think you should plead guilty by reason of insanity. Any psychiatrist that hears about our past will agree that a psychotic break could've been possible, leading you to do things you wouldn't have normally done," David says.

I lean forward and peer into David's eyes. "Is that what

you think happened? Do you think I went nuts and didn't know what I was doing?"

"I don't know, Billy. I'm just saying it makes sense given everything you've witnessed in your life. It helps me explain it to myself, so I'm guessing if I can buy it, so could a jury of twelve people," David pauses. "It's the only thing that makes sense to me, since the brother I knew and loved never could've raped and killed a teenage girl."

"I've become someone much different than the brother tucked away in your memories. Trust me, I wish I could be the person you've imagined." I have more to say but stop myself. "I need some time to think about this."

"We don't have much time. I need to let the courts know how we plan to proceed by the end of the year," Mr. Mc-Cabe states.

"I'll let you know before then. I need some time to think it all through."

Mr. McCabe signals to the guard outside of the counsel room to indicate our meeting is over and shakes my hand, saying he'll await my call. David hesitates and then gives me a hug, whispering in my ear that he loves me.

As the guard cuffs me, I watch Mr. McCabe and David walk towards the gate that will let them out of this godforsaken place. Watching my brother disappear beyond it reminds me of the day our grandparents took me away, and I watched him shrink away to nothingness behind me.

COLD CASE SOLVED NEARLY 20 YEARS LATER

By Lucinda Parlow

The Langston Messenger

December 20, 2008

Almost two decades after the body of a high-school senior was pulled from the Holcomb River, a Langston man has admitted to killing her.

William Dunkin pleaded guilty Friday, December 19, 2008, to involuntary manslaughter in the February 8, 1989, killing of 17-year-old Chelsea Marie Wyatt.

Dunkin was charged with aggravated murder and murder on January 31st of this year after DNA evidence from the Wyatt killing matched a sample of Dunkin's DNA collected while he was jailed for another crime.

Dunkin, a 42-year-old father of six, faces 10 to 25 years

in prison when sentenced in the Fairmont County Common Pleas Court by Judge Edward Sable. The sentencing date has not yet been set but is expected to take place in the next month.

According to the prosecutor's office, the Wyatt family agreed to the plea arrangement with conditions to be revealed at a later time. Prosecutor Justin Lockhart said, "My heart goes out to the Wyatt family and this entire community that has waited almost twenty years for some closure."

Wyatt disappeared after leaving her job as a hostess at *Landoll's Restaurant* on the night of February 8, 1989. Her burnt-out car was found the next day, and her body was found in the Holcomb River two days after she was initially reported missing.

Tom and Kendra Wyatt reported that although the wait has been unbearable at times, they always hoped in their hearts this day would come, and their daughter's killer would be found. They expressed relief at the guilty plea saying they were glad they wouldn't have to sit through a lengthy trial.

Local police authorities stated they are also relieved this case has finally been closed as it never left their radars even though so many years have passed. This unsolved murder has touched many people's lives in the Langston community for the past two decades. Hopefully, the guilty plea will allow the community to sleep a little more peacefully tonight.

TOM

19 YEARS, 11 MONTHS, 15 DAYS AFTER
JANUARY 23, 2009

SINCE William's guilty plea, life has felt almost normal between Kendra and me. She moved back into our bed instead of the guest room down the hall, where she's slept since
returning from Kent's in October; her anger seems diminished;
and, we can actually have a whole conversation in which I'm
allowed to share my opinions without her storming off. We've
talked many times about William's plea and are relieved we won't
have to sit through a trial listening to every detail of those painful
days and our daughter's horrific death. There are only two steps
to go through, and then we can truly move on, knowing William
is behind bars for the crimes he committed against Chelsea.

Today we're meeting with Mr. Lockhart as part of the

plea agreement reached with William. In exchange for his guilty plea to involuntary manslaughter, William agreed to answer questions posed to him from the prosecutor so we could have details about how our daughter died. Kendra and I helped prepare a list of questions for Justin to ask William.

The final step in the process will take place on Monday at the sentencing hearing. Justin explained what the events of that day will be. William will again state his guilty plea for the court; friends and family will have the opportunity to address William and the courts; his attorney will make his statement to the judge on behalf of his client regarding sentencing recommendations; the judge will sentence William for the crimes to which he pled guilty. Kendra and I have started working on the statements we plan to read aloud at the hearing. We're writing them independently and not sharing them with each other beforehand, so we can ensure that we're each saying what we need to without the other's judgment.

Kendra walks in the kitchen as I'm starting a fresh pot of coffee. I see the nervousness about the upcoming meeting in her eyes.

"Hey, c'mere," I say, pulling her into an embrace. I kiss her on top of the head as she clings to me. "You okay?"

"I don't know. We've waited for these answers for so long now," Kendra says, tightening her grip around me. "Part of me wants to hurry up and get the meeting over with so we know. The other part of me dreads hearing what Justin will tell us."

"I know. I'm anxious about it too. I'm trying to remember that having some information is truly an answered prayer," I say. "I'm glad we're getting them, as painful as they may be, and that we're getting them here instead of a courtroom."

"Hopefully, more of the truth will come out this way. A trial only paints a picture the attorney wants the jury to see instead of giving us the truth," Kendra says. "I know I've said this a lot over the last month, but I really hope that this guilty plea means William knows how he's destroyed our lives, and he's finally taking responsibility for his actions. Maybe he's changed since he's been in jail."

"Me too. Maybe after today's meeting, we'll be able to tell," I add.

As we continue talking, I again realize how much I've missed my wife. Even though we've been living in the same house, I've lost her to her anger so many times over the years. It's definitely turned her into a different person, one that feels like a stranger most of the time. It's nice to be able to sit and discuss this situation, sharing our fears and anxieties. It feels like the days of our marriage before Chelsea was murdered.

Our conversation is interrupted by a knock. Butterflies work their way from my stomach to my throat. I give Kendra's hand a slight squeeze and open the door. I exhale loudly at the sight of Nicole, expecting that Mr. Lockhart would be on the other side. I pull Nicole into an embrace.

"Thanks for coming. Would you like some coffee? I just made a fresh pot," I ask as Kendra hangs Nicole's coat in the closet.

"No, thanks. I'm too nervous for anything right now," Nicole replies. "How are you guys holding up?"

345

"We're doing okay," I say. "Anxious to get this all done with. Are you okay? You look like you might pass out."

"I don't know how I'm doing really. One minute I'm okay and the next I'm crying. I didn't sleep last night because I kept imagining the things that Mr. Lockhart will tell us today. I guess I'm afraid of what'll come out. I came up with my own answers over the years—ones I've learned to live with, ya know? Just wondering how I'll learn to live with the truth," Nicole says with teary eyes.

Kendra sits on the love seat next to Nicole, pulling her into a hug. Kendra whispers comforting words to her. I'm filled with gratitude that Kendra's anger has dissipated enough that she can actually be a consolation to someone instead of always being on the warpath. I'm making my way into the kitchen to refill my coffee when the front door opens.

Kent tosses his coat on the chair by the front door. "Hey, guys. I made it—even have a couple of minutes to spare, I see," he says as he looks around the living room.

I give Kent a hug, and he makes an awkward attempt at returning it before he frees himself to take a seat on the couch. I resume my task of freshening my coffee, leaving the three of them to chat.

I pause in the kitchen, offering a quick prayer for the meeting we're about to have. *God, I beg you to be with us today. Please keep Kendra's anger under control, help Nicole with her anxiety, help Kent to...just help Kent. And help me to stay mentally sound through all of this. Help us deal with the pain of whatever we're about to hear. We need your strength.*

346

Before I get the Amen out, there's a knock on the door. Since we're only waiting on one person to arrive, I know it's Justin, with our answers.

*   *   *

NICOLE

As Mr. Lockhart walks in, I'm on the verge of hyperventilating. No matter how hard I try, I can't get a full breath. If I've ever needed a Valium, now is the time. Even before the thought fully forms, I remind myself that it isn't an option. I attempt some positive self-talk to ease my anxiety, but when that doesn't work, I run to the bathroom without excusing myself. I splash cold water on my face, ruining what little make-up I wore today. I don't understand what I'm so afraid of. I've waited for almost twenty years for these answers, and now that I'm about to get them, I'm falling apart. I can't even begin to make sense of my feelings.

I sit on the toilet and let the dam of tears fall, easing some of the pressure in my chest. *C'mon Nicole, get a grip. Everyone's out there waiting on you. You gotta be strong. Suck it up and get out there. Do it for Chels.*

Thinking Chelsea's name makes the tears fall harder, and a sob breaks free. I picture my beautiful friend, hear her boisterous laughter, feel her arms around me, offering comfort. I hear Chelsea whispering to me, as I have so many times throughout the years, telling me she's in a better place, everything will be okay, and to find peace in remembering.

Part of my fear is that my memories will somehow be

347

tainted with the new knowledge I'm about to receive. I don't want the recollections of my friend's face, voice, and laughter to be replaced by the images I'm sure will be conjured by the discussion to come. I don't want to picture Chelsea hurt and dead. I want to remember her laughing, smiling, and full of life. I've fought for too many years to be able to have the good memories without the intense pain of my loss, making me turn to pills or alcohol. I'm afraid that after today, I'll have to begin that fight again.

As I let the tears flow, there's a knock on the door. In a raspy voice, I announce that I'll be out in a moment.

"Nicole, let me in so we can talk a minute, 'kay?" Kent's voice comes from the other side of the door.

Hesitantly, I rise to open it.

"I'm sorry," I say as Kent envelops me in his arms. "I don't know what's wrong with me."

"It's okay. I get it. It just brings it all back, like it was yesterday," Kent says.

"Yea. It does. It shouldn't hurt this bad after such a long time," I add. "I feel like an idiot. I'm a grown woman, and here I am crying like a baby over something that should help bring some closure."

"Well, you could be doing worse things...like finding something to keep the tears from falling." He chuckles, but there's no joy in it. I break our embrace to study his face.

"Trust me, the thought's there. But I've been there, done that, and it didn't turn out so well for me," I say.

"I understand that one," Kent chuckles. "Pretty sad

when you have to do a couple of shots at nine-thirty in the morning just to work up enough courage to come to your parents' house to hear the gory details of your sister's murder almost two decades ago. Talk about pathetic."

"Not pathetic, Kent. You're just lost and not sure if you want to be found." Talking with him has helped. My muscles no longer feel like they're about to snap in two.

"Well, how about this pathetic crybaby and this pathetic drunk go hear what the man has to say," Kent says, making us both laugh. "We'll get through this...you sob if you have to and I'll take a quick trip to my car for a swig if need be. It can't be much worse than what we've already been through, right?"

I'm finally able to draw a deep breath. I nod and grab his hand. "C'mon, little bro. Let's get this over with."

*   *   *

KENDRA

I'm getting up from the couch to go tell Kent and Nicole to hurry when I hear them coming down the hall. I sigh deeply and sit back down next to Tom. It seems like they've been gone for an eternity, and my head might explode if I have to listen to any more of Tom and Justin's idle chit-chat.

Nicole has obviously been crying. There's not a hint of make-up left on her face, and her nose is bright pink.

"I'm sorry about holding everyone up. My emotions got the best of me," Nicole says as she and Kent sit.

Tom and Justin give Nicole an empathetic look, and I wish I could muster the same, but instead, I find myself saying,

"Okay, we're all here. Can we move forward?" My urgency to know what William said far outweighs my need to be delicate with Nicole.

"Sure," Justin says and clears his throat while pulling notes from his briefcase. "As you know, I met with Mr. Dunkin and his attorney, Mr. McCabe, to ask the questions we prepared. Let me first say that some of the information I'll share with you will be hard to hear, but it will answer some of your questions.

"William states that on the evening of February 8, 1989, he worked until six p.m. at *Fill N Go* gas station, which used to be on the corner of Maple and Main Street. He was a cashier there at that time. After work, he went to the *Golden Axle Bar* on Main Street. He said he had a few shots, a few beers, and played a couple of rounds of pool with some buddies. According to William, he bought a joint, smoked it in his car, and then started to head home. As he was driving past *Landoll's*, he felt what he described as a—give me a second to check my notes—okay, here it is. To quote, *an incredible pull, like some kind of force, was telling me to stop there.*

"William admitted he was drunk and high. He pulled into the restaurant parking lot at around ten 'til eight and parked, saying he wasn't sure what he was looking for. He said after a few minutes, he got out and started walking toward the restaurant. He was almost to the entrance when he saw a girl walking out towards a row of parked cars. He said it was the weirdest feeling he'd ever had and, that again, he felt *drawn* to her. He called it an *instant attraction*."

I sigh in disgust, and Justin pauses a moment.

"William said he followed her toward her car. When she got into the driver's seat, he got in on the passenger side and started talking to her. He claims that he just wanted to talk to her.""Oh my god, she must've been so scared," Nicole says with a gasp. "What'd she do? Did she scream? Did she try to get out?"

"Unfortunately, he didn't give us that information. William said after getting in the car and seeing she wasn't going to talk to him, he had to get more forceful. For the next forty-five minutes to an hour, he made her drive around town. He wasn't specific about what took place during that time, where they drove exactly, or what they did. He said at that point, he still just wanted to talk and get to know her," Justin pauses. "Is everyone doing okay so far?"

We all nod, each lost in our own thoughts. Tom sits, staring directly at Justin as he speaks. Kent picks at his cuticles. Nicole is perched on the edge of the loveseat, eyes wide, as if she might bolt for the front door at any moment. I shift my attention back and forth between Justin and the framed eight by ten senior picture of Chelsea sitting on the end-table, mesmerized by her smile and beautiful blue eyes.

"William then had Chelsea pull over on Sandstone Road, back where there weren't many houses, and he raped her."

Tom gags beside me, and Nicole's tears fall freely down her cheeks. Kent continues to pick at his fingers. My thoughts race. *My poor, poor baby girl. You must've been so afraid. My poor Chelsea. I'm so sorry we weren't there to help. How you must've been praying and screaming and crying for help.*

"After that, he forced Chelsea out of the car and made

her walk back toward the restaurant."

"Oh my God, he made her walk? It was freezing cold, with inches of snow on the ground," I sob. "And her shoes, they didn't find her shoes! Was my baby girl barefoot, walking in the snow, and freezing? That has to be about four miles. Oh my god!"

I again look at Chelsea's smiling face, beaming at me from the picture frame. I can't imagine it twisted in the pain and fear she had to be feeling that night. I can't begin to comprehend the horrors my daughter was forced to live through.

"I'm not sure, Kendra. Let's hope she had them on, and they were lost in the water. I'm sorry. I know how hard this must be for you to hear."

No one speaks. The only sounds in the room are the ticking of the clock and our sniffles, trying to choke back the tears.

"William said they walked alongside the Holcomb River to get back into town. He said they were almost back to the restaurant when Chelsea slipped on some rocks and fell into the water. He claims she must've hit her head on something because, by the time he got to her, she was gone."

"Bullshit," I yell. "That's such bullshit. He either hit her in the head or held her under or something. He killed her. It wasn't an accident. How can he say it was an accident? He's still not owning up to what he did."

For the first time since the meeting started, Kent speaks. "Mom, just let Mr. Lockhart finish. He's only sharing what he heard—he's not the one who did it. Besides, we don't know what happened. We've got to go with what we're given."

I'm enraged. "Go with what we're given? Go with what we're given by some crazy guy who rapes and murders teenage girls? No, I don't have to go with anything that man says. Tom, you know its bullshit, right?"

Tom doesn't respond, only shrugs.

I look to Nicole, "Nicole? You know?"

Through her tears, Nicole replies hoarsely, "I don't know what to think. I hope...I hope it happened that way. That it was an accident. I want to believe it happened that way."

I throw my hand in the air in disbelief. "I can't believe what I'm hearing. I can't believe you're all taking this guy at his word. Sure, we agreed to let him plead to involuntary manslaughter as a way to hopefully get the truth. Obviously, we were expecting too much. He actually believes his own lies saying it was an accident. Was it an accident he raped her too?"

No one speaks for a moment. "Mom," Kent finally breaks the silence. "What does it matter if it was an accident or he killed her with his bare hands? She's still gone."

"What does it matter? I can't believe I just heard you say that. What does it matter?" I scream so loudly that my voice cracks.

"Kendra, can you calm down so Justin can finish?" Tom says quietly.

"I'll bite my tongue so Mr. Lockhart can finish sharing William's story of lies, but I won't *calm down*," I say as I point at Tom. "And, for your information, Kent, it does matter. It matters very much."

I sit back and cross my arms in front of me, anger pulsing through me so strongly that I might explode. "Go ahead, Justin. I promise you won't hear another word from me."

Justin clears his throat. "William said that after he realized Chelsea was dead, he panicked. He broke down during the interview and cried, saying he never meant to kill her and that he was sorry."

A slight chuckle escapes me, but I do as I promised and don't say a word.

"He said he walked back to where they'd left her car, drove it back into town, parked it in the field along the tracks where it was later found, and set it on fire."

Justin glances at his notes a final time. "That's all of the information I was able to get from him. I hope that answered most of your questions, even though they were probably the hardest answers you'll ever hear."

"Thank you, Justin. We appreciate all you've done to help us through this. Thank you for taking the time to meet with William, to meet with us. We know you care, and that means a lot," Tom says as he moves towards Justin to shake his hand.

Kent and Nicole rise as well, while I remain seated, arms crossed, staring intently at Chelsea's picture.

As Justin heads towards the door, the three of them talk about the sentencing hearing on Monday. Kent shakes his father's hand, gives Nicole a hug, and heads towards me. As he leans down to hug me goodbye, I push my hand against his chest to keep him from coming closer.

Through clenched teeth, I say, "Don't you dare. Don't

you dare touch me. I don't want you near me."

"Mom...c'mon. I love you," Kent says.

"What's it matter Kent? What's it matter? Isn't that what you said?" I spew at him. "If none of it matters, I guess it doesn't matter if we've lost each other, too."

Kent takes a step back, and I push past him, down the hall, and slam the spare bedroom door behind me.

*   *   *

KENT

My mind is swirling with bits of the information we just heard as I drive home. I can't help but conjure images to go along with each piece of the story. My heart races imagining the fear my sister must have felt at realizing a stranger had entered her car. I can envision the fear on her face and feel the quiver in my fingers as I grip the steering wheel, imagining what it must've felt like to be forced to drive somewhere with a stranger. Chelsea's screams echo through my body as they must have sounded when she was being raped, losing her virginity to a madman. Even though the heater in my car is on full blast, a chill creeps into my bones at the thought of a four-mile walk in the freezing February night with no shoes on.

I beg my mind to stop, but it won't. It can't. I wish I hadn't gone today so that these pictures wouldn't be consuming my mind, ravaging my soul. I want to remember my sister the way she was. I want to remember her smile, her laugh, her eyes sparkling as she was planning something mischievous. I want her voice to resonate throughout me, not her screams, the remnants of her fear causing my own body to tremble.

The fifteen-mile drive to my apartment has never felt so long. I keep checking the odometer and telling myself that Chels would've still been walking. I take a deep breath and have a moment's relief when I finally reach five miles knowing she didn't have to walk that far. Relief until the realization pounds me that, by the five-mile mark, she was already dead and floating in the icy cold river, awaiting discovery. I can't wait to get back and have a drink. The shots from this morning have fully worn off, and I'm more sober than I remember being in years. There's no way to describe how I'm feeling other than I *feel*. I feel it all—the one thing I've tried so hard not to do.

Once I'm in my apartment, I head for the unopened vodka bottle in the freezer, taking a drink straight from it. My thoughts turn to my mother. I'm sick of her anger and tired of being pushed away from her. I'm fed up with not being able to have a thought, a feeling, or an opinion around her. Does she think I'm some kind of puppet that will simply respond to her commands? I'm no one's damn puppet. Why am I always so damn pathetic when it comes to my parents? I'm like a little boy that's waiting and waiting for some attention, some love from them.

How could I be such an idiot to actually believe things would be different between Mom and me after the night she stayed a couple of months ago? I'd been surprised to wake up in the middle of the night to find my head resting on my mother's lap, her arms wrapped around me while she too slept. I was half-tempted to wake her and ask what the hell she was doing in my house. In the end, though, I laid back down, falling back to sleep in the comfort of her arms, not remembering the last time I had felt anything other than judgment, anger, and condemnation from her. Curling up with her on the couch brought back warm memories of the *before* days in our life, when things were normal. She really was a good mom before. Up until I was about nine, each night I'd crawl into her bed for snuggle time where I'd lay wrapped in her arms and talk about my day. That was back when her smiles and laughter would reach her eyes, making them shine with joy. Back when she loved being a mother to both of her children. Back when she was whole.

The next morning, when I woke up, my mother had cleaned up the apartment and was in the kitchen frying bacon and making French toast. When she saw me stir, she brought me a cup of coffee with just the right amount of cream and sugar, as if remembering how to make the perfect cup of coffee for your child is a requirement of motherhood. We ate together and talked, with no judgment, condemnation, or invasive questions. She didn't even mention the previous night and my drunken stupor. It was the best conversation I'd had with my mother in years and the most love I'd felt from her in what seemed like a lifetime.

What a damn fool I was for thinking anything would be different. Today, she showed her true colors by, once again, being an angry, heartless bitch.

I sit with the bottle in one hand and mail in the other. The first four envelopes are bills and get tossed, unopened, onto the coffee table. The next envelope is from the Fairmont County Child Support Enforcement Agency.

"What the hell?" I say aloud as I tear open the envelope.

My eyes quickly scan the paper seeing *subpoena to appear, paternity test, Christy Callahan mother, Jenna Lynn Callahan (dob 11/2/08), minor child.*

"What in the world?" I yell this time, followed by a long, hard swallow of vodka. I take a deep breath and read through the paper more slowly.

A paternity test has been scheduled for me on Friday, February 9, 2009, at the Fairmont County Child Support Enforcement Agency to establish paternity for Jenna Lynn Callahan who was born on November 2, 2008, to mother, Christy Callahan. I read it three times, the information still not penetrating. I desperately try to come up with a face to match the name Christy Callahan—too many nameless faces enter at once. There have been so many women, in so many drunken stupors, half of them I can't recall, let alone the names.

I pace my apartment with the bottle of vodka, trying to make the names and dates in the letter conjure a face. I'd be happy if I could even remember a body to go with the name. Whoever Christy Callahan is, she's obviously trying to say this kid is mine. That would be next to impossible. First of all, anyone who came home with me has probably taken similar trips with many other men. Secondly, what are the chances that some chick would get pregnant with my kid on a one-night stand? A lot of people sleep together for years before a slip-up happens. There's absolutely no way I could be the father of this child. I'll show up for the paternity test as required but know that will put an end to whatever Christy Callahan is trying to pull. It will definitely come back negative.

I take a drink, close the bottle and stick the remainder back in the freezer. I grab my keys, deciding to head to the bar. I don't need to be alone right now. I need a distraction from this day of craziness. I'll find exactly what I'm looking for in the first woman who shows the willingness.

NICOLE

19 YEARS, 11 MONTHS, 18 DAYS AFTER
JANUARY 26, 2009

MY nerves are shot as I sit in the crowded courtroom next to Kendra, sitting rigidly and paying attention to nothing but William Dunkin. She's been staring at him since he was led in by the deputies in handcuffs and leg shackles. Judge Sable is reading aloud the original charges, the details of the plea agreement reached, and the purpose of today's proceedings—allowing the family and friends of Chelsea to share with the courts our thoughts regarding sentencing. I try to listen and make sense of Judge Sable's words, but my heart is racing, my palms are sweaty, and I feel like I'm going to pass out. I'm the first one scheduled to speak to the courtroom full of spectators—I hope my voice isn't riddled with the anxiety coursing throughout my body. I unclasp my hands and am not surprised to see how shaky they are.

I look briefly at William Dunkin, who sits slumped forward toward the defense table, his head resting on his handcuffed hands, eyes cast downward. He's wearing a dark blue jumpsuit with the Fairmont County Jail logo on the left breast pocket. Shivers race up my spine—the hands on which he now rests his chin are the same ones that groped Chelsea's body.

I force myself to break my gaze and instead look around the courtroom, recognizing a few of the faces. My mother and father are in the back row—my father gives me a wink as I look at them. The media has its own reserved section directly behind where we'll be standing to read our statements. I wish I could face them rather than looking at William the entire time, although the statement I intend to read is directed towards him. Speaking the words aloud is one thing; saying them while he potentially looks into my eyes is another matter altogether.

"I understand that several family members and friends of Chelsea Wyatt have prepared statements to read before the court," Judge Sable's voice booms.

"Yes, your honor, they do," Justin Lockhart says from behind the prosecution table. "The first person to speak today is Nicole Lansing."

Justin rises and meets me at the gate to grant me entrance into the inner sanctum of the court. My knees tremble as I rise, and I say a silent prayer for my legs to carry me to the podium. As I work my way through the crowd, Kent gives me a thumbs-up sign, which gives me the strength I need to walk the

361

remaining two feet.

Once behind the podium, I lay my written statement down and clear my throat several times before I try to speak.

"As Mr. Lockhart stated, I am Nicole Lansing. In 1989, I was Nicole Spriggs, and Chelsea Wyatt was my best friend. We met our first year in middle school, and our friendship was immediate. From that moment on, we were inseparable—she was the sister I never had. Chelsea was one of the most full of life people I have ever met. Her laugh was contagious. Her smile was beautiful; and, she had the most amazing blue eyes that sparkled with her joy for life. Before she was killed, we'd been looking at colleges and trying to make plans for where we would go, together of course, and what we wanted to do with our lives. Chelsea wanted to be a nurse or a doctor—her greatest desire was to help people in whatever way she could. She never got that chance." Tears burn my eyes, and I clench the sides of the podium to try to stop the tremble in my hands.

"I cannot describe for you the hell I went through as a seventeen-year-old girl when Chelsea went missing. I went through so many different emotions in the days before she was found. The biggest part of me always clung to the hope that it was all some sort of joke and Chelsea would stroll back into school one day, laughing at how worried we all were. But that didn't happen. I never got to hear her laughter again." I pause and clear my throat several times, trying to swallow the lump of grief lodged inside.

"I had to watch my best friend get buried. Along with her body, my hopes, dreams, and desires for the future got bur-

362

ied as well. They were replaced with an intense fear and sense of failure. I was afraid of everything and everyone for many years, including myself and my feelings. I didn't know who had killed Chelsea—if it was a friend of ours, her boyfriend, a family member—therefore, it was best to trust no one. I lived in constant fear of death, knowing that at any moment, my life could be stolen from me as Chelsea's was. In many ways, I lost all motivation for life at the age of seventeen." I raise my gaze from the paper and look towards William. He hasn't moved an inch, and I wonder if he hears a word I'm saying.

"I figured it didn't matter what I did or didn't do because I could die at any time. I started college and then dropped out. I got married and then divorced. I made friends and then failed to keep in touch with them. Nothing mattered. I'd already lost what mattered most—my best friend and my hope. I was also afraid to allow myself to feel anything during that time, good or bad. If I was happy, I felt guilty because Chelsea didn't have the chance to be there with me. If I felt sad, I was afraid to let the tears fall, fearing they would never stop. The only emotion I was comfortable with was the fear gnawing at me day in and day out, hour after hour." As if talking about it, gave it permission to rear its ugly head, those old fears rush into me as crushing anxiety. A weight on my chest, making it hard to catch a breath.

"To keep myself locked inside of me, where it was safe, I turned to pills and alcohol, which only worked for so long. With the drinking and pills, my life fell completely apart until things were such a mess that I had no choice but to get help. Today, I'm proud to say I'm sober," I look at Kent, and he smiles. "I have a wonderful husband and two beautiful daughters that I love more than life itself."

"There are days I still miss my best friend so badly that there's an ache inside me nothing can fill. On those days, I cry a lot, I try to remember our good times, and I give my kids lots of hugs. I wish I could pick up the phone and call my best friend, who always knew how to make me feel better—but I don't have that choice. One day, maybe my heart will accept that."

I pause and look up from my notes to the defense table. William is still in the same position with his eyes downcast, as still as a statue.

"William," I pause for a moment, waiting for him to look up. When he doesn't, I continue.

"You stole so much from me through your terrible actions that night. You stole my best friend, my sense of security, my hope, my future," I pause to wipe the tears trailing down my cheeks. "But when I got sober and started to deal with all of this, I realized I couldn't give you any more power over my life—I had given you enough already. Even though I still have my struggles, I've taken back my life and have tried to rebuild it into something Chelsea would be proud of. Sometimes, I still hear her speaking straight into my heart, and I know what she'd want me to say to you."

I choke back a sob and wipe my tears before continuing. "She would want me to tell you I forgive you because that's the kind of person she was. And, the strange thing is, I do. I have nothing left to give you—whether it be my anger, my hatred,

364

my fear, my guilt. The only thing left to give is my forgiveness. I hurt so many people I love during my using days; I would be a hypocrite to judge you any more harshly than I've judged myself. I hope you hear me say that I forgive you, and I know Chelsea does too. Even though I would do anything in the world to have her back, she's in a better place, and she's okay. Even though I can't still see her face-to-face, she will live forever, right here," I say and pat my hand above my heart.

"I know I'm supposed to speak today about what would make me feel like justice has been served," I stop and look at the judge. "I can't do that, Your Honor, because the only true justice would be me getting my best friend back and Chelsea living a long, happy life. I'm praying you have the wisdom to make the right decision because I truly don't know."

The judge nods slightly at me. "I'd like to thank the courts for their time this morning and for allowing me to share a bit of Chelsea with you."

I head back towards my seat and notice the tears in Kent's and Tom's eyes. Kendra shows no emotion, her eyes still glued to William. I take a deep breath, thankful I'm finished, and sit down, realizing William never once looked up from the table.

*　*　*

KENT

I'm seriously regretting my decision not to drink this morning as a way to honor Chelsea. Knowing it's soon my turn to speak has my stomach in knots and me wishing I had something to calm my nerves. I wrote a statement but don't think I'll be able to get through the first sentence of it, let alone the entire two pages. Hearing Nicole speak, and everything she said, rattled me to my core. I'm still trying to wrap my mind around it all when the prosecutor calls my name.

I walk quickly to get behind the podium, so I'll have something to help steady me. I wait several moments before speaking, hoping like hell my voice won't fail me.

"Your Honor, thanks for the opportunity to speak today. My name is Kent Wyatt, and I was...um... am Chelsea Wyatt's little brother. I was ten when my sister was kidnapped and murdered—just a little boy. At the time, I didn't fully understand what had happened, I just knew I missed my sister. Now, as an adult, I realize how profoundly Chelsea's death affected my entire family."

I now know it is pointless to read my prepared statement, so I re-fold the papers and put them in my pocket.

"I guess the best way to describe it is in befores and afters. Before Chelsea was murdered, our family laughed a lot. After, there were hardly ever smiles, let alone laughter. Before Chelsea was murdered, I cannot ever remember hearing my parents argue. After, that was the only conversation that filled our house for years. Before I never saw my father, or any man for that matter, cry. After, it was as common to see him with tears as it was to see a cloud in the sky," my voice catches as an image of my father in tears overtakes my thoughts. I take a couple of deep breaths before continuing.

"Before, I had a mother who loved me, one who com-

366

forted me when I had bad dreams and tucked me into bed each night. After I had a mother who was so busy working and volunteering at church, I'd sometimes go days without seeing her. Before, I didn't know what words like rape meant. After, I had details of sex that a ten-year-old boy should never have. Before, I was a child who trusted the adults around me to take care of me. After, I thought all the adults in my life no longer noticed my existence or cared if I was alive. Before, I had so many hopes and dreams for my future. After I didn't care about anything, especially my future—sometimes, it's hard to just make it through the day.

"I could stand up here for hours and give you the details of my sob story about how Chelsea's death destroyed my life and my family but, in the end, it wouldn't make a bit of a difference. She'd still be dead, and our lives would still be in the exact same mess. I really don't want anyone's pity. Life simply is what it is.

"What I do want is for William Dunkin to pay for the endless days of pain, torture, and grief he's put my family through. If justice were to really be served, he'd have to serve extra time for the pain he's caused each one of us sitting here today," I pause and look at the judge. "Since that can't happen, I'm begging you, Your Honor, to give him the maximum sentence allowable under the law. I wish each year he spends behind bars would erase a moment of our pain—but, I know it won't. Our loss won't be lessened, but perhaps he'll realize the devastation he's caused. Thank you, Your Honor, for the chance to speak today."

I'm flooded with relief as soon as I step away. My gaze

shifts towards the defense table for the first time since I entered the courtroom. The man sitting there, head down, staring at the floor, looks broken and defeated—the same way I feel most days. I realize as I take my seat that looking at William is a lot like looking in a mirror at my own reflection.

*   *   *

KENDRA

I push past Kent as he's coming down the narrow aisle to take his seat. The others sitting on the row must stand to give me room to get through. I make eye contact with no one, looking only at William as I've done since he entered the room. Each forceful strike of my heels against the wooden floor echoes in the silence. I take my place behind the podium just as Mr. Lockhart says my name.

I've waited almost twenty years for this chance—I'm not about to waste a moment on formalities or introductions.

Without hesitation, before Mr. Lockhart sits, I begin.

"I am Kendra Wyatt. And unlike my son, who couldn't decide what tense to use when referring to Chelsea, I *am* her mother. Mr. Dunkin, could you give me the respect of looking at me while I'm speaking to you?" I pause a moment allowing him the chance to meet my request.

When no acknowledgment comes that he heard my demand, I continue.

"I guess it should come as no surprise that a man who is enough of a coward to rape and murder a child, would be too much of one to look me in the eye." My voice is probably louder

368

than necessary in such a small space, but I don't care.

"On February 8, 1989, you snatched my daughter from the restaurant parking lot, raped her, forced her to walk four miles in the snow, and then you murdered her. You claim it was an accident, but a mother's heart knows the truth. The truth, in this case, is that you killed my daughter with your own two hands. Everyone else today has talked about the impact Chelsea's death has had on them. I'm not going to waste my time doing so because, I know a cold, heartless being like yourself doesn't care. You lived for almost twenty years, knowing what you'd done, and never had the guts to come forward. You worked; you got married; you had lots of children—all things my daughter will never have the chance to do because of you." I point my finger at him. "It doesn't really matter how this affected me. What matters is the pain, fear, and torture my daughter went through because of your sick and twisted mind. What matters is that you stole my daughter's virginity and defiled her in every way imaginable with your disgusting body."

My voice quivers with rage. I take a shaky breath and continue. "What matters is that you dumped her body in a cold, icy river, burnt her car, and continued on about your way, living your life, for the past twenty years—not man enough to face up to what you did. What matters is that my daughter never had the chance to graduate from high school, go to college, pursue a career, get married. My daughter never got the chance to have a child and know the unconditional love that comes with motherhood."

Tears of wrath sear my eyes, threatening to spill onto my

cheeks. I will not cry in front of this man. I refuse to give him the satisfaction.

"Being here today is all about Chelsea. If it were up to me, I wouldn't waste my breath speaking to you. You don't deserve it. But today is Chelsea's day. It's the day she can celebrate that you'll finally have to face what you did to her. Regardless of what lies you've told yourself throughout the years, you know the truth, and so does Chelsea. Your denial may have allowed you to believe your own sick lies all these years, but it doesn't change the facts. I'm here now, and I pray that my voice, and my daughter's face, haunt you for the remainder of your days on earth.

"As far as justice being served," I chuckle. "That's not possible. The only justice would be if you had to endure the exact same punishment my daughter did in her final hours. Hopefully, behind bars, you'll get to experience at least some of it, as others violate you as you did to Chelsea. I hope each time it happens, you remember it's exactly what you deserve."

I finally pull my gaze away from William and towards Judge Sable. "Your honor, I beg you to give him the maximum sentence possible. I assure you even that won't be enough to erase the pain he's caused my entire family. I wish the death penalty were possible because I would be in the front row watching him take his last breath, as he watched Chelsea take hers. Please, Your Honor, show him no mercy—he surely did not show any to Chelsea. Thank you."

The anger pulsing through my veins makes my blood boil. I wish I could have five minutes alone with William to release some of it before I explode. I want nothing more than to see his face writhe with pain and horror, as Chelsea's surely did.

As I take my seat, an overwhelming sense of sadness crushes me because I don't feel one iota of relief. This anger has festered for almost twenty years; I thought getting some of it out would take at least a tiny bit of it away. Instead, it's only grown larger, consuming my soul.

*　　*　　*

TOM

I try to make eye contact with Kendra as she sits, to see if her outpouring of anger has helped. She refuses to look my way, continuing only to glower in William's direction. Even though I know the extent of her fury, her outburst shocked me. As I rise to take my place as the next speaker, I wonder if the kind, patient, loving woman I married will ever resurface. I've heard it said by many different couples throughout the years that they "didn't know the other person anymore." I used to find such a statement laughable, but now, I fully grasp their meaning. Kendra is a complete stranger to me and one I would never even stop to speak to if we passed by each other on the street. Her anger is etched into every line in her face; her fury pronounced clearly in every word. I can't believe she's the same woman who used to lecture our children about the importance of forgiveness. Now there isn't an ounce of it within her.

I walk twelve steps to the gate. Ten more steps to my place before the court. I wait two seconds and carefully lay out my typed notes on the podium. I then place the eight by ten senior photo of Chelsea on the table in front of me, facing William.

I clear my throat several times, trying to find my voice.

"Mr. Dunkin, I am Chelsea Marie Wyatt's father, Tom. I brought a picture of Chelsea today to remind you of the beautiful person you took from this world. I hope you find it in your heart to at least honor Chelsea's memory, and those of us who love her, by taking one look into the smiling, innocent face of my daughter—the person she was before you took her from us." I pause, continuing to look at William, waiting for him to raise his eyes towards the picture, if only for a moment.

His eyes never rise from the table, and after waiting for thirty seconds, I continue.

"On average, an adult takes twenty-three thousand, forty breaths each day. Assuming I'm average, I've taken one hundred sixty-seven million, nine hundred eighty-four thousand, six hundred and forty breaths in the seven thousand two hundred and ninety-one days since my daughter has been gone. On many of those days, each of those breaths felt like a struggle, and I found myself often wondering where I would find the strength to take the next one. Even though so much time has passed, my heart still aches every time I realize that, this side of heaven, I'll never see my daughter again. There are mornings I still awaken, and I'm in that state between sleep and reality, when I could swear I hear my daughter's laughter from down the hallway or hear her whispering in my ear. I cannot describe for you the pain I feel when alertness fully hits me, and I must face that regardless of what my mind has concocted, she's no longer here with us.

"I've had so many questions for you over the years—questions that have tormented me, causing me to lose sleep, my hair," I chuckle, as do several people in the courtroom, as I point to my slightly balding head, "and even my sanity for a while. For a long time, I didn't think I could live without knowing the answers to my questions, like who killed my daughter? Why her? How did it happen? When did she take her last breath? Somewhere along the way, I realized I would have to learn to live again without the answers, for I didn't know if they'd ever come. I must tell you that when you killed Chelsea, you took half my heart with you. She was my angel. While it wasn't easy learning to live with only half a heart and with so many unanswered questions, I did it. I went to work each day; I went to church; I had friends; I loved my wife and son. Each time the nagging questions would rise up in me, I would squelch them down with the information I did have, with what was right in front of me—my family, my friends, my home, my job, my memories. If I had allowed those questions to remain with their daily torment, I would not be able to stand in front of you today, because I would be lost within my own mind." A shudder works its way through me at the memories of my time in the hospital.

"In going on with life, despite my unanswered questions, I found something else that I never thought would be possible for a father of a murdered child—peace and forgiveness. Even though I only recently found out your name and the circumstances surrounding my daughter's murder, I forgave you many years ago. It wasn't even a conscious, or wanted, choice—I simply had to if I wanted to be able to move forward in my life.

373

Now, you have answered some of the questions that I wanted answered so long ago, and to many people, this may seem like it'd be a relief. But, to me, those answers really don't matter anymore. Having them doesn't make my heart heal; they don't erase my daily struggles; they don't change the fact that my daughter is dead. People may think the answers would help bring closure; please understand I had to find closure many years ago, without the answers, so I could continue to live and face each new day." I look at Chelsea's picture. Her blue eyes and radiant smile fill me with a sense of peace.

"I cannot begin to describe the toll that Chelsea's murder took on our entire family and the price we have each paid throughout the years. A price no family should ever have to pay. Despite what we've been through and what we've lost, I need you to hear me say I forgive you. I was surprised to see you in person for the first time because, in my mind, I believed only some kind of monster could've done this to my child, to my family. But then, upon seeing you, I realized that you're just a man. I still don't know the reason you did what you did; but, to forgive, I don't need to know the reason. God has commanded us to forgive one another if we seek forgiveness; so, I must forgive you if I want it for myself. I'm not saying the process has been easy, rather, the journey started long before I ever even knew your name.

"Just because I forgive, doesn't mean I believe you should escape the consequences for your actions. I ask the judge to give you the maximum sentence that he can. Even if you spent the rest of your life behind bars, it truly wouldn't be enough to make up for what you've done. I pray that your time in prison brings you healing, repentance, and a desire to move forward in a different direction."

I look up from my notes and stare at Chelsea's picture as I continue. "Some people may think I'm crazy for what I'm about to say, and maybe I am; but, I know my daughter doesn't want me to hate you. To hate makes me focus on my daughter's death, not her life. I hear her sometimes, whispering straight to my soul. She wants me to remember her smile, her laughter, the joy, the good times. You may have caused my daughter's death; but as long as I remember her, you can never take her life from me. That life continues to live on in my memories of her."

Finally, I move my gaze to William. "We all have choices. I must make a conscious choice every day to celebrate the person my daughter was, instead of focusing on what you did to her. I choose to allow her to live on. I ask once more, father to father; please take a moment to look at my beautiful daughter who I will cherish as long as I live."

After waiting a full sixty seconds, which feels like a lifetime of silence, I sadly shake my head, thank the judge and walk back to my seat. Cold fury emanates from every pore in Kendra's body, telling me she was incensed by my statement. All that matters is I am at peace and know Chelsea is smiling.

*   *   *

BILLY

I take a deep breath as Mr. Wyatt steps away from the podium, realizing I've been holding my breath through most of the statements. I was intent at following my attorney's advice of tuning out what was being said and not making eye contact. He said it was the only way to ensure that I appear calm and stable throughout the hearing. Finally, after sitting as still as possible for the past hour, I shift in my seat and raise my eyes slightly, enough only to see the reporters across the courtroom furiously scribbling on their tablets.

The prosecutor announces that Mr. Wyatt is the last person to present a statement for the prosecution. Judge Sable addresses my attorney and me, asking if anyone would like to speak on behalf of the defense prior to sentencing.

Mr. McCabe rises, "My client does not wish to make a statement. However, I would like the floor for a moment if I could Your Honor?"

"Certainly," Judge Sable says.

"As the courts are aware, my client pled guilty of his own volition because of his desire for the family to not have to suffer any more by sitting through a trial," Mr. McCabe pauses when a sarcastic laugh comes from Chelsea's mother. "My client admits that he committed egregious crimes against Chelsea Wyatt almost twenty years ago and, for that, he is sorry. Prior to sentencing, I ask the courts to consider the extreme alcohol and drug addiction problems that have plagued my client for years and take into account the role these addictions played in his actions that night."

I'm trying to tune out Mr. McCabe's voice because his excuses sound like bullshit even to me—I can't imagine what the Wyatt family thinks.

A rustle of bodies shifts in the courtroom behind me as a man's voice shouts out, excusing himself. I want to see what the commotion is about but don't want to accidentally meet the eyes of anyone in the Wyatt family. Mr. McCabe stops speaking and turns towards the rows of observers. The judge pounds his gavel and is ready to speak when he's interrupted by a familiar voice. I turn around for the first time since the hearing started and see my brother. He has a wild-eyed, frantic look as he steps towards the gate.

"I'm sorry for the disruption, Your Honor, but I would like to make a statement before sentencing," David says.

Judge Sable bangs his gavel once. "And you are?"

"I'm David Dunkin, William's brother, and also an attorney," David's words rush out. "Once again, I'm sorry. If you could please give me a few moments of the court's time."

"Mr. McCabe, were you aware of Mr. Dunkin's desire to speak?" Judge Sable asks.

"Not entirely, Your Honor. But I have no objections to it if the courts and Mr. Lockhart are in agreement," Mr. McCabe seems dumbfounded by David's interruption, and I'm sure the judge sees it too.

"Mr. Lockhart?" the judge asks.

"Your Honor, this certainly is an unexpected interruption, but the prosecution has no objection to hearing what Mr. Dunkin has to say," Mr. Lockhart adds.

"Mr. Dunkin, you may make a statement; however, I must say, you, of all people, being an officer of the court, should have known better than to interrupt in this fashion. I don't allow

377

my courtroom to be turned into a circus. I'm sure you are well aware that I could ask for you to be removed; however, now that we're all off track and curious about what it is you have to say, you may proceed," Judge Sable sternly announces.

David makes his way purposefully to the podium. Once there he looks more at ease as if his mind automatically slips into lawyer-mode the minute he's this close to the raised bench of the judge. David asked me if he could speak today; I was adamant he didn't. In fact, I made it clear to my attorney that David was not to speak on my behalf; obviously, my request was completely disregarded. I don't want David to stand up in front of everyone and claim his allegiance to me—his brother, the murderer. I don't want David to have to admit any connection to me whatsoever. He has a successful career, a wife, a child—his life is complete. Associating himself with me will do nothing but complicate things for him, and there's absolutely nothing he can say or do to change the outcome. I confessed; the girl is dead. David won't be able to say anything to influence the judge's decision about my sentence.

I now stare directly at my brother, hoping he'll look my way. After a few seconds, David meets my eyes, and I slightly shake my head to tell him to stop. He gives a single nod in my direction and then turns away, towards the observers.

"Again, I'm sorry to everyone for the interruption. I'm David Dunkin, and William, known to me as Billy, is my older brother. Mr. and Mrs. Wyatt, Kent, and Nicole, let me first tell you how sorry I am about the murder of Chelsea. From everything I've heard about her today, she sounds like she was a wonderful person, and I can't imagine the loss you must continue to feel every day," David says with tears in his eyes.

"I didn't plan on speaking today, so I have no prepared statement; instead, I'll speak to you from the heart. I've heard a lot here today that left me no choice but to share with you how my brother went from the boy in this picture with our mother and me," David has a framed four by six picture that he places on the edge of the table in the exact same spot where Chelsea's picture sat earlier, "to the man pleading guilty to involuntary manslaughter and who is responsible for taking a life."

My heart aches as I look at the picture. It's one Mrs. Lawson took of the three of us in front of the bakery. Mom is standing in the middle in her pink uniform, an arm around each of us boys, drawing us close to her. We are all smiling. I can smell the cinnamon rolls baking as though they are here in the court-room. Our mother was beautiful and happy, with the light shining all the way to her eyes. I had forgotten she was ever happy. I didn't know any of the pictures of my mother survived the fire.

"Please know that I'm not here to make excuses for my brother's reprehensible actions. I'm here simply to give you a glimpse of how he became who he is today. I won't go into all the details for there are far too many and none are pretty. Billy is two years older than me, and when we were younger, he was my hero. We were raised in a home with an extremely abusive father. Our mother was initially the target of his abuse, but our dad's wrath often turned to Billy because he'd try to defend her. Billy often took beatings in my place as well—he was my protector, making sure I stayed quiet or got out of the house when our fa-

379

ther was in one of his rages. We watched my father try to drown my mother, leaving her for dead on the bathroom floor, when Billy was seven, and I was five. That was one of the more severe beatings Billy got, requiring him to get stitches in his head."

Old fear starts rising up in me that I always felt as the young boy David describes. The memories of watching our father repeatedly plunge our mother's head into the tub full of water fill my mind. My ancient screams of terror echo in my head. Feelings of overwhelming loss and hopelessness bombard me, like when I thought our mother was dead. Why is my brother rehashing all of this for these strangers who hate me? I want to stand up and scream, telling him to shut up, that none of it matters. But I can't, and David continues.

"My mother left with us several times but was never able to stay away for long, for a variety of reasons—she had no money, nowhere to go, no family to support her. We always ended up right back where we started, with our father, in our house of misery. Our father ended up," David pauses, his voice choked with tears, "excuse me ... ended up killing our mother when Billy was eleven, and I was nine. Our father caught our house on fire, with our mother and Billy trapped inside. Billy escaped and attempted to save her but couldn't. Instead, my eleven-year-old brother had to watch our home and our mother go up in flames."

The heat from the blaze burns my throat, my eyes, my hands, my heart. My mother's screams of agony from within the inferno now mix in my mind with Chelsea's screams of fear as I raped her. The two voices have merged into one, and I can

380

no longer differentiate which scream belonged to whom. I still see the blaze which has burned its image into my memory. The fire that killed my mother now merges with the one I was responsible for in the burning of Chelsea's car. I recall hearing my mother's screams of terror coming from the burning remnants of the car. I watched it burn, mesmerized by the licks of flames as they hashed out their destruction, unable to turn from it, as it was when I was younger. Tears build in the corners of my eyes, threatening to scald my cheeks if I release them.

I turn to my attorney and whisper, "Please make him stop."

My attorney holds up his hand to silence me, never taking his gaze from David, too enthralled with the story. There's nothing I can do to make David stop. I drank so much over the years and took so many drugs, trying to block all of this from my mind. Now, here I am shackled, stuck in a roomful of strangers, being forced to listen to my history—the one I've wasted my entire life trying to run from.

"After her murder, my brother and I were separated. I went to live with our neighbor, Mary Jones, a wonderful woman who gave me as normal of a life as possible, given my first nine years. Billy was sent to live with my mother's parents—people who had turned away our battered, bruised, and crying mother years earlier when she went to them trying to escape my father's abuse, and who never had a relationship with us throughout the years. I don't know much about Billy's life after that, other than bits and pieces. What I do know is he became a different person. He drank a lot, just like our father used to. He used drugs.

He stole. He hurt people. All I can assume is that his heart had hardened beyond repair and, in his desperation to run from his past, he kept living it out over and over by hurting everyone who crossed his path."

David pauses and finally looks at me for the first time since he started speaking. He holds up the picture and lifts it towards me.

Maintaining eye contact with me, David continues. "This is my brother who I've never stopped loving, my hero, my protector. The man sitting right there, shackled and handcuffed, is the product of a murderous, abusive father and a mother who was never able to leave. I'm sorry Chelsea had to encounter the man he became instead of the one he could've been, given a different life."

Tears now spill down my cheeks. I want to wipe them away, but the handcuffs won't allow it. David doesn't make an attempt to wipe his away, letting them flow as if they can wash away our pasts.

"Your Honor, Billy needs to be punished for his crimes. Please remember, as you determine his sentence, the punishment he's already received and will continue to live with for the rest of his life, whether he's in jail or not. I love you, Billy, and I'm sorry. I'm so sorry."

David walks away. I slump back in my seat, the memories of my past so heavy that it's difficult to hold my head up. One thing is perfectly clear as I sit awaiting my fate, I've become the thing I hate most in this world. Regardless of the plea agreement and what I told them about how Chelsea died, I am a murderer, just like my father. I know the truth. I know whose face I saw as Chelsea took her last breath. The resemblance between her and that caseworker, Veronica, from so many years ago was uncanny. The hatred I'd carried for Ms. Walters for years rose up in me the moment I saw Chelsea cross the parking lot. She could've been the younger sister or daughter of that caseworker. My mind couldn't distinguish between the two of them. I wanted Veronica to hurt like she hurt me. Instead, the wrong person suffered at the hands of my wrath.

If there were a way for me to end my own useless life right this moment, I would do it. Had I known who I would become, I would've made sure to end it all before I had the chance to exact my punishment on poor, innocent Chelsea Wyatt.

DUNKIN SENTENCED — CASE CLOSED

Closure comes for Wyatt family after nearly 20 years of waiting

By Lucinda Parlow

The Langston Messenger

January 27, 2009

Chelsea Wyatt's father, Tom, placed her senior picture next to him on the table while he addressed the courts. His desire was for her killer to look at her one last time, seeing the person he stole from them almost twenty years ago. Regardless of Mr. Wyatt's pleas, William Dunkin never looked.

Throughout the proceedings, he didn't glance up from the table where he sat, until his own brother, David Dunkin, took center stage and shared information about their abusive upbringing with the courts. As his brother described their father murdering their mother, tears could be seen in William Dunkin's eyes. David did not make a plea for mercy from the courts, only a sense of understanding for how the person who took Chelsea's life was created.

Judge Sable announced to Mr. Dunkin, prior to his sentencing, that he was "extremely disturbed by his utter lack of remorse" towards the Wyatt family as exhibited in his unwillingness to meet the one small request of Mr. Wyatt, to look at his daughter's picture. Sable also expressed disgust that William did not offer any apologies to the family.

Sable ordered him to serve seven to twenty-five years in prison. A full five years of his sentence must be served before he's eligible for parole. However, Sable said he will recommend to the parole board that Dunkin finish the entire twenty-five-year sentence since he evaded law enforcement for almost twenty years. Time that Chelsea Wyatt didn't have.

After the sentencing, Tom Wyatt spoke openly with reporters. He reiterated statements made earlier in court, regarding how hard this has been on their entire family. In response to the question as to whether he felt justice has been served, Mr. Wyatt responded that after hearing about William Dunkin's life today in court, he is no longer sure what justice truly is. He stated, "Perhaps, true justice would've been someone intervening in William's tragic life when he was younger, and then he never would have murdered Chelsea."

Tom stated that, after today, the family could begin to have closure and everything they said during the proceedings was in honor of Chelsea's memory.

KENT

B EFORE I leave, I look around one last time, making sure everything is in place. I'm impressed. The last time my apartment looked so good was before I moved in any of my belongings. All my nervous energy was put to good use by making the place more presentable for today's visit.

I can't believe today is finally here after the last several months of trying to reach an agreement with Christy. It's my first visitation alone with my daughter, Jenna Lynn Callahan. Whenever I think, *my daughter*, a smile spreads across my face. It's taken quite some time for those words to bring a smile instead of a panic attack.

After the paternity results initially came back, I fell

apart. I thought God must be playing a cruel joke by giving me, one of the most careless and irresponsible people in the world, a child. I felt sorry for the kid. I couldn't even take care of myself most days, let alone a child. My buddies told me not to worry about it—I could make my monthly child support payments, and nothing about my life would need to change.

For two months, that's exactly what I did. I only did what was necessary to stay out of trouble—fill out the forms at work to have sixty dollars and eighty-four cents taken from my paycheck each week to go to Christy Callahan. Even though the money was going to Christy and the Child Support Agency determined I was the father of a child named Jenna, I still couldn't picture the woman who had given birth to my daughter. We had no reason to come face to face as everything was handled by mail, e-mail, or phone. For two months, I was drunk more often than I was sober, with a different woman in my bed each night. I tried everything to make myself not care that I was a father to a little girl I had never met.

In the middle of May, I had been out partying with some buddies and co-workers. I drank more than I could remember, snorted a lot of coke, and took a handful of pills, not knowing or caring what they were. It was one of the few nights I went home alone, a little after four in the morning. I was lying in bed trying to calm my racing heart, desperately needing to sleep off my high, but the sound of a baby crying kept filling my head. I couldn't get it to stop no matter what I tried. More Vodka didn't work. More pills didn't work. Banging my head repeatedly against the wall didn't work. The baby wouldn't stop crying. My desperate pleas to God to stop the noise went unanswered.

I finally picked up the phone, deciding that maybe talking to someone would help. I needed to stop the baby's crying, so I could go to sleep—having a conversation would distract me from the uproar in my brain. I didn't have a person in the world I felt I could call at four in the morning while ranting like a raving lunatic about a crying baby. My buddies would laugh it off, and I'd be the butt of their jokes for months. My parents weren't an option—I really couldn't deal with a lecture about my lifestyle choices with the baby screaming in my head.

As clear as crystal, a voice interrupted the crying and simply said, "Nicole." I could've sworn it was Chelsea.

I looked through my cell phone, found her number and called. She answered on the fourth ring and listened to my ramblings for a few minutes before telling me she'd be right over. Within fifteen minutes, she was at my door, still in her pajamas and sleep heavy in her eyes. I don't remember much about our conversation other than what Nicole later told me.

Nicole sat with me for hours as I went back and forth between weeping in her arms and pacing my apartment in a rage at the world. I kept telling her about the baby crying and saying I had to get to it to make it stop. Sometime during the conversation, I broke down sobbing and told Nicole I had a daughter—I'd told no one other than my drinking buddies before that moment. She listened and held me in her arms until I eventually fell asleep.

She was still with me when I finally woke up the next day. She filled in the blanks in my memory about the previous night, and we talked for a long time. As Nicole was getting ready to leave, I stopped her and said the words that had needed to come for a long time, *I'm ready.*

I didn't have to offer any more to Nicole for her to understand my meaning. She drew me into a hug and told me to come with her. We went to her house so she could shower and get dressed. Afterward, Nicole took me to my first ever twelve-step meeting. The person speaking at the meeting seemed to be telling my story, and I was teary throughout the entire thing. Nicole introduced me to a man, Jim, at the end of the meeting, suggesting we go out for coffee and talk. Jim hadn't touched drugs or alcohol in twenty-five years, although he was quite a wild one during his using days. Even though I didn't fully understand the commitment, Jim agreed to be my sponsor by the time we finished our fourth cup of coffee.

Jim became the father I wished I had—one that listened to me, could relate to my fears and pain, gave me advice instead of nagging me about my screw-ups. For the first time in my life since Chelsea died, I chose to obey rather than rebel and vowed to do whatever Jim told me to do. Ninety meetings in ninety days. Stay away from old places and old faces. Take it one day at a time. Pick up the phone instead of picking up a drink. And, to my amazement, it worked. It has been six months since I've taken a drink or a drug.

I had only been sober for about a month when I told Jim about my daughter. He was by my side every step of the way to get to today, through all the phone calls, e-mails, letters, court appearances. Jim was with me when I initially got to see her, hold her, and fall in love for the first time in my life.

Our first meeting was September sixteenth, and Jenna was already ten months old. The visit was at Christy's mother's home on the east side of town. I was thankful Jim went with me. I was so nervous that if I'd been on my own, surely I would've made a pit stop at the liquor store to drink my anxieties away. Christy answered the door. She was a young, beautiful woman with tears in her piercing blue eyes. I couldn't remember ever seeing her before, let alone making a baby with her. I pulled her into a hug, partly to comfort her as I could tell this meeting was also hard on her, and partly to hide the fact that I couldn't remember.

"Well," Christy said, removing herself from my embrace. "Would you like to meet Jenna?"

We followed Christy to the family room where Jenna, with her blond curls and big blue eyes, was sitting on a blanket on the floor, surrounded by toys. She looked up at us when we entered the room, and her face broke into a huge grin, a dimple in each cheek. That's all it took— I was in love. The first time I held her in my arms, and she gazed at me with her innocent eyes, I felt complete. I knew I'd never again be the same.

Over the next month, Christy and I met several times, sometimes with Jenna, other times without, for coffee or dinner, trying to get to know each other. She knew I had no memory of our night of passion and helped fill in the empty spaces, including reminding me of how I'd forcefully discarded her the morning after. I discovered through our conversations that I really liked her and found myself looking forward to our get-togethers. Christy finally agreed to let me have some unsupervised visitation with Jenna, after being fully convinced that I've really stopped drinking.

I still haven't told my parents about Jenna because I'm not ready to share her with them. Outside of "Uncle" Jim and "Aunt" Nicole, I've kept her a secret—not out of shame, but out of greed. I am still savoring every smile, every tear, every new word spoken, every milestone accomplished. I don't get to see her often enough to have to share her with anyone else.

I ring the bell and Christy comes to the door, carrying Jenna. Immediately, my daughter reaches out her arms to me, saying *Daddy* with a smile that melts my heart. As I pull her close, the scent of her fills me. Whatever happened in the past, whatever happens in the future, this is my present, which makes it all worthwhile—the love of my daughter.

NICOLE

20 YEARS, 10 MONTHS, 16 DAYS AFTER
DECEMBER 24, 2009

I pass out presents to each of the children sitting in a semi-circle on the floor in front of me as their mothers watch from their seats. The smiles on the children's faces are priceless; their eyes so trusting. It amazes me that children who have suffered so much in their lives can express such glee at a simple act of kindness. The faces looking up at me now are completely different from when they arrived at the *Divine Sanctuary Women's Shelter*, where I've worked for the past six months as the Program Director.

While handing over their presents, I recall some of their stories. Michael, a seven-year-old boy, watched his mother get beaten within a centimeter of her life by his father. When Michael and his mom, Carolyn, arrived at the center, he was withdrawn, wouldn't make eye contact, and spoke only in whispers. Now, Michael's eyes sparkle, and he shouts out "Thank you, Mrs. L." and jumps up to give me a bear hug when I give him his gift.

Natasha, a six-year-old girl, had been raped repeatedly by her mother's boyfriend over the course of four months, while her mother, Josie, was too terrified to intervene, fearing her next beating would be the one to kill her. Natasha and Josie have only been here about a month, but the fear and sadness are already starting to leave Natasha's eyes. She's still withdrawn and wakes up almost every night screaming but manages a slight smile as she's handed her present.

Sammy, a two-year-old boy with bright blond hair and big brown eyes, is barely able to sit still because he's so excited. When Sammy and his mother, Julie, arrived they both were bruised from head to toe, and Sammy had a cast on his little leg, making it impossible for him to walk. Julie's husband had gotten mad because Sammy spilled his milk on the floor during dinner, and she didn't do anything to prevent it. One glass of spilled milk resulted in a broken leg, a bruised kidney, and two broken ribs for Sammy; a fractured jaw, concussion, broken nose, and two busted lips for Julie.

There's a story for each of the faces before me; each one breaks my heart. Each one also fills me with gratitude for my life and my struggles, which feel insignificant compared to theirs.

When David Dunkin spoke in court about the life he and William had endured as children, I was left with no doubt that if someone would've intervened in their mother's life, giving her a fresh start, a way to live without suffering at the hands of her husband, I would still have my best friend. I left the courtroom completely convinced that William, given a different beginning, wouldn't have become a murderer. I left court that day on a mission—to help the William's and David's of the world, and their mothers, so they don't become monsters that exact their rage on innocent bystanders. So that no other seventeen-year-old girl has to lose her best friend.

It didn't take long to find the position here. My work is fulfilling; however, some days, I leave so depressed that it takes all my energy to plaster on a smile for my own children. Other days, I want to take a child and run away with it, knowing the mother is going to return to the man who hurt them so badly.

Then, there are days like today, when their resilience shines in the sparkle in their eyes. Their laughter fills the room, and there's genuine warmth in their hugs. These are the days I pray the children will remember years from now—days they know they are loved, special, and that they matter. Days they are safe. I pray this will be a place they can return to, if only in memory, to keep them from hurting someone else because of the pain they've suffered.

I snap pictures as the children open their gifts. I plan to give one to each mother and child. Then they'll have something to remind them that there can be happiness despite the pain. There can be healing, no matter how deep the wound. There are choices.

KENDRA

I place the bouquet of pink roses in the vase attached to the side of Chelsea's headstone. The pink looks startling next to the drab gray marble that signifies my daughter's life.

"Happy Birthday, Chelsea," I say, running my hand along the smooth stone, wishing instead I was able to feel the warmth of my daughter's cheek beneath my fingers. "You'd be thirty-nine today."

I sit on the ground and lean back against the headstone, imagining that I'm lying directly above my daughter's body, wishing I could hold her in my arms as I speak. Instead, the moisture and coldness from the damp earth seep into my jeans, causing me to chill. I don't care though; I just want to be close to my daughter.

"I still miss you so much—every second of every day. I wonder how you would've changed over the years, who you'd be now. I wish you were here.

"Some exciting news! Kent has a daughter, our first grandchild. She's absolutely beautiful and reminds me so much of you when you were little—the way she laughs whenever we make a silly face at her, the way she eats all of one food at a time before moving onto the next, the sparkle in her blue eyes whenever she's being mischievous. Her name is Jenna, and she's amazing. I wish she'd gotten the chance to know her aunt, Chelsea. You would've loved her."

Tears stream down my cheeks as my anger rises. "It's not fair, Chelsea. You were supposed to be the one to give us our first grandchild. You should've had two or three by now. We should be having big Sunday dinners after church with you and your kids, Kent and his. We should be laughing together and building memories. I shouldn't have to come here to tell you happy birthday.

"I'm just so damn mad. I'm mad at God for allowing you to be taken from us. I'm mad at William Dunkin for killing you. I'm mad at your father for forgiving that horrible man. I'm mad at your brother for moving on with his life, seeming to forget you and us. I'm even mad at you. Why didn't you put up more of a fight? Why didn't you run away when he was forcing you to walk across town? Why did you leave us?"

I bury my head in my hands, sobbing and unable to continue for a few minutes. "Mostly, I'm mad at myself. I'm mad that I can't move on; I can't let go; I can't forgive. This anger's killing me but I'm so afraid— scared that if I let go of it, I'll have nothing left to keep me going. Without my rage, I'll be completely empty. I know if I want to enjoy any part of the rest of my life though, I've got to find a way. I just don't know how, Chels. I don't know how to let you go, how to truly accept that you're gone."

I rest my forehead against my knees, tears burn my eyes, and sobs shake my entire body. I wish I could lie down and die right here with Chelsea. Catching her killer didn't bring the closure and help me move on as I hoped it would. Knowing what happened that dreadful night so long ago is killing me. Dreams of my daughter screaming in pain as she's raped often wake me from sleep. Seeing my daughter's lifeless body, floating in the ice-covered river, creeps into even my waking hours. William Dunkin's face infiltrates almost every thought, whether I'm awake, asleep, laughing, or crying. I can't get him out of my head.

"I want to see you again, to hold you, to love you. I just want to be with you Chels."

The wind blows through the trees, and suddenly its warmth envelops me, despite the chill in the air. It gently dries my tear-soaked cheeks. For the first time since my daughter was taken from us, I hear her voice speaking directly to my soul. *Let go, Mom. As long as you remember, I am with you. I am okay—I am free, and I am soaring. I want you to be free—to forgive, to laugh, to love.* The kiss of my daughter has touched my cheek, and Chelsea's arms have embraced me in the gentle breeze.

I laugh through my tears, relieved to have heard, if only for an instant, my daughter's voice. Grateful to have felt my daughter's kiss. "I remember honey...I remember."

I sit for a while longer and finally rise to go home. I turn towards my daughter's gravestone. "I will try, Chelsea. For you, I will try. It hasn't been, and never will be, easy; but I'll do my best. Thank you, sweetheart. Thank you."

TOM

"HIGHER, Pop-Pop, higher," Jenna giggles.

"Hold on, little lady, the rocket is headed into outer space," I say as I give her a push.

Her laughter swells my heart to its fullest.

I took a vacation day to spend with my favorite little lady in the world. I picked her up from Kent and Christy's and headed to the park. Her first stop was, of course, the swings where she'd be content for hours if I'd let her. I may just do that because there's nothing that makes me feel better than her smiles and laughter.

This little girl has stolen my heart. I was completely dumbfounded when Kent showed up at our door a little over

seven months ago, baby in tow and introduced her as our grand-
daughter. It took me a full minute to stifle my shock enough to
be able to absorb what Kent was saying. It took me about twenty
seconds to cross the room to meet Kent and the baby at the front
door. It took two seconds for a smile to cross Jenna's small face
and for me to fall completely, head over heels in love.

I've spent every possible minute with her since our first
meeting. Each time, Jenna manages to wrap me a little more
tightly around her finger. I love everything about her. Her bright
blue eyes. Her bouncy blond curls. The way my heart melts
when she smiles at me. The way her little arms wrap around my
neck, while she says, "I wuv you, Pop-Pop!"

For seven thousand eight hundred and fourteen days, if
someone would've asked me what I would give to get my daughter back, my answer would've been anything. And I would have
given *absolutely anything*—my life, my job, my home, even my
wife or son. In some ways, it feels like I've already sacrificed each
of those at one time or another throughout the years. But, in
the two hundred and thirty days I've known Jenna, my answer
has completely changed, so much so, that it often shocks me to
realize the depth of transformation this little angel has brought.
I don't have an answer other than a firm knowing, deep in my
soul, that whenever God closes one door, another always opens.
I still miss my daughter. I wish she could be here with us. I realize, though, that the gift of Jenna has to be enough.

Kent and I have spent a lot of time in the past several
months talking and trying to work on our relationship. I'm enjoying getting to know my son, and I'm amazed to see what a

good father he is. Watching Kent with Jenna reminds me of how enamored I was with Chelsea when she was a baby. I know, without a doubt, Kent would give his life for this little girl. During one of our conversations, Kent told me he still misses Chelsea but can't imagine life if she hadn't been murdered. He said that his life, our family, would be different, and the paths he'd chosen would've looked nothing the same. Kent explained that even though his journey was painful and full of choices he later regretted, he wouldn't do a thing differently because he wouldn't have ended up with his daughter, and soon to be wife.

"Down, Pop-Pop, down," Jenna yells.

"Alright, sweetie. What'cha wanna do next?" I ask, freeing her from the swing.

"Catch me!" she yells, taking off in the field beside the park

I watch as her little legs, pumping as hard as they can, take off in the field of dandelions before me. The sun shines down on her, and her blond hair glows, making her look like an angel. She turns to see if I'm close and bursts into laughter. I remember my own little girl, so many years ago, running through a similar field, her laughter filling the air. As I catch up to Jenna, I pull her into a hug and kiss her chubby cheeks. I feel Chelsea here, looking down on us and smiling. I know, without a doubt that she will always be here, as long as I remember.

BILLY

I sit on the bed in my cell holding the stack of letters, some of the envelopes yellowed with age. Despite my protests, David sent the letters from my father anyway. I received them over a month ago and, so far, have gotten no further than holding them in my hands. Part of me wants to destroy them all unopened; the other part wants to know what my father had to say, if he had any remorse over what he'd done. There are fifteen letters in all, but I have no idea when he started writing them.

I was transferred to the Mason County Correctional Institute, ironically enough, on February 8, 2010—exactly twenty years to the day since I abducted and killed Chelsea Wyatt. It was a sign from God telling me I'm exactly where I need to be.

In the seven months I've been here, David has come to visit twice. I hate him coming anywhere near this vile place, and I felt overwhelmed with guilt on both of his visits. My brother never would've seen the inside of a prison were it not for me. David tells me that he doesn't blame me for the path I took in life—he blames our parents and the broken system. Still, I know that I had choices, and unfortunately, throughout the years, I continuously made the wrong ones.

I pick up the top letter in the stack, deciding to read at least one. If it's full of shit, I'll rip them all to shreds without reading them.

I open the letter and am surprised at the sight of my father's handwriting. I can't ever remember seeing it before. It's very much like my own.

> *June 3, 1987*
>
> *William,*
>
> *Today is your 21st birthday. I hope you had a good day.*
>
> *I'm writing this letter to you from my cell at the Landon County Correctional Institute where I've been for nine years. I have at least eleven more years to serve before I'm eligible for parole.*
>
> *Life here has been hell, but it's given me a lot of time to think about the things I've done and how I've screwed up. Like with you and David. This probably doesn't mean much after the hell I put you through, but for what it's worth, I'm sorry. I loved your mother, and I wish I could go back in time and do it all over again. I love you*

too, even though I never showed it very well. I'm not trying to make excuses, but my dad was a mean bastard, just like me. He used to beat my mom and me. I guess I thought that was how it was supposed to be. I don't know why I did the things I did, and I wish I could take them back, but I can't.

My birthday wish for you is that you turn out nothing like me and that you're a good dad to your kids someday. I don't want you to have to be sitting in a room, locked up with all your regrets, like I am.

I'm sure that I'm the last person you want to hear from, and I don't blame you after what I did to you and your mom. I hope someday you'll know how sorry I am. I don't expect you to forgive me—what I did can never be forgotten, I know that.

Love,

Dad

I don't know whether I feel relief at Dad's apology or disgust that he thought an *I'm sorry* would even begin to erase the hatred in my heart for him. Granted, the man in the letter sounds nothing like the father I remember—he never apologized for a damn thing.

My emotions are all over the place, my thoughts jumbled together. Memories of the beatings, my mother's screams, my father's rages, don't go with the words I just read. How could my father call his feelings for my mother love? He tortured her repeatedly over the years. At least when he killed her, her punishment stopped, and she was free from him. And using his parents as the excuse for his behavior? Maybe that's why David annoys me so much with trying to say it is okay that I've turned out this way because of our childhood. A screwed-up childhood doesn't mean you have the right to hurt everyone around you.

Desperately needing a break from my thoughts and emotions, I lie down to nap. My dreams are of my mother. We're running through the park in the rain, laughing. The rain beats down on us so hard that we're drenched from head to toe and can barely see through the downpour. We rush inside to escape, into a home I don't recognize, filled with the smell of baking bread and vanilla. Mom grabs a towel for me and dries me off, both of us still laughing with water dripping from our eyelashes, our noses, our hair. My mother puts her hand under my wet chin and forces me to look into her eyes.

"Billy, look at me. Listen to me," she says with urgency. "I've got to go now."

I start crying—I don't know if I'm a child or an adult in the dream or a combination of the two. "Don't go, Mommy. Please stay."

"Billy, I have to go. Remember, I love you, my little prince. I'll always be here with you. Your pain doesn't have to be passed on. No matter what, remember, I love you."

My mother fades away in the dream as I scream, "Come back! Come back!"

I wake myself with a start, drenched in sweat. This is the first dream I've had since my mother's death where she didn't disappear engulfed by flames, rather she simply faded away. Even though the dream unsettles me, it's better than the nightmares I've had for so many years. Her voice is still in my head, saying

I love you. I still feel the warmth of her kiss on my cheek. I had forgotten the sound of her laughter—it brings me a sense of comfort and peace to be able to remember it now.

I now know what I have to do before it's too late. I get out my tablet and pen and start the letter I'm not sure I'll ever send. As I start writing to my oldest son, Robby, I recall the first time I held him and the fierce love I felt. I remember the promise I made to myself at that moment, that I would give him the love of a father that I never knew. I also vowed to never hurt him; never become the man my father was to David and me. As I put pen to paper, I begin my attempt at explaining why I've fallen so short as a father, broken so many promises, and how truly sorry I am.

ROBBY

22 YEARS, 7 MONTHS, 23 DAYS AFTER

OCTOBER 1, 2011

DESIRE burns within me, a raging fire threatening to consume everything in its path. I turn the corner towards the woman to try to smother the flames. I need to know her, have her next to me. I have never wanted anything so badly in my life. The fire within leaves me no room for logical thinking or choice. It is in absolute control.

I slow down as I approach her. She is now running, sensing my presence, feeling the heat of the fire. She must know it will devour her too if she doesn't flee. But like any fire, it burns stronger as she flames it with her fear. She cuts through yards, where my car can't follow. I quickly abandon it and take chase on foot. Her little dog's barks slice through the calm night air. Her energy, her fear, her anxiety vibrates within my soul, drawing me to her.

I am almost within reach of her. The desire to touch her, if only for a moment, is the only thing that matters, the only thing I need. She is so close; I can feel her heat burning hotter than the fire inside me. She glances over her shoulder to see how close I am, and our eyes meet. Suddenly, I am lost in an ocean of blue; its waters drown out the inferno.

My mind flashes back to a night over twenty years ago when I was only five years old. A night where I was filled with the same fear that I now see written all over the face of this beautiful woman in front of me. I can't escape the memory. Now that the fire has been extinguished, the past absorbs me.

I had been awakened from a dream to the sounds of my parents arguing yet again. No matter how hard I tried to slip back into sleep, I couldn't because my parents were yelling too loudly. I sneaked down the hallway as quietly as possible to see if everything was okay.

"Just tell me where the hell you've been," my mother yelled.

I hated it when she'd yell at him because it always fueled his anger. My dad had a beer in his hand, as usual.

"I don't have to tell you shit," he said as he pushed past her. "Go back to bed and leave me the hell alone. I need a drink."

"I have the right to know where you've been until almost four in the morning. I am your wife, Billy," my mother said.

My father looked like he'd been in a fight with his dirty

work clothes, torn pants, and scratched face. The smell of smoke filled our house, emanating off him. I know now that this was *the* night. The night he killed her.

"Yeah, I know you're my wife. You're not my mother… just back off," my father yelled as he stormed off to the kitchen, out of my sight.

My mother followed behind, insisting he tell her where he'd been, what he'd been doing. Shortly after, I heard a loud crash and my mother scream. I knew I shouldn't do it, but I ran to the kitchen doorway where my mother was lying on the ground with my father kicking her in the stomach and head.

"Daddy, stop!" I ran to him and grabbed a hold of his leg before he could land another kick on my mom. "Please stop."

My father grabbed me by the hair, yanking me off her and tossing me to the ground like I was a dirty rag. My mother yelled at me to go back to my room. Even though I knew I should listen to her, I couldn't leave because she was hurt and bleeding. Instead, I ran to her.

"Mommy, are you okay?" I whispered into her ear.

She begged me to go back to my room, whispering empty assurances that she was okay. My father jerked me up by the arm so hard I felt something snap.

"You think you're a big man now that you're five, huh? Big man trying to save your mommy," he yelled in my face. "Stand up here then and fight me like a man."

I feel the first kick hitting me in the stomach as if it's happening right now. His first punch made blood gush out of my nose, and my head snap back against the wall. His second kick made me buckle to the ground.

My mother screamed as I tried to prepare myself for the next blow by curling into a ball on the floor. "Billy, stop. Please stop! You'll kill him! He's just a little boy!"

I remember the surprise I felt when my father actually stopped. He bent down and picked me up, cradling me in his arms like a baby. Tears streamed down his cheeks.

"I'm so sorry, Robby. It'll never happen again—I promise. I'm so sorry," he said.

I didn't believe him though, because he'd made so many promises before that he'd broken.

My mother grabbed me from my father's arms and kissed me tenderly while she carried me to my room. My father's wails filled our home, bouncing off the ceiling, echoing off the walls, racing across the floors, and thundering in my aching heart.

As my mother cradled me in her arms and hummed a lullaby, I remember hearing my father's screams fill the air. The words he yelled—those that could be coming from my mouth right now. "What have I done? Oh, God, what have I become?"

The one thing that kept going through my mind that night as I tried to find sleep again, now cuts deep into my soul. I repeated it over and over to myself that night, hoping I wouldn't ever forget. *I will never be like daddy. I will never be like him.*

I buckle to my knees in the wet grass as the realization crashes over me that I was about to become him in more ways than I already have. Tears stream down my cheeks as the woman disappears from sight. My wails of despair and brokenness fill the night air. I don't know what I'm going to do, where I'm going to go, or how I can possibly repair all the damage I've done so far. I do know that I need to hold onto the words of the five-year-old boy still inside me. It is time for the madness to stop. I have to be the one to break this, to stop the trail of misery in my family.

With memories echoing inside of my soul, I head back to my car. Without knowing if it's even possible, I decide to try. I don't know if there is a way to stop this cycle that began so many years ago. As I start my car and pull away, something opens inside of me. Something that feels like a new beginning. I also hear what sounds like an ending.

Perhaps it's the end of echoes.

ABOUT THE AUTHOR

Dawn Hosmer is the author of psychological thrillers and suspense. She is a lifelong Ohioan. She received her degree in Sociology and spent her career in Social Work; however, writing has always been her passion. She is a wife and the mother of four amazing children. In addition to listening to true crime podcasts, drinking coffee, and coloring, Dawn is busy working on her next novel.

For more information, visit www.dawnhosmer.com or follow her on Twitter @dawnhosmer7, Instagram @dawnh71, Tiktok @dawn_hosmer, or Facebook. Dawn can also be found on Goodreads and Bookbub.

ACKNOWLEDGEMENTS

THIRTEEN years ago, I decided to attempt to write my first novel. The End of Echoes is the result of that endeavor.
It is truly the story of my heart because it touches on so many important topics that have profound impacts on people's lives, as well as society as a whole. I've spent my career in social work and have seen firsthand the destruction that domestic violence, alcoholism and addiction can wreak on people's lives. I've seen the difference that one person can make in the life of another hurting person. I've witnessed the tragic loss of someone I care about at far too young of an age. I've encountered so many hurt-ing people that don't know what to do with their pain, so they unwittingly unleash it on others. But, I've also witnessed the beauty in healing, in recovery, in breaking the cycles of the past. This book is to honor all those I've encountered on my journey who have found beauty amongst the ashes, who have used the pieces of what seemed like a shattered life to create something lovely.

While the subjects in this book are heavy, I hope readers leave with a sense of hope. No life is beyond repair. One person can truly make a world of difference in another person's life. Our tragedies and hurt do not have to define us. We do not have to take our pain and use it to hurt others. There can be healing.

I spent many hours alone writing and editing this book, but I could not have done it without the help, support, and love of so many others along the way. I'd like to take a moment to thank some of the people who have been instrumental in making my dream a reality.

In addition to God, I'd like to thank my husband, Steve, and children (Krystyna, Jesi, Dominic and Gabriel). You have been by my side, cheering me on, every step of the way. You are my why, the rea-sons I carry on. I'd also like to thank my mother, Joyce. Your love and support are a constant in my life. I wouldn't be who I am without your love.

A huge thank you to Gestalt Media and Jason and Anna Stokes for first publishing The End of Echoes. I have so much gratitude to Rebecca at Black Cat Graphic Design for working tirelessly to help me get the second edition up and ready. I'd be completely lost without her help. Also, a shoutout to Carol Beth Anderson who is instrumental in this self-publishing process.

I would like to thank all of those who took the time to read my work and offer their valuable insight and feedback: Heather Har-rison, Erinne Lansing, Amy Gail Hansen, Jen Yan, Shelley Trenholm, Jan Watts, Laura Wilson, Sheryl Mumby, Jodi Jensen, Renee Hurteau, and Shawn Burgess. This book would not be the same without the feedback, love, and support from you.

Words cannot express how grateful I am for each of you. Some of you I've known for what feels like forever, while others have come into my life more recently. All of you are dear friends and hold a special place in my heart.

I would also like to thank the Writing Community on Twitter for all of the love, encouragement, and support you've given me over the past year. You've all inspired me to keep pursuing my dream and have shown me more support than I ever could've imagined. A special shout-out to my Huggers for Puppers/Yoga group friends. You all keep me laughing and make me feel better on the worst days. I would've lost my mind several times along the way without all of you.

Also a special thank you to Kate Minear Sorenson for your friendship and for using your mad photography skills to do my author photo. Also, much gratitude to Rachel Hopmoen for convincing me to join Twitter.

I also have so much gratitude for all those who have entrusted me with parts of their own painful stories throughout the years. Each of you that have shared a part of your heart with me have impacted my journey and taught me so much about myself and the world.

Thank you to every single person who lets me into their life by reading my words. I cannot describe for you what an honor it is that you invest your time, energy, and money to support my dream. I am touched beyond words.

Independent Authors rely on reviews to help spread the word about our work. Please take a moment of your time to leave a quick review on Amazon and/or Goodreads. Reviews are one of the few ways we, as writers, know whether you enjoyed (or hated) what we wrote. Thank you so much!

*A special thank you and so much gratitude to all of the con-
tributors to my pre-order campaign through Indiegogo. Your
support means the world to me. My heart is full.*

Lakiesha Edwards

Ian Cahill

Colleen Brown

Blanche Lucyk

Shelly Strosnyder

Stephany Husemann

Sam Henson

Dominic Ritchey

Monica Reents

Gay Leigh Henson

Peggy Replogle

Julia Koval

Chad Walter

Janet Watts

Kimberly Wilkin

Donna Mickey

Alain Davis

Kimberly Prats

WB Welch

Beth Anderson

Shawn Burgess

Amy Kemper

Jacqui Castle

Rachel Hopmoen

Kathy Riebel

Jennifer Yan

Anna Ray Stokes

Jaime Cooley

Curt & Tonya Spires

RESOURCES

(IN THE UNITED STATES)

National Center for Missing & Exploited Children

www.missingkids.com

1-800-THE-LOST (1-800-843-5678)

National Domestic Violence Hotline

To find help, options, and resources for you or someone you love

www.thehotline.org

1-800-799-7233

Substance Abuse and Mental Health Services Administration

To seek help for you or someone you love who is struggling with alcoholism, addiction or mental health issues

www.samhsa.gov

1-800-662-HELP (1-800-662-4357)

The Childhelp National Child Abuse Hotline

www.childhelp.org/hotline

1-800-4-A-Child (1-800-422-4453)

Alcoholics Anonymous

If you are struggling with alcoholism or addiction, please visit the website to find meetings near you

www.aa.org

Narcotics Anonymous

If you are struggling with alcoholism or addiction, please visit the website to find meetings near you

www.na.org

1-818-773-9999 (NA World Services)

Al-Anon

If you are worried about someone with an alcohol or drug problem, please visit the website to find meetings near you

www.al-anon.org

1-757-563-1600 (Al-Anon Headquarters USA)

National Mentoring Organization

To find out about opportunities to serve as a mentor to someone in need, contact

www.mentoring.org

617.303.4600

U.S. Department of Health & Human Services

For information on health insurance, social services (assistance with child care, child support, cash assistance and food assistance), and prevention & wellness

www.hhs.gov

1-877-696-6775

My name is Mackenzie Bartholomew, or at least it was. I'm staring at my dead body, lying in a casket. I was a healthy, thirty-nine-year-old, mother of three.

I have so many questions but very few answers. Was I murdered? Did I commit suicide? I don't know if I'm in some sort of purgatory or if I've gone straight to hell.

I'm stuck somewhere in between life and death, forced to travel back in time to relive moments from my past, ones I'd rather forget. I'm desperate to piece together the details surrounding my death. If I don't, I fear my soul will never find rest.

Chock full of family drama, secrets, betrayal, and lies, Somewhere in Between is a Psychological Thriller with wicked twists that will keep you hooked until the last page.

MOSAIC

*A collection of very short stories, ranging
from scary pieces to those full of hope.*

Dawn Hosmer

Mosaic is a collection of very short stories, ranging from scary pieces to those full of hope. Through these stories, I hope to provide glimpses into what it means to be human. Each of us is made up of many different pieces that, when fit together, make a beautiful, messy whole. Those tiny pieces in and of themselves don't mean much and are easily overlooked. But, when we put them all together, a full picture of what it means to be human starts to form.

〜

A chance encounter with a stranger traps Tessa within the mind of a madman.

Tessa was born with a gift. Through a simple touch she picks up pieces of others. A "flash" of color devours her—the only indication that she's gained something new from another person. Red equals pain; purple, a talent; yellow, a premonition; orange, a painful memory; and blue, a pleasant one. Each flash blurs the lines between her inherent traits and those she's acquired from others. Whenever she gains bits of something new, she loses more pieces of herself. While assisting in search efforts for a local missing college student, Tessa is paralyzed by a flash that rips through her like a lightning bolt, slicing apart her soul. A blinding light takes away her vision. A buzzing louder than any noise she's ever heard overwhelms her, penetrates her mind. As the bolt works its way through her body, images and feelings from someone else take over. Women's dead eyes stare at her as her hands encircle their throats. Their screams consume her mind. Memories of the brutal murders of five women invade her. Will she be able to find the killer and help save the next victim? Can she do so without completely losing herself? Bits & Pieces is a fast-paced, riveting Psychological Suspense with supernatural elements that leaves the reader guessing until the end.

~

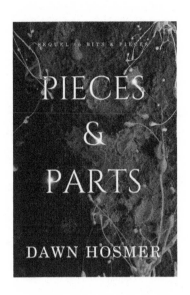

COMING SOON
SEPTEMBER 2021

Book 2 in the Bits & Pieces Series

The highly anticipated sequel to Bits & Pieces, the psychological thriller that kept readers up at night.

For the past five years, Tessa has lived a normal life, the kind she always dreamed of. One without her gift and the flashes that tormented her for as long as she can remember.

All of that changes on a winter's day when, out of nowhere, the flashes return. Only this time they're different.

Along with the flashes, Tessa makes a gruesome discovery on her property. Images haunt her. Voices from beyond the grave plead for her help. She is thrust into a quest to find and stop a murderer. Time is running out.

Tessa scrambles to fit all the pieces and parts of this hideous puzzle together before someone she loves becomes the next victim.

Pieces & Parts is a spine-tingling psychological thriller with a touch of the supernatural that will keep you guessing and turning the pages until its chilling end.

∼